A Love Forbidden

Books by Kathleen Morgan

BRIDES OF CULDEE CREEK
Daughter of Joy
Woman of Grace
Lady of Light
Child of Promise

THESE HIGHLAND HILLS
Child of the Mist
Wings of Morning
A Fire Within

HEART OF THE ROCKIES
A Heart Divided
A Love Forbidden

All Good Gifts
The Christkindl's Gift
One Perfect Gift

Giver of Roses
As High as the Heavens

A Love Forbidden

A NOVEL

KATHLEEN MORGAN

Revell

a division of Baker Publishing Group
Grand Rapids, Michigan

Published by Revell
a division of Baker Publishing Group
P.O. Box 6287, Grand Rapids, MI 49516-6287
www.revellbooks.com

Printed in the United States of America

Library of Congress Cataloging-in-Publication Data
Morgan, Kathleen, 1950–
    A love forbidden : a novel / Kathleen Morgan.
        p.   cm. — (Heart of the Rockies)
    ISBN 978-0-8007-1971-5 (pbk.)
    1. Sisters—Fiction. 2. Ranchers—Fiction. 3. Ranch life—Colorado—Fiction. I. Title.
PS3563.O8647L68 2012
813'.54—dc23   2012000771

This book is a work of fiction. Names, characters, places, and incidents are the products of the author's imagination or are used fictitiously.

The internet addresses, email addresses, and phone numbers in this book are accurate at the time of publication. They are provided as a resource. Baker Publishing Group does not endorse them or vouch for their content or permanence.

12   13   14   15   16   17   18   7   6   5   4   3   2   1

God grant me the Serenity
   to accept the things I cannot change;
The Courage to change the things I can;
And the Wisdom to know the difference.

                    Reinhold Niebuhr

Prologue

Colorado Rockies, June 1870

There were times—just a few—when Shiloh Wainwright truly, fervently hated her sister. And this was one of those times, the twelve-year-old thought as she watched her older sibling take the half-breed Indian youth's hand and lead him into the barn.

Why in tarnation—her fists clenched the wooden post as she peered around the corral fence—*did I think any good could come of Jordan making friends with Jesse? Once she works her wiles on him, he won't even know I exist, much less want to be my friend!*

It had seemed such a good idea. Though Henry Wilson, their ranch foreman, had only hired the seventeen-year-old Jesse Blackwater two months ago, it hadn't taken long for Shiloh to convince the handsome youth to allow her to tag along while he did his chores. And, after a time of guarded interactions on Jesse's part, they had gradually formed a bond that had blossomed into an actual friendship. It was just as apparent, however, that their friendship was the only one he had made.

Shiloh puzzled over that for several days, before coming right out and asking Jesse about his lack of other friends. "Not everyone likes Indians, even those with half-white blood," he soberly informed her. After digesting that surprising revelation—well, maybe not all *that* surprising, Shiloh admitted, recalling some remarks made in passing by certain schoolmates—she set to work remedying that problem.

Shiloh now watched the barn door slide shut behind Jesse and her sister, all the while recalling the plan she had hatched to help Jesse make friends. *The other hands just don't know him like I do*, she had thought. *They all sure want to get to know my sister better, though. Not only is Jordan older, but she's beautiful and without any ugly freckles like me.*

At fourteen, Jordan Wainwright caught the breath of every man who laid eyes upon her. Well, every man save her father and two stepbrothers, anyway, Shiloh amended. If she could get her sister to favor Jesse . . . well, every other man on the ranch would surely fall over himself to befriend the half-breed in the hopes of finding similar favor with Jordan.

After a few rough patches, the first stage of Shiloh's plan had seemed to be working. At first, Jordan had shown interest in Jesse as a favor, after Shiloh had hounded her mercilessly, regaling her with tales of Jesse's expertise in breaking the most unbreakable broncs and roping cattle no one else could even come near, and about all the tracking secrets he'd taught her. Well, after all that *and* the surrender of the precious music box their father had purchased for Shiloh on the day of her birth.

But she wasn't going to linger over something as material as even a beloved music box. What mattered, above all, were people. Loving them, helping them. Shiloh had always loved helping others.

And people around here needed a passel of help to see

beyond Jesse's Ute Indian heritage to the good and wonderful person he was inside. A friend who ignored her coltish, clumsy body and homely face, her wild red hair and embarrassing overabundance of freckles. A friend who didn't discount her as the baby of the family but looked past it all to see straight into her heart. To see her on so many levels, to really *know* her and, in the bargain, like what he found.

One couldn't ask for more than that. All the same, Shiloh thought, her apprehension rising as the minutes ticked by and the barn door remained closed, she regretted—fiercely regretted—ever pushing Jordan to take notice of him.

Not that, at this point, there was much she could do about it. Jordan no longer talked to Jesse just as a favor to her. These days, her sister actually sought him out, stealing him away from Shiloh at every opportunity. And something no longer seemed quite right about her motives.

For several minutes more, Shiloh waited for the pair to reappear. Then, with a disgruntled sigh, she turned and headed back to the white frame ranch house. She had laundry to take down and she'd better do it soon, she thought, casting a glance at the gray clouds building over the valley. Emma, their housekeeper, wouldn't be happy if the freshly laundered bedding she'd hung out this morning got wet all over again.

Fifteen minutes later, a basketload of folded sheets resting on her hip, Shiloh headed through the back door and into the house. She deposited the basket on the kitchen table and glanced around, wondering where everyone had gone. The murmur of voices rose from the front of the house, so she set off in that direction. At the open entry door stood Emma and Martha, Shiloh and Jordan's mother.

"Do you think we should get Mr. Nicholas?" Emma was asking their mother. "With Mr. Edmund gone to town, I mean."

Martha gave a sharp nod. "Yes. There's no one else with enough authority to stop that brute. He certainly won't listen to either of us."

As Shiloh opened her mouth to ask what they were talking about, a sharp crack shattered the silence. She edged closer and glanced around the two women standing in the doorway.

"What's going on? Who's using that old bullwhip of Pa—"

Her breath caught in her throat. At the corral not more than fifty yards away, the same corral she'd hidden behind just a short time ago, someone was tied, hands over his head, to a tall fence post. He faced away from her, his shirt ripped open, and several oozing lash marks crisscrossed his bare back.

Even as she and the two other women watched in horror, Henry Wilson threw back the hand holding the whip. Then, in a swift, hard motion, he snapped it forward. As the thin piece of leather met flesh, the recipient of the whip went rigid, then reared back in agony. Not a sound, however, passed his lips.

The tilt of the head in that single, swift moment gave away the victim's identity. It was Jesse.

"No!" she whispered on a swift, sudden exhalation of breath. "No!"

In the split second between realization and action, her mother grabbed for her. Shiloh was too fast. She dodged the outstretched hand and scooted instead around Emma.

"Shiloh! Don't!" Martha Wainwright cried, but Shiloh was already across the front porch and scrambling down the steps.

"Emma, go after her," Shiloh heard her mother say, but then the sickening sound of the bullwhip meeting flesh once again filled the air. Everything around her narrowed, converging on the sight of Jesse yet again jerking in silent agony.

Her booted feet pounded against the dry earth, sending up puffs of dust with each stride she took. Her arms pumped furiously.

Jesse. I've got to reach him. Protect him.

"S-stop!" she screeched even as she neared the half-circle of men who'd gathered around Jesse and the foreman. "Stop it! Stop hurting him!"

Henry Wilson paused in surprise, lowering the whip he'd raised yet again. When he caught sight of Shiloh, his gaze hardened.

"Someone. Anyone. Grab and hold her," he snarled, then turned back to the task at hand, unfurling the bullwhip behind him.

A pair of hands nearest her reached out. Shiloh pivoted sharply, just managing to evade the man. She twisted, nearly losing her footing, then righted and threw herself between the foreman and Jesse, covering Jesse's now-ravaged and bleeding back with her own body.

"No! Blast you, girl!"

Shiloh shot a swift look behind her. Henry Wilson staggered backward in an attempt to halt the forward flight of the whip he'd just unfurled forward. Yet, though he threw all his weight into the effort, it was too late.

The whip's leather tip caught Shiloh a passing glance on her upper right cheek, slicing open a tiny cut. It burned like fire. She choked back a scream. If Jesse could take such punishment in silence, so could she.

"S-stop it!" As a thin stream of blood trickled down her face, Shiloh wheeled about to face the now panic-stricken foreman. "Stop it, right now!"

For a fleeting moment, Henry stared in disbelief. Then a firm resolve darkened his eyes. An angry flush gave color to his formerly pasty white face.

"Clay. Go. Get a hold of her. I aim to finish what I started. As long as I'm foreman of this ranch, no half-breed piece of trash is going to take liberties with the boss's daughter!"

11

The hand named Clay hurried to do what he was told. This time, Shiloh was too shocked to resist. He took her by both arms and pulled her away from Jesse, dragging her to stand behind the other men.

Liberties? With the boss's daughter?

The blood pounding through her brain, Shiloh fought to make sense of the man's words. Then, as comprehension flooded her, she turned, searching the gathering until she finally found her sister standing several feet behind the men.

Jordan's flawlessly groomed hair was mussed. High color pinkened her cheeks. She was, however, quite obviously unharmed. Their gazes met, and the look of guilt in her sister's eyes was almost instantly replaced by one of defiance.

Oh, how I know that look! Shiloh thought. *She uses that ploy all the time to wriggle out of any trouble she's gotten herself into.*

Fury filled her. "What did you do?" she shrieked at her sister. "This is all your fault, isn't it? Isn't it?"

Jordan gave a sharp shake of her head. "No. I went in the barn with Jesse, but I didn't cause any of this. He . . . he wouldn't leave me be. He wouldn't stop when I told him to stop . . ."

She couldn't quite manage to meet Shiloh's gaze at the end. Still, the action was so subtle Shiloh doubted anyone who didn't know her sister as well as she did would've caught it.

"Liar," she muttered softly. Though no one heard the bitter accusation, the expression on her sister's face changed ever so slightly, signaling her recognition of the charge. Shiloh turned away in disgust and began to struggle in the ranch hand's clasp.

"Let me go. You've got no right—"

"Do as she says," a deep voice intruded just then. "Let my little sister go."

Clay froze, then turned in the direction from which the command had come. He looked to the brown-haired man sitting in a wicker wheelchair, Martha Wainwright behind him, then at Henry Wilson standing not far away, the bullwhip curled limply at his feet.

"S-sure thing, Mr. Wainwright."

The foreman gave a quick jerk of his head. As if he'd been burned, the ranch hand released Shiloh. At the reprieve her stepbrother had bought her, she wasted not a moment. Running to Jesse's side, she pulled out her small pocketknife, flipped it open, and began sawing at the rope binding his hands to the corral post.

"I'll have you free in a minute. Just hold on, Jesse," she whispered, leaning close to him.

He lifted his head, turned to look at her. The expression in his rich brown eyes chilled Shiloh to the marrow of her bones. Fury burned there. Fury overlaid with a soul-searing pain the like of which she'd never before seen.

It was as if a blade had sliced clear through to her soul.

"Jesse. Oh, Jesse . . ."

Then the bonds fell away. With a shuddering breath, Jesse forced himself to straighten. Then, ever so slowly, he turned to face them all.

"I'm sorry about all this, son," Nicholas Wainwright, oldest son of the ranch's owner, said. "Come on up to the house and let us see to those wounds."

"No."

Shiloh reached toward him. "Please, Jesse. If they're not cared for, those wounds could fester and become infected."

"No!" He jerked back, shaking his head with a savage intensity. "Don't touch me. Don't any of you touch me!"

On unsteady feet, he headed to where his unsaddled horse was tied near the barn, unfastened the reins, and swung up on the animal's bare back. For a long moment Jesse just sat there, hunched over in pain, the loose, blood-soaked bits that remained of his shirt fluttering in the breeze. Then, with what Shiloh knew must be a superhuman effort, he straightened. Gathering up the reins, Jesse turned his horse in the direction of the road leading from the ranch.

Clutching the tooled silver eagle hanging from the chain around her neck—a gift he had given her just a few days ago—she watched him ride away. For the longest time Shiloh stood there, her heart cracking open in her chest, immobilized in horrified disbelief. Finally, though, the blood began to course once more through her frozen limbs. With a wild cry, she ran after him only to be scooped up by one of the ranch hands and hauled back to the house.

Inconsolable, Shiloh bawled for days. Then she tucked away the memory of Jesse Blackwater into a secret place in her heart and forced herself to think no more of him. Not so with her sister, whom she couldn't forgive for the part she'd played that terrible day.

She tried, oh, how Shiloh tried, but she just couldn't.

1

Castle Mountain Ranch, Colorado Rockies,
early March 1879

"Mark my words, Shiloh Wainwright. It's bad enough you've thrown the whole family into an uproar with this rash decision to quit your job in Denver and head out to that Indian Agency. But your head-in-the-clouds need to save the savage Utes is going to be the death of you yet. And that," Jordan added, one dark blonde brow arched in a knowing look, "will be the very *best* you can hope for."

It never stops, does it? Shiloh clamped down hard on her rising irritation. Lowering her gaze, she folded yet another skirt and placed it in her leather travel trunk standing beneath the window of her former bedroom. *No matter how old we get, she's always going to try and have the last word.* And *maintain her bossy ways and superior airs.*

The fact that they were both young women now—Jordan married and the mother of a six-month-old baby girl, and Shiloh to be twenty-one years old the beginning of next month—hadn't softened the long simmering animosity between the sisters. Two years of teacher's education, plus another six months instructing at that fancy girls' boarding school in Denver, still didn't hold a candle to Jordan's greater age.

No matter that her sister had been quite content to finish school and immediately wed her longtime beau, while Shiloh had gone on for a higher education. No matter that, while *she* possessed the means to support herself, independent of any man, Jordan was now but a simple wife and mother. Indeed, there were times when Shiloh wondered if her sister was as content with the life she had chosen as she claimed that she was.

There were no more adoring suitors to stroke her eternally inflated self-esteem. Well, none, anyway, who'd dare risk revealing their admiration in the presence of her sister's hulking, ever-possessive husband, Robert Travers. Indeed, thanks to her husband, in many ways Jordan's ability to come and go as she pleased was severely limited these days. And her sister had never been one to tolerate any constraints on what she could and couldn't do.

Maybe that was why Jordan seemed so dead set against her heading off on yet another adventure, Shiloh mused, corralling her thoughts and herding them back to the present. Why, when her two stepbrothers had sent word of Shiloh's arrival and surprising plans, her sister had hightailed it from her own home twenty miles to the southwest of here. Because marriage and motherhood were choking the life out of her. Because she wanted—and wanted desperately—to be as footloose and fancy-free as her younger sister.

The possibility filled Shiloh with a grim satisfaction. For once, just once, her older sister might actually envy her. Might desire something only her younger sister could have.

"Head in the clouds, notwithstanding," Shiloh replied, restraining a smug grin with only the greatest of efforts, "taking the job at the White River Indian Agency is what I aim to do. So maybe we should agree not to discuss the matter further. You've got your opinions. I'm not going to budge.

And there's plenty of other topics far more pleasant. Like, did little Cecilia enjoy her new rattle? I thought it was so pretty, with those pink and red roses painted on the white porcelain."

For a moment, Jordan looked as if she wasn't ready to relinquish their current discussion. Then, with a sigh and shake of her head, she apparently let the topic go.

"Yes, I think my Ceci will love it, once she's older. I know you can't understand the ways of babies, not having one of your own, but if I were to give it to her now, she'd soon have it in a million pieces." A self-righteous smile lifted her sister's lips. "So, I'll put it away for a time. It's far too pretty to risk breaking."

Shiloh chose not to rise to the bait. One way or another, Jordan was determined to win every argument. Instead, she walked to the dresser and picked up an armload of books. Her precious books that she'd use to teach the Ute Indian children.

The image of dark eyes peering intently back at her from sun-bronzed faces filled her mind. One of the few Indian bands that had yet to be torn from their beloved lands and relegated to the dreaded "Indian Territory" in Utah, the White River Utes were a free-spirited and intelligent people. Her old nursemaid, a Ute Indian and Buckskin Joe's wife, had regaled her for years with tales of their life and culture. Thanks to Kanosh, Shiloh also spoke fairly decent Ute. Her impressive educational credentials and glowing recommendation from her last job notwithstanding, she suspected that her knowledge of the Ute language had most helped sway Nathan Meeker, the White River Agency's Indian agent, to hire her.

Currently, his daughter, Josephine, though not teacher trained, was struggling to set up classes for the Ute Indian children. Her success so far, however, had been minimal. Apparently the Utes were suspicious of the effects of the white man's education on their children. They feared it would incline their offspring to leave the traditional Ute ways and the reservation.

It was expected, however, that Shiloh's professional training would be sufficient to induce better attendance at the Agency school. Still, for a fleeting instant, Shiloh wondered if she perhaps hadn't "oversold" herself and her abilities. Though she firmly believed education was the only hope for the Utes' survival in a world rapidly changing around them, she wasn't certain she could single-handedly alter their opinion of what they wanted versus what they truly needed.

One couldn't know if one didn't try, though. And she'd never been one to shy away from a challenge. Especially not a challenge that meant so much to her as this one did. With all her heart, Shiloh wanted to help the Ute Indians, to make a difference in their lives. A difference that would educate not only their minds but also their hearts with the knowledge of the love of the Lord Jesus Christ.

"You do what you deem best with that rattle," she said as she carefully placed the books in one corner of her trunk. "And, in the future, I'll try to purchase more appropriate gifts for little Cecilia."

Jordan rose from her spot on the edge of the bed. "That would be appreciated." Her glance strayed to the necklace dangling from Shiloh's open-necked blouse as she leaned over to tuck a box of fountain pens and bottles of black ink in the upper corner of her trunk.

Shiloh looked up just in time to catch the direction of her sister's gaze and the resulting grimace of distaste. "What's the matter now, Jordan?" she asked wearily.

"That Indian trinket you insist on wearing along with the cross of Christ. Do you have any idea how sacrilegious that must appear to anyone who sees it?"

As her hand rose to protectively clasp the small silver eagle suspended from the same chain as her silver cross, Shiloh stiffened in anger. "Not only do I cherish these in honor of my two dearest friends," she said tautly, "but because the Indians revere the eagle as a carrier of prayers and for its special connection to the Creator. So I hardly find it sacrilegious or unworthy to hang alongside the cross."

"Well, I'm willing to bet some of the folks who work at that Indian Agency will think differently. But suit yourself. You've never been one to listen to those older and wiser—"

In that instant, something in Shiloh frayed and broke. Her patience, most likely. She'd never been overly patient.

"Enough, Jordan!" She slammed down the lid of her travel trunk and stood there, her hands fisted at her sides. "It never ends with you, does it? The constant belittling? The poorly contained, eternal displeasure?"

Her sister's mouth dropped open in surprise. "I-I was just—"

"No. Don't say it." Shiloh held up a silencing hand. "I don't give a tinker's darn *what* you think you meant! I'm leaving for the White River Agency tomorrow morning, and nothing you can say will sway me from that intent. So, let's try and make the passing hours between us pleasant, if not for the sake of our relationship, then for the sake of our family."

"Fine." Jordan's mouth snapped shut. Her lips thinned to a white line. "I'll see you at supper then." With an indignant toss of her blonde head, she stomped from the room.

Shiloh rolled her eyes. Leave it to her sister to take offense whenever she didn't get her way. Shiloh was mightily, mightily tired of the games and manipulations. The only blessing in any of this was she no longer had to live with Jordan or long endure her silly, self-centered tantrums.

Her mouth quirked in wry realization. If only Jordan

19

realized how great was Shiloh's desire to run off to be with the savage Utes! Especially in comparison to enduring even one more day in *her* irksome presence.

Surprisingly mollified, Shiloh completed her packing, then headed downstairs for a bit of fresh air before supper. The independent life definitely had its benefits. And one not so insignificant one was that she was no longer compelled to put up with the likes of her sister.

The Ute brave known as Nuaru paused on a rise over-looking the valley where the White River Indian Agency lay. Below and south of him, past a large fenced and plowed field, spread a small community of buildings neatly laid out in a north–south pattern.

First and foremost was the granary, community well, and agent's house. A long dirt street separated all that from the adobe-walled milk house. Directly south of the agent's house were the employee quarters, and across the street from them were the storerooms that held all the annuity supplies that were periodically and, at least from the Utes' view, very parsimoniously doled out. Next came another storeroom building and a boardinghouse.

Just before the White River carved its undulating way south lay the tepees of Chief Douglas's band, a large pony corral, and the house and tepees of Chief Johnson. Though Nuaru generally preferred to keep as wide a distance between Agent Meeker and himself as he could, he had agreed to spend the next few days with his best friend, Persune, who was part of Douglas's camp. And, now that he'd delivered all the slain mule deer but one to his own chief, that time was finally upon him.

Admittedly, Chief Douglas wasn't any more fond of Meeker than was Nuaru's chief, Captain Jack. But Douglas and most of his band *were* overly fond of the annuity handouts of flour, oats, plug tobacco, and blankets that Meeker dispensed on an almost weekly basis, and so settled for Agency living. Despite Nuaru's repeated warnings that these government supplies came with a price, and that price was the ultimate surrender of the Ute way of life, few were willing to listen. But then, he thought bitterly, they had yet to experience how swiftly—and viciously—the white man could turn on his Indian brother.

Today, however, Nuaru was compelled to enter the Agency. And, tomorrow, the first day of spring, was the official start of the annual Bear Dance. On that day, no Ute male was exempt from the ceremonies, nor allowed to refuse any woman who asked him to dance. At least not if he wished to avoid having a bear later find him in the mountains and kill him, Nuaru thought with a wry twist of his lips.

He nudged his pony down the rock-strewn incline, pulling the packhorse loaded with the remaining mule deer carcass with which he intended on gifting Chief Douglas. Just a few days in the oppressive atmosphere of the White River Agency, he promised himself. Then he'd be free, once more, to come and go as he pleased. Or rather, come and go until the white man no longer pleased.

***

"You'll like Josie Meeker. Everyone does."

Two weeks later, and for the umpteenth time, Shiloh swatted a maddeningly persistent fly from the vicinity of her nose, adjusted the broad brim of her straw hat to minimize the sun on her face, and glanced over at the man who sat beside her on the big freight wagon bench, driving the team of four mules before him. Joe Collum, hired to bring in some farm equipment from Rawlins, Wyoming, to the White River Agency, seemed a decent enough sort, if a bit loquacious. She'd been fortunate to hear about his pending Agency trip when her train had arrived in Rawlins, and she'd soon run into him loading supplies. If not for him, Shiloh would've been compelled to hire someone to take her the rest of the way.

Though she'd have far preferred just admiring the scenery on the way south back into Colorado to the Agency, Shiloh did her best to keep up some semblance of a conversation with the man. He was likely a bit hungry for womanly conversation, she supposed, if the scant amount of females in these mountain towns was any indication. And, though she was no Jordan Wainwright, Shiloh knew she had finally grown into a passably attractive young lady. Well, that was what several suitors for her hand in those months teaching in Denver had said, anyway. But then, the severe shortage of women in these parts probably helped to make even the plainest female seem pretty attractive.

No matter. She wasn't looking for or even wanting a husband. She had more important—more worthwhile—plans than tying herself down to a man and a passel of squalling babies. Not that she had anything against babies or a husband . . . someday. But not now. And not anytime soon.

"So, you've met Josie Meeker, have you?" she asked, now that Joe had finally introduced a topic that piqued her interest.

The big freight driver nodded. "Yep. To be honest, she's not quite the looker you are, ma'am, but she's tall, slender, with dark blonde hair and a straight, no-nonsense air about her that sets well with most men. And, if there's a need, there's nothing that gal won't take on." He chuckled. "Word is she was quite the tomboy in her youth."

In her youth . . . Shiloh smiled to herself. Josephine Meeker—the only one of three surviving Meeker children to come with Nathan Meeker and his wife, Arvilla, to live at the White River Agency—was barely a year older. Shiloh hoped the closeness of their ages and the fact they were both college-educated, independent women would lead to a fast friendship.

"Yep," Joe continued on, apparently oblivious to the fact that the conversation was again rapidly becoming one-sided. "I even heard tell that Miss Josie used to challenge the boys to horse races in the streets, when she lived in Greeley with her family."

"Well, then we'll have a lot to talk about," Shiloh replied, giving a firm nod. "I grew up on a cattle ranch and know my way around horses. It'll be fun to have someone to go riding with."

"Well, beggin' yore pardon, ma'am, but that might not be all that safe, what with the problems of late with the Utes, and—"

Just then, they topped yet another hill. The mule team paused. Below them spread a small, verdant valley, pierced on its southern end by a river. It was the tidy layout of buildings, corrals, and a scattering of tepees, however, that took Shiloh's breath away. She turned to the freight driver.

"It's the Agency, isn't it?"

He nodded, then slapped the reins over the backs of the mules, urging them forward. "Yep, sure is. Another ten minutes or so, and you'll finally be home."

Home . . . The word had an unexpectedly foreign ring to it. Shiloh swallowed hard, suddenly overcome with a wave of homesickness overlaid with an acute edge of trepidation. This was it. She was here, and now reality must substitute for all her dearly held dreams. But what if . . . what if things didn't turn out as she hoped? What if she wasn't sufficient to the task at hand?

With a resolute shake of her head, Shiloh banished the doubts and fears. Nothing was served allowing such thoughts to undermine her confidence. She would do the best she could, changing the things within her power and finding peace and acceptance with what couldn't be changed. That was all anyone could do. The rest was in the Lord's hands.

As they headed down the hill, someone apparently gave word of their approach. A small crowd formed outside what must be the Agency office, if the American flag flying there was any indication. A distinguished-looking older man—gray-haired and who appeared to be in his early sixties—with an older woman of similar years at his side, stood directly beneath the flagpole. A younger woman with two small children walked up to halt nearby. And then, a slender, dark-blonde-haired woman, drying her hands with a dish towel, strode from the building just down from the Agency office.

"That's Miss Josie," Joe offered. "The tall one in the white blouse and blue skirt."

"And the older man and woman?" Shiloh leaned toward him, as they were almost within earshot. "I assume they're Nathan and Arvilla?"

"Yep."

She shot the big freighter a quick glance. The clipped way he had replied was out of character, and she wondered why. It almost seemed as if . . . as if he wasn't overly fond of the senior Meekers. If so, was it both or just one?

Shiloh was tempted to ask him, but it was too late. Joe Collum, even then, was leaning back, pulling the mules to a halt.

All eyes turned in the direction of Nathan Meeker. With a squaring of his shoulders, he stepped forward and offered his hand to Shiloh. She took it and climbed down from the wagon.

"Welcome, Miss Wainwright," Nathan said, his voice cultured and mellifluous. "We've been awaiting your arrival with the greatest anticipation. Haven't we, my dear?" he asked, half-turning to the older woman standing behind him.

She walked up and nodded. "Yes, indeed we have."

"May I introduce myself?" he next said. "I am Nathan Cook Meeker, the agent for the White River Indian Agency. And this is my beloved wife, Arvilla Delight Meeker."

Shiloh accepted the woman's proffered hand. "It's so wonderful to finally make both your acquaintances. I've been looking forward to working with you."

"Well, no more than *I've* been looking forward to working with *you*," the dark blonde young woman said, pushing her way past the others standing about. "Though I dearly love trying to recruit and teach the Ute children, with all the other tasks Father's assigned me, I must confess I'm in dire need of assistance."

She thrust out her hand to Shiloh, her blue eyes sparkling. "I'm Josephine Meeker. Everyone, though, calls me Josie, so you should too. And you did know, didn't you, that you'll be helping with the meals at the boardinghouse, and with the weekly laundry, and maybe even with some doctoring if you've got the skills?"

"Josie, why don't you show Miss Wainwright to her room and help her get settled in?" her father brusquely interjected just then. "Time enough later to drown her with an excess of information."

His daughter laughed. "As you wish, Papa." She looked to Shiloh. "Did you bring a trunk or something with all your things?"

Shiloh nodded. "Yes, a trunk and a carpetbag." She turned to the freight driver. "Could you hand me my traveling bag? And see that someone brings my trunk to wherever my new lodgings will be?"

"Sure thing, ma'am." Joe tipped the brim of his big, floppy hat at her. "It was a pleasure traveling with you, ma'am."

"I enjoyed your company as well, Mr. Collum."

25

A Love Forbidden

"Well, now that *that's* settled," Josie said, grabbing hold of Shiloh's arm, "let's get you to your new room. Supper's in an hour, so you'll have just enough time to unpack a bit and freshen up. But only if we hurry."

Shiloh had to quickly lengthen her stride to keep up with the long-legged Josie. So much for proper introductions and getting to meet everyone right off, she thought. But maybe it was for the best. She really was travel weary, and it'd be nice to settle in a bit before supper.

Then, if all went well, she might be able to make an early day of it. Right about now, a nice bed in a quiet room sounded the closest thing to heaven she'd find on this earth. The stop-over last night in that tiny town hadn't yielded the most comfortable of sleeping quarters. Not upstairs of the town's only saloon, which didn't close down until at least three or four in the morning. Indeed, even the prior nights of sleeping under the stars had provided better rest.

"You mustn't take offense when Papa gets a little short," Josie said just then, wrenching Shiloh's thoughts back to the present. "He's just under such duress at times, trying his mightiest to please the Utes and the Indian Bureau. And believe me, most times what the Utes want is in direct opposition to what the Indian Bureau wants."

"And what would those opposite desires be?" Shiloh asked as they passed two buildings across from each other and then headed for the one in the southeasternmost corner of the little complex.

"The Utes want to live as they've always lived, free to hunt and roam as the seasons dictate. And the Indian Bureau wants them to give up their ancient ways, settle down on reservations, and become farmers."

"That does sort of put your father smack in the middle, doesn't it?"

26

Josie nodded. "Yes, it does. Unfortunately for the Utes, my papa pretty much agrees with the Indian Bureau. And when he sets his mind on a task . . ." She shook her head. "Suffice it to say, I feel sorry for the Utes."

She paused at the door to a two-story building that appeared to be newly built. "Well, enough of the politics. Come on in and let me show you your room."

That was a very interesting bit of information, Shiloh thought as she followed Josie into a small foyer with a set of stairs at the back that led to the second floor. A colorful hooked rug graced the hardwood paneled floor, and a tiny carved wooden table stood just to the left of the door, set with a crystal vase adorned with a handful of pine bough greenery. It was all very charming and rather unexpected in such a high mountain valley so far from civilization.

As she followed her hostess up the stairs, however, she couldn't keep from harking back to Josie's most recent words. They were very interesting indeed, but best not delved into too deeply just now. She had plenty of time to get the lay of the land, figure out where everyone stood on things. And tomorrow was definitely soon enough to begin.

The next morning after a hearty breakfast of oatmeal, biscuits, ham, and eggs, Shiloh helped Josie and her mother clear the table in the boardinghouse dining room, scrape plates in the kitchen, then wash and dry the dishes. It was Shiloh's first opportunity to actually meet sixteen-year-old Flora Ellen Price, wife of Shadrach Price, an Agency employee who worked as a farmer, and little May and baby Johnnie, their two children. Though Flora had been in the group to welcome her yesterday, Josie had hurried Shiloh away before she could greet everyone. And then Flora hadn't felt well that evening and so had missed the supper meal at the boardinghouse, where she and her family lived with most of the other employees.

Shiloh immediately liked the shy young woman and was heartened by the fact she'd have two potential friends in Flora and Josie. Hopefully, their companionship would help ease her transition into Agency life, which, at present, still felt rather foreign and awkward. So foreign and awkward that she hadn't slept well last night, even after unpacking all her things and attempting to make her bedroom as homey as she could.

But that was to be expected, she hastened to reassure herself. Her first job at the girls' school in Denver had been a challenging transition from her two years spent at teacher's training at Peru State Normal School in Nebraska. And, Shiloh sheepishly reminded herself, she'd nearly given up from severe homesickness and gone home while there.

She was a grown woman now, though, and would rather die a thousand deaths than slink back to Castle Mountain Ranch because of yet another bout of homesickness and the self-doubts that always seem to hover just below the surface of her self-sufficient, confident façade. Not to mention she'd never hear the end of it from Jordan. No, if it was the last thing she ever did, she'd finish out her year's contract. By then, she would have made a place for herself here or begun looking for employment elsewhere. She wasn't about to tuck tail and head home.

Josie entered the kitchen just then, returned from putting the clean dishes back in the cupboard in the dining room. "As soon as you're finished with those forks and knives," she said, glancing at the silverware Shiloh held, "we can head down to Chief Douglas's village by the river. They're getting ready for the first day of the Bear Dance."

Though Shiloh had heard of the Utes' traditional three- to

four-day annual ceremony held in late March to celebrate the coming of spring, she had actually never seen one. All she really knew was that the Utes believed that the first spring thunder awakened the bear from his winter's hibernation, and that the dance would not only placate their friend, the bear, but awaken him for his hunting. The Bear Dance was a time to make new friends and rekindle old friendships. A time to thank the Creator for their surviving another harsh winter and to celebrate the renewal of life with the coming of spring.

Excitement filled her. This was why she had come to the White River Agency. To immerse herself in the Ute life and culture, to gain a deeper understanding of their needs, hopes, and dreams. It was the only way she might have a real chance at effecting any change in them and their lives. The only way she might be able to help them avoid the same sad fate as all the other Indian tribes, relegated to bleak, barren Indian reservations far from their ancestral lands, dependent on the United States government for even the food they ate.

Shiloh quickly finished drying the last of the silverware, placed the pieces in the drawer beside the sink, and put away the dish towel. "Give me a moment to run upstairs and get my coat and mittens," she said as she untied her bib apron and hung it on a peg near the wall cabinet. "I'll meet you in the entry."

"Don't tarry," Josie replied. "I want to get us a good spot where we can see everything."

With a quick nod, Shiloh hurried from the kitchen and bounded up the stairs to her bedroom. Morning sun still streamed into her single, white-lace-trimmed curtained bedroom window, making the small space a bright, cheery place. A simple, iron-framed bed covered with one of her mother's colorful handmade quilts graced the wall catty-corner to the window, and on the opposite wall, a plain little table with a chair served as her desk. Near the door was a chest of drawers with a mirror atop it. Her traveling trunk sat beneath the window, and though it provided a handy seat, the view of the storehouse across the street didn't encourage a lot of time spent gazing outside.

She had yet to unpack all her books, or hang the few framed prints she had brought with her, or lay out the rag rug beside her bed, but her family photographs already sat on one corner of the table. Putting out the tintypes of her two older stepbrothers—Nicholas and Cord—as well as one of her now-deceased stepfather standing with her, Jordan, and their mother, and the very grainy one of her father, dressed in Union blue, taken just a few months before his death in a battle against the Confederates, was always one of the first things Shiloh did when she was away from home. The photographs were the closest thing to actually having her family with her, and their presence seemed to help lessen some of her homesickness.

She grabbed up the heavy, black woolen coat she'd left laying on top of her trunk and donned it. Briefly, Shiloh considered whether to bring along her knit hat, then decided against it. The day was cloudless, sunny, and no wind blew. She'd be warm enough in her coat, mittens, and wool skirt, in addition to a woolen vest over her pleated white blouse, woolen stockings, and boots.

Pausing before the chest of drawers, she did a quick check of her hair in the mirror. In a vain attempt to contain it, she had pulled back her dark auburn, irrepressibly curly tresses at the nape of her neck and tied them with a black ribbon. Still, as hard as Shiloh had tried to tame the flighty mess, some of the shorter, more wayward tendrils escaped to frame her face.

She inwardly sighed. With the wild mane she possessed,

not to mention its color, she was sure to be the center of attention with all the Utes. But it couldn't be helped. The good Lord had His reasons for everything, and sooner or later even the Utes, who were certainly not used to curly red hair, would get used to it.

For an instant longer, Shiloh's gaze caught on the silver chain that lay over her buttoned blouse, the silver cross and tooled eagle glinting at her throat. Jordan's claim that it was sacrilegious to wear the two together echoed in her mind. Was her sister correct in her scathing assessment? Was she pushing the boundaries of good taste and decorum wearing the two together?

After a moment of indecision, Shiloh decided not to hide the necklace beneath her blouse. She was proud of both. Indeed, perhaps they might be of some help in bridging some of the cultural separation between the whites and Indians. If nothing else, the Utes should appreciate her honoring their beliefs by wearing one of their revered symbols.

The walk down to the White River from the Agency took about ten minutes, Josie chattering on about the Bear Dance preparations the whole way. "See that tall fence of sticks and branches?" she asked, pointing to a large circular brush corral between the river and Chief Douglas's tepees. "The opening to it always faces east, and inside is where the Utes do their Bear Dance. The men and women line up facing each other, and then each line takes two large steps forward and then three small steps back, everyone moving in unison. The men build the enclosure and make all the other preparations, including the feast afterward, to honor the women."

Shiloh shot her a quick grin. "It's nice to see that some men, anyway, like to cook. Our own people could stand to learn that custom."

Josie laughed. "Well, don't go getting your hopes up that

Ute men are any different than white men. In the Ute culture, cooking the food is usually the woman's job. All the men are expected to do is provide the food. And, aside from protecting his family when the need arises, that's pretty much all Ute men do. Well, aside from racing their ponies."

She paused, her smile fading. "My father had such high expectations of changing their ways when he first came to the Agency. He wanted to turn the Utes into progressive, self-sustaining farmers. So far, all my father's been able to get them to do is dig one irrigation ditch, and to get them to do even that, he had to threaten to withhold their supplies. Now, he just shakes his head and says they're lazy."

Unease rippled through Shiloh, and she quickly ignored it. Nathan Meeker's letter in response to her application for the teaching position had certainly not made mention of such difficulties. He had, instead, written a glowing account of all he'd accomplished since his arrival last July, and all he still intended to do to help the heretofore nomadic White River Utes adapt to a farming lifestyle. His letter had excited and inspired Shiloh, who had always wanted to play a part in helping the Indians of Colorado.

Whether the Utes realized it or not, their days of roaming their beloved mountains were numbered. Since the end of the War between the States, the influx of settlers seeking a fresh start was rapidly growing. And, with the discovery of gold deep in the southern Utes' territory of the San Juan Mountains of Colorado in 1858, soon followed by the unearthing of additional gold and silver veins throughout the Rocky Mountains, the relentless onslaught of miners had only compounded the problem. The Ute way of life required they have a vast territory to roam in pursuit of game and other food, and the white interlopers couldn't understand why such a small number of people needed such large amounts of land.

Sooner or later, these two opposing ways of life were bound to clash. Unfortunately, past events had already proven that the Utes wouldn't come out well.

"It takes time—and education—to change long-held beliefs," Shiloh replied instead. "Surely we can find some common ground on which to build a mutually respectful relationship. The Utes are as much God's children as we are, after all."

"Yes," Josie said with a nod, "they are. Father isn't very good, though, at hiding his opinion of the Utes as exactly that. Children. And they resent him for that, among other things."

Shiloh sighed. "The ones I've known have been far from childish. They're kind, friendly, generous people. But they're also proud and fiercely independent."

"Oh, you won't get any argument from me on those counts," her companion said with a chuckle as they neared the brush corral and a crowd of Utes milling around outside. "I like them very much."

There was an air of excitement mixed with much laughter and joviality in the colorfully dressed people slowly filing into the enclosure. The women wore moccasins and long, soft, white buckskin dresses covered with buckskin capes that were beaded with porcupine quills and elk teeth, the sleeves of the dresses fringed, as were the hems. Their long, thick, black hair was parted in the middle and either hung loose or in two braids. The men were garbed in heavily fringed buckskin shirts with the traditional V flap in front, and fringed leggings with moccasins on their feet. Some of them decorated their braids with animal fur coverings, and others wore their braids unadorned.

"Those are their ceremonial clothes," Josie offered. "Usually the men wear trade cloth shirts with their leggings, and the women's dresses can be a combination of trade cloth and buckskin. When it's really cold, they add buffalo robes and fur hats or robes made from gray wolf or coyote or badger fur."

"But not today," Shiloh added with a smile.

"No, not today. Their buckskin clothes are pretty warm, and it's not that cold."

Josie paused to survey the Utes inside the corral. "Oh, good," she said at last. "There's Persune. He's a member of Chief Douglas's band." Her mouth tilted upward in a smile. "He's married, but he keeps asking me to be his wife. He says he loves me."

Shiloh looked over at her. "And are you going to accept his offer?"

Her companion giggled. "No. Though I like and respect the Utes, I'm not interested in permanently living like one. When Papa's time here is over, I'd like to travel and maybe find some sort of government work in our nation's capital. I don't want to be tied down to any man. Leastwise, not for a long while to come."

"Me, neither," Shiloh replied with a resolute nod. "Not for a long while to come."

Josie grabbed her arm and began to pull her forward. "Let's go stand with Persune and his friends. The Bear Dance is about to start."

As they wound their way through the Utes who were beginning to take their seats around the outer edges of the corral—the men sitting on the north side, the women on the south—others moved forward to form the two lines facing each other in the center. Several older Ute men sitting beneath a brush shelter on the western end of the corral began to sing and scrape a short piece of wood down a long, notched stick. The sound was harsh and rasping.

Shiloh knew the notched stick, in the Ute language, was called a *morats* and was supposed to imitate a growling bear.

The *morats* was a special ceremonial tool only used for the Bear Dance.

As they neared the spot where Persune stood talking with two other Ute men, one of the men, much taller than his compatriots, turned slightly in their direction. For a moment, he seemed not to take much notice of their approach. Then he abruptly stopped and blatantly stared at them. Or, rather, stared at Shiloh.

An expression of disbelief then shock, as his gaze traveled from her hair to her face to finally rest at her throat, swept over his face. Shiloh felt the blood rush to her cheeks. She had expected some unwelcome gaping at her red hair, but this Indian's response bordered on outright rudeness. Her eyes narrowed in irritation and, unconsciously, her hand rose to the base of her neck. As her fingers brushed the cross and eagle hanging there, a sudden realization shot through her.

She looked back up at the tall Ute, whose own eyes at that moment lifted to lock gazes with hers. Eyes that were the most intense, rich shade of brown she'd ever seen. Eyes she'd recognize anywhere, even after all these years.

Shiloh's throat went dry. Her heart began a wild hammering in her chest. And, with the greatest difficulty, she forced a name to her lips that she hadn't uttered in almost nine years.

"Jesse," Shiloh whispered. "Jesse . . ."

2

Jesse . . .

He saw her utter his name. *Jesse* . . . A name he hadn't used since the day he'd ridden into the camp of his mother's family and asked Captain Jack for a new name, a better name—a Ute name. And, since he had arrived on the cusp of a powerful windstorm, that had been his name ever since. *Nuaru.* Wind.

As he gazed into Shiloh Wainwright's soft, beautiful green eyes, however, Nuaru knew the past had come rushing back to confront him. Once again, whether he wished it or not, he'd be torn between two different worlds. Torn between Jesse Blackwater, the white side of him, and Nuaru, the Ute.

The admission didn't sit well with him. Anger stirred then flared into a blazing conflagration. Suddenly, he couldn't remain there, breathing the same air as the young woman who, by her mere presence, evoked such painful memories.

"I must go," he said, leaning over to whisper in Persune's ear. "I feel ill."

His friend turned, a look of incredulity on his dark bronze face. "But it isn't permitted. Besides, you'll disappoint far too many maidens who hope to choose you for the dance. And that, my friend, is not a wise move."

"I'm well aware of that, but it can't be helped. I need—"

"Persune!" a feminine voice called out.

Nuaru winced. Too late. Now he couldn't get away without appearing impolite.

With a sigh of resignation, he turned along with Persune to greet the two women hurrying up to them. Josephine Meeker he already knew, though he tried to give the outgoing young woman as wide a berth as he did her father and the rest of the Agency employees. And, truth be told, he knew Shiloh as well, indeed better. Or at least he had nine years ago, when she was but a girl of twelve.

However, she wasn't a girl anymore but instead a radiant young woman. True, her long red hair seemed almost as unruly as it had when he had last known her, but the color had deepened to a pleasing shade of auburn. The freckles she had loudly and frequently bemoaned had faded and were but a faint, charming sprinkle across her nose. Her sparkling eyes were a gold-and-brown-flecked green, her skin was pale but perfect, and her lips . . .

With an abrupt shake of his head, Nuaru wrenched his thoughts back to the moment at hand. It didn't matter what kind of woman Shiloh Wainwright had grown into. She was part of another life. A life he had permanently and gladly turned his back on.

"Oh, I'm so glad I found you!" Josie said just then, glancing at Persune. "This is my new friend, Shiloh Wainwright. My father hired her because she's a trained teacher and sure to accomplish far greater things with the children than I ever have."

Persune looked to Shiloh. His hand moved to a lock of her hair that had fallen onto her shoulder. He fingered it curiously before letting it go.

"Very red . . . like a mountain sunset. Pretty."

Shiloh smiled. "Thank you."

At his friend's action and Shiloh's response, Nuaru felt a surprising stab of jealousy overlaid with a fierce protectiveness. She was just innocent enough to imagine that, even with that hair and pale skin of hers, she wouldn't be a lure to nearly every Indian brave within a hundred miles of here.

"You're Nuaru, aren't you?" Josie next asked, turning to him.

He nodded. "That's my Ute name, yes."

She took Shiloh's hand. "Well, this is Shiloh Wain—"

"I know who she is."

He supposed he could've phrased it more kindly, but for some reason he dreaded what Shiloh would next say. That she'd reveal his white name and set all sorts of questions into motion that he didn't want unleashed yet again. There wasn't much he could do, though, to stop her.

Josie glanced from him to Shiloh. "Oh?"

"He's an old friend," Shiloh said. "He used to work for my stepfather on our ranch." She extended her hand to him. "It's so good to see you again, Jesse."

Nuaru stared down at her proffered hand for a long moment, then took it and gave it a brief squeeze before releasing it. "Edmund's a fool to have let you come here. This is no place for you."

Her gaze narrowed. "Well, to catch you up on things, my stepfather died last year. And, for another, I'm a grown woman now and don't have to account to any man for what I choose to do."

"So, you're not married?" Somehow, that revelation both irritated and pleased him.

"No."

His mouth twisted wryly. "That shouldn't surprise me, I suppose. You always were a headstrong, independent sort."

Shiloh's chin lifted a notch. "And what about you? If

memory serves me, you were always pretty headstrong and independent yourself. Ever find a woman good enough for you?"

"My woman died three years ago of the smallpox. Seems the Agency got hold of some infected blankets, and unknowingly passed them on to a few unlucky Utes. Onawa was one of them."

"Oh no." She flushed. "I'm so sorry, Jesse. I shouldn't have said that the way I did. Please forgive me."

"It doesn't matter. It's over and done with." Once again, he turned to Persune. "I'm leaving. I can't stay here."

His friend's brow furrowed, and Nuaru knew he was trying to sort through the conversation—both verbal and non-verbal—that had just transpired between Shiloh and him. He needed to cut that line of thought short, or risk some embarrassing questions.

"It was nice to make your acquaintance again, Miss Meeker," he said with a slight nod. "And you too, Shiloh."

As he turned to go, however, Shiloh grabbed his arm. "Wait, Jesse. We've just met each other again. And there's so much I want to know about you and your life since . . . since that day you left. When can we meet again and talk?"

He hardened his heart to her sweet entreaty and even sweeter expression. No good was served dragging this out between them. She needed to leave here before things exploded, and they were surely going to do that sooner rather than later. Agent Meeker was oblivious to what was going on around him. All it would take was just the right inflammatory incident and he'd have a full Indian uprising on his hands. And both the half-Ute Nuaru and half-white Jesse Blackwater didn't want to see Shiloh caught in the middle of it all.

She had been his friend once—his only true friend—and he would never forget how she'd stood up to the foreman that day. How she'd shielded him with her own body, and still bore the faint scar on her cheek of the whiplash she'd taken for him. No, for what she'd done for him that day in the guise of friendship, he would try his best to send her back to where she'd come from. Before it was too late. Before he would be forced to turn his back on her and stand with his people against her and her kind.

"I don't have the time or interest in renewing old acquaintances," Nuaru ground out. "That life is over. And with it went our friendship."

He spun around and stalked away, the harsh rasp of the morats and rhythmic singing following him as he headed across the brush enclosure and out the entrance. But not before he saw the hurt and confusion that darkened her eyes. He feared he'd carry that image with him to his dying day.

As Shiloh watched Jesse walk away, her emotions roiled within as crazily as they had that day he'd ridden from the ranch. More than anything, she wanted to run after him, grab his arm, and force him to turn around and talk to her. To tell her why he now seemed to hate her, and what she had done to cause that. To beg him to forgive and be her friend again.

But pride and a refusal to make a scene before the very people she had come here to help stiffened her spine and quashed what was surely nothing more than a childish impulse. He had all but insulted her, she realized as the haze of pain slowly faded. He didn't have the time or interest . . .

Shiloh's gaze narrowed and her hands clenched at her side. The nerve of him! The sheer, unmitigated arrogance! Well, *she* didn't have the time or interest to spare on *him*, either.

Around her, the scrape of the morats and rhythmic singing

took on an almost irritating tone. She suddenly felt hemmed in, smothered. She had to get away.

"I-I think I should leave," she managed to stammer out, turning to Josie. "I'm sorry."

Understanding shone in the other woman's eyes. "It's all right. Would you like me to walk back with you?"

"No." Shiloh shook her head. "Stay and enjoy this. I'll be fine on my own."

Josie took her hand and gave it a quick squeeze before releasing it. "Go on then. I'll check with you later. If you feel up to it by then, I can show you around the Agency in more detail, and even take you to our little schoolhouse."

"That would be wonderful." She managed a wan smile. "I'll see you later."

With that, Shiloh turned and made her way through the crowd, sudden, unexpected tears filling her eyes. Angrily, she swiped them away. Barely here a day, and already she was crying. And about what? Because a man she used to know—and apparently no longer knew—had rejected her overtures of friendship?

She was a fool, pure and simple. It had been almost nine years since they'd last seen each other, and who was to say what Jesse had gone through in that time? Could she really blame him for wanting to put that unpleasant time at the ranch behind him? Still, he could've been a tad more polite in refusing to renew old acquaintances.

Shiloh sighed, glad to pass under the portal of the brush enclosure and head out into the open. It wasn't the end of the world just because Jesse had briefly reentered her life, then just as quickly departed it again. She hadn't come here, after all, in the hopes of finding him. She had come to be a teacher to the Ute children and to make a difference in their lives. Jesse or no, that hadn't changed.

With every step she took back to the Agency, Shiloh's mood improved. Once before, she had been forced to put Jesse out of her heart and mind. She could—and would—do so again. This time, though, she at least had the comfort of knowing he lived and had found a new and hopefully happier life with the Utes.

⁂

"Excuse me, Miss Wainwright."

Shiloh jerked around, trying to balance on one foot as she tugged off her snow-laden boot in the entry foyer of the boardinghouse. Still deeply immersed in her thoughts on the way back from the Bear Dance, she had failed to hear Nathan Meeker's footsteps as he exited the dining room.

After a second or two of hopping around while still attempting to remove her boot, Shiloh gave up the task temporarily and stood on both feet. "Yes, Mr. Meeker? Is there something I can do for you?"

"I need to speak with you and my daughter." He glanced around as if hoping Josie would appear at any moment. "Do you know where she might be?"

"Likely still down at the Bear Dance. I just arrived back from there myself."

He frowned, his thick gray brows nearly joining in the middle. "That girl involves herself too frequently and familiarly with those Indians. And, contrary to what she may believe, they're not as friendly or benign as they may appear. I hope you will take greater care and keep a proper distance around them, Miss Wainwright."

She didn't know how to reply to his comments about Josie, so thought it best to address his request of her. "Since I'm to be the children's teacher, I believe a professional demeanor—both with the children and their parents—is appropriate at all times."

42

As if digesting that bit of information, Meeker paused, then nodded his approval. "Good. Good. Perhaps some of that will rub off on my daughter. We try our best, Arvilla and I do, to instill proper Christian morals and attitudes in our children. Josie, however, has always been a bit unruly and strong-willed. Perhaps a young woman closer to her own age is just what she needs."

Shiloh managed a smile, all the while holding her opinions tightly reined in. "I'm sure Josie and I will both profit from our acquaintance."

"Yes. I'm sure you will." He paused again. "Well, I've work to do, but as soon as my daughter returns, would you and she join me in the Agency office? I've a plan to discuss regarding how to win over the Ute parents, so they'll finally allow their children to attend school."

Somehow, Shiloh doubted there would be much "discussion" on the plan, but wisely decided to forego expressing that observation. She felt a twinge of guilt at so swiftly taking Nathan Meeker's measure, but she'd learned at an early age to trust her instincts. Instincts that generally proved very accurate.

Still, he was the Indian agent and ultimately in charge of everything that went on at the Agency. Shiloh made a mental note to keep her opinions to herself. Well, at least for now anyway. And, hopefully, once she got school going, he'd stay pretty much out of the teaching side of things. After all, it *was* why he'd hired her.

"I'll be sure to tell Josie, just as soon as I see her, sir."

"I'm sure you will. Good day, Miss Wainwright." He grabbed his coat from a peg by the front door, donned it, and departed without another word.

Shiloh watched him leave, then resumed the removal of her boots. Boots that now were free of the snow that had melted into puddles of water on the pine plank floors. She picked up her boots, carefully stepped around the water, and headed for the kitchen to retrieve a mop.

Two hours later, just about the time Shiloh had finished unpacking everything, written a letter home, and decided on a nap, Josie arrived at her door. The other woman stood there out of breath, her eyes sparkling, her cheeks and nose pink from the cold.

"Oh, it was so much fun!" she said. "I wish you would've stayed."

"By the looks of you, maybe I should've." She swung the door wider. "Come on in while I get my boots back on. Your father asked that we meet him in his office just as soon as you returned."

"Really?" Josie grimaced. "Well, I reckon he can't mean to chide me for attending the Bear Dance if you're there, so guess it's about something else."

"He mentioned discussion of a plan to win over the Utes to allowing their children to attend school."

"Oh? That should be interesting." Josie chuckled. "Considering I've tried everything short of kidnapping and outright bribery."

"You've been having that much trouble, have you?" Shiloh asked from her spot on the chair as she finished pulling on her boots.

"After all these months, I've only managed to get one little boy to come to school—Chief Douglas's son, Freddie."

"Only one child? Oh, my, then we really do have a problem."

As Shiloh followed Josie from her room and back down the stairs, her thoughts raced. It was all starting to fall into place now. She had always wondered why Nathan Meeker

44

had seen the need to spend extra money for a professionally trained teacher, when his college-educated—and quite intelligent—daughter should've been sufficient for the task. It wasn't as if the US government required that the Indians be given a high level of education, but rather just enough to change their outlook and old ways. Still, if there was a mandate placed on the White River Indian agent to produce results, and Meeker had hit a brick wall with stubborn parents . . .

The niggling unease that had been with her since shortly after her arrival flared into outright concern. Had she been given an impossible task and all but set up for failure, however unintended it might have been? Or was it, instead, a studied attempt by Nathan Meeker to absolve himself of blame? After all, if a professionally trained teacher couldn't get the school going, what could a mere Indian agent hope to do? And he could lay the fault squarely on her shoulders.

Shiloh hated even to think such unkind thoughts about her new employer. Not only was it a poor beginning to a working relationship, but it was uncharitable. And Meeker was said to be a God-fearing man.

"Don't lose heart, Shiloh," her friend said as they paused in the entry to put on their coats. "It takes time to win the trust of the Utes. But once they get to know you and see your skill . . ."

"They're good people. They only want the best for their families," Shiloh replied. "I just pray that your father can give us the time we may need."

Josie nodded as she opened the front door and they walked out. "If the timetable of things was up to him, likely he would. The Bureau of Indian Affairs, however, isn't known for its patience. And, seeing as how they're far away in Washington and probably don't know much of anything about how things are out here, I'm not sure how much more time they'll give us. That's what's got my father worried."

"He's in a difficult position," Shiloh said by way of agreement as they walked up the street to the Agency office. "Stuck right in the middle between two vastly different cultures with vastly different needs."

"Unfortunately, only one can come out on top," the other woman said as they finally paused in front of the Agency office door, "and I don't think it's going to be the Indians."

✦

"So, here's what I want you to do." Nathan Meeker glanced directly at Shiloh. "Beginning tomorrow, visit all thē Ute camps on this reservation—which, for starters, includes Chief Douglas's, Chief Johnson's, and Captain Jack's—meet with each set of parents of school-age children, and procure their commitment to enrolling their children in your school."

He paused to glance down at a calendar. "I'll give you until the end of April. That should be more than sufficient time to get the children enrolled and everything set up to start lessons on May first."

A little over a month, Shiloh thought. Meeker must be feeling a lot of pressure from his superiors to spare so little time. But then, Josie had been trying since her arrival last summer with no appreciable results. And another summer would soon be upon them.

"I'll do my best, sir," she said. "It might take awhile, though, for the Utes to get to know and trust me, much less accept my reasons for why they should send their children to school."

"Unfortunately, Miss Wainwright," the agent said with a sigh, "I don't have awhile. And neither do the Utes. I've been very patient with them, tried to be a benevolent father and bend over backward to accommodate them. Yet, for the most part, all I get in return is an avid interest in procuring all the government annuity supplies they can get their hands on and then going their merry way. It never seems to enter their childlike brains that to continue to receive, they must also give."

"They don't have a lot of choice, do they, sir, when the government requires they remain within the confines of the reservation? They can't find much game or gather much food that way, and so need the annuity supplies to survive."

Nathan Meeker's head jerked up from a note he was making on his calendar, and his glance turned to Josie, then Shiloh. "I see my daughter's already been filling your head with her thoughts on the treatment of the Utes."

"No, actually, sir," Shiloh replied, "I've been of that opinion for a while now. It's pretty much common knowledge amongst those who care to look past the white man's needs to those of the other inhabitants of this state."

He arched a graying brow. "Indeed, Miss Wainwright?"

She could tell by the angry glint in his eyes that she needed to tread carefully here. Nathan Meeker meant well. It was evident, though, that he was deeply frustrated. Whatever his initial plans had been for the Utes, things hadn't gone as he'd first envisioned. He seemed a man near the end of his resources and patience. He needed help, or the next steps he took might lead to very unpleasant consequences. Unpleasant not only for the Utes but the Agency employees as well.

"Indeed, sir." She paused, trying to choose her next words with all the tact she possessed. "From your letters to me when I was first seeking employment here, I was most impressed with your vision for the Agency and the Ute Indians. That you would lead them from sin to a new life of Christian virtues. That you would teach them to once again become self-sufficient within the confines of their reservation by learning how to farm, raise cows and other livestock, and settle into warm, snug, permanent homes. It might not be the old way of things for them, but it's the only way. And they get to remain in their beloved mountains."

His angry look now mellowing to one of consideration, Meeker rested his chin in his hand. For several long, tortuous seconds, Shiloh watched him, wondering, fearing that she may have just talked herself out of a job. But she had told the truth. There wasn't more she could say. Either they shared the same vision or she couldn't remain here anyway.

Finally, the Indian agent lowered his hand and nodded. "As much as I'd like to give you more time with the schooling issues, Miss Wainwright, I can't. I will, however, try to ease your way with them by sending one of the more trustworthy braves to escort and introduce you. And, if doling out a few trinkets to the squaws can help smooth things over for you, I'll gladly provide some extra gifts from the annuity supplies. Are you willing to join me in this endeavor? I can surely use your aid."

Shiloh supposed it was the closest thing to an admission that he desperately needed her that she might get. "I'll do my best for you, sir. I truly believe education will be the key to the Utes' salvation, both on this earth and in the life beyond."

He shoved back his chair, came around the desk, and took her hand in his. "As do I, Miss Wainwright. As do I." He paused. "Is tomorrow too soon to begin? With the unpredictable mountain weather this time of year, we're sure to lose more than a few days to the snow and cold. So each day of good travel is best utilized."

"If that's what you want, sir, I—"

"Father," Josie interjected just then, "the Bear Dance goes

on for another two days. Hardly anyone will be home at their tepees, including the children."

Meeker's mouth twisted in irritation. He released Shiloh's hand and stepped back. "Ah yes. That infernal spring celebration of theirs. I suppose we've no choice but to wait until it's over."

"It'd be the respectful thing to do, Father."

He sighed. "Yes, I suppose it would be. Too bad the respect isn't returned in kind." He looked down at Shiloh. "Two days from today, then. Make the most of the time in planning what you'll do and say. And send me a list of the gifts you'll want from the storehouse.

"You may go, Miss Wainwright. And, as for my daughter," he added, casting her a stern look, "I'd like for you to stay. I've a few things I need to discuss with you."

Shiloh nodded. "Good day to you, sir." She shot Josie a swift smile as she turned to leave. "See you later."

Her friend returned the nod, then walked over to her father. "I've a few things to discuss with you too, Father," Shiloh heard her say as she opened the office door and stepped outside. "Including an excellent candidate to escort Shiloh when she visits the camps . . ."

The good weather held for the final days of the Bear Dance, but as if it had been planned all along, a fierce winter storm blew in the very next morning, bringing below-freezing temperatures, fresh snow, and frigid winds. Still, Jesse thought three days later as he angrily covered the distance from Captain Jack's camp to the Agency office on his horse, he would've far preferred braving the wind and snow in order to put Meeker and his restrictive policies behind him. After all these years, he knew the mountains and all the warm places next to water and with sufficient game to get him through the rest of the winter. And now, more than ever, he wished to be as far from the White River Agency as he could get.

Since that first day of the Bear Dance, he had managed, quite successfully, to avoid Shiloh. Not that he'd actually expected her to come looking for him after the way he'd rejected her overtures of renewed friendship. Still, he kept sensing her presence, and not a few times, he'd whirled around to find no one there.

What aggrieved him the most was the acute sense of disappointment he'd always felt when that happened. It made no sense, indeed bordered on sheer lunacy, to want to see her again. He needed to put her from his mind and, in the doing, put as much distance as he could between them.

Fate, at the very least, though, seemed dead set against him. Nothing he could say would convince Captain Jack that he wasn't the man for this particular job. Agent Meeker had specifically asked for him, his leader had said, and he could see no reason not to comply.

It had been on the tip of Jesse's tongue to enumerate all the reasons *he* could see not to carry out this summons but decided it wouldn't make a lot of sense to Jack. It was also none of anyone's business.

From a distance now, he noted two women awaiting him outside the Agency office. Both were bundled up against the cold; though the day was sunny once again, it was still a bit crisp. A dun-colored horse stood tied to the hitching post nearby, an overstuffed set of saddlebags tied behind the saddle.

Captain Jack, apparently not without his own reasons to make the trip today as difficult as possible for Shiloh, had directed him to bring her back to their camp where Coal Creek flowed into the White River, a good two hours' ride east of here. Jesse was well aware of Jack's feelings about

Meeker and his efforts to turn them all into farmers. Was it possibly Jack's plan to nip Meeker's new endeavor in the bud by intimidating Shiloh? If so, Jack might well be in for a surprise. That is, if the adult Shiloh Wainwright was anything like the girl had been.

Be that as it may, Jesse had no intention of making her task any easier either. She'd soon learn that her devious attempt to force him to meet with her, under the guise of needing an escort and interpreter, was doomed to failure. If she thought his earlier refusal to have anything to do with her had been cruelly worded, she was mistaken.

For her own good, he had to drive his point home today. For his own good too, Jesse reluctantly admitted. And he aimed to do just that, if it was the last thing he ever did.

3

"This won't do," Shiloh whispered, her pulse beginning to pound crazily. "This won't do at all."

"Of course it will," Josie muttered from beside her. "In fact, I'd almost call it providential."

"Providential?" Shiloh turned from the tall figure riding toward them and glared at her friend. "I hardly think the Lord had anything to do with Jesse Blackwater being chosen as my escort today. But you, on the other hand, did have a hand in this. Didn't you?"

Josie pretended to find some bit of lint to brush off her wool coat. "I may have mentioned his name to my father in passing, but in the end, it was Captain Jack's call."

"Tell that to Jesse," Shiloh said between gritted teeth. "Otherwise, he's going to assume I orchestrated this."

"Rather, I suggest letting him assume what he will."

"No." Shiloh grabbed Josie's arm. "You tell him. Please!"

Her friend made a cautioning sound. "Shush. He's too close now. He'll overhear."

With an exasperated sigh, Shiloh released Josie's arm, struggling all the while to regain some semblance of composure. Jesse's expression, however, as he finally drew up before them, wasn't at all conducive to maintaining a calm demeanor. Though his face was impassive, the taut line of his lips and glacial glint to his eyes told her more than she ever cared to know.

"Ladies," he said by way of greeting, even as his furious gaze never wavered from Shiloh's.

"It's good to see you again," Josie quickly offered. "I'm so glad Captain Jack decided on you for Shiloh's escort. You are perfect in so many ways."

"Am I?" Jesse's mouth twisted sardonically. "Well, that remains to be seen, doesn't it?"

An edge of warning hovered on his words, and Shiloh felt a frisson of unease. What exactly did he mean by that?

Her chin went up, and she shot him a defiant glare. "I'm sure it'll all work out for the best. Now," she said as she walked to the nearby hitching post and untied her horse, "let's be on our way. I don't wish to take up more of your valuable time than is absolutely necessary."

With that, she moved to the side of her mare, gathered the reins in her left hand, put her foot in the stirrup, and lithely mounted. A moment more and she was firmly settled in the saddle.

"Well, Mr. Blackwater," she then said, "shall we be going?"

"Suits me just fine." He turned his horse about, then paused to glance down at Josie. "Don't plan on her being back before later this afternoon. This latest snowfall is going to slow us down even more."

The other woman nodded. "I'm not worried. I know you'll take good care of Shiloh." She looked up at her friend. "Good luck. And remember, Captain Jack can be a bit . . . er . . . difficult at times. You don't have to win him over with just this first meeting."

Jesse gave a snort. "Now that's an understatement, if ever I've heard one. I'll tell you right now that Jack isn't interested in anything you have to say. Even now, it's not too late to call it all off."

Shiloh's mouth tightened in irritation. If he thought to scare or intimidate her, he had another thought coming. The only reason she even needed him was to show her the way to the Ute encampment and provide protection against potential renegades or ruffians. Otherwise, she'd have far preferred going it alone.

Jesse wasn't coming along because he wanted to. And her gut told her that he'd no intention of making things any easier for her than he could. But then, nothing about this undertaking was going to be easy. Nathan Meeker had made that apparent from the start.

"Let's get going, shall we?" she gritted out. "And, for what it's worth, your counsel has been duly noted."

"Yeah, I just bet it has." He smirked, then nudged his horse forward. "For what it's worth."

As they headed east along the White River, Shiloh vowed a thousand times over that she'd not be the first to speak. No matter how she needed any and all information that might aid her in her attempt to win over first Captain Jack and then his people. Perhaps she could blame her stubbornness partially on wounded pride, but Shiloh also sensed Jesse didn't plan to be forthcoming. It'd be a lost cause to humble herself and beg him.

She would've, though, if she'd thought her pleas would move him. Too much depended on her success with the Utes to allow pride to get in the way. It wasn't just about her, anyway, but about her employer and all the people who worked at the Agency. It was also about the Utes and their welfare. And she firmly believed that education and adopting the white man's ways were their only hope.

"It's a fool's quest, Shiloh," Jesse said just then, almost as if he was reading her mind. "The People don't want to learn the white man's ways. They want to honor their ways, the old ways, the ways of their ancestors. They don't want to farm. They don't want to be limited to just a small area for the rest of their lives. They're hunters. They're mountain people. It's in their blood, in their hearts, to roam the land, to follow the seasons and where the food is at the different times of the year. You, of all people, should know that."

Shiloh clenched the reins in her hand. Jesse was right. She *did* know what the Utes wanted. But that no longer mattered. Yet how could she even speak such words, much less convince him to agree and to help her?

"The old ways don't work anymore." She looked over at him. "And wishing it were so and digging in one's heels and refusing to change is even worse. The People have got to change or they'll lose whatever freedom they still have."

"Adopting the white man's customs hasn't helped them so far." He turned his head to meet her glance, and the look in his dark eyes wasn't at all encouraging. "The government still keeps lying to them and stealing their lands."

"As true as that might be, I can't do anything about it," she replied, her exasperation rising once more. "All I can do is help them adapt and learn to live with what they now have. And education is paramount if they are to survive with any of their traditions intact."

"Well, good luck." Once more, Jesse riveted his gaze straight ahead. "You'll get no help from me."

A sudden anger filled her. What a patronizing, officious, narrow-minded boor!

"And exactly why not?" she demanded. "You've lived with both whites and Indians. If you'd an ounce of brains in your head, you'd know what's to come if the Utes remain on the path they're currently taking. Or don't you care?"

He reined his horse to a halt. Startled, Shiloh did the same. Ever so slowly, Jesse impaled her with an icy glare.

"Insult my intelligence if you want," he ground out. "Obviously, you share Meeker's opinion of our mental capabilities. But don't ever imagine that I don't care what happens to the People."

"Then why won't you help me with this? Help me convince the parents to allow their children to be schooled?"

Jesse sighed and nudged his horse back into a walk. "It's not that simple. You don't understand."

Shiloh urged her own horse forward again. "Then help me to understand, Jesse. I want to understand."

"It wouldn't make any difference. You're just like Meeker. You've already decided what's best for us."

"Well, someone's got to. The Indians sure haven't been very successful dealing with the government so far."

"Yeah, I know. Because every time they agree to yet another treaty, the government ends up ruling in the favor of any and all land-grubbing settlers or miners, and eventually chips away at the treaty until there's nothing left. It doesn't matter what the People do or how educated or domesticated they become. Their needs will never matter much to anyone but themselves."

"If I believed that, I wouldn't be here, Jesse."

"Then you're worse than a do-gooder. You're totally out of touch with reality!"

This conversation was going nowhere fast. And if she couldn't even convince Jesse, who was privy to both the white man and red man's outlooks, how would she ever succeed in convincing the Utes of the dire danger they and their lifestyle were in?

"So, there's no hope. Is that what you're trying to tell me?"

"No hope of you succeeding, that's for certain." He

expelled a deep breath. "Now, enough of this, Shiloh. I should've never broached the subject to begin with. Let's just finish this trip and be done with it. The sooner I do that, the sooner I can complete this task Jack's put on me, and be gone from this valley."

It was on the tip of her tongue to make mention of the fact that he wasn't allowed to leave the reservation any more than any of the other Utes, but decided that observation wouldn't be taken well. Especially since she still needed his help.

"That's fine with me," she said. "Just one favor, if you will."

"And what's that?"

"If you won't help me with Captain Jack and his people, will you at least agree not to sabotage my efforts with them?"

He shot her a disbelieving look, then laughed. "Sure. I'll agree to that. In fact, if you can manage to win over Jack, I'll eat my saddle blanket."

The twelve-pole tepees, covered with either buffalo or elk hides sewn together, stood in neat parallel lines on the snow-packed earth. Gray smoke wafted from many of the tepees through the open smoke holes at their tops, and Shiloh suspected most of the women were inside cooking the day's main meal. Buckskin-clad children played outside, and most of the men either stood talking in groups or sitting outside their tepees on buffalo robes, sharpening knives or fashioning various tools and weapons. A few others worked with the horses corralled a short walk from the camp.

Shiloh counted ninety tepees. She wondered how many held children of school age. If even half did so, combined with the children of Chief Douglas and Chief Johnson's people, she might need Josie's help after all. But she was getting ahead of herself. First, she had to convince the parents even to send their children to school.

She looked to Jesse as they rode into camp. "Which one is Captain Jack's home?"

He pointed toward a tepee standing nearly straight ahead. It appeared a bit bigger than the others and was painted with various symbols. As did all the other tepees, its entrance faced east so the occupants could always greet the morning sun. As they approached the hide dwelling, the flap covering the entrance lifted, and a man stepped outside.

From the look of him, Shiloh instantly surmised this was Captain Jack, the chief of the camp. Tall for a Ute, he was dressed in a blue trade shirt and brown vest, buckskin leggings and moccasins, and he wore a bear robe that he pulled tightly to him as he exited his tepee. His long hair was worn in two braids, and a large, round earring hung from each ear. His cheekbones were high, his lips full, and his nose long and straight.

His eyes were narrowed and piercing, however, as he glanced first to Jesse, then Shiloh. And it was quite evident, from his scowling expression, that he didn't appear at all happy to see them.

Shiloh inhaled a steadying breath, squared her shoulders, then swung down from her horse. Without even waiting for Jesse to join her, she marched right up to the Ute chief and nodded in greeting.

"My name is Miss Wainwright, and I've come at the request of Indian Agent Meeker to meet with you," she said in the Ute language. "I am the new teacher for the Agency school, and I—"

Jack lifted a hand to silence her and turned to Jesse, who had halted at Shiloh's side. "So, Nuaru, do you now let a woman speak for you?"

Jesse smiled and shrugged. "Remember, I'm only her escort. It was her wish to pay you the visit. And, as you can see, she speaks very well all by herself, without any assistance from me."

The Ute chief's mouth quirked in grudging admission. "That she does. I don't know many white women who are quite so forthright, though."

"If you wouldn't mind," Shiloh interjected just then, turning to Jesse, "could you bring me my saddlebags?"

"Glad to be of service, ma'am," he said with an edge of mockery in his voice, then promptly turned and headed back to the horses.

His lips quirked in amusement, Captain Jack watched Jesse walk away, then riveted his attention back to Shiloh. "You're a bold one. I've heard tales about red-haired white women."

"And all of them complimentary, I'm sure," Shiloh softly muttered.

The Ute cocked his head. "What did you say?"

She shook her head. "It doesn't matter." She plastered on her most winning smile. "As leader of your band, you make all the important decisions for them. So, I've come to ask your permission for the children to attend the Agency school. I'm a professionally educated teacher, and I've many exciting plans to discuss with you—"

Jesse sauntered up just then, and Captain Jack immediately turned his full attention on him. "Though I told Meeker I'd loan you as her escort, knowing full well how I feel about the white man's school, I thought you'd have done a better job of convincing her not to come."

"I warned her you wouldn't be pleased, but she insisted on coming anyway," Jesse said, apparently not at all daunted by Jack's flare of anger. "Out of courtesy and hospitality, the least you could do is hear her out. Besides," he added, holding up the full saddlebags, "she brought gifts."

Jack eyed the saddlebags with thinly disguised disdain. "It'll take more than a few trinkets for me to send the children to the school. Unlike some of my brothers, I'm not so cheaply bought."

"Nonetheless," Shiloh said, "there's no harm done bringing gifts for the women and children. It's my way of introducing myself and offering my friendship."

The Ute chief stepped aside and indicated the entrance to his tepee. "You are welcome to visit as a friend. Please, enter my home and share some food and drink."

Shiloh nodded. Then, lifting the tent flap, she stooped a bit and walked inside.

A half hour later, they were on their way back to the Agency. Though he and Shiloh had been able to visit with Captain Jack and his family, sharing a meal of fry bread made from some of their annuity flour and a pot of rich venison stew from which they all ate with horn spoons, the Ute chief refused to allow her to meet any of the others. He accepted the trinkets she offered, promising to distribute them and credit her as the gift giver, all the while denying her even that small way of making contact with his people.

Jesse knew Shiloh was frustrated, but he had repeatedly warned her that her overtures would be rejected. That was exactly what had happened, and likely would continue to happen. Still, he couldn't help but feel a little sorry for her. She meant well. Her concern for the People was heartfelt and genuine.

He just couldn't seem to get it through her head that the problem was far bigger and more complex than a simple need to educate the poor, ignorant savages. She was, in actuality, a helpless pawn in the ever-widening catastrophe that was the annihilation of the Indian way of life. And he, too, felt more helpless with each passing day. Helpless and caught up in it nonetheless, as if he were trying to swim against a raging torrent. A torrent that would soon sweep him—and all that he held dear—away.

The difference between them, however, was that he knew the fate that ultimately awaited the Utes, and had still chosen to remain, to stand with his people no matter what the outcome. The people who had always accepted him just as he was, welcoming him with open arms. What Jesse didn't want was for Shiloh to get entangled in it all. She had tried to protect him once. In return, he owed her that much at the very least.

Problem was, how to get the stubborn little redhead to admit defeat and go back to where she belonged, where she'd be safe. As they rode along, he shot her a covert glance.

She was paying him no mind, and instead gazed at the snow-covered peaks, the dark green pines piercing the bright blue, cloud-strewn sky, and the ice-clogged river on their left. Her expression was one of delight and wonderment. It was obvious to anyone who cared to observe that Shiloh loved this land the Utes called the Shining Mountains.

Her cheeks and tip of her nose were pink with the cold, but it only made her seem prettier. Her deep auburn hair, where it peeked out from the scarf she had wrapped around her head, glinted with many shades in the sunlight. And her form, even bundled up against the chill weather, was most appealingly female.

Jesse marveled at what an attractive woman the coltish, almost homely tomboy had grown into. He had once thought her sister the most beautiful girl he'd ever seen. But her beauty, he soon learned, only touched the surface. Shiloh's beauty went far deeper.

Her face had glowed with pleasure as she'd met and talked briefly with Captain Jack's children. When she'd explained how to use the little top she'd given to Jack's son, Jesse caught a glimpse of her love of teaching. And she was still as plucky as she'd been all those years ago. That was more than evident in the way she'd stood up to Jack. Though she may not have realized it, she had already won the Ute chief's respect. Jesse suspected, given enough time, Shiloh would achieve the same results tomorrow with the other two chiefs who lived even closer to the Agency.

Had it been more than a coincidence that they, after all these years and separated by hundreds of miles, had crossed paths again? Had the Creator willed it that Jesse should repay his debt and free himself, once and for all, from the final link binding him to his white blood? For Shiloh and their youthful friendship were surely the last pleasant memory he had of his ill-fated interactions with his father's people.

His first instincts had been right. He needed to get her to leave the White River Agency. And the sooner the better.

⁂

"So, how did it really go?" Josie asked that evening after supper, as the two women visited in Shiloh's bedroom. From her comfortable perch on her big trunk, Shiloh glanced up from the scarf she was knitting and across to where her friend sat in the room's only chair.

"Pretty much exactly as I told it to your father," she replied. "I saw no reason to leave anything out."

"Oh, I didn't mean how it went with Jack," Josie said with a giggle. "I meant how did it go with Jesse?"

Shiloh could feel the warmth creep up her neck and into her cheeks. She looked back down at her knitting and realized she had just dropped a stitch.

"It went exactly as I suspected it would. He pretty much told me I didn't understand anything about the Utes or their plight. That I was a do-gooder and out of touch with reality." She expelled a weary sigh. "And he didn't help me at all with Captain Jack."

"Not at all?" Josie asked, her voice tinged with disbelief.

"Well, he fetched the saddlebag of trinkets for me," Shiloh admitted reluctantly, "and told Jack I was capable of speaking for myself. And he also," she added, "told Jack he should hear me out."

As if in thought, her friend pursed her lips, then nodded. "See, he did help you." She grinned. "Oh, I just knew it was the right thing to do, getting Jesse to be your escort!"

"So, you *did* have more of a hand in this than you first claimed." Shiloh narrowed her eyes. "I thought so."

Josie shrugged. "I think he's sweet on you."

"What?" Shiloh gaped at her in astonishment. "Who's sweet on . . ."

As the realization dawned that Josie was speaking of Jesse, Shiloh vehemently shook her head. "No. You're just an incurable romantic and seeing things that aren't there. Not only does Jesse now hate me for some reason, but he's five years older than me!"

"My, my," the other woman said, clucking her tongue, "nearly old enough to be your father, he is."

"Oh, come on, Josie. I didn't mean it was as bad as that. I guess when I was twelve, someone seventeen seemed so much older. Like I was a child and he was—"

"Almost a grown man?"

Shiloh nodded. "Yes. That's it."

"So now he's what, twenty-six, and you're soon to be twenty-one? Not so wide an age difference anymore, is it? You both being all grown up now."

With Josie putting their age difference in the proper per-spective, Shiloh couldn't help feeling like a fool. Still, it didn't really matter. Jesse wasn't now nor had he ever been interested in her in "that way."

"So what if our ages don't much matter anymore?" she demanded. "It doesn't change the fact that Jesse Blackwater likely blames me for what happened to him when he worked at our ranch."

Josie leaned forward to rest her forearms on her thighs, clasped her hands, and cocked her head. "I always suspected he had a story—a difficult one, I mean. What exactly hap-pened all those years ago? If you don't mind me asking?"

She supposed it didn't matter, telling about Jesse's whip-ping and all that had led up to it. And if it would help Josie understand the basis of what seemed to be Jesse's antipathy toward her these days, then it might squelch further romantic imaginings about them.

"No, I don't mind telling you," Shiloh said. "As I men-tioned before, when I was twelve, Jesse came to work for us as a ranch hand . . ."

It didn't take long to finish the story, and she tried her best to downplay her sister's considerable role in the event. Not that Shiloh didn't still hold Jordan fully responsible. She just felt her sister's behavior was family business and no one else's.

"Well, that explains the scars I saw on his back this past summer," Josie said when Shiloh had finished the tale. "And a lot, perhaps, of the basis for his hostility toward the Agency staff, and especially my father. But I wonder if just that one incident could've soured Jesse as badly as it has?"

Josie was beginning to delve a bit more deeply into Jesse's past than Shiloh was willing to reveal. "I never saw Jesse again after that day, until the Bear Dance," she said with a bemused smile and shrug. "A lot could've happened to him in those ensuing nine years."

"Yes, I suppose so." Josie paused. "Do you know if his father was white or his mother?"

Shiloh hesitated. She supposed she could answer that question and not tread too closely into more private matters.

"His father was white, a trapper. His mother was a Ute. He traded a pack load of furs for her. Never married her, though."

Her friend pondered that a moment. "I wonder if Jesse's mother was related to someone in Captain Jack's camp? Persune mentioned that Jesse was quickly accepted by their people."

"Maybe. If so, I'm glad. Everyone needs to feel they belong somewhere."

That ready acceptance would also explain Jesse's passion and commitment to the White River Utes, Shiloh thought. If they were actual relatives, they were probably his only remaining family. And considering that Jesse had dearly loved his mother, who had died when he was fourteen, and he had hated his abusive father . . .

She wondered if her knowledge of his past was yet another reason for his hostility toward her. Because she knew things of which he did not wish to be reminded and did not want spread around as a source of gossip or ridicule. Not that she would ever do that to him, but she supposed he didn't know that. Didn't know *her* anymore.

"Does it bother you that he's a half-breed?"

Her friend's query jerked Shiloh from her musings. "What? What did you just ask?"

Josie shrugged. "I wondered if his being a half-breed bothered you. Does it?"

Shiloh frowned in puzzlement. "Bother me? In what way?"

"In a romantic way, of course. That was the original topic of this conversation, wasn't it?"

Fine. Just fine. Josie was back to that again.

"If I were to be thinking of Jesse that way—which I'm definitely not—no, it wouldn't bother me," Shiloh replied. "If the man was good and strong and brave, and God-fearing too, of course, I wouldn't care what or who his ancestors were. But I also wouldn't go out of my way to seek someone of mixed or different blood. The cruel, intolerant people would make a life together difficult. And not just for us but for any children we might have."

"You're awful practical, aren't you?" Josie asked. "I'm not thinking that love, though, is felt that much with the head."

Exasperation filled Shiloh. "No, I suppose it isn't. It doesn't matter anyway. I'm not looking for a husband, be he white, Indian, or half-breed. I've got my hands full right now just trying to get this school going."

"Yes, I reckon you do." Josie straightened and stood up. "Well, it's getting late and you've got another big day ahead of you, what with meeting with Chiefs Johnson and Douglas. Will Jesse go with you, considering how close these two chiefs' camps are?"

Shiloh laid aside her now-forgotten knitting and rose to see Josie to the door. "Yes. He said he was ordered to accompany me to all the camps, and though my Ute is good, it's not fluent. So I might need him to translate if things get too complex."

"He's handsome, don't you think?" her friend asked as she paused at the bedroom door.

For an instant, Shiloh wasn't sure who Josie was talking about. Then the realization dawned that Josie had yet again returned to her matchmaking.

"If you think Jesse's so attractive," she said, "why don't *you* encourage him? Because I'm not interested."

Josie walked from the room then turned back. "Maybe I will," she said with an impish grin. "Maybe I just will."

4

Shiloh awoke to the first rays of dawn peeking through her curtains. She stretched, yawned, and then lay there beneath the thick quilt, savoring the sheer luxury of her warm bed. The smell of coffee and something frying—was it bacon?—wafted up from the kitchen directly below her bedroom.

As luck would have it, she wasn't assigned to breakfast duty this morning, so she hadn't needed to get up an hour earlier than the rest of the boardinghouse residents. She had a good half hour to do her morning ablutions, dress, and read a few verses from her Bible before the bell rang for the first meal of the day. And she was in no particular hurry to jump up and face the ice-cold room.

Just five more minutes in bed, she promised herself, *and then I'll get up and get dressed. Just five minutes more, and then I'll face the day ahead.* She tucked the quilt more snugly beneath her chin, closed her eyes, and allowed her thoughts to drift.

Today I have to meet with Johnson and Douglas.

After the failed visit with Captain Jack yesterday, the realization didn't fill her with any particular enthusiasm. Though both chiefs were said to be more friendly with Meeker, the reality was, of all the children in the two camps, only Chief Douglas's son had attended school so far. From that, Shiloh could only surmise that Douglas and Johnson had chosen not to require any of their people to send their children to school. And that didn't bode well for her attempts today to convince the two chiefs otherwise.

A sudden surge of frustration swept over her, followed quickly by fear. Fear that she was going to fail. That she'd accomplish nothing more than Josie had, and her contract would be canceled due to incompetence. That she'd be forced to leave in ignominious defeat, with no recommendation to ensure her finding a new job. That she'd have to slink home like some dog with its tail between its legs, pitiful and beaten. And oh, how Jordan would gloat.

Overcome with self-pity, Shiloh felt her eyes burn and a single tear trickle down her cheek. Angrily, she swiped it away. It wasn't fair. Nathan Meeker had withheld vital information when he'd written her all those letters. If she'd known how bad things really were . . .

Shiloh expelled an exasperated breath. "You'd have come anyway," she muttered to herself. "You'd have imagined you could accomplish what everyone else couldn't. That's always been your problem. Thinking you could do anything you set your mind to do."

One would've thought she would have learned her lesson after that fiasco with Jesse. She'd set her mind on getting him to fit in on the ranch, to become a friend to all, and look how that had turned out. But her overly optimistic outlook had led her to believe it was youthful audacity that had led her astray. And she had soldiered on, attacking every obstacle set in her path and pretty much conquering them all. Well, at least until now.

Funny how Jesse seemed to be a part of the few—the *only*—failures in her life. Was he just bad luck for her and perhaps she for him? Even the consideration of such a possibility filled her with sadness. She had seen, felt something strong between them even all those years ago. As if . . . as if he were her other half, her soul mate. He had always seemed to understand her, even when she didn't understand herself.

But that special bond had been torn asunder, shredded by nine years spent apart and lives lived in entirely different ways. Jesse had realized that from the start, there in the Bear Dance enclosure. She, though, naïve little fool that she was, hadn't.

Tears flooded her eyes once more. "Dear Lord," Shiloh prayed, "help me to let Jesse go, once and for all. I thought I had that day he rode away. I put him from my mind and heart, because to do otherwise was to endure a part of me being ripped away. But I know now that I hadn't. I knew the moment I saw him again.

"Yet I *must* let him go. I do him no favors by trying to clutch at the remnants of what we once had. So, help me, Lord. Give me the strength to do this for Jesse's sake, for I haven't enough to do it for my own."

As Shiloh wiped away the tears yet again, she gradually became aware of movement downstairs, of chairs scraping back in the dining room and voices lifted in laughter and talk. She flung back her quilt, sat up, and gasped at the cold air that assailed her. Then, gritting her teeth, she set her bare feet on the frigid floor and forced herself to hurry and dress.

There was no purpose served worrying about tomorrow, Shiloh resolved, harking back to a verse from Matthew. Tomorrow would take care of itself. Today had more than enough problems of its own to deal with.

By the time Shiloh exited the boardinghouse promptly at ten that morning, Jesse was already waiting outside. The day was cloudy with the sun struggling to break through, and a chill breeze blew, but it didn't appear as if any snow was imminent. She fastened the top button of her wool coat, pulled her knit hat down more fully over her ears, and tugged on her mittens.

"You haven't been out here long, have you?" she asked as she joined her scowling escort.

He was dressed in his usual buckskin leggings, shirt, and moccasins, and over it all he wore a long, fringed buckskin coat lined with wolf fur. His long black hair hung loose as always, and with his height, he appeared regal but very imposing. Yet again, Shiloh realized she no longer knew the man he had become.

"Worried about me, are you?" Jesse shot back, managing a halfhearted smile.

"Well, it is still winter in these mountains."

"And most of the rest of Colorado as well. But don't worry. I just got here a few minutes ago."

Their gazes locked just then, and silence fell between them. As he stared down at her, Jesse's glance flared hot and bright. Her mouth went dry. Her face felt warm. Then, as if suddenly realizing he was gawking, Jesse stepped back and indicated the encampment down toward the river.

"Let's head on out, if you're ready," he said, his voice gone strangely husky. "We don't want to keep them waiting."

Shiloh forced her legs to move, though she couldn't be sure exactly where she was placing her feet. Her head spun crazily for a brief moment and then cleared.

This was ridiculous! One look from Jesse and she was as giddy as some schoolgirl. Whatever was the matter with her?

"Who shall we visit first? Chief Douglas or Johnson?" she asked, trying to fill the uncomfortable silence with conversation.

"I thought Johnson. He's the medicine man. And you'll like Susan, one of his wives. She's Chief Ouray's sister."

"Really?" Shiloh totally forgot her earlier discomfort with Jesse. "Ouray, the chief of all the Utes? Oh, I can't wait to meet her!"

"I'd imagine so," he said, his tone dry and matter-of-fact. "Susan and her husband are among the few Utes on the reservation who actually try to live the way Meeker and the government want the People to live." He pointed to a house, with several tepees nearby, located to the southeast of the Agency near the river. "Meeker just recently built Johnson that house. He lives there with Susan and his other wives."

Shiloh felt heartened by the information. If Jesse was determined not to help her, then she'd just find someone else. And Chief Johnson and his family, especially Susan if she shared her brother Ouray's belief that the Utes should keep peace with the whites and learn their ways, might be just the allies she needed in her quest to get the children to attend school.

All the doubts and fears of earlier this morning slowly dissipated. If she was nothing else, she was determined and resourceful. And perhaps this was at least part of an answer to all her prayers of late. If she could make friends with Chief Johnson and Susan and engage them in helping her, then she'd be free of further interaction with Jesse. He could go his way, and she could go hers.

She shot him a quick glance as they walked along, the crisp snow crunching beneath their feet, the sun finally piercing the clouds to shine warm and bright upon their faces. He had matured into a strikingly handsome man, with his dark good looks and finely wrought features. He was tall, strong, and proud. And he seemed, for all his surly ways with her, at least content to be where he felt he belonged.

Thank You, Lord, she silently offered up a prayer. *Thank You for bringing us together again, just so I could know he lives and thrives.*

71

"I've been meaning to mention a few things," she said, deciding it was time to clear up any misconceptions he might have about her.

"Really?" He slanted her an inquiring look. "And what might they be?"

"I wasn't the one who asked for you to assist me. After how you acted toward me when we first met at the Bear Dance, I'll admit I wanted nothing else to do with you."

He halted and turned to her. "Look, I'm sorry if I came across rather harshly. I just . . ." Jesse sighed and shook his head. "Well, it doesn't matter. You know as well as I that no good can come of us resuming our friendship. Too much time has passed. Besides, you're not a little girl anymore."

For a brief moment, Shiloh was confused about what point Jesse was trying to make. Then her words to Josie last night rushed back with a vengeance, and she understood.

"If the man was good and strong and brave, and God-fearing too, of course, I wouldn't care what or who his ancestors were," she had told her friend. "But I also wouldn't go out of my way to seek someone of mixed or different blood. The cruel, intolerant people would make a life together difficult. And not only for us but for any children we might have."

Was that what Jesse was skirting, Shiloh wondered, when he made mention that she was a grown woman now? But if he was, did it mean he now found her attractive, even desirable? At the consideration, joy surged through her before she firmly quashed it.

No, it wasn't possible. Jesse had surely meant only that they were now both adults and knew how poorly looked upon a friendship between a half-breed and an unmarried white woman would be. He had only her best interests at heart. A serious involvement with Jesse, even a serious if platonic friendship, would surely jeopardize her employment here.

"You're right, of course." She turned and resumed their trek down to the Ute encampments. "I just wanted you to know I never brought up your name to Mr. Meeker."

"Well, I can guess who did then. Not that *that* matters either."

"No, it doesn't." Shiloh hesitated, choosing her next words carefully. "I also wanted you to know that nothing you ever confided in me will be shared with anyone else. I won't dishonor the friendship we once had by indulging in gossip about you."

"I appreciate that, Shiloh."

She wanted to say more, about how she'd always cherished his friendship, had cared so much about him, and had always wanted the best for him. But she also feared what might rush out if she dared crack open those floodgates. No possible good would be served if she did, so Shiloh clamped down hard on any response and nodded instead.

Fortunately, they drew near the house of Chief Johnson just then, which put an end to further conversation. It was a tidy little log cabin with a pen on one side, in which Shiloh noted chickens industriously pecking at a scattering of grain thrown atop the frozen ground. Two goats were tied nearby, calmly munching on a pile of dried brush. And behind the cabin was a corral that held several horses and three cows. A fallow garden patch stood on the other side of the corral.

Their approach must have been noted from a distance. As they paused before the front door, it opened, and a Ute male walked out. He was of medium height and wore the usual braids, buckskin leggings, and moccasins, and a dark blue trade cloth shirt with a yellow bandanna around his neck.

He extended his arm to Jesse and smiled. "So, are you enjoying escorting this pretty one around to the camps?" he asked in Ute. "You're the envy of all the young braves, you know."

Jesse's mouth quirked wryly as he clasped the other man's arm in greeting, then released it. "Let them be jealous. It'll do them good."

He turned to Shiloh and gestured to Johnson. "This is Chief Johnson. And this," he added, gesturing now to Shiloh, "is Miss Shiloh Wainwright."

Once again, she surprised another Ute by speaking their language. "I have heard many fine things about you from Mr. Meeker and am pleased to finally make your acquaintance."

Johnson laughed in delight. "Come, come." He stepped aside and motioned her into his home. "My wives will be happy to have yet another white woman who they can talk with. Susan will be especially pleased."

Susan was a large, handsome woman, and it soon became evident that she, above all of Johnson's wives, had the most influence over him. She was dressed in a pale, almost white, mountain sheepskin dress—which Shiloh knew to be a softer, thinner hide than deerskin and far preferred by the women— that was heavily fringed, painted, and decorated with beading and porcupine quills. On her wrists and arms, she wore silver Navaho trade bracelets; around her waist a wide, beaded belt; and on her feet, the usual moccasins.

Though the other wives were dressed similarly, Susan's garb was the most ornate, and Shiloh knew from the clothing of the women that Johnson was a successful man. She recalled Josie telling her that besides being the medicine man and a powerful chief, Johnson, along with Captain Jack, had been a scout at one time for the US Army. Both men understood a lot about the ways of the US government when it came to its treatment of the Indians and weren't to be trifled with. She only hoped Nathan Meeker fully appreciated this.

The interior of the house, though simply furnished, had a table to dine upon and crockery and dishes that were neatly stacked on shelves on the wall. A few colorful, woven rugs decorated the floor, and the spots not covered were swept scrupulously clean. Something savory-smelling was cooking over a pot at the fireplace, carefully tended by another woman Shiloh assumed was a wife.

She smiled and offered her hand when Johnson introduced her to Susan and then his other wives. Aside from Susan, the other women were shy and hurried back to whatever they were doing. Susan, however, soon motioned Johnson and Jesse away. Taking Shiloh by the arm, she led her over to sit at the table.

"You speak our language well," the Ute woman said. "How did you learn it?"

"When I was young," Shiloh replied, "my parents hired a Ute woman, the wife of Buckskin Joe, one of our ranch hands, to help with the housework and the care of my sister and me. Her name was Kanosh and I loved her. She taught me her language at first by playing games, and later, by conversing only in Ute. In turn, when I was older, I taught her how to read, which, I suppose, was the beginning of my dream to become a teacher."

"And your dream, as well, to become a teacher for the People?"

"Yes." Encouraged by Susan's friendly manner, Shiloh relaxed and continued. "Kanosh had given me so much over the years, and I saw how learning to read helped her and her husband in their dealings with their white brothers and sisters, that I came to realize I might be able to accomplish much as a teacher to the Indians. Especially the Utes," she added with a grin, "because I spoke their language and understood some of their beliefs and customs."

"But you've not been received well by most of our people, have you?"

Shiloh hesitated. How much should she admit to? Susan appeared to be a forthright woman who, through her husband, likely possessed some influence with the other Utes. And her being the sister of the chief of all the Utes was no small advantage either.

"No, not yet," she confessed. "But I've only just begun, and I know it takes time to win people's trust. If you've any suggestions—besides giving out gifts," Shiloh added with a chuckle, "I'd be most appreciative. I'm expected to start school by May first."

"Father Meeker doesn't always understand the ways of the People," Susan said, a small frown forming between her brows. "He expects us to change our customs just because he is told by his chiefs to have us do so. But those things take time, if they will ever change."

"It's not my intent or wish to change your customs."

Even as she spoke the words, she struggled with their veracity. Teaching the children to read and write *would* change the Utes. Progress always ended up changing some things. But she hoped learning the written word would help preserve many of the old ways for posterity.

A shrewd look came into Susan's eyes. "Nonetheless, we both know that with education, change will come."

"Yes, it will," Shiloh admitted. "But hopefully only change for the good."

"Ah, but that is the real question, is it not? Who will be the ones to determine that? The whites or the People?"

Susan had put words to a legitimate fear of the Utes, indeed likely a fear of all the Indian tribes. And, for the most part so far, it had been the white man's way that had prevailed. Still, though Shiloh was against a lot of the changes forced on the Indians by her own people, there wasn't much she could do about them. What she had control of, though, she intended to wield with the utmost respect for Ute traditions.

She released a long, slow breath. "All I want to do is teach the children the skills they'll need, as the life around them changes with the arrival of more and more whites. So that the Utes will possess the knowledge to ensure they are fairly treated. So they won't be so easily lied to or cheated out of what is lawfully theirs. So that they can take their rightful place alongside the whites in the growth and prosperity of this great nation."

Johnson's wife was silent for a time, and Shiloh knew she was carefully considering her words. Had she been too grandiose in her aspirations, sounding like a lot of the men who had promised the Indians many fine things and never meant a word that fell from their lips? She hoped not. It was her dearest wish to accomplish all the things she had spoken of. It was her dearest wish because she truly, and deeply, cared about the People.

"So, what do you think, husband?" Susan asked, glancing straight over Shiloh's right shoulder to where Johnson and Jesse stood not more than ten feet behind them. "Do you think we should try to help her with this task?"

Shiloh flushed with embarrassment. How had her impassioned words sounded to them and most especially to Jesse? Did he think her a bombastic, lying fool, like so many of her kind? And would he now speak his mind and destroy any chance she might have to enlist Chief Johnson and Susan's aid?

Instead of immediately answering his wife, Johnson turned to Jesse. "What do you think, Nuaru? Word has gotten around that you knew this woman many moons ago. Do you believe the truth of her words?"

Panic shot through Shiloh. Depending on how he replied,

Jesse held the power to ruin all her chances with his people. She stood and turned to meet his inscrutable gaze, trying with all her might to keep the entreaty she felt out of her eyes.

Say what you truly feel, Jesse, she silently thought. *Say it and be done with it, once and for all.*

"I believe," her self-appointed adversary finally replied, "that she means what she says. I've never known her to speak falsely, and I don't find her changed in that regard from when I last knew her. But I also believe she will not succeed in this undertaking of hers."

"And why is that?" Shiloh asked, struck with a sudden realization of how to turn his words against him. "Because, in spite of my professional training, you find me ill-prepared for the task? Or because you don't believe your people are capable of change, even when it's in their best interests?"

Comprehension of her intent flared in Jesse's eyes. A smile briefly twitched at one corner of his mouth.

"On the contrary," he said. "I think both you and the People are up to the task. I just think time, *and* the self-serving agenda of most whites, isn't on our side."

"So what do you propose instead? Give up and not even try?" she demanded, struggling to keep the rising irritation at his negativity from her voice. "Time may indeed be our enemy. And there are those who'd like nothing better than to send your people off to the Indian Territory where they hope the Utes will languish and die. But it might not happen if we try to educate the People. And it surely will if we don't."

Anger sparked in Jesse's eyes, but Shiloh was past caring. He had suddenly become the biggest roadblock to her success in getting the school going. And, though she didn't wish to shame him before his own people, it was time they realized how detrimental his pessimism was.

"Nothing's lost in trying, is there?" She looked from Jesse

to Johnson, and then over to Susan, who'd silently moved to her side. "And there's so much potentially to be gained."

"Well, husband?" Johnson's wife asked. "Will you speak with the men about the school, while I talk with the women?"

Chief Johnson shot Jesse a troubled glance, then slowly nodded. "I, too, have my doubts that schooling will help us, but just as I have tried to change some of my ways to please Meeker, I will also try to convince our people to give this woman a chance."

In her joyous relief, Shiloh rushed up to Johnson and took his hand, shaking it vigorously. "Oh, thank you. Thank you! You won't regret this. I'll honor your traditions as I teach the children. We'll play Ute games and sing their favorite songs, and when the children learn to read and write, we can transcribe all the old legends—"

Johnson laughed and placed his other hand over hers to still her continued shaking of his hand. "Not so quickly, young one. Though Susan and I said we'd try to help, there's no surety we'll succeed. We've already attempted to convince the others to take up living in houses and keeping a garden and some dairy animals. And surely you've already noticed how little we've yet accomplished?"

His words were sobering, but still the pleasure—that she had finally enlisted some Utes of importance to her cause—couldn't totally be dampened. "Yet you have accomplished something, and when the others see how much food you have from your garden and the dairy animals to tide you through the next winter, they may reconsider. And I'll teach the children how to grow vegetables by having a school garden, and maybe I can even get Mr. Meeker to give us a milk cow for the school, and then the children can learn to milk and make cheese. There's a lot of science that goes into cheese making, so they'll learn many things in the process. It'll be so much fun, and the children won't even realize they're in school."

"She has much enthusiasm, does she not?" Susan asked. "And Nuaru himself has vouched for her trustworthiness, so I think she'll be a good teacher for our children."

"Yes, I think so too." Johnson motioned to his other wives, who had come in with baskets of fresh fry bread and a pot of stewed meat. "Come, let us sit and eat together. Time later to speak more of your school plans."

The next few minutes were spent in preparing the table and settling into the chairs. All the while, Jesse was disconcertingly quiet. She supposed he was upset that, despite his efforts to the contrary, she had convinced Johnson and Susan to help her. But what was she supposed to do? Meekly take him at his word that all was hopeless and give up and run crying back home to the ranch?

If he imagined her a quitter, Jesse Blackwater had never really known her. Or, at least, he didn't understand the woman she'd become. For his own sake, he'd better pay closer attention from here on out. The Ute children weren't the only ones who were going to get an education.

She might just have a thing or two to teach him as well.

5

The following visit to Chief Douglas's camp yesterday didn't go nearly as well, Jesse thought as he brushed his pony the next morning. He'd suspected that Douglas, for all his seemingly friendly overtures to Meeker and the other whites, would eventually find some excuse to turn Shiloh down. And his suspicions were more than amply confirmed.

The failure to pay the Utes for the land they'd ceded to the US government and other treaty failures were just the beginning of the chief's diatribe, all of it directed at poor Shiloh. Then he'd launched into a speech about the arrears in annuity payments owed the Indians, and the rumors that they were to be moved to a reservation in the hated Indian Territory. To top it all off, Douglas finished with a complaint that Meeker refused to sell them the guns and ammunition they needed to do their hunting, forcing them to buy the weapons off the reservation at greatly inflated prices. All in all, it swiftly became apparent that most of the White River Utes—Douglas included—didn't particularly like the unbending, rules-and-regulations-driven Indian agent.

What exactly had set Douglas off yesterday was a mystery, but the end result was the same. Shiloh had barely been able to get a word in before or after the chief had begun speaking.

And once he was done, he'd stomped off with his wives in tow, leaving her standing there in stunned silence.

He'd been tempted, Jesse admitted as he moved next to picking out small stones and mud from his horse's hooves, to apologize for Douglas's rude and inhospitable behavior. Then, on second thought, he'd decided it best to leave things the way they stood.

After all, he'd never intended for her to succeed. And now, with Johnson and Susan's earlier agreement to assist her, Shiloh's growing optimism needed a bit of deflating. His plan had always been to get her so discouraged she'd give up and go home.

It was good, as well, that she begin to comprehend the general sentiments the Utes held about Meeker. So far, the point of view had all been one-sided—Meeker's side. Shiloh couldn't have a true concept of what she was facing until she began to hear what the People had to say. The *majority* of the People, who didn't subscribe to Johnson and Susan's belief that they should learn and live the white man's way.

"And what's so serious on such a fine day," a voice unexpectedly pierced Jesse's thoughts, "that'd make you wear such a forbidding frown?"

Jesse dropped his pony's hoof and whirled around. Persune sat atop his black pony, grinning down at him. "Rather, what's brought you all the way to Jack's camp?" Jesse asked his friend. "Your wives running out of things for you to do around your own tepee?"

Persune chuckled. "More like the harder I worked, the more they found, so I told them I was going fishing. If the fish are closer to the surface, we can try spearing them." He motioned to the spear tied to his back. "And if they're deeper, there's always the hook and line," he added, indicating the empty woven grass bag to hold his catch and several handmade fishing lines with bone hooks that hung from his belt. "Care to come along?"

The idea held much appeal. Though they were still eating the venison he'd caught over a week ago, some fresh fish would be a nice change of diet. Still, he had that war shield to mend and a lance tip and knife blade to sharpen . . .

"Yes. I'll come." Jesse made his way to his tepee and crawled inside. Ten minutes later, they were riding from camp and headed toward the river.

They didn't talk much until they reached the river, secured their horses, and tried for a time to spear fish. When that proved fruitless, the two men settled down to line fishing from a big boulder jutting over the river's rushing waters. The sun was warm, the rock's surface comfortable, and though the fish didn't seem to be in any hurry to accommodate them and latch onto their hooks, the time passed pleasantly enough.

"I was away when you brought the red-haired woman to our camp yesterday," Persune said after a while. "I heard, though, your visit with Douglas didn't go well."

At the reminder, Jesse grimaced. "You know how unpleasant Douglas can be when he's in a foul mood. I don't understand, though, why he chose to take out his frustrations with Meeker on Shiloh."

His friend shrugged, pulled up his line from the calm spot of water on the far side of the boulder, glanced at it briefly to see if the hook was still baited—which it was—and then lowered it back into the river. "Sometimes, when the dung gets stacked too high and deep, the heat builds up and the pile finally bursts into flame. For Douglas, this might have been one of those times."

"Perhaps so." Jesse sighed. "I just felt sorry for her."

From the corner of his vision, he saw Persune slant a curious look his way and belatedly wished he hadn't shared that particular insight. Though they could usually talk about anything and do so without regrets, Jesse instinctively knew he had made a serious blunder. A blunder that was soon confirmed.

"So, you have feelings for the red-haired one, do you?"

Jesse bit back an irritated curse. "No." He punctuated that reply with a shake of his head. "Or at least not in the way I think you mean. I'd feel sorry for anyone forced to endure Douglas's wrath. Well, at least anyone not deserving of it."

"Well, if that's so, I suppose it won't matter then that Broken Antler has expressed interest in the woman."

"What?" Jesse's head whipped around from the fishing line he was watching. "Broken Antler? What does he want with Shiloh?"

"He wants the same thing several other men want, once they saw her womanly face and form, and of course, that red hair. He wishes to offer for her to become his wife." As he replied, Persune's expression was suspiciously innocent. "And he was wondering, if you're not planning on asking her, what you thought might be a fair bride price for such a special woman. Four or five ponies?"

Jesse clamped down hard on his anger—and a surprisingly fierce surge of protectiveness—and forced himself not to add further fuel to his friend's curiosity. "Shiloh's worth a lot more than all the ponies in Broken Antler's possession. But it doesn't matter. White courtship customs are different from ours. You *did* explain that to him, didn't you?"

"How could I? I hardly understand them myself."

"She won't have him at any rate. Besides, her family lives far, far south of here. The usual bargaining with the parents would be impossible."

Persune scratched his jaw. "That would certainly make the courtship more difficult. But perhaps since she is independent of her family now, the choice is but hers. And how can you be so certain she won't have him? It's her decision, not yours."

. "Broken Antler already has a wife, and he doesn't treat *her* very well. Until he learns how, he doesn't deserve to take a second wife."

"That may be, but it's not really up to you or me, is it? After all, you've already said you've no feelings for the red-haired one. And if you're so certain she'll reject him, what does it matter anyway?"

As Jesse sat there, silently fuming as he cast about for some plausible counter to Persune's comments, the admission that he actually *did* care about Shiloh gradually penetrated his awareness. Maybe not in some romantic way, of course, he hastily clarified, but as someone who was concerned with her welfare. As an old friend if nothing else.

"Just tell Broken Antler to stay away from her," Jesse gritted out. "Shiloh's got enough on her hands right now without having to deal with a Ute courtship ritual."

"Oh, so now I'm the bearer of threats, am I?" The other man gave a disgusted snort. "And should I tell all the others, too, the same thing? That Nuaru says leave Red-hair alone or else?"

Jesse could just imagine a long line of braves waiting their turn to fight him. Not that the consideration concerned him— he was a feared warrior and could likely vanquish most or all of them, one by one. Still, the ludicrousness of such an act did give him pause. He didn't wish to court Shiloh himself, but he refused to allow anyone else to court her? He had to admit it didn't make much sense.

He released a frustrated breath. He couldn't protect Shiloh from every possible occurrence, and this was one of them. She'd just have to deal with it on her own. Which probably— the sudden realization flashed through Jesse's mind—wasn't necessarily a bad thing. He sincerely doubted she'd accept

Broken Antler's—or any of the other Ute braves'—offer of marriage.

What might happen, however, was that she'd find it yet another reason to cut short this futile and foolish undertaking of hers. The image of Shiloh being visited by one brave after another, a string of ponies and other gifts in hand, filled Jesse with amusement. Indeed, the offers of marriage could be just the thing to help hasten her departure.

"You've made a very good point, my friend," he said. "I don't have any right to interfere. Tell them all that they should do what they must. And if she rejects them the first time or two, encourage them to return again and again with even more ponies."

Persune's crestfallen expression was almost comical, and it was all Jesse could do to keep a straight face. His friend's response also confirmed a surprising matchmaking streak Jesse had never before noted. Perhaps, in some backhanded fashion, Persune hoped that if Jesse was successful in taking Shiloh to wife, Josie Meeker would more eagerly consider him.

That dream, however, was as doomed to failure as any Jesse could've had, *if* he'd chosen to have any. Which he didn't.

Just then something tugged on the end of his fishing line. Jesse glanced down and saw a flash of silver.

"I've got one!" he cried, and set to battling the fish who seemed quite adamantly determined not to be caught. And, blessedly, in the ensuing minutes, further thought of Shiloh Wainwright and the consideration of what a courtship of her would be like fled his mind.

❧

After four initial proposals of marriage, followed by two repeat offers in the course of one week, Shiloh was nearly beside herself with embarrassment. Nearly everyone in the boardinghouse was teasing her nonstop, and it had gotten so she actually dreaded mealtime.

Most of her Ute suitors were polite and kind, and it near to broke her heart to see the slump in their shoulders as she tried, as gently as she could, to explain she did not wish to marry anyone right now. One brave, however, a stocky, hard-muscled man with a long, ugly scar down the right side of his face and cold black eyes only seemed to get angrier each time she turned him down. And she didn't care for the hungry looks he gave her whenever they happened to see each other.

"When will it stop, Josie?" Shiloh all but wailed one Saturday afternoon two weeks later as they took their daily constitutional down to the White River and back. "Everyone finds this courtship endeavor amusing but me."

"Well, not a lot happens around here for entertainment," her friend replied, waving at Frank Dresser and Art Thompson, two of the Agency employees working on one of the storehouses they passed. "Father, unfortunately, isn't one for dancing or anything as frivolous as drinking, smoking, or gambling. So your goings-on with those Ute braves is quite the talk right now."

"I just hope they stop soon. I don't fancy being the topic of conversation or the butt of jokes, even as well meant as they might be."

"Oh, it's just good fun. When Persune was trying to court me awhile back, I too had to bear some teasing and talk." Josie's expression sobered. "Of course, Father quickly put an end to all that, scolding me soundly for encouraging Persune with the visits I was paying to the camps. When I asked him how was I to convince the parents to send their children to school if they didn't get to know and trust me, he finally calmed down a bit. Just count yourself fortunate that you don't have a father nearby to lecture you about your behavior around men."

Shiloh's heart twisted. "I think I'd rather have a father alive to lecture me than be without one entirely."

"Oh, Shiloh, I'm so sorry!" Josie halted and grabbed her arm. "That was thoughtless of me, complaining about my father, when you no longer have one. And you're right. I shouldn't be so hard on my father. He means well and only has my best interests at heart."

"I didn't tell you to make you feel badly." Shiloh's smile was wistful. "Only to remind the both of us that we should strive always to treat others with patience and compassion. One never knows, after all, how long one has with a dear one."

Josie nodded. "So true. So true." She paused and stared over Shiloh's shoulder. "Speaking of treating others with patience and compassion," she said, "there's someone headed our way who equally deserves the same kindness. Or rather," she added slyly, "*your* kindness. Personally, *I* have no problem treating him cordially."

With a sinking feeling, Shiloh turned to find Jesse headed their way. Whatever did he want? Considering she hadn't seen hide nor hair of him since the disastrous visit with Douglas two weeks ago, and that she really didn't need him until she chose to make another trip to Jack's camp, it was surprising to see him headed their way.

The Chief Douglas fiasco notwithstanding, she was at least making some progress with the women in Johnson's camp. And that was in no way thanks to Jesse. A lot of her good fortune was due to Susan paving the way for her in the past couple of weeks, but to Shiloh's credit, it was her own efforts that had won over Susan.

Still, Josie was right. Everyone should be treated with patience and compassion—at least to the best of one's abilities.

It was just that, at times, some people strained the limits of such actions, and one of those people was surely Jesse Blackwater.

Funny, she thought, how these days being around Jesse set her on edge. She'd never felt like that when they were younger. But then, in the days back at the ranch, they'd both been so young and inexperienced in the ways of the world. Her more so than Jesse, of course, but still . . .

As he drew near, Shiloh pasted on a smile of welcome and stepped forward to greet him. Best to seize the advantage, she resolved, and take charge before Josie got it into her head to do so. There was no telling where the conversation might lead if her gregarious friend got into another match-making mood.

"I haven't seen you in a while," Shiloh said to the tall man who drew up before them. "What brings you all the way from Jack's camp to the Agency?"

"Jack wants to see you again," Jesse replied without preamble. "When can you be ready to ride there with me?"

Shiloh took a moment to digest that interesting bit of news and, as she did, a frisson of excitement vibrated through her. Was it possible? Was Captain Jack reconsidering allowing her to speak with his people? Oh, let it be so!

"Any idea what Jack wants to see me for?" she asked, tamping down any outward display of pleasure at Jesse's curt pronouncement. Though he tried to hide it, she could tell he wasn't particularly happy with Jack's summons.

Jesse shrugged. "Who knows? I didn't think it was my business to ask."

"No, I'd imagine not," Shiloh muttered under her breath. She paused as Josie apparently decided it was time to join them. "Tomorrow's Sunday, so we can't leave then. But Monday would be a good day to go, I think," she replied as she sent her friend a quick glance, then looked back to Jesse. "Considering the long ride there and back, it's already too late to head out today."

"Suits me fine. The day after tomorrow at ten in the morning then?"

She nodded. A sudden thought struck her. "You won't ride all the way home today, then come back on Monday to fetch me, will you?"

"No." A wry grin tipped the corner of his mouth. "I figured you'd want to go in the next day or so. I told Jack I'd stay with Persune and his family until then."

"Oh. Good." Shiloh paused again, not sure what else needed saying, especially with the stilted conversation they were already having.

Josie, however, seemed to possess no such sense of reticence. "Perhaps you'd like to join us for supper at the boardinghouse then? We're having beefsteak pie and boiled cabbage, and chocolate bread pudding for dessert. You could sit with Shiloh and me, so you'd have people you know to talk with."

Yes, Josie was definitely back into her matchmaking mode, Shiloh thought with exasperation. Still, the consideration of spending some time with Jesse this evening wasn't altogether unpleasant. She doubted, though, that he'd accept. She wasn't disappointed.

"I've already made plans to share supper with Persune and his family," he said, smiling politely down at Josie. "But I thank you for the invitation."

"Well, perhaps another time then," the other woman replied, regret clearly written all over her face.

Jesse solemnly nodded. "Yes, perhaps another time."

An uncomfortable silence again fell between them. Finally, Shiloh couldn't bear it a moment longer. She turned to Josie.

"We really should be on our way if we want to complete our full walk before it's time to return to set the table for supper."

"I suppose you're right," her friend said, looking uncertainly from her to Jesse.

"And I need to go as well," Jesse said. "I promised to help Persune and a few of the others repair some of the pony pens." He caught Shiloh's gaze. "Until Monday then?"

"Yes." She gave a quick nod. "Until Monday."

With that, Jesse spun on his heel and strode away, heading back toward the river and Chief Douglas's camp. The two women stood there for a few seconds, then Josie smiled.

"He most definitely likes you."

Shiloh rolled her eyes. "Oh, Josie, don't start. Just don't start." She stepped out, leaving her friend standing there, a contrived look of confusion on her face.

"Start what?" Josie called to her. "Truly, sometimes I don't have the slightest inkling what you're talking about."

Then, apparently realizing Shiloh had no intention of discussing the subject any further, Josie gathered her skirts and ran after her.

Someone exiting the tepee and the tent flap slapping closed woke Jesse just before dawn on Monday morning. He yawned, stretched, and then pulled the buffalo robe up more tightly around his shoulders. Though it was almost the middle of April, the nights and early mornings still held a bitter chill to them. Not to mention the threat of snow this high in the mountains could linger until at least the beginning of June.

In the quiet of the darkened tepee, the only sound the slow, even breathing of its still-sleeping occupants, his thoughts soon turned to the day ahead. If truth be told, he wasn't particularly looking forward to it.

Though he had told Shiloh he didn't know why Jack had asked to see her again—and he technically *didn't* know as he hadn't outright asked—Jesse suspected his chief had given her last visit some thought and was reconsidering her offer to teach the children. Jack, after his time scouting for the US Army, could not only read but also understand better than most of the People how important it was to know the white man and his ways. Not to assimilate into the white culture, of course, but rather to comprehend the enemy better, and use that insight against him.

Nonetheless, Jesse didn't want Shiloh getting involved. Jack would use her until he didn't need her anymore, and then toss her aside. And *that* would be the best that could happen. Whether she realized it or not, she was fast becoming a pawn in the ever-escalating war between the US government and the Utes. For that matter, he supposed Meeker was caught in the middle as well, which, if Meeker actually realized his predicament, could explain some of the man's periodic frustrated and angry outbursts.

Still, as hard as he tried to discourage Shiloh, something always seemed to be happening to bolster her optimism that she would indeed succeed. First, Susan and Johnson joining forces with her, and now Jack's summons. Though she might have thought she'd successfully hidden her delight when he'd informed her of Jack's invitation, Jesse hadn't been fooled. She thought she was beginning to make some inroads with the People. And if things continued to play out as they had so far, he didn't hold much hope of convincing Shiloh otherwise.

Perhaps it was best just to give up and let things occur as they may. He couldn't protect her if she wouldn't let him. Better to just do as he'd planned. Fulfill his obligations to her, then stay far away from her from there on out.

With a sigh, Jesse flung aside the robe and sat up. The frigid air slammed into his bare skin, sending a spray of gooseflesh forming over his body. He quickly dressed, pulled on his moccasins, grabbed up his buckskin coat, and crawled across the hard-packed tepee floor and out the skin-covered door.

He needed to wash, eat breakfast, and make some plans. Plans that, he was certain, Shiloh would spend the rest of the day attempting to thwart.

Jesse's gloomy mood hadn't lifted by the time he mounted his pony later that morning and set out for the Agency headquarters. The sight of Shiloh standing outside the Agency office beside her horse, her eyes bright with anticipation, her welcoming smile wide and joyous, did little to sweeten his sour mood.

The ever-faithful Josie stood beside her, likely there to bid her a safe and fruitful journey. She was a nice enough young woman, even if she was slowly breaking his best friend's heart. Jesse, however, had to admit he was becoming mightily weary of having to listen to Persune's moanings and groanings every time he visited these days. Based on his friend's misery, unrequited love was not something Jesse ever cared to experience.

In the distance, a mule team pulled a loaded freight wagon over the last rise. Likely more supplies for the Agency, Jesse thought. If additional annuity goods were in that load, he knew word would travel fast among the camps, and in the next few hours, Utes would be swarming the area, eagerly watching everything that was unloaded.

Luckily, he and Shiloh would be long gone before all the chaos ensued. He drew up his horse a few feet from where she was standing and looked down at her.

"Ready to head out to Jack's camp?"

93

"Yes." She shot a glance toward the freight wagon slowly lumbering toward the Agency. "Would you mind waiting for a few minutes more? Until the freight wagon arrives? I just want to see if there are any letters from home."

Another fifteen or twenty minutes weren't going to immeasurably impact their trip. Besides, Jesse knew how important letters from her family must be to Shiloh. She had been such a tenderhearted person as a girl. From all he could tell, she still was.

"Suit yourself. It's up to you how soon you want to get to Jack's camp."

"It won't be long, I promise. In fact, I'll just ride out to meet the freight driver right now." She untied her horse, gathered up the reins, and quickly mounted. "I'll be back in a few minutes."

With that, Shiloh urged her horse into a fast walk that swiftly accelerated into a lope. As Jesse watched, she soon reached the wagon, and the driver halted. There was a brief interchange. Then the man reached behind him and pulled out a packet of letters, which he handed to Shiloh.

He pointed to the one on top and appeared to explain something. Shiloh immediately pulled that letter free and ripped it open. For a long moment she avidly read the letter, then ever so slowly looked in Jesse's direction.

Even from the distance separating them, he could tell something was wrong. His instincts were confirmed when Shiloh turned back to the freight driver, appeared to thank him, then urged her horse around and galloped back to them.

"Oh no," Josie whispered, moving closer. "I fear it must be bad news."

Jesse didn't reply, fixing his gaze on Shiloh as she rode ever nearer. Now, he could make out her pale, panic-stricken face and overbright eyes. His gut clenched. Whatever it was, it likely involved one of her family.

"What is it, Shiloh?" Josie immediately demanded when her friend reined in her horse before them. "Tell me, before I die of worry."

For a fleeting instant, Shiloh's tear-filled eyes met Jesse's. Then she looked down at her friend.

"It's a telegram. A telegram from home. My sister is gravely ill and m-may not live." She stopped and swallowed hard. "They said for me to get home just as soon as I can."

6

Jesse never thought he'd find himself sitting at the dining room table of the Agency boardinghouse. What made the experience seem even more unreal was the fact that Nathan Meeker and his wife sat opposite him, with Shiloh beside him and Josie on her other side. To add to the oppressive sense of crowdedness he always felt indoors, several of the Agency workers hovered in the background, most likely to keep an eye on him.

It seemed almost like a social gathering, perhaps after a Sunday dinner. A social gathering he felt out of place in, and decidedly uncomfortable in the bargain. Only Jesse's concern for Shiloh kept him planted in his chair.

She had barely learned of her sister's dire condition when she began making plans to pack a few belongings, borrow a rifle, and head south on her own. Only Josie's quick intervention and strong encouragement that Shiloh discuss her departure first with her father convinced the distraught young woman to pause and reflect on her impulsive decision. But only for a very short time.

"I appreciate your concern, sir," she was saying, gazing resolutely across the table at the Indian agent that afternoon. "But it's a six-day trip back up to Rawlins, and if I miss the train, another few days before the next one comes through.

And then it's a two-day trip to Denver on the train, then another day to Colorado Springs then Pueblo, and then another three days' ride from there to our ranch. Under the best circumstances—including good weather the whole way—I wouldn't make it home for nearly two weeks. On horseback, heading south instead, I could maybe make it in about a week. And time appears to be very much of the essence."

Meeker sighed, glanced briefly at his wife then back to Shiloh. "I understand that, Miss Wainwright. But it's far too dangerous for you to go alone, and I can't spare any of the men right now. So the safest course is to accompany Mr. Collum back to Rawlins on his freight wagon. He said he'd be happy to head out first thing tomorrow morning, just to get you there as quickly as he could."

From his position, half-turned in his chair toward Shiloh with one arm resting on the table, Jesse could see her jaw clench in stubborn determination. As a girl, she had always been headstrong and mule-headed, especially when she made up her mind. And Jesse sensed Shiloh had already made her decision. Nothing anyone could say would sway her. If she couldn't convince them of the rightness of her plan, she'd just wait until they weren't looking and do exactly what she wished.

He inwardly sighed. Meeker, for once, was right. It was indeed far too dangerous for Shiloh to head for home alone. But she was just crazy enough to attempt it.

"I'll go with her," he heard himself saying, wondering even as he spoke who the crazy one really was. "I know these mountains like the back of my hand, and the quickest way to her ranch. At the very least, she'll be safer with me than with any of your men."

With a cry of joy, Shiloh swung around and clasped the arm he had laid on the table. "Oh, Jesse. Thank you. Thank you so much!"

Despite his resolve not to let her touch his heart ever again, he felt himself drawn into her overbright eyes, floundering helplessly in the warm gratitude shimmering there. An answering warmth flared deep within him. A reluctant smile touched his lips. For an instant, it seemed as if they were the only people present in the room.

Then Nathan Meeker harshly cleared his throat. "An admirable offer, to be sure," the older man said, "but also unacceptable. Miss Wainwright needs a proper escort, or I'll never hear the end of it from her family."

Jesse went taut, then turned an icy gaze to the Indian agent. "'A proper escort'?" he asked, carefully enunciating the words in his rising anger. "One that isn't of Indian blood, I presume?"

The other man had the good grace to blush. "I'm not saying this because I doubt your honorable intentions. But I also have a responsibility to see to Miss Wainwright's reputation, and her family might take offense—"

"I assure you, Mr. Meeker," Shiloh cut in just then, "my family will take no offense if Jesse accompanies me home. He used to work for us, so he's well known at our ranch. And no one there doubts that he's a good and honorable gentleman."

If the situation wasn't so tense and Shiloh's desperation to get home as quickly as possible so evident, Jesse would've laughed out loud. Likely some folk still remained at Castle Mountain Ranch who remembered the terrible day of his whipping. And if Jordan recovered from whatever ailed her, fairly or not, she'd be the first to dispute his being an "honorable gentleman."

But no one present—save Shiloh—apparently knew that story. And he wasn't about to contradict her claims. Indeed, the more he thought about it, the more Jesse liked the plan. In making certain she'd get safely home, he might also manage to get her to reconsider returning to the White River Agency. It seemed the perfect solution to everything he'd wanted.

"There's still the issue of a chaperone," the agent said at last. "I wouldn't feel right sending you on such a long journey alone with a man not any relation to you. As a properly reared young lady, I'm sure you'd at least agree with me on that."

Shiloh paused, then nodded. "In most circumstances and places, yes, I would agree with you, Mr. Meeker. But Jesse is known and approved by my family; this is an emergency, and women living in the West aren't as bound to societal strictures as they are in cities out East. We can't be, or we'd never get anything done, much less survive very long out here."

"Nonetheless—"

"Sir," she politely but firmly interjected, "I had no chaperone when I first rode out here with Mr. Collum on his freight wagon. Why is this any different?"

For a long moment, Meeker didn't reply, evidently struggling to formulate some tactful response. Jesse locked gazes with him. "Let me help you," he ground out at last. "Mr. Collum was a white man, and that made all the difference in the world. Didn't it?"

"Mr. Collum is a married man," the agent finally replied. "You, young man, aren't."

The barely controlled anger flared hot and bright. "I still would be," Jesse snarled, half-rising from his seat before Shiloh grabbed his arm and pulled him back down, "if my wife hadn't used a blanket given to her from this very agency! A blanket that gave her smallpox!"

Nathan Meeker's eyes widened. He drew in a shaky breath. "I-I regret the death of your wife. Truly I do. But it isn't fair to blame me for something that happened before I arrived. I would've never allowed such a thing to happen."

Shiloh's fingers dug into his arm. Jesse knew she was

cautioning him to get control of his temper. He inhaled several long, slow breaths and willed his anger-taut body to relax.

"Likely you wouldn't have, if you'd known." He managed a wan smile. "And it's entirely possible the other agent didn't know he'd been sent contaminated blankets either. It's just when you claimed Mr. Collum was a better escort for Miss Wainwright because he was married, and I was found lacking because I wasn't . . . well, you touched on a sore spot."

"It's quite understandable." The older man sitting across from him actually looked contrite. "Please forgive my insensitivity to your loss."

Though Jesse was surprised Meeker would humble himself to apologize to any Indian, he decided it best to take the apology at face value. He still didn't trust the man or his intentions for the People, but nothing was served acting like an arrogant boor by refusing to forgive him.

"It's already forgotten," he softly said.

"So, it's settled then." Shiloh apparently decided to seize the opportunity that the embarrassing little aside with Meeker had given her. "Mr. Blackwater will accompany me back to our ranch."

Jesse watched the indecision slowly transform itself into resignation in Nathan Meeker's eyes. Though not for one minute did he imagine the agent truly approved of him escorting Shiloh home, Jesse knew the man probably also suspected he'd not win the argument. Shiloh always was one to wear her heart on her sleeve, and Meeker likely guessed she'd leave with or without someone to accompany her.

"I suppose I can accept your assurances, Miss Wainwright, that your family would find this man"—as he spoke, Meeker indicated Jesse—"a suitable companion. Once you arrive home, you will keep us apprised of the situation, won't you, and your expected date of return to the Agency?"

"Of course, sir. It's the very least I can do. And I promise I'll return just as soon as my sister's safely on the way to a full recovery."

Beside him, Jesse could see Shiloh visibly relax and smile in apparent relief. She was an attractive woman in any circumstance, but when she smiled . . .

He expelled a soft breath, already wondering what he had just gotten himself into. A week or more alone with Shiloh Wainwright promised to be fraught with complications, the least of which was keeping an emotional distance. He recognized that very clearly now.

His first impulse to offer to escort her home hadn't been very well thought out. He had reacted to her distress, wishing to protect her and diminish her pain. The consideration that this might finally be the way to get her to leave the Agency as well as to permanently assure she never returned had been much slower in coming. So slow, in fact, that Jesse recognized the danger he was in.

He cared for Shiloh. Cared for her as a grown man for a grown woman. Yet even as he admitted his feelings, Jesse knew there was no hope for them. For all practical purposes, he was an Indian. And she was a white woman.

No good could come of a relationship between them. No good at all.

As the first rays of dawn crept over the mountains east of the wide river valley, Shiloh and Jesse set off for Castle Mountain Ranch. Their saddlebags were laden with food, ammunition, and additional warm clothing. Bedrolls were tied to the back of their saddles, and each had a rifle in a scabbard and two canteens full of water hanging from their saddle horns. They were as prepared as anyone could be for the long trek ahead of them.

Jesse chose to wear his buckskins and fur-lined coat. Shiloh, however, to Mrs. Meeker's consternation and her husband's overt disapproval, donned a warm flannel shirt, denims, and boots, topped off with her wool coat and a wide-brimmed hat. She wasn't about to brave the mountain wilderness in long skirts, no matter what anyone thought of the propriety of the action. They were in the West now. And there were times when one had to set aside what might be considered unladylike comportment for what was not only practical but sensible.

Shiloh had left a hastily written note in Josie's custody, to be telegraphed from Rawlins just as soon as Mr. Collum arrived back there. It might or might not reach the town of Ashton, and subsequently her brothers at the ranch, before she and Jesse made it back there. Everything depended on the amount of delays they might encounter in their journey south, the very least of which might include the unpredictable late-spring, Rocky Mountain weather.

It seemed nearly all the inhabitants of the boardinghouse saw them off, as well as Mr. and Mrs. Meeker. Shiloh was surprised at the tears that sprung to her eyes as she and Jesse headed their horses away from the Agency toward the White River. Somewhere, in the past three and a half weeks, the Agency and most of its people had begun to feel like family.

She shot a surreptitious glance at Jesse, who rode to her left. His expression was inscrutable. But then, he likely didn't appreciate the presence of any whites on his precious reservation lands, and so wasn't at all bothered to be leaving the Agency folk behind. That he cared enough to embark on what would be at least a six-day trip through some frequently harsh terrain, just to help her out, was what mattered most to

Shiloh. It was the sort of thing the old Jesse would've done, and that gladdened her heart.

Little by little, he was beginning to lower his defenses against her, just like he'd done all those years ago. Little by little, he seemed to be trusting her again. That day he'd turned and walked away from her at the Bear Dance, Shiloh had thought she'd lost him forever. Lost him just as she had nine years ago when he'd ridden, bloody and beaten, from their ranch.

She knew now she couldn't bear to lose him again. That one time, long ago, had been more than enough. But how to convince Jesse to resume a friendship forged once in their youth and now on the verge of restoration as adults?

Well, Shiloh reassured herself, there'd be plenty of time alone together to work on that dilemma. And maybe the endeavor would help keep her mind—and worries—off her sister. If she still even lived . . .

Please, Lord, she prayed. *Don't let me be too late. Jordan and I didn't part very well that last time I left the ranch. I've always harbored so much resentment against her for what she'd done to Jesse, not to mention the tiresome, superior way she always treated me. Yet she's still my sister. I love her and desperately need to have her hear that. Oh, please, let me at least be able to tell her that!*

"If it's all right with you," Jesse said just then, piercing her painful thoughts, "I'd like as much as possible to avoid any settlements or camps along the way. A lot of folk won't take kindly to some Ute escorting a pretty white woman through the mountains. And the resultant 'discussion' with them over that could slow us down a lot. Not to mention, I'd prefer not to have to kill any of them, because then we'd have a posse of Indian-hating whites on our hands."

Shiloh expelled an exasperated breath, even as a frisson of pleasure at Jesse calling her "pretty" coursed through her.

"If that's what you want, that's fine with me. But you really should stop assuming all whites hate Indians. Because it's just not true."

"Problem is," he grimly replied, "it's kind of hard to separate the Indian lovers from the haters. Most times, you don't find that out until it's too late."

There was a thread of bitterness, likely well substantiated by many years of personal experience, in his words. Compassion filled her. She looked once again at him and saw the rigid set of his shoulders and tight line of his jaw. Though she yearned to know more about what his life had been like since he'd left the ranch, she also sensed he was in no mood to confide in her right now.

"Except for my red hair causing an occasional stir," she said instead, "I've never felt like I stood out in any crowd, or that I didn't belong. Not until I came to the Agency and first mingled with the People at the Bear Dance, and then when I visited the camps. But the sense of alienation, of being different and that I didn't fit in and maybe wasn't even wanted there, struck me so strongly then. And it wasn't a very pleasant feeling."

"We're from two different worlds, Shiloh." Jesse's expression turned pensive, sad. "Two worlds that unfortunately don't seem to understand each other very well or want to accept each other."

"And that's exactly why I wanted to come to the Agency and teach the children, Jesse!" In spite of her efforts to control it, excitement tightened her voice. "Because there's no reason why we can't come to understand and accept each other. We're all God's creatures. He loves us equally and we're called to love our neighbors because of our love for Jesus."

His mouth twisted in disdain. "For one thing, not all whites are Christians. And, for another, a lot of those who claim to be Christians don't think Christ's mandate to love extends to even some of their own kind, much less to heathen savages. You know that as well as I."

"I do know that," she said. "But you can't give up on your vision of life and how others should be treated because of the evil done by a few. Instead, you have to find and join with the good people to make this world a better place."

"Which I have. The only difference is I chose to try and make the lives of the Ute people better. I've no interest in involving myself with the whites anymore, at least not any more than I have to."

Frustration filled her. "But, with your shared Ute and white blood, you've been given the opportunity to make an impact on both worlds, for the good of both."

Jesse graced her with a disbelieving look. "Surely you're not that naïve to imagine I've any influence with the whites? As far as they're concerned, even one drop of Indian blood makes one an Indian. When they look at me, they don't see a half-white man. They see a full-blooded Ute Indian."

"And since when do you let another's view of you determine what you will or will not do or believe?" As much as she tried to hold on to her rapidly fraying patience with Jesse's negativity, she was beginning to lose her temper. "The Jesse Blackwater I knew nine years ago certainly didn't."

With an aggravated sound, he reined in his horse and turned in his saddle to lock gazes with her. "Look, I think it's past time we drop this particular conversation. Let's just agree to disagree. Because, if we don't, this is going to be a pretty long and miserable trip for the both of us."

Shiloh halted her own horse, then opened her mouth to explain herself further. After a moment's consideration, however, she clamped it shut again.

105

She had pushed too hard. She needed to back off. And Jesse was right. They did have a long trip ahead of them. Nothing was served making him angry right off.

"Fine," she muttered, urging her horse forward again. "Let's drop it then. You're obviously incapable of holding more than one narrow-minded, cynical opinion in that mule-headed head of yours."

"Oh, so now I'm the mule-headed one, am I?" He gave a sharp laugh, then nudged his horse to catch up with her. "If that isn't the old Shiloh, I don't know what is. You haven't changed much at all, have you?"

"Well, neither have you!" She punctuated that with an indignant toss of her head. All the while, though, she smiled a secret smile.

It was beginning to seem like old times, with her and Jesse trading quips and teases back and forth. Bit by bit, she was getting him to relax and open up with her. And, as he did, she was learning more and more about the man he had become. A man she was increasingly eager to know.

She had Jesse back again—or at least the opportunity to renew their friendship. And, the Lord willing, this time their friendship would forever hold firm and strong.

As soon as they crossed the White River, they urged their horses into a ground-covering canter, heading southeast, and eventually picked up Sheep Creek, which they then began to follow as it flowed southward. After several hours of hard riding, the mountains on their left gradually began to rise in elevation. They took a short break to eat a simple lunch of cheese sandwiches washed down with some apple cider, water the horses after they cooled a bit, and then set out again. By midafternoon, the towering behemoths in the distance grew closer and closer and began to form a jagged set of ridges with many streams running down their steep sides.

"The snow was heavy this winter," Jesse said as they finally slowed their pace yet again to allow their winded horses to catch their breath. "I expect, now that the spring runoff has started, that some of the bigger creeks farther south of us might be treacherous to cross."

"Well, lucky for us we're both good swimmers." Shiloh grinned at one particular memory of a hot summer's day nine years ago. "Not that you let on that you could swim until I was just about convinced you'd drowned."

Jesse's lips twitched. "You certainly were a very gullible little girl back then. I mean, anyone with even an ounce of Indian blood in them wouldn't know how to swim? It's one of the first survival skills we learn."

"Well, maybe so, but I didn't know how much Indian up-bringing you'd had back in those early days when I first met you. You didn't trick me like that again."

"Oh, I reckon, given time and the right opportunity," Jesse drawled, leaning back in his saddle to gaze up at the tall mountains on their left, "I could do so again."

Shiloh gave a disgusted snort, then followed his gaze to the pinyon-juniper woodlands that crept up the mountainsides. "What are they called? These mountains, I mean?"

He pointed to the jagged peaks undulating above them. "Do you see how the tops join together to almost form a spine? Well, I've heard this range called many things, but Hogback is one of them, because it resembles the back of a hog."

"You seem pretty familiar with this area. I suppose this is one of many Ute hunting grounds?"

Jesse nodded. "Yes, it is. We capture the red-tailed hawks and golden eagles that nest in these rocks and cliffs for our feather war bonnets. And there's also elk and deer in abundance roaming the steep hillsides. Occasionally, we even manage to outmaneuver a bighorn sheep up there." He chuckled. "Not too often, though. They're a lot more sure-footed on those rocks than we are."

Shiloh smiled, her gaze avidly taking in the scenery already kissed with the early green of spring. "It's a beautiful land, these mountains. I hope your people never have to leave them."

"So do I." Jesse sighed. "The People feel closest to the Creator in the mountains." He looked over at her as they rode along. "Have you heard any of the Ute legends?"

"Some of them. Kanosh, my Ute nursemaid, used to tell me some when I was a child."

"Ever heard the one of the Sleeping Ute Mountain?"

"No, can't say that I have," she replied after a moment's thought.

"Well, in the very old days," Jesse began, "the Sleeping Ute Mountain was the Great Warrior God. He came to battle the Evil Ones who were causing a lot of trouble. That's how the peaks and valleys of these mountains were formed, during the battle between the Great Warrior God and the Evil Ones, from them stepping hard upon the earth as they fought.

"In the midst of the battle, the Great Warrior God was injured, so he lay down to rest and fell into a deep sleep. And the blood that flowed from his wound turned into living waters for all of the creatures to drink. When clouds settle over the Sleeping Warrior God, it's a sign he's changing the blankets of the seasons. When the People see a light green blanket over their God, they know it's spring. A dark green blanket tells them it's summer. A red and yellow one means it's fall, and of course a white one is winter.

"The People also believe when the clouds gather on the highest peaks, their Great Warrior God is pleased with them and will send rain to water the land. They also believe he will someday rise again to do battle for them against their enemies."

Lulled by the rhythmic rocking of the horse beneath her as it walked along, warmed by the sun, and mesmerized by Jesse's rich, deep voice as he spun his story, Shiloh couldn't remember when she'd been more content or felt so complete with just the presence of another person at her side. She almost wished this day would never end.

But it had to. And another and another day would follow until they finally reached their destination. With that, Shiloh's happy mood evaporated. A wave of guilt washed over her.

Her sister was seriously ill or injured and could well die, if she wasn't already dead. As much as Shiloh wished it otherwise, this wasn't the time to fulfill girlish dreams of a romantic journey with Jesse at her side.

She straightened in her saddle, gathered up her reins, and glanced at Jesse. "Thank you for the wonderful story. It's time, though, that we move out again. This isn't a pleasure trip, after all. We need to cover as much ground as we can before nightfall."

With that, she urged her horse forward. The startled animal broke into a fast trot, then quickly settled into a lope. After a moment, Shiloh heard Jesse signal his own horse to follow.

He soon came up alongside her and, in a swift move, leaned over and grabbed her horse's reins. In but the span of a few more seconds, Jesse had her mount pulled to a stop.

His brow furrowed with puzzlement, he pointedly caught and held her gaze. "What's wrong, Shiloh?" he demanded. "And what was *that* all about?"

7

Shiloh sent Jesse a searing glare. Not only did she not want to talk about her muddled feelings right now, but she especially didn't want to talk to *him* about them. Jordan would surely be a sore point between them, and though she couldn't blame him for his feelings, Jordan nonetheless was her sister. The fact that Shiloh had enough of her own mixed emotions, and the resultant guilt over that especially now that Jordan might well be dying, didn't help things at all. Especially now, when she and Jesse had been sharing such a wonderful time of their own.

"Nothing's wrong," she managed to grit out in reply to his question. "I just forgot, for a moment, the reason for this trip. And I've got to get home before"—in spite of her best efforts, she barely caught the sob that rose in her throat— "b-before it's too late."

The confusion faded from his dark eyes. "Oh yes. Of course."

Now she'd gone and offended him. "I'm sorry. I didn't mean it was your fault. I just . . . ." She heaved a weary sigh. "I just need to stay focused, that's all."

"Feeling guilty for enjoying this beautiful day, are you?" Jesse asked, sudden realization dawning in his eyes. "And for the pleasure of my company?" he added with a wicked grin.

Hot blood rushed to Shiloh's face. "It wasn't like that at

all. Now, are we going to sit here and jaw all day or get on with our journey?"

He shrugged and released her reins. "Sure." He lifted his gaze to the sky, where the sun was already beginning its downward descent. "Let's make the most of the three or four hours of daylight we have. I know a perfect spot to make camp tonight."

With that, they set out once again, and the next few hours passed with some satisfying miles covered. Just about the time the sun started to set, they came upon a nice-sized creek flowing through the open meadows in the rolling foothills of the Hogback range. Enough small trees grew closely together in one spot near the creek to offer some shelter, and it was there that Jesse led Shiloh to make camp for the night.

"Tell you what," he said as they tied their horses to a nearby tree and proceeded to remove the saddles and other gear. "Why don't you start gathering a mess of firewood for a cook fire and to keep us warm tonight, while I go see if I can catch some fish from the creek? Some trout would sure taste good right about now, don't you think?"

Shiloh's mouth began to water at even the thought of fresh fish roasted over a wood fire. "I think that's an excellent idea. Just don't disappoint me, now that you've got me thinking about such a delicious supper."

Jesse laughed. "Give me a few minutes to fashion a spear from one of those saplings growing down by the creek, and you'll have your fish before you can even collect enough wood and get a fire going."

The earlier tension dissipated in the friendly rivalry as Shiloh set to work gathering twigs and pieces of wood. And, true to Jesse's challenge, she had barely gotten a good, hot fire going when he sauntered back, the mouth of a big cut-throat trout gripped in each hand.

As she set to work cleaning the fish of their innards, Jesse quickly fashioned a long, smooth, wooden spit to hang between two forked branches he'd rammed into the ground on either side of the fire. After shoving the spit through both trout and flavoring them with some salt from his pack, he set the spit on the forked branches. Soon the savory aroma of cooking fish began to fill the air.

From her saddlebags, Shiloh pulled out some slices of bread, a hunk of cheese, and a bag of dried apples. After cleaning off a relatively flat stone, she laid a cloth over it and placed the additional parts of the meal upon it. Jesse glanced at the offerings and then gestured to the bread.

"Let's save the bread for breakfast," he said, digging through his own saddlebags to extract a bag of flour. "I'll make some bannock bread for us tonight with my ration of annuity flour. It'll taste great with the fish."

Shiloh leaned forward in interest. "I've heard of bannock bread but never had any. How do you make it?"

"In its simplest version, which is what we'll have tonight, you just mix flour and water, roll the dough into a long snake, and wrap it around a green stick that you then hold over the fire to bake it." He grinned. "There are more complicated recipes that require butter and other ingredients, but that's too much to bring along when flour and water will do."

In another ten minutes, Jesse handed Shiloh her own stick with the dough wrapped around it and they both proceeded to bake their bread until it was a golden brown. By then the fish was done.

As they ate, Shiloh couldn't believe how delicious everything was. Between the two of them, they soon consumed an entire fish, some of the bannock bread, and most of the cheese and dried apples, washed down with the fresh, cold creek water. Finally, replete, she leaned back against her saddle with a contented sigh.

"Why is it food always tastes so good eaten out-of-doors?" she asked, pillowing her hands behind her head.

Jesse shrugged, popped his last bite of trout into his mouth, and chewed and swallowed before replying. "Likely because we've had a hard day of riding, and anything cooked over an open fire tastes better. Plus, it was all freshly caught or made. Well, the fish and bannock anyway."

She shot him an impish glance. "In addition to the most excellent company, of course."

He arched a dark brow. "Oh, so now after that brush-off earlier, I'm suddenly back to being excellent company? Fat chance of that."

At the memory of her chaotic mix of guilt and pleasure this afternoon, and her brusque behavior toward Jesse, Shiloh's smile faded. "I'm sorry for that," she said, her expression turning serious. "It was nothing you did. I just . . . I just was feeling badly, worrying about my sister."

"Well, I'm glad to hear I didn't offend you in some way. Considering I've managed to do that a lot since we first met again."

He rose and began gathering up the small pile of fish bones left over from the meal. After tossing them into the fire, he picked up a few thicker pieces of wood Shiloh had gathered earlier and laid them onto the slowly dying flames. In no time, the fire spread to the newly added limbs and rose high once again.

For a while, they watched the arcing flames dance, ebbing and flowing, throwing off occasional bright red embers to flare then dissipate in the darkness that enveloped them just outside the cozy haven of the fire's light. Sparks popped and crackled; the tangy scent of wood smoke permeated the air.

She followed the trail of a few sparks as they rose into the night sky, where her gaze snagged on the stars, intense points of light in the black canvas of the heavens. And, once again, Shiloh was overcome with a sense of gratitude and deep peace.

"You don't know how much this means to me," she said at long last, never taking her eyes off the stars. "The fact you offered to escort me home." Shiloh paused, then looked to Jesse. "It's bad enough I'm dragging you on a long and arduous journey. But the consideration of returning to Castle Mountain Ranch surely can't sit well with you, either."

"I put all that behind me years ago." Jesse heaved a weary breath. "I'm beginning to wonder, though, if you have."

For an instant, Shiloh was tempted to pretend she didn't understand what—or who—he was talking about. As much as she'd resented Jordan all these years for her condescending, older sister ways, the long-simmering and unresolved anger at her for the lies she'd told about Jesse was the true source of her guilt. She claimed to be a Christian, yet she couldn't let go of that anger or find forgiveness in her heart. And it was a shameful secret she'd never shared with anyone.

Leastwise, not until now.

"If you're asking if I've ever forgiven Jordan for what her lies about you caused," she said tautly, "no, I haven't. Not only were you brutally whipped and humiliated because of her, but I lost the best friend I'd ever had. When you rode away that day, Jesse, you took my heart with you."

She laughed, and the sound was softly considering. "After that day, I'd thought I'd successfully hidden you back in the deep recesses of my mind, never to be thought of again. Because I didn't dare think of you, or I might not long endure the pain. But I realize now that I did so for another reason entirely."

Shiloh hung her head and when, after a time, she didn't

continue, Jesse gently prodded her. "What was that reason, Shiloh? You need to face it, name it, before you can come to terms with it."

"Yes, you're probably right." The admission, though, was a hard one to make, even to someone who was the most likely to understand. "It's just that . . . how do you face the fact that you hate your sister? That, sometimes, you even wish her dead?"

Jesse stared at her, stunned. It was one thing for him to distrust and even hate the people who had hurt him, time and again. But he had never imagined that kind, happy, generous Shiloh would ever possess such feelings. She was light, brightness, and should never have had to experience such darkness.

And maybe she never would have if she hadn't met him. Bitterness filled him. No one who came to care for him ever had a happy ending. Not his mother. Not his wife. And now, it seemed the same might happen to Shiloh if she once more came back into his life. If he *let* her come back into his life.

"Don't be a fool," he snarled, picking up a twig and savagely throwing it into the fire. "Don't turn your back on your family because of what happened to me. I wasn't entirely innocent in that encounter with Jordan in the barn. She didn't hog-tie and drag me kicking and screaming in there, you know."

Pain darkened her eyes. "Yes, even then I knew that you went willingly. And maybe that's as much a part of my anger at my sister as anything else. That she stole you from me and didn't even appreciate what she had."

"Oh, Shiloh." A pitying look on his face, Jesse shook his head. "I wasn't any big catch."

"You were to me! And Jordan knew it."

Once more, Jesse was taken aback. He had known Shiloh cared for him but was surprised to hear how deeply her feelings for him had gone. As deep as his for her?

But would he have done differently that day, even if he'd known? Shiloh was but a child then, a mere twelve-year-old, freckle-faced, pigtailed girl. True, he'd immediately liked her, but part of that might well have been because she always looked up to him with such trust and admiration. A heady combination for a youth who'd rarely had a friend, certainly not one who thought so highly of him. Yet what normal male could've resisted the strikingly beautiful Jordan Wainwright?

"Well, though you might not have realized it then," he said, his tone grim, "you should now. Your sister was doing you a big favor. I wasn't any good for a sweet kid like you. And, even though I didn't force myself on her like she claimed, I still got what I deserved for being fool enough to think Jordan saw any value in me."

"So, anyone who loves you is a fool, is she?" Anger glinted in her eyes, and Jesse had the uneasy sense that they teetered on the brink of yet another argument. "So, is that what you thought of your wife too? That she was a fool for loving you?"

At the mention of Onawa, pain stabbed at him. He had loved her deeply, and she, him. He would never denigrate what they had by calling his wife a fool.

"Onawa saw me for what I was and accepted it," Jesse muttered. "But then, she was an Indian."

"And that's the difference, is it? No white possesses the ability to see you as you really are? And so, if they think they do, that makes them fools?" Her fists clenched, and she drew in a shaky breath. "Or is it just me? Do you just think I'm a fool for caring about you?"

Though it gladdened a part of him to hear her speak such words, it also frightened him. "I don't think you're a fool,

Shiloh," he softly replied. "But I don't understand what you want from me or where you expect this to lead."

Her eyes grew big. She swallowed hard. A grim satisfaction filled him. *So,* Jesse thought, *I've finally made her think about this, take it seriously.*

"I-I don't know where I expect this to lead," she whispered, never taking her gaze off him. "All I know is that I want to be your friend again, to have what we once had."

He gave a slight shake of his head. "And is that realistic, considering you're not a little girl anymore? To have what we once had?"

Shiloh expelled a breath and looked away. "Probably not. But we can still try and be friends, can't we? And take whatever else comes as it comes?"

She wasn't going to let things be. Jesse should've guessed it would come to this. And this was but the first day of their journey. What an idiot he'd been ever to agree to this trip!

Still, he had no choice but to see it through, for Shiloh's sake if not for his. And he'd do anything for her, he realized. Anything but let himself fall in love with her.

"Look, let's make a deal," Jesse said. "We can try the friendship thing. But you must also work on forgiving your sister. I don't want to feel responsible for getting in the middle of that. Especially now, when we don't even know if she'll survive whatever befell her."

"Have you forgiven her?"

"That's not the issue, and you know it. Your forgiveness doesn't hinge on mine. I'm not the Christian here, after all."

She managed a sad little smile. "You were once."

He steeled himself to the swift wave of yearning her words stirred. "Well, like a lot of other things, that's long gone." Jesse leaned over, grabbed a few more pieces of wood, and threw them on the fire. Then he climbed to his feet.

"We've a long day of riding ahead of us, if we hope to cross the Colorado River before nightfall. Let's get some shut-eye."

Something flickered in her gaze—another question or attempt to renew their discussion perhaps—then was gone. She sat up, turned around, and began to unfasten the bedroll from her saddle.

"Good idea," Shiloh said. "Not that it's likely I'll get to sleep anytime soon. You've given me too much to think about for that."

Jesse's smile was mirthless as he walked around to his own bedroll. "So have you," he muttered under his breath. "And the least of it will be the fact you'll be sleeping just across the fire from me."

Shiloh woke shortly after dawn, feeling refreshed and eager for the new day. She glanced across the now-smoldering ashes of last night's fire, expecting to see Jesse snuggled in his own bedroll. He wasn't there, and his bedroll was already fastened to the back of the saddle lying nearby.

She sat up and looked around. He was nowhere in sight. Both horses, however, were still tethered to a line running between two trees about ten feet away.

Likely he'd gone to wash up or hunt for small game, she thought. Climbing to her feet, Shiloh first stirred the ashes and found some still-red coals beneath them. She carefully lay some tinder atop the coals and, as the small bits of grass and brush began to smoke, leaned over and gently blew to encourage them to catch fire. When flames finally began to lick at the tinder, she added small twigs and then a few bigger pieces of wood, taking great pains not to smother the revived fire.

She filled the small tin pot she'd brought along with water from her canteen, slid a long stick through its handle, then hung it over the fire using the forked sticks still standing from last night. A nice cup of hot tea would taste wonderful and help take the edge off this chill morning, she told herself. Especially after she'd finished washing up a bit in an equally chill creek.

Though the night had been just above freezing, if the lack of frost on the dried grasses was any indication, it had just barely been so. Luckily, the day already promised to be a fine, sunny one and would warm nicely. Just not before she'd washed and they'd had breakfast and ridden down the valley for a few hours.

There was still no sign of Jesse, so Shiloh dug through her saddlebag again, extracting a wrapped bar of soap and a small towel. There'd be no privacy for a true bath while on the trip. There would also be no body of water worth washing in that would be warm enough this time of year, but she could at least cleanse as much as modesty allowed. And, in another day or two, maybe she'd attempt shampooing her hair.

She met Jesse heading up from the creek. His hair was wet and slicked back from his face. His shirt slung over one shoulder, he wore only his buckskins, loincloth, and moccasins. Droplets of water clung to his muscular chest and arms.

Warmth flooded Shiloh's face, as much from finding him half dressed as from the frisson of pleasure that coursed through her at the sight of him. He was a tall, well-made man and, to her way of thinking, far too attractive with his dark, exotic good looks. Well, she quickly amended, far too attractive for her anyway.

"Oh," she managed to choke out as he drew up before her a few feet away. "I was wondering where you'd gone off to."

"The same place it looks like you're now headed to." His mouth lifted in a smile. "You look like you could use a bit of cooling off."

Shiloh stared at him, taken aback at his comment. "What . . . what exactly do you mean by that?"

He shrugged. "Nothing much. You just look a bit flushed, is all. Kind of sweet, actually, along with that tousled mane of red hair."

If she'd blushed before, Shiloh's face felt as if it were on fire now. Her mouth went dry, her palms damp.

Kind of sweet . . .

So, he thought she looked sweet, like some little kid, while she was standing here trying not to ogle him. Frustration filled her. What would it take for Jesse finally to see her as the woman she now was, rather than the girl she used to be? And, even more to the point, would she dare try it, if she even knew?

"Well, just give me a little time to clean up and brush my hair, and I'm sure I'll look a lot better." With that, Shiloh stepped around him and hurried down the path to the creek. Behind her, she heard Jesse's deep chuckle.

Her cheeks still burning, she threw down her soap and towel onto some rocks on the bank of the swiftly flowing water. Kneeling, Shiloh splashed several handfuls of the frigid water onto her face before her skin began to feel normal again. Then she unwrapped her bar of soap, washed her hands, then scrubbed her face and neck. A few more handfuls of water to rinse off, towel herself dry, and she felt a lot better.

Pulling her brush from her jacket pocket, she then tried to tame her unruly hair. She ended up plaiting it into a loose braid down her back and then tying it off with a blue ribbon. With no mirror to check her appearance, and with the creek flowing too fast to offer any kind of reflection, she had to suffice with patting her hair to make sure the rest of it wasn't sticking out at any strange angles around her face.

Finally, after gathering all her supplies, Shiloh headed back to camp. She supposed it didn't really matter how she looked anyway. All Jesse seemed capable of seeing her as was some snotty-nosed kid.

He glanced up from his spot by the fire, where he was slicing the leftover trout from last night, and smiled as she made her way over to join him. "You clean up pretty good. Considering the primitive conditions and all."

"When you don't have to bother primping for hours in the hopes of captivating any admirers, it makes one's morning toilet quick and simple," she said, throwing down her soap and hairbrush before using her towel to remove the pot of now-boiling water from the fire.

She lowered herself carefully to sit beside her saddlebag, set down the pot, and began digging through one pocket of the leather pouches. Pulling out a tin cup and a small cloth bag, she looked to Jesse, who was watching her, a curious expression on his face. Though tempted to ask him what he was thinking, she decided to forgo that impulse. All it would likely do was get things all stirred up again.

"Want a cup of tea?" she asked instead, holding up the cloth bag. "I can't start my day without my Earl Grey."

"No, thank you," he said with a shake of his head. "I've never been much of a tea drinker."

"It's a luxury, I know." As she spoke, Shiloh shook some of the fragrant, dried tea leaves into her cup. "But I'd sacrifice a lot of other things just to have my tea." She picked up the pot with her towel and carefully poured in the hot water.

For a time, Shiloh just clasped the cup between her towel-protected hands, inhaling the fragrant scents of black tea and citrusy bergamot wafting with the steam up to her nose. She closed her eyes and for a moment imagined she was already home, back at Castle Mountain Ranch, sitting in the cozy kitchen in the midst of her family. If only her family would be intact and Jordan still alive when she arrived back home.

"Will some fish and the rest of the bannocks suffice for breakfast?" Jesse asked of a sudden, piercing her poignant musings. "I figured we might as well finish them and lighten the load a bit. Besides, the bread and cheese will make a quicker lunch."

Shiloh's eyes snapped open. "Sure. That sounds fine." She cautiously took a sip of her steaming cup. The tea had steeped well and tasted delicious. She smiled in contentment. "Perfect."

He handed over a large chunk of fish on an open piece of bannock. "The tea or the breakfast?"

"Both, of course," she replied, accepting the food.

They ate in companionable silence then finished packing their gear, making certain the campfire was thoroughly extinguished before saddling up. In less than a half hour, they were back on the trail, headed south along the Hogback range.

As the sun rose higher and higher as the morning drew on, the steep slopes of the mountains became dappled with shadows from the towering timber that grew up its sides. Waterfalls of melting snow poured down from high cliffs. The air smelled of pine needles and damp earth. And, just like yesterday, Shiloh relaxed and enjoyed the brief respite of walking the horses before once more resuming the pulse-pounding pace.

Lunch was a hurried affair. They ate and watered the horses, restocked their canteens, then set out again. And finally, in late afternoon, they began a slow descent toward where the Colorado River wound through a wide channel. The bracing scent of sagebrush and pinyon began to fill their nostrils, and the sound of rushing water reached their ears.

A river of dark, churning water came into view. When they

neared its banks, Jesse reined in his horse. He studied the river for a time, a frown on his face. At long last, he turned to her.

"I was afraid of this. With the warm days lately, the snow-melt has started earlier than usual. The river's up a lot higher for this time of year. And it's flowing a lot faster."

"So we'll have a little more trouble fording it." Shiloh shrugged. "I'm not worried. I've forded worse than this."

"Maybe you have," Jesse said. "But the worst thing you can do is get too cocky. Things out there in the water can change at a moment's notice."

"Well, sitting here and wasting time worrying over what may or may not happen isn't going to get us across this river. Let's just figure out how we're going to do this, and then get on with it."

Jesse eyed her, then gave a chuckle. "Okay, Miss Impatient. Here's how I propose we do this . . ."

A few minutes later, Jesse then Shiloh urged their horses into the water. Though she knew it was going to be a frigid crossing, she still couldn't restrain a soft gasp as the icy waters swiftly rose to her hips. Gritting her teeth, she continued to urge her horse onward. After a time, she couldn't feel the cold quite so much. Numbness, Shiloh knew, had set in.

The current was strong, but the horses seemed to handle it. Her teeth began to chatter, and she couldn't control the shivers that racked her body. At the halfway point, she released a breath of relief. *Almost there*, Shiloh told herself, glancing down at her knuckle-white hold on the reins. *Just . . . a few minutes . . . more.*

"Shiloh, watch out!"

She jerked her gaze to where Jesse stood near the opposite shore, pointing upstream. As her glance followed the direction of his hand, panic swamped her. Coming directly at her was an uprooted tree.

"Move!" he roared. "Now!"

For an instant too long, she stared at the behemoth barreling toward her. Then she snapped into action, kicking her horse full force in its side.

"Go! Go!" she screamed at the now-frightened animal.

The mare leaped forward then reared in terror. Shiloh grabbed for the saddle horn and tried clamping her legs to stay on the horse's back, but her fingers and limbs were too numb. With a cry, she slid off and into the churning waters. She went under and after several frantic seconds fought her way back to the surface.

"Shiloh!" she heard Jesse yell. "Watch out!"

Turning, paddling with all her might to stay above the roiling waters, she caught a glimpse of something big looming almost over her. Then the tree turned in the current and slammed into her.

Pain exploded in her head. Everything went black.

8

Jesse had just reached the river's far bank and turned to assure himself that Shiloh was following safely behind him when he caught sight of the uprooted dead tree headed directly toward her on the fast-flowing current. He yelled to warn her, then leaped from his horse, turned, and dove into the water. Even as he did so, he knew he'd never reach her in time.

Once more the icy temperature took his breath away. The river current was strong, and he had to fight his way back to the surface. As he did, the old pine, now a scant ten feet away, began to pass him. He saw Shiloh's horse rear, wheel around, and throw her into the river.

The tree, rolling about in the current with roots leading, swept over the spot where she'd just sunk below the river's surface. He swam toward the tree as the massive pine swept by, hoping to find Shiloh as she resurfaced. Instead, she rose several yards downstream, just as the end of the tree passed over her.

Her hair, broken loose from her braid, tangled in some of the roots. The tree rolled over again, pulling her beneath the water. Jesse flung himself forward. By some stroke of luck, he managed to grasp a long, broken branch protruding near the top of the big pine, before being jerked downstream along with it.

Water, churning around him and splashing into his face, obstructed his view down to the end of the tree slicing through the middle of the river. Flinging his arm around the rough bark, he inched his way down toward the roots. He saw a flash of red and flailing arms as Shiloh managed to fight her way to the surface. She gasped, drew in a frantic breath of air, and tore at her hair still entwined in the myriad sharp, dried roots.

Then the tree bounced off a large boulder, and the impact sent it rolling again. With a cry, Shiloh was jerked back beneath the rushing water. The twisting trunk almost pulled Jesse under as well, but he kicked away from it just in time. As soon as it righted, he swam back and grabbed hold of it again, desperately making his way down toward where he'd seen Shiloh disappear.

For a brief time, the river calmed a bit. He grabbed a long root, swam around the tree base, and looked for a sign of Shiloh. Just then, a hand rose amongst the roots. He saw faint strands of auburn hair entangled in the finer tendrils splaying off the main roots. He reached out, grasped the hand, and pulled. In the space it took for Shiloh to surface and take a breath, he held her up.

Her face was pallid, her lips blue. But recognition flared in her terror-darkened eyes.

"Hold on!" Jesse yelled above the river's roaring tumult. "I'll get you loose."

He began to tear at the bits of her hair that he could see caught in the roots. Then the tree glanced off another boulder and rolled yet again. He was forced to let go of Shiloh or risk breaking her arm. This time, though, he followed her beneath the water. It was that or risk becoming caught in the roots himself.

Blinded in the dark, churning water, Jesse thrust out wildly, trying to find Shiloh. His hand glanced off something soft. His numb fingers clenched around a human limb. An arm.

Frantically, Jesse used his other hand to reach her head and work its way up to the hair still caught in the roots. He jerked down hard, tearing the ends of her hair free. Then, slipping his free arm about her waist, he held her down as the rest of the pine sailed over and past them.

As Jesse kicked his way to the surface with his now-limp burden, the big tree slammed into a huge boulder jutting from the middle of the river. The wooden hulk spun around, its end barely missing Jesse. He swung his body to protect Shiloh just as a jagged, broken branch caught him in the right side.

Burning pain shot through him. He thought the flesh was surely being ripped away. Then the tree caught in the boulders, its farthest end nearly at the riverbank. Jesse seized the fleeting opportunity this presented and swam the few feet back to the tree. Still holding onto Shiloh with one arm, he used the other to pull his way down the tree toward the shore.

He made it just in time. With the last of his strength, Jesse dragged Shiloh up onto dry land. He lay there for a moment, gasping for breath and gritting his teeth against the searing agony in his side.

Don't you dare pass out, he fiercely ordered himself, fighting the blackness that threatened to take him. *Shiloh needs you. Needs you as much as you needed her that day.*

His fingers digging into the soft earth, Jesse made himself sit up. Then, as gently as his numb hands would permit, he turned Shiloh over on her stomach and began to try and push water from her lungs. For the longest minutes of his life, she didn't respond, only lay there limp and lifeless.

"B-breathe," he cried. "Don't you die on me! I can't lose you too. I just c-can't!"

His words caught on a sob. He was so tired. His head

spun. And he was so very cold. But still Jesse pressed on. Shiloh couldn't die. Not while there was breath still left in his body . . .

Water began to gurgle from her mouth. She gagged, choked, and then began to cough. Her arms flailed at her sides.

Jesse rocked back on his heels. He lifted his gaze to the sky in silent gratitude. Then the edges of his vision began to gray. He blinked hard against the encroaching darkness, fighting to stay conscious. It didn't work for long. He toppled forward.

It seemed forever before she could draw in a full breath, as water kept rising from her lungs to spew from her mouth. The choking kept going on and on. Finally, blessedly, however, the moment came when Shiloh found she could breathe again. And, for what seemed the longest time, she just lay there, savoring the experience.

At last, she rolled onto her side and levered to one elbow. Bone-deep shivers racked her. The recollection of her near drowning flooded back with terrifying intensity.

How did I get free . . . ? The memory of a darkly handsome face filled her mind.

"Jesse!" she whispered, her voice little more than a ragged croak.

Her bleary gaze took in her surroundings, the river racing past only a few yards away, the scattered bushes and chokecherry trees, and the greening grass beneath her. There was no sign of Jesse, though.

Fear lanced through her. Had he drowned trying to save her? She forced herself to a sitting position and, looking over her shoulder, found him.

Jesse lay there motionless, only inches from her, facedown on the ground. His hair and buckskins were dark and wet, but what sent Shiloh's heart to hammering was the blood she saw seeping from a long gash in his right side.

She turned around to face him and after a brief struggle managed to get him onto his back. His skin was pale, his lips blue. But he was at least breathing, thank the Lord.

The continued bleeding, however, was worrisome. Shiloh pulled up his buckskin shirt and soon found the reason why. Something had pierced Jesse's side and torn a ragged hole in his flesh.

Panic, this time bordering on hysteria, filled her. Here she was in the middle of nowhere, their horses missing—and with them had gone all their supplies. Jesse was badly wounded and bleeding. In the bargain, they were both soaking wet and night would be here soon. A very cold night.

"Oh, dear Lord," she whispered, her chest rising and falling in rapid sequence until she began to feel light-headed. "Help me. Help me to see what I must do and how to do it."

Clasping her hands before her, Shiloh clenched shut her eyes and prayed. Little by little, her breathing slowed. Her muscles began to relax. Her confidence returned.

The land would give her what she needed. Her Ute nursemaid had taught her much about herbal remedies. How to recognize the many healing plants even in spring, before they regained their full growth and color.

Shoving to her feet, Shiloh forced her cold-stiffened limbs to move her back down toward the river. She walked along the bank, checking for patches of green amongst the rocks and sandy shore. And, finally, she found several mounds of moss in the shallows between some rocks, already beginning to green in the warming days of spring.

It was a simple enough matter to dig up big handfuls of the absorbent plants, which she unceremoniously shoved into her jacket pockets. First order of business was to get Jesse's wound to stop bleeding, she decided, then move him to some sort of shelter. Next, she had to locate one or both of their horses. Without them, and the bedding and supplies they carried, both their lives might yet be forfeit.

Jesse was still unconscious when she returned, and Shiloh was more than thankful for that. The wound itself was surely painful. Packing the moss into the wound would be even more so.

A scant ten minutes later, the moss firmly pressed against his side and bound in place by strips she'd torn from her chemise, Shiloh finished dragging Jesse's inert form a short ways downstream to rest beneath a small chokecherry tree. Already, its leaves were beginning to swell. Not the best shelter in the world, but hopefully the branches would provide Jesse with a bit of visual haven from any who might venture by.

Any humans at least, she amended as she next set out to hike upstream in the hopes of finding their horses. Jesse's blood and its scent could easily attract several kinds of non-human visitors. She had done the best she could for the time being, though.

The activity of hiking uphill, combined with the still warm sun, eventually rejuvenated her, stimulating the blood to flow back into her benumbed limbs. If not for her wet clothes, Shiloh would have felt almost comfortable again. She only hoped the sun was helping to warm Jesse too.

After a half hour's brisk walk, Shiloh's efforts were rewarded far beyond what she had dared hope. Both of their horses stood near each other, placidly dining on the bits of spring grass poking up through the winter-killed foliage. They glanced briefly at her, then resumed their grazing. They were easily caught.

A quick check revealed their bedrolls were still tied to the back of each saddle, the rifles and saddlebags as well, and three of four canteens still remained. Neither horse was hurt or lame. Shiloh soon mounted her mare and, leading Jesse's pony, headed back downstream.

Thank You, Lord, she thought, relief and gratitude filling her. *Now, if Jesse survives through this night, and we can get him to some town or friendly settler's house, I'd be most thankful.*

The return trip was a lot less strenuous and a whole lot swifter. Shiloh jumped down when she reached the choke-cherry tree, tied the two horses to it, and quickly unfastened the bedrolls from both saddles. Both sets of double blankets were wet. Shiloh spread the four blankets atop some nearby bushes to hasten their drying.

An examination of Jesse's wound revealed the moss had done its work. The bleeding had stopped. Jesse was still unconscious, however.

She used the time to good purpose. After gathering a load of tinder and scrap wood from the shrubbery and trees growing along the river, she fashioned a fire pit ringed with rocks, then set up the wood and tinder to make a fire. Within one of the saddlebags, the flint and steel lay in its waterproof pouch. With those invaluable aids, it was a simple enough matter to create sufficient sparks, and it didn't take long before Shiloh had a small fire going. She added additional twigs until the fire flamed hot and bright, then paused to pull Jesse as close to it as she dared.

Next, she found her lidded pot, fashioned a spit, and headed to the river to fill the pot with water. After hanging it over the fire to heat and adding some bigger branches to the flames now leaping into the rapidly darkening sky, Shiloh checked on Jesse once again. His wound was still doing well and he was finally beginning to stir.

Retrieving her knife from her saddlebags, she next headed

to a willow tree a short distance down the river. Reaching up as high as she could, she cut off a sizable length of several newer, smoother-barked branches. Her booty in hand, Shiloh hurried back to the fire, where the pot of water was steaming. She stripped the bark from one of the branches, cut it into pieces, and popped a few into her tin cup. Then she carefully filled the cup with the now-boiling water.

"Sh-Shiloh?"

"I'm here." She set down the cup to allow the tea to steep, and scooted over to him. "How are you feeling?"

"Like I've swallowed half of that blasted river." He tried to push himself up, then grimaced and fell back. "And my side feels like it's on fire. But otherwise, not bad. Not bad at all."

Though he accompanied his last few words with a wan smile, Shiloh knew he was in a lot of discomfort. "I packed some moss into your wound to stop the bleeding. And I've got a cup of willow bark tea almost ready for you. It should at least take the edge off your pain."

His lips quirked. "Trying some of the old Indian remedies, are you?"

"Well, it's not like we've got an apothecary in the neighborhood." She paused. "How did you get that wound?"

"I'd just freed you from those tree roots when the tree hit some rocks and ricocheted back toward us. I got in the way of a branch." He glanced up toward her head. "Just so you know, I had to break off some of your hair to get you free of those branches. There wasn't time to slowly unwind it all, considering what was going on at the time. But I'm sure your hair will look just fine . . . in a year or two."

At the twinkle in his eyes, Shiloh reflexively touched the top of her head. There were definitely some spots of shorter hair up there. "Well, considering the other option, I reckon it was a good trade-off. And," she added with a grin, "if it ends up looking too awful, I'll just cut it all short and start over. Maybe start a new fashion trend."

He used his good arm to reach up and touch the damp curls tumbling over her shoulders. "I think it'll be just fine without you having to cut it."

The tenderness of his gesture and the unguarded expression of affection in his dark eyes found an answering chord in Shiloh. Her breath caught in her throat, and she blinked back tears.

"Oh, J-Jesse . . ." Her voice wobbled. She swallowed hard. "I'm *so* sorry. I should've never insisted on taking such a dangerous trip just to get home faster. We both could've died today."

"But we didn't. I took care of you, and now you're taking care of me. As long as we each do our part, we'll get you home safe and sound." He inhaled a deep breath, then caught himself as the pain in his side apparently fiercely reminded him of his wound. "Er, do you think that willow bark tea has steeped long enough by now?" he asked, shooting a questioning glance at the cup sitting beside her.

"Of course it has." She picked up the cup, leaned down to slip her other hand beneath his head to raise it, and held the cup to his lips. "Sip it carefully to make sure it's not too hot for you. Then, try and drink it all down. It'll be bitter, but I'm thinking you can use a bit stronger dose for a time or two."

He grimaced at the taste but dutifully emptied the cup's contents in just a few swallows. She laid him back down. Scooting around to her saddlebags, she pulled out a bag of oatmeal and two smaller containers.

"Do you prefer your oatmeal sweet or salty?" She held up both small containers.

"I don't recall ever having oatmeal, so I couldn't say."

"Even at the mission school? What did they serve for breakfast then?"

"Some sort of gruel. It tasted like glue."

"Well, oatmeal's a lot better tasting and better for you."

"I'd prefer a haunch of roast venison."

Shiloh laughed. Jesse might just make it after all. "Not tonight. Let's start with something gentler on your stomach, shall we? Besides, it's getting too dark for me to go out deer hunting."

He glanced around and sighed. The night had settled in, Shiloh thought, and the air had taken on a decided chill. She tossed a few more branches on the fire, then rose to go and check how the blankets were doing.

If they weren't dry enough by bedtime, they were in for a long, cold night.

***

As she feared, the blankets weren't dry enough to use for cover that night. By dint of not much sleep, she managed to keep the fire going and the area near it relatively warm. She made Jesse lie as close to it as he could tolerate, and she then tried to shield his back as much as she could by snuggling up behind him. Still, as the night wore on, and despite additional cups of hot willow bark tea, Jesse couldn't seem to shake off his shivering until, near dawn, he took a fever.

His face became flushed, his forehead and body hot. He was harder to rouse and tossed and turned restlessly. Though hesitant to remove the moss packing, afraid its extraction might set off fresh bleeding, Shiloh knew she needed to do so.

"Jesse," she said at last, when she had all her supplies ready. She laid a gentle hand on his shoulder to waken him.

After a time, he opened his eyes. Their gazes met, and Shiloh knew he was awake enough to understand her.

"I need to clean out your wound with some of the willow bark tea then repack it with the moss. Are you all right with that?"

It took him a long moment before he nodded. "Do what . . . you must." He licked his dry lips. "But first, a little water, please."

She grabbed a nearby canteen, lifted his head, and held the opening to his mouth. "Drink as much as you want. It can only help."

His intake was minimal before he fell back exhausted. Shiloh wet a cloth with some of the water and wiped his sweat-sheened face with it.

"That . . . feels good," he murmured, smiling softly.

Shiloh laid him down, set aside the cloth and canteen, and began to untie the bandage that held the moss in place. "I'll do it again, once I've got this wound taken care of. And I'll try to be as gentle as I can."

Less than ten minutes later, Jesse's wound was examined, cleaned of a few stray splinters, flushed with the willow bark tea, and repacked with fresh moss. The wound edges were inflamed, which worried her. She could only hope the antiseptic properties of the tea and the moss dressing would help with that. There wasn't a lot more she could do, save pour more tea down his throat at appropriate intervals, encourage him to drink a lot more water in between times, and keep him warm.

What she really needed was to get him to a doctor, or at least to someplace with better shelter and more access to a variety of food and medical supplies. But, as ill and weak as he now was, she didn't think there was much chance of getting him onto his horse, much less him staying on it for very long. The other alternative, however, of leaving him to try and find help, didn't set very well with her either. So far, they hadn't come upon any towns or individual ranches. And there was no telling how long it might take her to find anyone.

A wave of despair overwhelmed her. What would she do if Jesse got worse? Sit beside him and watch him slowly die?

The sense of helplessness of such a passive act grated on her normally practical, take-charge nature. She lifted a fervent prayer for aid, then rose, walked to Jesse's saddlebag, and pulled out the small hand ax. After ascertaining that he was sleeping soundly, she headed out toward the nearby hills toward a stand of aspens.

Two hours later, sweaty and sore, Shiloh dragged the first of two felled aspen saplings into camp. She'd found the hand ax did the job, just very slowly. It worked a lot better, though, in stripping off the branches to make relatively smooth, long poles.

Twenty minutes later, the second sapling was back at camp. By noon, she had a reasonably sturdy travois tied to Jesse's pony's saddle with the coil of rope they'd brought along and two blankets sewn onto the bottom half of the poles. After making herself a sandwich for lunch and eating it, she woke Jesse and fed him the jerky broth she'd made.

"We need to try and get you somewhere where we can get better care for your wound. Can you get up and make it to the travois?" she asked as she spooned the broth into his mouth. "If not, I'll drag you over to it on your blanket, then pull you up onto its bed."

He swallowed the broth in his mouth, then gazed up at her with a confused look in his eyes. "A travois? Where . . . did you find . . . a travois?"

"I didn't find it, Jesse. I made it."

"M-made it?"

She nodded. "Yes. If a Ute woman can make one, I reckon I can too."

"Well, let's see . . . how well it holds up first. Before you get . . . too cocky."

"For that comment," Shiloh said with a grin, offering him another spoonful of broth, "I should dump you on your head no matter how good a job I did on that travois."

Jesse took the spoonful, then managed a wan smile. "You're . . . too good to me."

"Yes, I am." She scooped up some more broth. "Now, no more talk. You need to finish this so we can be on our way."

For the next several minutes, Jesse silently complied. Then as he lay resting, Shiloh filled one canteen with the remaining willow bark tea, filled the other two from the creek with fresh water, and packed up what was left of their supplies. Jesse was dozing when she returned.

Kneeling, she gently shook him by the shoulder. "Jesse? Time to go. Do you think you can walk to the travois, if I help you?"

"I-I think so," he replied, shoving to one elbow.

"I brought it close, so you won't have to walk more than maybe ten feet or so."

He was very weak and unsteady on his feet, but with Shiloh's help, he made it to the travois. After eyeing it for a moment, he nodded. "Looks . . . pretty good."

Even with Shiloh's assistance, it was difficult for him to climb onto it. By the time he did so, he was pale and winded. She covered him with the other two blankets.

"I'll try and go slow enough not to jerk you around a lot," she said. "But I can't promise I won't give you a rough ride at times."

"Do what you have to," Jesse whispered, closing his eyes. "I'll be . . . fine."

Her heart twisted. He was so weak, so ill, and she feared his wound was beginning to fester. What frightened her the most, though, was that he was totally dependent on her. She literally held his life in her hands.

Well, actually the Lord held Jesse's life in His hands, and she was but His handmaiden. *Don't let me lose him*, she prayed, *just when I've finally found him again. Please, Jesus. Help me to be Your hands in saving Jesse's life.*

Tears welled and fiercely, almost savagely, Shiloh brushed them away. *Stop it. Stop it now*, she ordered herself. *You don't have the time for weeping. All that matters is keeping Jesse alive long enough to get him to better medical care. And you're the only one who can do it.*

Shiloh checked one more time to make sure he was securely tied down to the travois, then went to fetch her mare, lead it over, and fasten a long lead rope onto its bridle. Rope in hand, she next mounted Jesse's pony.

Signaling the horse forward, Shiloh set out across the valley. Their journey, with the travois trailing behind, was slow. Still, they were finally on their way. On their way to find other people.

She only hoped *that* discovery wouldn't be long in coming.

9

Late that afternoon, after no sign of any other human being, Shiloh came upon the small farming settlement of Carbonville. About twenty homes spread out on the rich, fertile river bottomland and a cluster of homes surrounded a small village consisting of a mercantile, saloon, hotel, bank, sheriff's office, livery stables, and a doctor's office.

Her heart rejoicing, Shiloh headed straight for the doctor's office. Her arrival with the two horses and travois brought out the folk from the various businesses to stand there talking with their neighbors, but she had no time to worry about their thoughts or possible reactions. She tied the two horses to the hitching post in front of the doctor's office and hurried inside.

At her arrival, a middle-aged man dressed in black trousers, a white shirt unbuttoned at the throat with sleeves folded past his elbows, and a dark brown vest walked from a back room, drying his hands on a towel. He was tall and strongly built, his dark hair thinning to form a deep V on his forehead, and he wore a pair of spectacles perched on his nose. His smile of welcome was friendly, though his teeth were tobacco stained.

"What can I do for you, missy?" the man asked, laying aside his towel.

"I need a doctor."

He paused to look her up and down. "Well, I'm Dr. Michaels, but you don't look much in need of any doctor to me."

"It's not for me. It's for my friend outside on the travois. He's got a wound in his side from a branch that stabbed him while he was rescuing me in the Colorado River. I've done the best I could to treat it, but didn't have much to use save for some old Indian remedies."

He motioned toward the door. "Let's bring him in and have a look."

A crowd of men had gathered around the travois in the short time Shiloh had spent inside with Dr. Michaels. By the looks on most of the faces, they weren't very happy.

"Step aside there," the doctor ordered. "We've got a sick man to get into my office."

The men reluctantly parted to allow him and Shiloh through. Dr. Michaels bent over Jesse, touched the back of his hand to Jesse's forehead, then glanced up at Shiloh. Jesse never stirred.

"He's burning up with fever. We need to get some fluids in him and treat that wound of his pronto." He looked up at the men standing around. "Jim and Otto. Help me get this man into my office, will you?"

The two men exchanged a hesitant glance. "Er, Doc," the taller of the two men said, "you do realize this is an Indian, don't you? Likely even a Ute?"

"Yeah, Doc," the other one chimed in. "And surely you haven't forgotten how they rode in last Wednesday night, stole some of Bart Hancock's horses, and burned down his barn, have you?"

The doctor straightened and impaled them with a steely look. "No, Jim, I haven't forgotten. But it wasn't this man."

"Still," the tall one who was apparently Jim said, scratching his unshaven chin, "we don't need to take no chances of housing some Indian. Once he's better, he'll take a good look-see at what we have here, then hightail it back to his camp and tell them all about it. They're all thieves. No good will come of helping this one."

Anger filled Shiloh. "Jesse's no thief. He's a good man and he saved my life. That's how he got hurt. And, if it makes you feel any better, he's only half Ute. He's also half white."

"With that long hair and way he's dressed," the other one who by process of elimination was Otto, "looks to me like he's taken on the Ute ways. And since they're all murderers and thieves . . ." He paused to eye her closely. "And what's a pretty white woman like you doing with him anyways? Did he steal you away from your kinfolk or something?"

"No, of course not!" Shiloh struggled to keep the exasperation at these two ignorant louts out of her voice. "I'm the new teacher at the White River Indian Agency. When I got word my sister was seriously ill, Jesse offered to escort me home by the fastest route possible." She turned to look at the doctor. "Could we please get him inside now?"

Doctor Michaels arched a brow at Jim and Otto. The two men exchanged a glance between them, then shook their heads.

"Sorry, Doc," Jim said, "but I'm not helping some dirty, thieving Ute, no matter who she claims he is." Still shaking his head, Jim, joined by Otto, shouldered his way through the crowd.

Anger swelled within Shiloh. What a narrow-minded, ignorant pair, she thought, followed swiftly by the realization that this was what Jesse possibly had to deal with whenever he met a white man. Would he be accepted or judged and found lacking, just because of his heritage?

Once again, she was struck by the cruelties people who were different had to endure. Her lifelong dissatisfaction with her freckles and the color of her hair were nothing—absolutely nothing—in comparison.

She looked to the doctor. "With your help, I think you and I can carry Jesse inside. I'll not be begging the likes of those two men, or any like them, for help. They're not even worthy to touch him."

"You're a feisty one, for sure," Doc Michaels said with a grin. "Still, can't say as though I blame you." He moved to Jesse's right side and grasped the blanket firmly in both hands.

"Now, if you get a good hold on the other side of him—" he then said when he was suddenly interrupted.

"Let me help you there, Doc," said a heavyset, sandy-haired man wearing a cleric's collar. He moved to stand beside Shiloh, tipped the brim of his hat at her, and motioned for her to move aside. "If you'd accept my assistance, ma'am."

Gladness filled her. At least there were a few good-hearted souls in this place. And one of them was a parson who actually seemed to live the kind of life he was vowed to.

"Thank you," she whispered and stepped back.

In but the span of five minutes, the two men had lifted Jesse from the travois and carried him into the back room of the doctor's office, where they laid him on the examination table. With Shiloh's help, they got Jesse's buckskin shirt off him. Doc then picked up a set of scissors and began cutting away the bandages.

"I'll need to examine the wound for any foreign bodies like splinters, then flush it out real good, pack it, and rebandage it," he said, turning to Shiloh. "Why don't you and Reverend Bauermann take your horses to the livery? This might require some work, and that way you've got the horses all settled in and cared for."

Shiloh eyed Jesse uncertainly. "I-I'd rather stay here with him."

"You'll have plenty of time to do that, Miss . . . ?"

She stared at him uncomprehendingly for a moment. "Oh, I'm sorry. I'm Shiloh Wainwright."

"Well, Miss Wainwright, it'll only take you a short time to get your horses seen to."

"I suppose you're right," she said after a brief hesitation. "For all they've done for us, the horses do deserve a nice stall with some hay and water." She glanced at Reverend Bauermann. "I'd be much obliged if you could help me get the horses to the livery."

He smiled, and his teeth were startlingly white against his tanned skin. "No sooner said than done, ma'am."

"Shiloh. Please, call me Shiloh," she said as she followed him from the room.

Once outside, Shiloh was relieved to see the crowd had dispersed. She moved immediately to untie Jesse's pony and hand the reins to the parson. "I'm assuming you know your way around horses, Reverend Bauermann?"

He nodded. "I grew up on a ranch, before deciding to attend seminary. There aren't very many horses I can't manage."

"Good. Jesse's pony is a bit skittish around strangers but settles down nicely once he realizes he can't get away with anything." She unfastened her horse from the hitching post, then indicated that the reverend should lead the way.

It didn't take long to reach the livery—basically a small barn with six stalls. After removing the travois and laying it just inside the barn door along a wall, she discussed the cost and care she desired with the liveryman. Then she led her horse into a stall beside the one the parson delivered Jesse's pony to.

"I don't know just yet how many days I'll need to board our horses," she said to Tom, the liveryman, "but I'll check back each day to pay you and keep you updated. You'll take good care of our horses, won't you, Tom?"

"Tom is a good man," Reverend Bauermann said, clapping the other man on the shoulder. "You can trust him. Can't she, Tom?"

The liveryman's head bobbed in nervous agreement. "Sure thing, Reverend."

"And, if there's any trouble, you'll come first thing and let me know, right?"

"Trouble?" Tom's eyes widened. "What kind of trouble?"

"Oh, just maybe Jim and Otto skulking around." The parson shrugged. "You know how they can't seem to keep their noses out of other folks' business. But if they do come around, you just fetch me and I'll take care of it."

Tom nodded again. "Okay, Reverend."

Reverend Bauermann turned to Shiloh. "Would you like me to escort you back to Doc Michaels's office, or do you think you'll be all right on your own?"

Shiloh grinned. "I think I'll be just fine. You're not the only one who was raised on a ranch."

He smiled. "Somehow, I figured you weren't the helpless sort. Not after seeing all you've done to keep your friend alive and get him here."

Her smile faded. "He would've done the same for me. One couldn't ask for a better friend than that."

The parson's mouth quirked. "I'd wager he's more than just a friend. Leastwise, as far as you're concerned."

She could feel the heat rise to her cheeks. Instead of commenting upon his wry observation, Shiloh held out her hand.

"Thank you for all your help, Reverend. It's so very much appreciated."

"It's nothing more than what Christ admonishes us to do for our fellow man," he replied, taking her hand and shaking it. "Be ye therefore merciful, as your Father also is merciful . . ."

"Indeed, Reverend. Indeed." She released his hand, stepped back, then turned and headed down the street to the doctor's office.

All the while, though, a poignant thought assailed her. Mercy . . . It seemed a virtue in short supply these days, least-wise when it came to the Indians. But then, there were plenty of whites who feared the Indians, and for good reason. If only both sides could sort the good ones from the bad and not inadvertently punish the innocent.

Problem was, the most expedient solution to a lot of whites was also the cruelest. For to them, the only good Indian was a dead one.

Jesse woke slowly, and the first thing he noticed was he was lying on something very comfortable. Silence surrounded him. For an instant, he wondered if he had died and gone to heaven.

Then common sense reminded him he was no longer a Christian, nor did he believe in the Christian god. So it couldn't be heaven.

And if it were the afterlife of which the People spoke, it wouldn't be quite like this. He would, instead, be outside where the weather was perfect and the game teeming. And he'd likely be clasping a bow, with a quiver of arrows slung across his back.

Inching open one eye, Jesse realized his assessment had been accurate. He lay on a bed in a room. The door to the room was shut, but beyond it he could now make out the sounds of someone moving about. He turned away from the door to the room's single window. Ruffled white curtains hung there but just outside he saw other houses nearby. He must be in some white man's town.

So, Shiloh had managed to find help. He smiled. When she set her mind to something, there seemed nothing she couldn't accomplish.

He levered himself to one elbow, and the sudden pain in his right side made him wince. Flipping back the colorful quilt covering him, he noted the neat, clean bandages covering his wound. Jesse wondered if Shiloh had done that, or someone else.

Now that he considered it further, where *was* Shiloh? He pushed to a sitting position, his legs dangling from the side of the bed, and noted he no longer wore his buckskin leggings and breechcloth. Instead, a pair of long woolen drawers covered the lower half of his body.

Briefly, as he sat up, his head spun. The feeling, however, soon passed. Just as he was leaning forward to touch the floor with one foot, the door opened and Shiloh walked in with a tray in her hands. Jesse quickly sat back on the bed and flipped the quilt over to cover his lap.

She almost dropped the tray as she turned from closing the bedroom door and saw him sitting up.

"J-Jesse! You're awake."

"Yes," he said, stifling a smile, "it appears I am. How long have I been asleep?"

Walking over, she laid the tray on the bedside table. "Nearly a day and a half. Since we got to Carbonville, I mean, and Doc Michaels took you in and treated you. Your fever took a while to beat, but it broke late last night. Then I finally knew you were going to make it."

"Well, I'm glad to hear I'm going to make it," Jesse replied after a moment of contemplating the possible contents of the covered bowl on the tray, "because I sure am hungry."

Shiloh grinned and uncovered the bowl with a flourish. "Then our timing's perfect. Harriet, Doc Michaels's wife, and I were debating when you'd wake, and we decided to go ahead and make a nice pot of chicken soup for you." She waved her hand over the soup, coaxing the scent of the steaming liquid toward him. "Doesn't it smell wonderful?"

He inhaled deeply and nodded. "Yes, it does. Are you going to let me have some or just torture me with the smell?"

She paused, giving him a considering look. "Next time, maybe we can get you up in a chair to eat, but for the first time, let's have you do it in bed, okay? You're bound to be pretty weak, after the fever and not eating anything for over two days."

The idea of eating in bed didn't sit well with Jesse, but he decided Shiloh was probably right. Better to suffer one meal as an invalid than risk staggering over to the chair in those ridiculous drawers, and maybe even falling. That possibility was more humiliating than remaining bedridden awhile longer.

"Fine with me," he said as he swung his legs up and beneath the covers. "But just this one time. I plan to be out of bed and walking just as soon as I can."

"Then the sooner you start getting some food into you on a regular basis"—as she spoke, Shiloh picked up the tray and placed it on his lap, then leaned over to prop his pillows farther up behind him—"the sooner you'll regain the strength you need for walking."

The few seconds she had bent close to him sent Jesse's heart to thudding. He'd felt her warmth, smelled her delicate scent, and if not for the tray of food on his lap, he thought he might have pulled her close. Which, on second thought, was an absurd idea. Besides upsetting the tray, he'd likely have hurt his side in the doing. And that was in addition to the fact that Shiloh would probably have taken offense.

His cheeks flushed warm, but Jesse doubted it was from the return of his fever. He hid his embarrassment by fumbling with the spoon and finally dipping it into the soup.

"Here, wait a minute." She grabbed the big cloth napkin from the tray and laid it across his bare chest. "Just in case the soup gets messy."

She didn't lean quite as close this time, but it was all Jesse could do to suppress a groan. What was the matter with him? Had his injury and subsequent infection weakened more than just his body? Had all the defenses he'd put up against her been burned away in the heat of his fever?

All he knew, as he watched her pull over the chair and sit beside him, was he wanted, needed her, and the intensity of his desire all but unmanned him. If only he could take her into his arms and hold her close, brush his lips against the smooth, rose-tinted skin of her cheek, rest his face on her silky, red curls . . .

With a savage jerk of his thoughts back to the reality of the moment, Jesse picked up his spoon and forced his trembling hand to steady as he scooped up some of the soup. The flavor was delicious and the liquid the perfect temperature as it slid down his parched throat. He took another spoonful and momentarily savored the tender morsels of chicken and noodles before swallowing.

"This is the best chicken soup I've ever had," he said, finally daring to meet Shiloh's expectant gaze. "Would you please thank Mrs. Michaels for me?"

She smiled in joyous relief. "Oh, I will. I'm just so glad

to see you awake and eating. If you only knew how worried sick I was . . ."

Shiloh turned away, but not before Jesse noted the suspicious brightness and moisture in her eyes. Did she care so much for him that the thought he might die had affected her so strongly? Though he knew he shouldn't let it, the thought gladdened him more than he cared to admit.

"Well, you needn't worry or make yourself sick over me anymore," he growled, the anger at his weakness making his voice take on a harshness he hadn't intended. "I'm going to be all right."

Her head jerked back around, and Jesse could tell from her pained expression that he had hurt her. Silently, he cursed himself for his insensitive words.

"Look," he said as he scooped up another spoonful of soup, "I didn't mean to sound ungrateful for all you've done. I guess I just . . . just have a hard time depending on someone else or being in their debt. So, I get angry and take it out on the other person, when it's really myself I'm angry at. For being so weak and all . . ."

The look she sent him was reproachful. "I don't like feeling weak and helpless either, but I don't take it out on others."

He swallowed the soup he'd just ladled into his mouth before replying. "Well, maybe that's because you're a fine, upstanding human being, and I'm not."

It took her a moment to catch the teasing look he sent her, and then she relaxed and laughed. "You're probably right about that." Shiloh waved toward his bowl of soup. "Now, no more talk. Finish your soup while you still have the energy. Because if I don't miss my guess, you won't have it for long."

Though he was tempted to dispute her claim that he wouldn't hold up, by the time Jesse got to the last few spoonfuls of chicken soup, he had to admit she'd been right. The spoon seemed to weigh several pounds, and the effort it took for him to wield it was almost more than he could manage. Finally, in exasperation, he laid down the spoon, grabbed the bowl, and emptied it.

"There," he said, falling back against the pillows, "I finished the soup. What do you have planned for me next? A walk outside? Splitting some firewood?"

"Oh, most certainly," she said, chuckling as she stood up, took a step toward the bed, and retrieved the tray. "Just as soon as you take a nice long nap. Then we'll discuss the chores I've got lined up for you."

Jesse managed a wan smile. "You're a hard woman, Shiloh Wainwright. But I always knew that about you."

"Did you now?" She laid the tray on the bedside table, then moved back beside him to take away one of the extra pillows that had helped prop him up. After putting it down in the chair, she turned to him. "Then I guess you know all my secrets."

He gave a disbelieving snort. "As if any man ever knows all of a woman's secrets."

"Well, then it'll give you something to think on until you fall asleep." She leaned down as if to give him a comforting kiss on the cheek.

In that instant, all the frustrating emotions he'd barely been holding in check seemed to burst past his iron control. Jesse reached up, gently caught her chin, and turned her face to his. Before she could react or he could reconsider, he kissed her.

❧

Shiloh froze. She thought she must be dreaming. Jesse Blackwater was kissing her? Had she lost her balance when she'd bent down to give him a quick, friendly peck on the cheek, and inadvertently hit his lips instead?

But no, she thought as the initial shock wore off, *he* had taken her by the chin and kissed *her*. And, as his warm lips slanted softly, tenderly over hers without ever pulling back, she realized Jesse had intended—wanted—to kiss her. The realization filled her with a swift, soaring joy, and she sank to sit on the edge of his bed and ardently returned his kiss.

Long seconds passed and Shiloh thought she'd never felt or tasted anything as wonderful as Jesse. She moaned, the sound rising from deep within her. A sound full of yearning, pleasure, and warm, womanly satisfaction.

Jesse released her chin and jerked away. She sat back, confused.

"What . . . ? D-did I hurt you, Jesse?" Even as she spoke, the traitorous warmth rushed to her face.

He wouldn't look at her. "No. I'm sorry. I shouldn't have done that."

She reached toward him, touched his shoulder. He shrugged her hand away.

"Don't."

His command stabbed through her, and into the gaping wound rushed an agonized shame. Shiloh pulled back her hand.

"I'm sorry too," she forced herself to choke out the words. "I thought you wanted to kiss me, liked kissing me."

"Of course I liked kissing you!" Jesse whirled around to face her and, at the sudden movement, he caught at his side and grimaced in pain.

Instinctively, Shiloh reached toward him.

"I said don't!" He halted her with his free hand outstretched before him. "Please, don't make this any worse than it already is. You and I know there's no hope of any good coming from . . . from . . ."

Anger began to smolder within her. "From what?" she demanded. "From letting ourselves care for each other? For opening our hearts to love?"

His eyes widened. He dragged in a deep breath, which made him wince. Then his jaw went taut, his lips tight, and he managed a harsh laugh.

"Who was talking about love?"

She stared at him, her thoughts colliding with her chaotic emotions. "But you kissed me! What else would I be thinking but that—"

At the sordid implications that flashed through her mind, Shiloh leaped from the bed. "You didn't mean . . . you wouldn't do such a thing!"

"In case you haven't figured it out yet," Jesse said as he gingerly lay back on the bed, "you're a beautiful, desirable woman. And I'm a normal man. But I also intend to be a man of honor and deliver you home in the same condition you left the Agency. So, let's forget what just happened. Because it never would have if I'd been right in my mind and body."

She wanted to cry and at the same time was so furious she could hardly think straight. She wanted to slap him senseless as much as she wanted to fling herself on him and beg him to hold her, kiss her, and tell her he truly and deeply loved her. Because she, Shiloh realized with a sudden piercing insight, truly and deeply loved him.

But had she ever known who Jesse Blackwater really was? She wondered. One thing was certain. Right about now she certainly didn't like him.

"Well, please let me know when you're back in your right mind and body then," she said with no small amount of sarcasm. "Because until then, I won't force myself on you in any way. Mrs. Michaels can see to your care. And when you deem yourself fit enough to resume our journey, I'll be sure to avoid any further sort of behavior that might besmirch your blasted honor!"

10

Though she had taken great offense at the mixed messages Jesse had sent with his kiss, Shiloh couldn't long hold a grudge. Well, she quickly amended, at least not with anyone other than her sister. Besides the fact they still had a three- or four-day's journey ahead of them, there was the reality he had saved her life at great risk to his own.

For those reasons, and no others, she kept trying to convince herself she owed him civil if not compassionate behavior. Well, perhaps just *one* other reason, she thought two days later as she knocked on his bedroom door, a breakfast tray in her hand. Her Christian conduct toward him had been sorely lacking of late. She must amend that for the love of her Lord, if not so much for any charitable feelings for Jesse.

"Come in," a deep voice responded from the other side of the door.

Shiloh inhaled a fortifying breath, lifted a quick prayer for strength, and pressed down on the door handle. As she entered, Jesse, seated in a chair near the window, looked up from a book he was reading.

He was dressed once more in his leggings and breechcloth, moccasins on his feet. Instead of his buckskin shirt, however, he wore a softly faded, red flannel shirt that she ventured to guess was one of Doc Michaels's. The color only served to enhance his darkly handsome good looks, and for an instant, Shiloh forgot her resolve not to allow her emotions regarding Jesse Blackwater to get the best of her again.

"Mrs. Michaels was busy," she said, forcing a smile, "so I offered to help her by bringing you your breakfast."

His glance lowered back to the page he was reading. "That's very kind of you. Especially since you must loathe being in my presence these days."

So, he wasn't going to pretend to a tenuous truce. But then, she supposed she deserved that, and the responsibility to be the first to extend a peace offering would have to fall to her. She was, after all, the one who claimed to be the Christian.

"You'd be wrong if you thought that," Shiloh said as she walked across the room and set his tray on the bedside table. "I might get angry at you and think you're a low-down, no-account varmint at times, but I don't—and haven't ever—loathed you."

"Really?" Jesse lifted his gaze from his book and impaled her with a disbelieving look. "Then, Miss Wainwright, you're either a very sweet liar, or you're denying what you truly feel. Because I have been a low-down, no-account varmint. And, for that, I beg your forgiveness."

She stared back at him, struck speechless by his unexpected apology. She had taken two days to work through her anger at him and had come to the acceptance that she must be the one to turn the other cheek. Well, figuratively anyway, because she didn't plan to get close enough to him to offer her cheek or anything else.

"Generally," Jesse offered dryly, "when someone apologizes, the other person is supposed to be gracious enough to accept it. Even if they don't really mean it."

Shiloh jerked her attention back to him. Irritation flared. Why did it seem that Jesse was always one step ahead of her?

"It's not that. That I don't want to accept your apology," she quickly amended. "It's just that I came to ask *your* forgiveness, even if you refused to claim any responsibility for . . . for what happened the other day."

"And I beat you to it, is that it?"

"Well, yes . . . so to speak, anyway."

His mouth quirked. "I'll bet that makes you mad."

"What?" She blinked, trying to break through the fog of confusion swirling about her. "What do you mean? Why would I be mad that you apologized?"

He shrugged. "Because I come out the better person, yet again?"

Her gaze narrowed. Jesse was toying with her, but for what reason? Why did he sometimes seem so warm toward her, while other times . . .

A sudden realization struck her. His actions were so contradictory because his feelings for her confused him as much as her feelings for him confused her. And he did have feelings for her. As much as he might have wished it hadn't happened, he'd revealed what he really felt in that kiss. A kiss he had turned from a friendly peck on the cheek into one far more ardent.

Though Shiloh didn't know from where the certainty came, her instinct on this was sound and sure. And with it came a confidence she'd never before experienced.

"And you *are* the better person," she said with a smile that only widened more at his look of utter surprise, "for your courage in daring to step forward and apologize. Especially considering how terribly rude and angry I was the other day. But I promise to do better in the future."

"So, you're accepting my apology?" Jesse looked like he couldn't believe this was happening.

"But of course," Shiloh replied with a firm nod. "And I humbly ask your forgiveness in turn."

He rubbed his chin. "Apology accepted," he mumbled finally, sounding less than sincere. Or maybe, she thought on second consideration, sounding even more confused and disgruntled. Like somehow his plan to keep her off balance and at arm's length had been thwarted.

"Well, good." She gestured to the breakfast tray. "Better eat this while it's hot. Mrs. Michaels made flapjacks with maple syrup, bacon, and a nice strong cup of coffee. I already ate, and it's as delicious as always."

Jesse laid aside his book and rose. Shiloh watched him make his way over to sit on the side of the bed and begin uncovering the plate of food. He still moved stiffly, but he appeared remarkably stronger than two days ago when she'd last brought him a meal. And knowing Jesse, just as soon as he could mount a horse, they'd be resuming their trip.

But that wouldn't happen for at least a few more days. Time enough to get the lay of the land when it came to him and his feelings for her. Because of this much she was certain: the terrain of their relationship had changed with just a simple kiss.

They left Carbonville early one morning just before dawn, a little over a week after they'd first arrived. After saying their good-byes and reiterating their deepest thanks to Doc Michaels and his wife yet one more time, Shiloh and Jesse headed down to the livery to fetch their horses. Several days before, Shiloh had disassembled the travois, leaving the poles to be cut into firewood and retrieving the blankets to add to the rest of the ones they'd need for the trip ahead. It took only a short time to bridle and saddle their horses, then mount and ride from town.

They soon reached the Roaring Fork River valley and began their trek down it. Eventually, though, they had to divert off to some smaller creeks that crept through side valleys more tightly surrounded by mountains, some of which soared high into the heavens. Snow still capped the tallest peaks, piercing the sky with majestic grandeur.

Jesse tried to ride until near sunset each day, and though he didn't meet that goal the first day, each day of travel increased the amount of distance they covered. He wasn't up to any hunting or spearfishing, however, and they had to suffice with the food they'd brought with them, supplemented by freshly made bannocks and hot tea each evening.

Shiloh didn't talk much, save to garner information or discuss what he'd like at mealtimes. For that, Jesse was grateful. He didn't quite know how to approach her these days, leastwise not since that morning she'd decided to heal the breach caused by his ill-advised kiss by graciously accepting his apology.

Ever since then, there had been something different about her. She appeared calmer, more confident, and nothing he could say seemed to rile her. It was almost . . . almost as if she possessed some secret knowledge. Some knowledge that had leveled the playing field between them.

He was no longer an adult male dealing with a young, inexperienced girl. Almost overnight, it seemed, Shiloh had turned into a woman. And that both worried and enthralled him.

Best that he safely deposit her at the front steps of Castle Mountain's main ranch house, then turn and hightail it out of there, Jesse decided the day they hit the top of the last hill separating them from view of the ranch. He caught himself in midthought.

Hightail it out of there . . .

Exactly how many times, since Shiloh had come back into

his life, had he told himself he needed to run as fast and as far away from her as he could get? However many times it had been, it was too many. When he had finally decided to put down roots with the People, he had vowed never to run from anything again, be it man, battle, or any hardship that could befall him. Yet now a pretty young redhead threatened to send him scurrying away with his tail tucked between his legs.

Or rather, Jesse quickly amended, not Shiloh actually but his chaotic mess of feelings for her. It was one thing to fight some enemy that originated from outside yourself. But how did you fight your own heart?

Shiloh abruptly reined in her horse. Bemused, Jesse did the same.

"Is there something wrong?" he asked, glancing at her curiously.

Her lips tight, her shoulders rigid, she stared straight ahead and shook her head. "No. I just . . ." She inhaled a ragged breath. "Yes, there *is* something wrong."

Turning in her saddle to face him, Shiloh met his concerned gaze. "I'm afraid, Jesse," she softly said. "I'm afraid that we didn't get here in time, and Jordan's already . . ."

Tears filled her eyes, and she swallowed hard. "I'm afraid she's already—"

"Already dead?" Jesse cut in, saying the words she couldn't find the heart to say.

She nodded. "I-I don't know if I could bear it. We've . . . never gotten on since . . . since that day."

What Shiloh had left unspoken, Jesse well knew, was the fact that she hadn't made her peace with Jordan. And, if Jordan was now dead, Shiloh would never be able to do so. Living with such guilt could suck the life out of you, even before you were dead.

But what could he possibly say to comfort her, to make things right? Jesse hated seeing Shiloh so miserable, so fearful. If it was within his power, he'd gladly protect her from that pain. Still, though he wondered if Jordan was truly worthy of Shiloh's love, she was her sister. And most familial bonds were forged strong and hard.

"We got here as quickly as we could," he said, thinking even as he spoke how lame his words sounded. "You did your best, Shiloh. You can't do better than that. And if Jordan didn't make it, she didn't die alone or unloved. Her family was with her. I'm sure if there was any way for her to hear it, they told her you were on your way."

"Yes, I suppose you're right." She sighed, then wiped away her tears. "Guess I need to go face it, whatever it is. Nothing's helped by sitting here."

He managed an encouraging smile. "That's the spirit. Let's go get it over with."

A tender light flared in her eyes. "You'll stay with me, won't you? At least for a few days? I don't know what I'll do if you leave."

How could he refuse her, Jesse thought, in her time of need? How could any man deny such a request, couched as it was and falling from such sweet lips? He stifled a silent groan. Yet again, circumstances were drawing him ever closer to her.

"Yes, I'll stay for a few days," he said. "Though I think you'd get a lot more comfort from your kin than you ever would from me."

Gratitude glowed in her big, tear-bright eyes. "Don't sell yourself short, Jesse Blackwater. You've always been a very special friend of mine, and you always will be."

A very special friend indeed, he thought wryly, recalling their brief but heated kiss that day in Carbonville. A very special friend who, in spite of everything screaming at him not to do it, wanted to be so very much more.

They must have seen them riding down the road to the main house. By the time Shiloh and Jesse pulled up before it, her stepbrother Cord was just wheeling their older brother Nicholas out onto the front porch. Sarah, Cord's young wife in her fifth month of pregnancy, stood nearby with her little brother Danny. In her arms she held Jordan's daughter, now a chubby, nearly eight-month-old.

As she and Jesse dismounted and tied their horses to the hitching post, Cord hurried down the steps and walked over to them. Shiloh exchanged a searching look with her brother, then stepped into his welcoming arms.

"I came as fast as I could," she mumbled from the depth of his embrace. "Is . . . is Jordan okay?"

Cord released her but still kept his hands on her arms. "Jordan's still alive," he said solemnly, "but we don't know how okay she is. She was unconscious for almost two days and even now can just barely take in enough water and broth to sustain her. And she's yet to speak a single word."

"Unconscious? Can't speak? But how? How did that happen?"

Shiloh's gut clenched. Her relief at hearing that her sister still lived was almost immediately extinguished by the news that she'd been so debilitated for so long.

Her older brother's expression darkened. "Robert beat her so hard that it fractured Jordan's skull. If Doc Saunders hadn't been a Union surgeon during the war and had experience with removing skull fragments, Jordan wouldn't even be alive today."

"Robert . . . Robert beat her?"

She couldn't believe what she was hearing. True, Jordan's husband was a possessive man, but her sister had never mentioned him ever hurting her. It was almost too much to comprehend.

"Seems he'd been treating her rougher and rougher over the course of their marriage," her brother said. "She kept it hidden for a long while. Guess Jordan was too proud to admit she'd made a mistake in marrying him. And, once Cecilia was born, he soon resented the time she had to spend with the baby. When it got to the point Robert was threatening Ceci, Jordan had had enough. She took the baby and came home."

Confusion filled Shiloh. "Then how did Robert get a chance to hurt her so badly?"

Cord sighed. "After a few days he came riding in all contrite, begging her to come back, swearing he was a changed man and would never lift a hand to her or the baby again. We tried to talk some sense into Jordan, telling her a leopard didn't change its spots so quickly, but she wouldn't listen. She said it was her duty to give him a chance, to help him mend his ways. And I think she still loved him, in spite of it all. At least enough to try and reconcile with him."

"I didn't know," she murmured, feeling so heartsick and shamed that she and Jordan hadn't been able to talk about such private things. "If I had, I would've tried . . ." She dragged in a shuddering breath. "Well, it's too late to prevent what happened. All we can do now is take the best care of her we can, and pray she recovers."

"Yes, that's all we can do." Cord gave her another quick hug, then pulled back. "I'm just so glad you could get here." He paused, his glance sliding to where Jesse stood a few feet away.

"Who's your friend?" he asked bluntly.

Shiloh turned toward Jesse, embarrassed that she'd all but forgotten about him. "Cord, this is my good friend Jesse Blackwater," she said, glancing back to her brother. "He used to work for us. He now lives on the White River Ute reservation, and I made his acquaintance again when I started my job at the Indian Agency there. When I got word about Jordan, Jesse offered to escort me home through the mountains."

She then turned to Jesse. "This is my brother Cord. He was already gone from home to attend college when you were hired here."

Jesse hesitated, then moved forward to extend his hand. "Pleased to meet you, Mr. Wainwright."

Cord took Jesse's outstretched hand and gave it a firm shake. "Likewise. I'm beholden to you for taking such good care of my little sister." He shot her a teasing glance. "She didn't talk you to death, did she, or try to order you around?"

"Not too much. After a while, I think she ran out of things to say."

Her brother gave an incredulous laugh. "I find *that* hard to believe."

"Well, it doesn't matter much anyway," Shiloh said, feeling a bit miffed to be an amusing topic of conversation between the two men. "If you don't mind, I'd like to say hello to Nick and Sarah, then head inside and see Jordan. A cool drink would be nice too, after such a long ride."

"Suit yourself." Cord stepped aside and, with a mock bow and flourish of his hand, indicated for her to proceed ahead of him.

She turned to Jesse. "You come too. I'm sure you can use something to ease your thirst, not to mention someplace to sit down and rest a bit."

"I'll be along in a while," he said. "First, I'd like to put up our horses and get them settled down with some fresh hay and water."

"Okay." She paused. "You won't leave, will you? You said you'd stay a few days."

"Yes, if it's all right with your brothers, I'll stay a few days."

"Cord?" Shiloh glanced his way.

Her brother nodded. "Of course you can stay. Any friend of Shiloh's is a friend of ours. Might have to put you up in one of the bunkhouses, though. Space is kind of tight in the ranch house, what with Jordan here, and now Shiloh."

"The barn will suit me just fine. No need to put anyone out."

"You won't be putting anyone out. We've got a few empty beds in one of the bunkhouses. You can eat your meals with us, though, in the main house. We'd enjoy your company."

"That'll be wonderful," Shiloh said, not giving Jesse a chance to back out of eating with them. "But be sure and return to this house after you're done with the horses. I want to introduce you to Cord's wife, Sarah."

Jesse's expression was less than thrilled, but he nodded his assent. "I'll do that. Now, why don't you go see your sister? She *is* the reason we made such a long trip, after all."

She smiled in gratitude and deep affection. "Yes, she is. She is indeed."

As still as death, Jordan lay in the bed in the bedroom she'd had as a girl. She was thinner than Shiloh had ever seen her, her head was swathed in bandages, and Shiloh couldn't discern any evidence of her sister's beautiful, long blonde hair. At the consideration that, due to Jordan's injury, it might have had to all be cut off, Shiloh's throat clogged with tears.

Ever so softly, she moved closer to the bed. It was then that she noted the yellowing bruises on her sister's pallid face, the almost healed split lip, and the broken nose that had apparently been reset. Jordan, if she survived these brutal injuries, would always have a small bump there to mar her flawless profile.

One arm was also bandaged, and both hands bore evidence of old scrapes. Shiloh gently lifted the quilt covering her sister and found more yellowing bruises up and down her legs. She laid the quilt back down.

A fury she had never known before filled her. How could anyone, and especially one's husband, do such things? She wished she'd thought to ask Cord what had happened to Robert after the beating was discovered. She couldn't help herself. She hoped her brother—a professional boxer at one time—had given Jordan's husband a taste of his own medicine.

Pulling up a chair close to the bed, Shiloh sat and took her sister's hand. The long fingers were so cool and lifeless. She turned a bit so she could cradle Jordan's hand between her own two hands. It wasn't much, but Shiloh felt that if she could at least bring some warmth to her sister, it was something. Some contact, some act of life-sustaining comfort, some proof of her love.

At the action, Jordan stirred and her eyes opened to stare, unfocused, straight ahead. Shiloh's heart gave a great leap, then commenced a rapid rhythm beneath her breast.

"It's Shiloh," she whispered, struggling to keep the tremor from her voice. "I came as quick as I could, once I heard that you were ill. And here I'll stay until you're better."

Swallowing hard, Shiloh fiercely blinked back her tears. "I don't know if you can hear me or not. But just in case you can, I want to tell you how sorry I am for the way I've always been with you. No matter what comes between us, you're still my sister and I love you. Please forgive me. Please . . ."

She rose, lifted the quilt, and laid her sister's hand beneath it to keep it warm. Then Shiloh leaned over and kissed Jordan on the cheek. "Get well, big sister," she said, her voice hoarse with emotion. "I so miss our little squabbles."

As she straightened and glanced down at Jordan's pale, expressionless face, Shiloh's breath caught in her throat. A single tear rolled from Jordan's eye and trailed down her cheek.

11

Two days later, Emma Duncan, the housekeeper who had been with the Wainwright family for almost twenty years, was finishing up Jordan's bath with Shiloh's assistance when she gave a soft cry. "Land sakes, Miss Jordan. You're awake! You're really and truly awake!"

At the older woman's words, Shiloh, who was busy pulling out a fresh nightgown for them to put on her sister, whirled around. Her heart pounding, she hurried over to the bed. Sure enough, Jordan was staring straight at Emma and appeared to be gazing at her in recognition.

"Jordan?" Shiloh took up one of her sister's hands. "Jordan, look at me."

After what seemed hours instead of just seconds, Jordan turned her glance to meet Shiloh's. Confusion clouded her eyes. Her lips moved, but only a low moan escaped.

"Jordan," Shiloh said, leaning closer. "Do you know who I am?"

She nodded, then a pink tongue escaped to lick dry, cracked lips. "W-water," her sister croaked.

Emma was immediately at the bedside table, pouring a glass of water from a small pitcher and handing it to Shiloh.

"Remember to raise her head," the housekeeper warned, "and only give her a tiny sip at a time. Otherwise, she'll choke on it."

Shiloh did as instructed. After a moment while Jordan held the liquid in her mouth as if she didn't know what to do with it, she finally swallowed. A few more sips, and Shiloh finally set aside the glass.

"That's enough for now," she said, smiling down at her sister. "But in a little while, you can have more."

Jordan reached up and touched her sister's hair. "Pr . . . pretty," she murmured. "Shi . . . loh."

"Oh, you do remember me," Shiloh cried joyfully. "That's a good sign, isn't it, Emma?" she asked, turning to the other woman, who had moved around to the other side of the bed.

"Yes, it is. The fact that Jordan can speak, hold up a hand, and remembers you are all very good signs." She looked down at Jordan. "Honey girl," she said, using the nickname she'd always called her, "do you remember me?"

Jordan turned to her, blinked a few times, then closed her eyes. "T-tired. Sleep . . ."

Emma smilingly nodded, took up Jordan's other hand, and bent to gently kiss her cheek. "Just let us get a clean nightgown on you, and then you can take a nice nap. Plenty of time later to talk."

Working together, Emma and Shiloh soon had Jordan dressed in a pretty, white cotton nightgown trimmed with rows of lace down the top front. Then, after pulling up the quilt to tuck it beneath Jordan's chin, Emma motioned for Shiloh to join her in exiting the bedroom.

Once outside with the door closed, Emma engulfed Shiloh in a big hug. "Oh, thank the Lord! Thank the Lord. Jordan has come back to us."

Shiloh enthusiastically returned the embrace. *Yes, thank*

You, Lord, she thought. *My dearest desire was for my sister to live, and that I might have the chance to tell her how much I love her. You are indeed merciful to a sinner such as I.*

Then, disengaging herself from Emma's clasp, Shiloh stepped back, grabbed up the housekeeper's hand, and pulled her down the hall. "Let's go tell everyone the good news. Then we'd better get started on a big pot of chicken and dumpling soup. I'm thinking it won't be long and Jordan will be asking for a lot more than water and broth."

A short while later, leaving the rest of the family happy, relieved, and talking excitedly among themselves, Shiloh threw on a shawl and headed outside. She had seen Jesse ambling off toward the barn about ten minutes ago and guessed he'd gone to check on his pony. She wanted to be the first one to tell him about Jordan's return to full awareness.

As she entered the barn, however, she heard voices, and none of them were Jesse's.

"Stinking 'breed," one man scornfully said. "You've got a nerve, riding in all high and mighty with Miss Wainwright."

"Yeah, like you owned her or something," another voice added derisively. "I've half a mind to beat the living tar out of you."

From inside the stall where the two ranch hands were standing just outside came Jesse's calm voice. "You're sure welcome to try. You're going to need more than half of that mind of yours, though, to succeed."

"Well, maybe I'll just help Dan out a bit," the first hand said. Hands fisted, he took a threatening step forward.

"That's enough!" Shiloh cried, hurrying to join them. She glared up at the two hands, who quickly jumped back to stare at her with wide eyes.

"We—we didn't mean no harm, ma'am," the man named Dan stammered. "Stu and I, we was just fooling with him.

He didn't take it none too well, though. These 'breeds just don't seem to have much sense of humor."

"Well, neither do I, when I see a Wainwright guest treated so rudely by our hired help." Shiloh didn't break gaze with the hand. "And you can be sure my brothers will be hearing about it too."

"Now, you don't need to be telling them about this, ma'am."

"Don't I? Then maybe you two should make your apologies and make them quick."

Stu and Dan exchanged a quick glance.

"Beggin' yore pardon, sir," Dan said.

"Yeah," Stu added. "Beggin' yore pardon."

Shiloh looked to Jesse. "Is that sufficient for you?"

He gave a snort of amusement. "Sure." He turned back to the hoof he was picking.

She shot the two hands a stern look. "Get on with whatever you were doing."

Stu and Dan all but fell over each other scurrying to the door.

"Shiloh, I don't need you always standing up for me," Jesse said quietly, interrupting her troubled thoughts. "I can take care of myself."

"I know you can." She turned around to face him. "I just get so mad when I hear talk like that. They're the ones so high and mighty, thinking they're better than you."

"I long ago ceased to care what people like that think of me. I'd have to value someone and his or her opinions before I'd let myself care."

She knew he was right, but she still couldn't shake off her anger. "The only way people like Stu and Dan are ever going to change is if people like us make them see what they do is unacceptable. We can't just stand by and let them get away with it. By not hearing anything to the contrary, they'll think that everyone goes along with them."

Jesse released his pony's hoof and moved to the next one. "True enough. But you also need to pick your battles. And have the sense to know when there's a chance of winning and when there's not."

Shiloh considered that for a moment, then nodded. "Well, likely you're right about that too. I just need more practice to know which battles are worth it and which aren't."

He finished with the hoof, put it down, and straightened. "I'd imagine you do. It's not as if you're faced with men like those two every day." He grimaced. "Only when folk like me come around."

"Folk like you can come around anytime they want. I much prefer your kind anyway." She paused, reminded of why she'd originally come to find Jesse. "I've got some good news. Jordan opened her eyes just awhile ago, looked at Emma and me like she knew us, and even said a few words."

"I'm glad to hear it." He walked over to stand before her. "It must be quite a relief to you and your family."

She gazed up at him, thrilled by his nearness even as she fought to keep her focus on the subject at hand. "Yes, it is. The Lord has heard our prayers and brought our sister back from the edge of death."

"I'd wager Doc Saunders's medical expertise and all the good nursing care had a lot more to do with it than God," he said as he walked over to a water bucket and washed his hands, then shook them dry.

His cynical words muted a little of Shiloh's joy. It pained her that his regard for the Lord was about as high as that for most whites. Which, in truth, wasn't very high at all.

"Reckon that means I can head back home now," Jesse said, wrenching her from her troubled musings. "Now that I know your sister's out of the woods and on the road to recovery."

"So soon?" She laid a hand on his arm, her heart twisting within her. "You've only been here a little over two days. Stay a few more days at least. Emma's good cooking will put a little more meat on your bones, and a bit more rest will only strengthen you for the trip back."

"I can manage the trip back just fine." Jesse covered her hand with one of his own. "I only stayed this long because you asked me, so I'd be here for you if something . . . something happened to your sister. But now that she seems to be on the mend, there's no sense me hanging around. I'm of no use here, save for showing up for three squares a day and taking up space in the bunkhouse."

Guilt filled her. She'd been so worried about Jordan and so involved in her care that she'd given little thought to what Jesse did much of the day. She'd expected him to remain at her beck and call, and then she'd hardly spent time with him except for meals and a brief visit or two each day.

"Oh, Jesse," Shiloh exclaimed on a remorseful breath. "Please forgive me. I've been so selfish and gave you so little thought these past few days. I imagine you've been near to going out of your mind with boredom."

He smiled ruefully. "Well, I spent a lot of time down by that little creek, dozing in the sun. But I didn't begrudge you that. I understood where your attention had to be. And my job was just to be there if you needed me."

His generosity of spirit touched her deeply. "As I'll always be there for you, if you ever need me. Oh, Jesse," Shiloh said, impulsively moving to hug him, "you're such a good man and a wonderful, wonderful friend!"

For a long moment, he just stood there, arms at his side. Then with an anguished groan, Jesse wrapped his arms about her and pulled her even more tightly to him.

"Shiloh," he murmured, his lips nuzzling the top of her

head. "This isn't right. And you need to stop tempting me like this."

His words gladdened her more than she could say. Shiloh leaned back against the circle of his arms and smiled. "But that's where you're wrong. If we both want it, it *is* right."

The sound of a throat pointedly clearing behind them wrenched them back to reality. Immediately, Jesse released her and stepped back. Shiloh whirled around to find Cord and his wife Sarah standing there. From their garb, they looked like they were headed for town.

Her brother's dark gaze swung from Jesse to Shiloh, and she cursed her easy propensity to blush as the heat flamed in her cheeks. She took a step forward, her hands lifted in supplication.

"Cord, it's not what you may think—"

"And what exactly would I be thinking, little sister?" he demanded curtly. "That this man seems to have a taste for secret meetings in the barn with both of my sisters? Meetings that always seem to end up with him taking inappropriate liberties?"

Exasperation filled Shiloh. "Oh, for Pete's sake, Cord! I was only giving Jesse a hug of thanks for all he's done for me. I hardly think that's an inappropriate liberty."

"And, because he was too polite to hurt your feelings, he was hugging you back, is that it?" Cord gave a disgusted snort. "Come on, Shiloh. You'll have to do better than that."

She scowled and fisted her hands. "Whether it was or wasn't what you thought it was, what does it matter? I'm a grown woman and can hug whomever I choose!"

"Not as long as I'm your brother, you can't!" He was making a move toward her when Sarah grabbed his arm.

"Cord, this isn't the time or place for a discussion of this sort," his pretty blonde wife said. "And besides, Shiloh's right.

She's a grown woman now, whether you want to accept it or not. She's old enough to know what she's doing."

Her husband turned and glowered at her. "Maybe that's what *you* think, but I'm not so sure about that."

"Oh, well, thanks a lot for that compliment!" Shiloh's fists settled on her hips. "So nice to be considered so highly. And by my own brother, no less."

"Look," Jesse said just then. "I hate to break up such a tender family get-together, but for one thing, I'm getting tired of being maligned in the third person. And, for another, I've fulfilled my obligation to Shiloh and am heading home. So, you don't have to worry about me and my dubious intentions anymore."

"No, Jesse!" Shiloh whirled around in dismay. "Don't go just because my brother's being such a knothead. He'll calm down in a bit and see reason. He always has before."

"Oh, I will, will I?" Cord gave a harsh laugh. "Don't count on it, missy."

"Cord, come on," his wife urged. "We came out here to fetch the buggy whip and then head for town. Not to get in an argument with Shiloh. So are we going buggy riding or not?"

A moment passed while Cord stood there, looking back and forth between Sarah and Shiloh. Then he heaved a huge sigh.

"Fine. Let's go get the whip." With that he stalked past Shiloh and Jesse, heading down the aisle to the tack room.

Shiloh turned to Jesse. "I'm sorry. My brother's still a bit too protective of me. But he'll see reason. I know he will."

Jesse smiled sadly and shook his head. "He has every right to be suspicious of me. Because I've done exactly what he said."

"That was nine years ago, Jesse. I'm thinking it's past time everyone needs to forgive and forget."

"Yeah, maybe we all do." His expression went solemn. "But it doesn't look like that's ever going to happen. I'm not wanted here. Never have been. And I'm not one to stay where I'm not wanted."

Tears stung Shiloh's eyes. "But you *are* wanted, Jesse. *I* want you."

He had made a move to head back to his pony, but at her impassioned words, he turned back to her. He grabbed her by both arms.

"Don't say that," he cried, an agonized look in his eyes. "Don't even think it! I'm riding out of here just as soon as I can get my pony ready and my gear collected from the bunkhouse. Riding out of here and out of your life, once and for all. And I don't want you coming back to the Agency. There's nothing you can accomplish there. Nothing. Stay here where you're safe. Stay with your family."

Jesse released her, walked over to the stall, and took down the hackamore. Without sparing her another look, he proceeded to place the headstall on his pony.

Shiloh watched him, the tears welling then tumbling down her cheeks. Myriad protests formed on her lips, some logical, some pleading. All formed then died away, never to be uttered.

She was sick of how he pulled her close, then pushed her away, over and over and over again. Only a fool would keep coming back to take such abuse. And she was no fool. She wouldn't let herself be, no matter how much her heart wanted to do otherwise.

Better to be like Jesse. Just turn and walk away, never to look back. She had given up on him once before. Surely she could do so again. If he was such a coward when it came to following his heart, then she didn't want any part of him.

Angrily, Shiloh swiped the tears away and squared her shoulders. "Fine, have it your way!" she shouted after him.

"You go and I'll stay here because my sister needs me. But just know one thing, Jesse Blackwater. What I told my brother applies to you as well. I'm a grown woman and can do whatever I choose. And if I choose to eventually return to the Agency, I will!"

With that she turned on her heel and, in high dudgeon, stomped from the barn.

⌘

The rest of the day, Shiloh's anger at Jesse gradually abated until, by suppertime, she was acutely regretting her decision to allow him to ride away without trying one more time to convince him to stay. She was also acutely missing him.

Though the meal of beef stew, fresh-baked wheat bread, followed by a dried apple pie was likely delicious, Shiloh found she had little appetite. Just as soon as she could, she excused herself and went outside to sit on the front porch. She needed time to be alone and think.

The sun soon set behind the mountains, and the day quickly darkened to night. The sound of voices rose inside the house, talking and laughing, the clink of forks against plates as they finished their dessert in the parlor. Finally, everyone departed for the kitchen to wash and dry dishes or for their favorite spots in the house.

The sounds were familiar, even comforting, but possessed a quality Shiloh had never noticed before. It was as if she recognized it all but it still seemed strange, as if she wasn't an integral part of this oh-so-familiar and beloved life. As if, in a sense, she didn't truly belong here anymore.

She'd heard it said that you can't go home again, thinking it'd all be as it once was. This realization both confounded and pained her, even as she accepted it as truth. Too much had changed in her life. Even if she'd wanted to, she couldn't go back and be who she once was. Funny, though, but until now she had never noticed that.

Things had certainly taken a dramatic turn of late. She had gone to the White River Indian Agency and found her new job to be supremely difficult and challenging. After all these years and quite unexpectedly, she had stumbled upon Jesse, an encounter that had freed all the long-buried emotions, emotions that would never be contained again. Emotions that were now so different and so much more intense. And then Jordan had almost died.

In a curious sense, she now sat here feeling almost torn in two. Part of her wanted to be here, where she could help in the task of bringing Jordan back to a full and productive life. Even if she might never be a wife to Robert Travers again, her sister could still be a mother to her infant daughter.

Yet another part of her wanted to be far away from here. Far away, riding at Jesse's side wherever that might take her. For when he'd left today, just like before, he'd taken a part of her with him. A part she had given him when she had given him her heart.

The front door creaked open. Shiloh glanced toward it and saw her brother. She inwardly groaned. *Here comes the lecture.*

Cord closed the door and walked over to where she was sitting on the bench. "Mind if I share that with you?" he asked, indicating the empty spot beside her. "After such a fine meal, which I of course ate too much of, I'm in need of some fresh air."

"Suit yourself." She scooted over to make even more room.

He settled himself beside her, leaned back with his long legs stretched out before him, and sighed. For a time they sat there, neither of them speaking, with Shiloh growing tenser by the moment. Finally, she could bear it no more.

"There's something you should know about what happened between Jesse and Jordan," she blurted out. "Something no one's known save Jordan, Jesse, and me."

"Really," he asked with an arch of a dark brow. "And what would that be?"

Shiloh inhaled a deep breath. "Jordan was the one who did the enticing that day in the barn. Jesse just went along with it."

Her brother seemed to take awhile to ponder that revelation. "It's not fair to make such accusations at a time when Jordan can't defend herself. And why now, after all these years?"

"Because I'm sick and tired of everyone blaming Jesse. Like you blamed him yet again today, if with a different sister."

"Well, he was definitely caught both times alone in the barn with one of my sisters. What did you suppose I would think?"

"That maybe both times, your sisters wanted him to hold them, kiss them? Because you would've been right to think that. The only difference is, I'll admit that I wanted it. And I won't blame him for getting caught."

Cord scratched his jaw but never once looked her way. "And Jordan lied about it, is that it?"

Though the truth would likely not sit well with her brother, it was still the truth. "Yes," she said. "She lied because she was afraid of what the consequences would be for her. Afraid it might besmirch her spotless reputation." Shiloh gave a sardonic laugh. "As if any man on the ranch, outside our family, thought her reputation was so spotless."

"And what exactly are you implying about our sister?" Cord demanded, pivoting on the bench to lock gazes with her.

Startled, Shiloh leaned away from him. "I'm not implying anything. Because I don't know how far she allowed things

178

to go with any of the hands she took a fancy to. All I know is Jordan was a tease, and she enjoyed testing her feminine wiles on any man who paid her the slightest attention."

"Sounds like there's a tinge of jealousy in those claims."

"Cord," Shiloh said in exasperation, "I long ago accepted I'd never attract men like Jordan always did. So I concentrated, instead, on being a good friend and improving my mind. And now, after what's happened to Jordan, I'm even more convinced I chose the better path."

"I didn't realize, all this time, that you held such a grudge against your sister."

She gave a mirthless laugh. "And you think it's because I envied Jordan her beauty and easy ways with men?"

"Isn't it?"

"No." Shiloh shook her head, sad that Cord would think her so petty, but determined to tell the truth and stand up for Jesse. "Until that day she betrayed Jesse and, in the doing, set him up for that whipping, I didn't hold any grudges against her. Sometimes she made me mad, but all sisters and brothers do that to each other. No, after that day, I just lost all respect for her and never trusted her again. And, as ashamed as I am to admit it, I couldn't forgive her either. I tried and tried, but I just couldn't."

"Then why did you even bother coming home, when we sent you word of how bad off she was?"

She clasped her hands together in her lap and looked down at them. "Because I realized I might lose her. Because in spite of it all, I still love her. And finding Jesse again began to make me think about things, like mercy, compassion, and acceptance."

"You have feelings for him, don't you?"

"Yes." Shiloh lifted her gaze to his. "Yes, I do, and I'm not ashamed to admit it."

"Even though—"

"Even though he's a half-breed?" Shiloh asked, finishing the sentence.

"No, actually," her brother said, shooting her a sardonic look, "I was going to say, even though he's a very angry man who doesn't seem to know where he fits in."

"Jesse has decided to live with his mother's people. They seem far more willing to accept him than his father's people ever have."

"So where do *you* fit into all of that, little sister? Got a hankering to live like a Ute now, have you?"

She was loath to admit she hadn't given that much thought. All she knew was she wanted to be with Jesse. But, now that the subject had been broached, could she truly be happy living with the Utes?

"I don't know, Cord. It hasn't gotten that far between us. And maybe it never will."

"Well, that would suit me just fine." He stood. "Because I'm not so sure he's good enough for you, little sister."

"Well, if you hadn't run him off today . . ."

"My point exactly. If he isn't willing to fight to have you, then maybe that should tell you something."

Shiloh didn't know what to say to that, so she just quietly stared up at her brother.

"I'm going to turn in. So should you."

She nodded. "In a few more minutes. I just want to sit out here awhile longer."

"Well, good night then."

"Good night." Shiloh hesitated. "No one else has to know what I told you about what Jordan really did that day. I wouldn't even have told you, if you hadn't been so hard on Jesse today."

"So, no one in the family knows? Why's that?"

"Who would've believed me? They'd all have decided that I was jealous. Just like you did."

"That's a lot of baggage to carry around for such a long time."

"Yes," she said, filled with the sudden realization that keeping such a secret was like closing over a festering wound and never allowing it to heal. "It was, and I think it didn't serve me or Jordan very well."

"Maybe not." Her brother leaned down and gave her a tender peck on the cheek. "Now all you've got to decide is where the Lord fits into all of this, and what He'd want you to do."

12

Somehow, Jesse managed to keep his thoughts from wandering to his parting from Shiloh that morning. Managed, that was, until he made camp for the night. Then he had nothing to distract him. Then there was nothing to do such as racing his pony, fording streams, climbing hills, and constantly scanning the terrain for anything unexpected or unfriendly.

But in the quiet of a star-pierced, blackened night, with only the company of his pony and a crackling fire, Jesse's head was flooded with memories and his heart with emotions. Emotions that were, at best, bittersweet.

Once again, he had fled rather than face what was happening between him and Shiloh. That he loved her and wanted her for his own. But the confrontation with her brother had only confirmed what he'd always known. That he would never be considered good enough for her, that his motives would always be suspect.

And, in truth, what could he offer Shiloh? Life on a reservation, living like a Ute? Not that it was such a bad life, just one he knew she wasn't accustomed to. But at least there they'd be accepted as a mixed-blood couple.

If he chose instead to take her off the reservation, they'd have to face the ostracism and unkindness of many of their neighbors. As would any children they might have.

Could any love long endure such obstacles thrown in its way? His own parents' relationship hadn't, but then Jesse wasn't convinced it had ever been a love match to begin with. He'd never seen any affection shown to his mother by his father. And, as the years went by, his father became more and more abusive. Until Jesse was old and big enough to finally stop him.

He tossed that unpleasant memory into the fire along with another piece of wood. His parents' fate didn't have to be his. Nonetheless, he didn't have much hope of a lasting marriage with Shiloh.

She loved her family, and if Cord Wainwright's reaction was any indication, it didn't look like they'd be eagerly stepping forward to accept him. Jordan, if she ever regained any semblance of a normal life, likely wouldn't either. To do so would require her to acknowledge her part in the fiasco that had been their liaison. And Jesse doubted that day would ever come.

No, he thought as he leaned back on his bedding and cradled his head in his hands, as hard as it had been today to ride away from Shiloh, he knew he'd done the only thing he could. In time, Shiloh would realize that too. All that was needed was for them to put as much distance between each other as they could.

And each remain where they truly belonged.

In the ensuing days, it soon became apparent that Jordan's recovery was going to be a long, tiring, and frustrating one. Though she could remember Emma, her two brothers, and her sister, she had no recollection of Sarah. And, though she knew she was the wife of Robert Travers, she had no memory of the night he'd almost killed her. She was also unaware that baby Cecilia, even when shown to her, was her own child.

As the three women of the household took turns caring for her and working to help her regain her memory, the full scope of what Jordan had lost with her brain injury was gradually revealed. She had trouble identifying the names of some objects, while others she immediately knew. Her usually flawless handwriting was greatly impaired, and at first they couldn't even decipher what she wrote. She could barely read above a first grader's level.

Jordan's days of progress, however minuscule it sometimes seemed, were usually followed by a few days' relapse when she fell back into exhaustion and pain. Her mood was frequently very low as well, in the moments when she'd realize how much she had to relearn. The only bright spot was that, though she was weak and unsteady, she had good use of her arms and legs. With help, she soon managed to walk around in her bedroom, then down the hall, and finally out onto the front porch to sit in a comfortable rocker for some fresh air.

One hot, late June afternoon almost three months after her horrifying beating, Jordan and Shiloh decided to cool off by sitting on the front porch. As Jordan contentedly watched the ranch activities, Shiloh busied herself shelling some freshly picked peas. The mild spring weather this year had encouraged a bumper crop of peas, spinach, and salad greens. The pole beans, summer squash, potatoes, and various other warmer weather vegetables had just been planted a few weeks ago. If the weather continued to be favorable, this would be a good year for putting up a lot of vegetables to enjoy through the next winter.

Shiloh loved working in the garden, digging in the rich dirt, planting seeds and watering them, and then watching as the first leaves broke through and reached toward the sun. She found the picking of the harvest produced by the lovingly nurtured plants satisfying, and the preparation of all the vegetables for storage comforting and reassuring. But then, she'd always reveled in almost all the chores of ranch life. Even the smelly work of shoveling manure into the compost pile, which eventually turned into rich nutrients to add to the garden soil.

"Here," Jordan said of a sudden. "Let me help." She reached over to take the bowl of unshelled peas from her sister.

"Oh, it's okay," Shiloh said. "I enjoy doing this."

"Yes, but I need to use my . . . my . . ." A look of confusion spread across her face. "What do you call this?" she asked, holding up a hand.

"It's a hand." Shiloh smiled. "Can you spell it, Jordan? The word *hand*?"

As if in intense concentration, her sister scrunched up her brow but finally shook her head. "It's there, just beyond my reach," she said. "But I just . . . can't . . . remember."

Shiloh leaned over and handed her the bowl of unshelled peas. "It'll come. It's just going to take time and a lot of patience. And you spell it h-a-n-d."

Jordan thought about that for a moment, then nodded. "Yes, I do remember that." She lowered her head and began to expertly open a pea pod and then slide her thumb down its interior to expel the plump, light green peas.

Pulling up the small table that held their glasses of cider, Shiloh placed the other bowl of shelled peas between them, then reached over and took a handful of pea pods to work on in her lap. They labored in companionable silence for a while, Shiloh stealing occasional covert glances at her sister. It was almost as if she still couldn't believe Jordan had survived, and needed a reassuring reminder from time to time.

The bandages had been removed for good about a month ago, and Jordan's head, which had been shaved for the surgery, was now covered in short blonde curls. The terrible bruises had completely faded, and her split lip had healed save for a faintly darker red line. She was still thin and pale, but her appetite seemed to be improving with each passing day. Save for any unexpected complications, Doc Saunders had pronounced her well on the road to recovery.

Robert Travers's trial date was set for a week from today. Cord, a trained lawyer, would prosecute the case. His considerable criminal trial skills, combined with the community outrage at the severe brutality of the act and the Wainwrights' influence in the area, would likely ensure Robert's conviction. Even his own family had distanced themselves from him, despite his claims that Jordan had driven him to hit her, and that she had fallen against the stone fireplace mantel and cracked her skull. The injuries were just far too severe to claim they were all "accidental."

Shiloh struggled with the need to forgive him, though she knew her religious faith required it. She tried, but then every time she saw her sister, how she looked and how she fought to regain her memory of things that had always come so easily for her, Shiloh's fury at Jordan's husband would flare into a fiery conflagration yet again. After a time, she decided to lay her conflict at the Lord's feet and just concentrate on helping her sister.

Surprisingly, these days she found herself actually looking forward to being with Jordan. Something had changed in their relationship. Shiloh knew part of it was that her sister wasn't the same as before. Jordan was unsure, physically weak, and mentally struggling. But it was more than just Shiloh holding an unaccustomed position of superiority over her.

Jordan was so appreciative of even the smallest things done for her. She thanked everyone profusely. She didn't pretend to be happy, that everything was wonderful, when it wasn't. She was open and honest.

Perhaps, in time, her sister would regain enough of her memory to become the old Jordan again. If that happened, Shiloh knew she wouldn't begrudge her, for it would mean Jordan had fully recovered. Still, she couldn't help but enjoy this special time. She'd been given a great gift in the chance to make amends for her part in the sisterly estrangement. And she meant to make the most of it.

Even the passing thought of the cause of the estrangement, however, soon stirred memories of Jesse. By now, he'd been back at the White River reservation for about two months. Shiloh wondered if he ever gave her a passing thought. All the hard work she put in every day from dawn to dusk did little to banish *him* from her mind.

The sensible thing to do, she well knew, was to take him at his word and leave him be. The sensible thing to do was to use the quite legitimate excuse of her sister's care needs to end her employment at the Agency. Doing so would effectively—and quite permanently—sever any contact with Jesse. But every time she sat down to write a letter to Nathan Meeker to include in a weekly letter she always wrote Josie, something always held her back.

The Indian agent, via his daughter, kept informing her to take all the time she needed to help her sister. He assured her that her position would remain open for at least another few months before he would be compelled to begin looking for another teacher. And so Shiloh put that decision on the back burner as well.

As the days and weeks passed, Jordan ever so gradually improved. If one looked at her handwriting on a day-to-day basis, one saw little progress. But Shiloh wisely saved weekly samples, and when her sister would get discouraged, she'd pull out earlier ones to show the slight but encouraging gains. There were still memory issues and what seemed, over time, to be lasting changes in Jordan's personality. She continued with balance issues, but with the help of the cane her brother Nick fashioned for her with a cunning horse's head at the top, she was finally able to get around independently.

Still, an aura of melancholy hung over her. Though gradually Jordan ceased disavowing that little Ceci was her daughter, it was more than evident that something was blocking her true acceptance of that fact. Shiloh suspected her sister's denial hinged on her continued muddled memories of Robert Travers and the night he'd nearly killed her. Muddled memories and sudden if lessening attacks of panic and near hysteria.

Both Shiloh and Sarah tried all sorts of activities to cheer up Jordan. Like today's picnic lunch down by the creek that ran through the ranch property, just over the hill separating them from view of the main house. It had been a sweltering, very dry summer with many wildfires burning throughout the Rockies, and the three women had longed for any excuse to get out of the overly warm house. So, one hot day near the end of August, Sarah had convinced Shiloh and Jordan that a picnic would be a most splendid idea.

Since Sarah, by now, was in her last month of pregnancy, and Jordan had all she could manage just walking down to the creek, Shiloh offered to carry the blanket and picnic basket. The smells of Emma's delicious fried chicken, buttermilk biscuits, thick-sliced garden tomatoes, and still warm from the oven applesauce raisin cookies made her mouth water. The ever-thoughtful housekeeper had also included a big jar of cider, tin cups, and, besides a plate for the tomatoes, large cloth napkins to put the rest of the food on.

Even burdened with the basket and blanket, Shiloh soon left the other two women behind. She found a nice drooping willow tree that provided excellent shade but didn't block the wonderful, cooling breeze, laid out the blanket, and set down the picnic basket. She retrieved the big jar of cider, walked to the creek, which was just a few feet away, and lodged the jar between some rocks. The cold creek water would soon cool the cider to a refreshing temperature.

By the time Sarah and Jordan arrived fifteen minutes later, both were perspiring, flushed, and winded. Shiloh jumped up, helped Sarah work her awkward way down to the blanket, then steadied her sister as she sat.

"This is perfect," Cord's young wife said as she maneuvered to lay on her side, the flat of one hand propping her head. "I may just set up house here and stay until the summer's long gone."

Jordan chuckled. "Would that be with or without our brother?"

Sarah shrugged. "Oh, he'd be welcome to visit anytime he wanted. Just as long as he didn't snore. With this huge belly, I have enough trouble sleeping these days, without him waking me up."

"I'll bet Cord would deny he snores." Shiloh pulled out the tin cups. "Anyone ready for a cool drink of cider?"

"I sure am." Sarah raised her hand. "And you're right. He does deny it, then turns around and accuses me of snoring. Can you imagine?"

"It's just his way of diverting the discussion away from him," Shiloh said and looked to her sister. "Isn't that the way Cord always liked to win any arguments he had with us? Because he knew he couldn't outtalk us."

Jordan nodded slowly. "Yes, I do believe I recall that. Probably where he first learned his wily lawyer ways."

As the other two women laughed amongst themselves, Shiloh climbed to her feet and headed to the creek to fetch the jar of cider. It had chilled nicely, she thought as she carried it back. Just what all of them needed.

After a couple of cupfuls each, the three women lounged back to rest a bit before they tackled their picnic meal. Shiloh soon rejoined them after depositing the cider jar back in its rocky niche in the creek to stay cool. Profoundly content, she smiled at Sarah and Jordan.

"I'm so glad everything's turned out as it has," she said. "You marrying Cord, Sarah, and soon to have your first child. And you doing so well, Jordan."

"Well, I'm glad you're home again where you belong."

Her sister's pronouncement took Shiloh aback. True, there had been occasional glimpses of the old Jordan at times, but she wasn't so sure she wanted to continue on the tack her sister seemed to be taking. If Jordan started in again on her job at the Agency being a fool's endeavor . . .

Before she could even offer up a silent prayer for patience and a gentle rejoinder, her sister hurried on. "Oh, I didn't mean it quite the way it sounded," Jordan said. "It's just that I love having you home. We've got so much lost time to make up." She paused, glancing down for a moment. "I do remember that we never got on very well, after that . . . day . . ."

Relief flooded Shiloh. She smiled. "And I love making up for that lost time."

"So, are you ever going to write that man—Nathan Meeker, isn't it?—and tell him you're resigning?" her sister prodded, lifting her gaze to Shiloh's. "Or are you of a mind to return to that job?"

It was Shiloh's turn now to look down. "I haven't decided."

"But isn't the deadline he gave you about ended?"

The passing thought that Jordan's memory could be surprisingly acute, despite her head injury, flitted through her mind. "In another month, so I've still got time. But I need

190

to get a letter off in the next day or two so he'll know what I intend to do."

"What exactly is holding you up, Shiloh?" Sarah asked, concern shining in her eyes. "From deciding, I mean."

How could she share her feelings about Jesse? Shiloh still hadn't sorted them out herself. Despite the ensuing months since he'd left, time and distance hadn't soothed the tumult she felt whenever she thought of him. It had only clarified the certainty that she loved him, and that he indeed had feelings for her. Whether they were ones of love, however, Shiloh didn't know.

All she knew was she'd never have the answers unless she confronted him, and to do that, she had to return to the Agency. There was also the growing conviction that she should honor the agreement to fulfill her year's contract. Problem was, she was now fully aware of the difficulties awaiting her if she returned. The difficulties of getting any straight answer out of Jesse, as well as the demands of her contract. Even before she'd left to rush to Jordan's side, Shiloh's doubt that she'd be able to get the Utes to allow their children to attend school had reared its ugly head.

No, she decided, she couldn't tell Sarah and Jordan about Jesse, but her concerns about her teaching job seemed safe enough to share. "I suppose I'm just enjoying being home too much, and I dread the task awaiting me back at the White River Agency," she finally replied.

With the other two women's encouragement, Shiloh soon had the tale told of the Utes' reluctance to have their children schooled, and Meeker's problems establishing a lasting, positive relationship with the Utes. "And then," she finished, "the unrealistic demands and unfulfilled promises of the US government to the Indians haven't helped much either."

"It puts everyone in an untenable position," Jordan said. "Indeed, a no-win situation."

Shiloh nodded. "The Utes most of all. But I still haven't given up my hopes to help them by educating their children. I truly believe that it's their only chance of survival in a world that's so rapidly changing around them."

"First, though, they must face the fact that there's no going back, no matter how badly they wish it so." Sarah reached for the picnic basket and pulled it over. "If you can just accomplish that, you'll have given them a great gift."

The thought heartened Shiloh. She didn't know how she was going to accomplish such a thing, but at least she had a definite, if less grandiose, goal to work toward now. A baby step, to be sure, instead of the giant ones she'd first envisioned, but hopefully the first of many steps. Because it was truth, what Sarah had said. There was no going back for the Utes, or any of the tribes for that matter.

"Thank you," she said, her heart full of gratitude.

Sarah's brow furrowed in puzzlement. "For what?"

"For clarifying some things for me." Shiloh motioned to the picnic basket. "So, are you going to hold on to that all day, or are we going to eat some lunch?"

"Oh, are you hungry?" Her brother's wife shot her an impish look. "And I thought it was just me, having to eat for two and all."

Jordan laughed. "Hardly. The smells coming out of that basket have been driving me crazy for the past half hour." She scooted closer to Sarah. "Let's eat!"

They enjoyed a tasty meal, full of laughter and camaraderie, and even argued over who'd get the last piece of fried chicken before deciding Sarah and the baby needed it most of all. As they cleaned up and put all the remnants of the lunch back in the basket, Sarah winced and put her hand to her belly.

"Is something wrong?" Shiloh was quick to ask.

"Oh, no." Cord's wife shook her head and managed a

smile. "Just some prelabor contractions. I've been having them for the past few months. They come and go. Doc Saunders says it's my womb practicing for the big event. Though, usually they don't hurt or last so long." She leaned back and began rubbing her distended belly.

"Just give it a few minutes and it'll be gone," Jordan offered, then stopped short. "Now, how did I know that?"

Shiloh bit her lip. Though Jordan helped with Ceci's feeding and care these days, she remained distant and stiff with the child. But this unexpected comment on the childbearing process was encouraging, actually the first one Jordan had made since her injury.

"Guess you're starting to remember the birth of your own child," Shiloh said, ignoring the enigmatic look her sister sent her. She looked to Sarah. "Is the contraction going away yet?"

Sarah nodded. "Yes." She sat up again. "That was a strange one, though. I've never felt one like that before."

"Well, you are getting close to your confinement, aren't you?" Shiloh set the picnic basket aside.

"Still have a couple more weeks before it's really safe to deliver." She picked up her tin cup. "Any cider left in that jar in the creek?"

"Just a little." Shiloh rose. "I'll go fetch it for you."

They finished up the cider, put away the cups, and stretched out on the blanket for a nap. Despite the heat, it had been a perfect day, Shiloh thought as she lay there, watching the long, limp willow branches gently sway in the breeze. Her time here at Castle Mountain Ranch had been pleasant, especially once Jordan began to recover. It wasn't the same as it had been when she was a child, but it was pleasant nonetheless.

Soon, however, she must head back to the Agency. Perhaps not for long, or for the extent of the full year. That would depend on Nathan Meeker. It would also depend on how things went with the Utes. But she was determined to give it her best try.

The White River Agency and the Ute people were where God had called her. She'd known that from the start, and the certainty hadn't faded. True, she'd been very discouraged at times, and she wasn't sure if, despite the Lord's summons, she'd ultimately be successful.

Well, successful in the eyes of men, anyway, Shiloh quickly amended. She needed to change her way of viewing things, she well knew. Most times, she saw things with human eyes rather than the eyes of God. Her notion of success was so shallow, going no deeper than the superficial perception the world took of things.

She yawned. A heavy drowsiness settled over her. She levered up on one elbow and took in the sight of her two companions, both sleeping soundly.

Let them doze for a while longer, she thought. No harm done. She'd stay awake and keep an eye on things. Keep thinking about what it would take to change her outlook, to see everything in a new and better light.

To accomplish that, however, she'd have to do something about her infernal pride. She didn't like to fail. Perhaps, though, a lot of that was caught up in how others might see her if she failed. As hard as she tried to deny it, she was very much directed by the opinions of others.

Yet Christ had never let the opinions of others direct Him. Indeed, He'd instead emptied Himself of His pride to the point of becoming a servant. He hadn't viewed His role as being and acting godlike, but solely in doing His Father's will. And that was the view of success she must take from here on out. Becoming a servant of others, being obedient, doing the Lord's will.

A warm, soft breeze caressed her face. Birdsong came from somewhere up in the willow, sweet and soothing. She felt replete, at peace. Her lids began to droop, and this time Shiloh didn't fight to remain awake.

Sometime later, she was jerked awake by a soft cry. She pushed up, rubbed her eyes, and looked around. Sarah was kneeling there, both hands clutching her belly, rocking back and forth.

"What is it, Sarah?" Shiloh asked anxiously. "What's wrong?"

Tears filled Sarah's eyes and trickled down her cheeks. "The baby . . . I think the baby's coming . . ."

13

Early the next morning, Sarah delivered of a son. Though the dark-haired infant was small and a few weeks earlier than expected, he was vigorous and strong. Cord and Sarah named him Caleb after her brother who had died before his time.

Shiloh couldn't recall Cord ever looking quite so proud. She had also, she thought with an affectionate grin of remembrance, never seen him so frantic and scared as when Doc Saunders had pronounced his wife to be in true labor. Emma, always the one to take charge in an emergency, had soon shooed him from their bedroom where Sarah labored, assigning his brother Nick to keep Cord occupied and out from underfoot. Jordan had been given charge of young Danny and the infant Ceci. And Shiloh had been appointed to assist Emma and Doc Saunders with the delivery.

Actually, she mused as she set the bloodstained bedsheets to soak in a tub of cold water late that morning, she'd really mostly run errands from the upstairs bedroom down to the kitchen and back. It amazed Shiloh how many bed linens and nightgowns a person could go through in the process of birthing a child. It was her first chance to view a human birth, and she found it both messy and beautiful. And, though Sarah's labor certainly didn't last near as long as some, according to

Doc Saunders, Shiloh was nonetheless relieved for Sarah—and Cord—when it was over and done with.

Emma soon hurried everyone from the room, so Cord and Sarah could spend a few moments enjoying their new son in private. But, after a time, the cleanup began. For the women, anyway. Nick, Danny, and baby Ceci were soon in bed, fast asleep, and even though Jordan offered to help with the chores, it soon became evident that she had also expended nearly all of her energy.

So, it was left to Shiloh and Emma to serve Doc Saunders breakfast and several cups of black coffee, then send him on his way, and to finally see to the laundry. Shiloh didn't mind, though. She was still too keyed up from the excitement of the birthing and knew she'd only have lain awake for a long while if she'd gone to bed right away.

As she leaned over the washtub and tried to scrub out as much of the blood as she could from the sheets and night-gowns before they actually washed them, her thoughts turned to Cord's and Sarah's happy expressions as they gazed down at their firstborn. As she watched them, something had changed within her. She'd felt a yearning rise from deep within, a yearning to hold a child of her own in her arms. Her and Jesse's child.

The revelation was surprising, to say the least. In all the years of her youth, unlike her sister, Shiloh had never been one to play much with dolls, dream of a fine wedding, or pretend at married life. She'd much preferred riding and rop-ing, climbing trees, catching tadpoles down by the creek, and helping the menfolk with chores. Indeed, when there was opportunity for conversation after supper, Shiloh naturally gravitated toward the men rather than the women. Talk of babies, favorite recipes, dress patterns, and the like bored her to no end.

But the thought of the joyous pride on Jesse's face as she handed him their first child, all wrinkled and red, filled her with happy anticipation. Working beside him as they built their first house, dug their first garden, and raised their first barn was the stuff of dreams. Together, they'd make a life for themselves and their children. And if that required her to cook, and wash, and sew, then she'd do it.

Because the necessary, if tedious, times would be far outweighed by the satisfying moments. Moments spent together after a long day, sitting on their porch watching a glorious sunset. Playing with their children. And lying in each other's arms at night, after everyone was in bed. To spend a life with Jesse, to raise their children with him, and then to grow old alongside him was surely as close to heaven as she could get on earth.

"A penny for your thoughts, honey."

Shiloh jerked up her head from her intent scrubbing of a nightgown. She rinsed it then held it up for examination. She'd about gotten out all the stains.

"Oh, I was just daydreaming, Emma," she said as she twisted the nightgown free of excess water and laid it aside. "Seeing Sarah and Cord with little Caleb just got me thinking, that's all."

"About having babies of your own someday?" Emma smiled. "Maybe with that handsome young man who brought you home?"

She could feel the heat creep up her neck and into her cheeks. "You mean Jesse?" She feigned a nonchalant shrug. "Oh, maybe. Or maybe not."

"Well, I don't know. The whole time he was here, you two near to couldn't take your eyes off each other. And when one wasn't looking, the other sure was. Land sakes, I don't recall ever seeing such hungry looks in all my days!"

"Emma!" Shiloh covered her burning cheeks with her

wet hands. "Now you've gone and done it. I'll bet I'm as red as a beet."

"Yes, you sure are, honey." Emma wrung out the towel she was scrubbing and placed it with the other laundry awaiting the final washing. "But you needn't be embarrassed. The good Lord created man to want woman, and vice versa. To love and cleave to. Are you sure, though, that your Jesse's the marrying kind? Leastwise, when it comes to marrying a white woman?"

The housekeeper had hit the nail square on the head. She knew Jesse was the marrying kind. He'd married that Ute woman. But it seemed these days he was trying his hardest to see himself as a Ute, and only a Ute, all the while reject-ing his white blood. That might well be part of the problem between them. He didn't want to live as a white in any way. And perhaps every time he was with her, he feared being with her would inevitably compel him to do so.

She suspected, though, that it was more than just that. Even when she'd known him the first time, Shiloh had sensed that Jesse bore a terrible secret. A secret that had a lot to do with how he viewed himself and his place in the world.

And, as self-confident and capable as Jesse was, beneath that façade he didn't think all that highly of himself. Shiloh wondered if that poor self-image, that sense of unworthi-ness, was part of the reason he'd so easily gravitated toward her when she was a child. Because she looked up to him, imagined him perfect in every way. Her hero worship likely stroked his ego.

Not that her opinion of him was the only source of their friendship. Even as young as she then was, she knew there was a special bond between them. They'd understood each other, shared similar views on things, and felt so comfortable in each other's presence.

On the journey from the Agency to home, there'd been moments when Shiloh had experienced that same comfort and bonding again. It had been like old times, only better. Better because now the mutual attraction had been electrifying, setting her heart to pounding, her mind reeling, and an intense yearning to rise within her. And she'd seen, known with a woman's instinct strong and sure, that Jesse had felt the same things.

But were their high emotions and desires for each other enough to overcome the obstacles that society and personal demons would place in their way? Shiloh didn't know. Indeed, *was* Jesse the marrying kind when it came to a white woman?

She sighed. "Truly, Emma, I don't know if Jesse would wish to marry me and live the white man's life. Not after how he's been treated all his life by whites, including his own father."

"So, what is it about him then that makes you even think of him for a husband? Surely you're not trying to save him out of pity?"

"Pity?" Shiloh laughed. "Oh, and wouldn't Jesse just love that? There's not much he detests more than pity."

"Well, that may be," the housekeeper said. "And I'm not looking to pry into your private matters. I just think a woman should give a lot of thought to why she's attracted to one man and not another." She paused. "Knowing that he was educated in a mission school for several years, do you think it's possible he's at least a Christian?"

Jesse's obvious ability to read and his education at a mission school had become common knowledge around the ranch when he'd first come to them nine years ago. Only Shiloh, however, had ever been privy to the actual details about the mission school near where he and his parents lived. The first teacher, Brother Thomas, had been a gentle man filled with the love of the Lord and the children under his tutelage. He'd seen no difference in them, be they half-breed or full-blooded Indian. Jesse had come to love the burly, bearded man and had finally accepted instruction in the Christian faith and baptism.

In time, Brother Thomas had been called to another mission farther north in Wyoming. Brother Isaac had soon arrived to take his place. By then, Jesse was fourteen, and from the start, Jesse and Isaac had butted heads.

Some of the friction between them arose from the increasing difficulties at home, as Jesse's father became more and more abusive to Jesse and his mother, keeping Jesse unsettled and constantly on edge. Some of it was the result of the normal heightened emotions and rebelliousness of a boy edging into manhood. But a large part of the conflict stemmed from the fact that Brother Isaac was not Brother Thomas.

Brother Isaac didn't particularly cotton to wasting his valuable instruction time on what he considered unappreciative children, and he wasn't above punishing any student he deemed disrespectful, unprepared for his daily lessons, or who dozed off in class. And, thanks to the turmoil at home, Jesse found it increasingly difficult to study, complete his homework assignments, or stay awake in the afternoons. He, however, though stoically accepting punishment for his own academic failings, found it increasingly difficult to tolerate the beatings some of the younger students received.

His schooling abruptly terminated one late spring afternoon when he intervened in the caning that a seven-year-old Indian boy was to receive. One thing led to another, angry words were exchanged, and when Jesse didn't back down, Brother Isaac turned the full brunt of his outrage on Jesse. The teacher was only able to land one blow with his cane before finding himself flat on his back, looking up at Jesse.

As Shiloh recalled, the details were vague after that. Jesse was expelled from school. His father tried to punish him;

201

his mother intervened, and somehow she was hit trying to protect her son. She fell to the floor, striking her head hard on the fireplace hearth. Nothing could be done for her, and she'd died the next morning.

Jesse had ridden out, never to return, just as soon as his mother had been properly buried. A few years later, he'd shown up at Castle Mountain Ranch, already an experienced ranch hand. And, though he'd finally come to trust her enough to tell her the story of his earlier years, he had also made it plain that he was through with the white man's schooling and God. Shiloh had decided it best not to broach the subject of either.

But Emma hadn't asked for a long-winded tale, Shiloh reminded herself. All she wanted was a simple answer.

"I believe, in the depths of his heart, Jesse still believes in God," she replied. "Maybe he doesn't give much thought to Jesus Christ anymore, but I think he still believes in a good and loving Creator. And I believe he tries to live his life by those beliefs. That he is a kind, generous, loving man."

"Well, sounds like you're giving this a lot of thought," Emma said, wringing out the last towel. She threw it into the basket, wiped her hands on her apron, then picked up the pot of steaming water on top of the cookstove. "In the meanwhile, I think we've got a load of laundry to wash."

Shiloh grinned, grabbed hold of the basket, and followed the housekeeper outside to the big washtub.

Jesse was busy skinning a rabbit he'd caught earlier that morning, when Persune rode into camp. Jesse didn't immediately jump up to greet his friend until he'd finished removing the rabbit's pelt and draped it over a nearby bush to dry. Since he'd already gutted the rabbit, he then quickly wrapped the carcass in a piece of hide and put it into a lidded basket and back inside his tepee to keep the meat safe from any inquisitive camp dog.

By the time his friend tied up his pony and ambled over, Jesse had cleaned both his knife and his hands. "What brings you all the way out here?" he asked as he stood and clasped the other Ute's forearm. "Your wives making more unreasonable demands of you?"

"No." Persune shook his head. "This time, it's Josie. She asked me to fetch you. Seems she has some important information to tell you about the red-haired woman."

Jesse released his friend's arm and stepped back. "If luck is with me, it's that Shiloh has decided not to return."

His friend shot him a curious look. "You don't wish to see her again? And here I'd hoped that the journey with her back to her family had helped to strengthen the bond between you. That perhaps you'd even made her your woman."

At the thought of Shiloh consenting to any untoward advances, much less her agreeing to bed him without being married, Jesse's mouth quirked in amusement. But then, Persune's view of how things should be between a man and a woman were colored by his Ute culture. It didn't matter anyway. Shiloh could never be his.

"No, I didn't make her my woman," he said in reply. "Nor will I."

"Well, I think you're making a big mistake, but you can be certain there'll be many braves who'll be happy to take your place."

"A lot of good it'll do them," Jesse muttered softly.

"So, when can I tell Josie you'll be meeting with her?"

"Still trying to win her favor, are you? Even stooping to becoming her messenger now?"

Persune's eyes narrowed in irritation. "You turn your nose

up at a pretty white woman, then begrudge me my love for Josie? You're not being fair, my friend."

No, he wasn't being fair, Jesse thought, remorse filling him. He was being unkind, peevish, and a bit jealous. And taking it all out on his best friend.

"You're right. I'm sorry for my foul mood." He gave Persune a playful punch on the arm. "If you can wait about an hour while I cook up this rabbit, we can eat it and then head out for the Agency. Assuming, of course, I can spend the night in your tepee?"

The Ute grinned. "Stay for a few days, if you wish. My wives always enjoy your company. And so will some of their friends."

Jesse rolled his eyes. He'd managed to forget what inveterate matchmakers Persune's wives were. Still, some of their friends were rather pretty. And their friendly company might help take his mind off of a certain redhead.

On the other hand, that possibility seemed rather unlikely, Jesse glumly amended. At least for a long while to come. But nothing was accomplished pining after what one couldn't have. And if he was nothing else, he was a realistic man, he thought as he turned and headed back to his tepee.

"No," Jesse said in disbelief the next morning as he stood outside the Agency office, listening as Josie finished reading Shiloh's last letter. "I told her not to come back. Why is she coming back?"

Josie eyed him caustically. "Maybe because she's a grown woman and can do what she wants? Whatever gives you the right to tell Shiloh what to do?"

Jesse sighed and shook his head. "Obviously, nothing. Nothing gives me the right."

"She just wants to fulfill the contract she made with my father," Josie said, softening her tone. "And I think, as well, Shiloh felt like she left things unfinished. Her work here, the friendships she was beginning to forge with some of the Ute people . . ."

"None of that will do her any good. She won't succeed."

"You don't know that!" Once again, anger flared in Josie's eyes. "Shiloh was becoming good friends with Susan and Johnson and some of their camp. And Jack liked her, even if he tried to hide it."

He gave a disparaging snort. "She may have won Jack's respect, but don't ever imagine he would trust or befriend her. He's long past trusting any white man."

"Well, then that's his loss," she snapped, fisting her hands on her hips. "As it apparently will be yours too."

Jesse clenched his jaw. "Is that all you wished to tell me then? That Shiloh's on her way back and will be here around the 25th of September?"

"Pretty much. For what it's worth."

"Then I thank you for the message. I don't intend, though, to be part of the welcoming party on her return." He turned on his heel and began to walk away.

"Oh, really?" Josie cried after him. "And where exactly do you intend to go to avoid her?"

He didn't look back but just kept on walking. "Who knows? It's hunting season. Maybe I'll just take a long trip into the mountains and stay there for a while."

Autumn was glorious this year, Shiloh thought from the front bench of the freight wagon as they headed south from Rawlins to the White River Agency. The aspens were already beginning to turn golden and, combined with the deep, dark green of the pines and firs higher on the mountainsides and the rich blue skies, she didn't know when she'd seen anything more beautiful. But then, she'd always loved these mountains and their verdant valleys slashed with rushing, ice-cold rivers and streams.

"Quite a difference from when you first came this way," Joe Collum said from beside her. "March was pretty bleak around here, if I recall."

"Bleak and cold." Shiloh shot him a quick smile. "I'm thinking I like this time of year a whole lot better."

He nodded, then slapped the reins over the mule team's backs to urge them to pick up the pace. "Me too. The summer was pretty hot, though, and miserable. Not a lot of rain, so it got pretty dry. And lots of wildfires, which set folks on edge. The Utes got blamed, and the settlers put pressure on Meeker to keep them on the reservation. And, of course, that didn't sit well with the Utes, who needed to travel farther into the mountains to get their summer hunting in."

In her letters, Josie had intimated that things had gotten pretty tense between her father and the Utes this summer. Josie, however, hadn't provided a lot of details. Shiloh hoped, with the coming of cooler weather in the next month or so, that the high emotions on both sides would also begin to cool. The summer heat always seemed to bring out the worst in everyone's tempers.

"So, how did all that end up?" she asked. "Was Mr. Meeker able to keep the Utes at home?"

Joe gave a disdainful snort. "Fat chance of that ever happening. Every time I bring in supplies, I get an earful of Meeker's complaining about the Utes. Things aren't going well for that man. Not well at all."

"I'm sorry to hear that."

"Word got around that Meeker went so far as to ask help

from Governor Pitkin, requesting soldiers to assist in keeping the Utes on the reservation. Pitkin then went to the Indian Bureau, demanding that troops be sent to move the Utes to the Indian Territory. And, somehow, Chief Douglas and Captain Jack found out about that."

Shiloh's heart sank. Governor Pitkin was well known to hate the Utes and want them all gone. And now, if Douglas and Jack knew what was in the works for them . . .

In spite of the day's warmth, she shivered. What exactly was she heading into?

"I don't mean to alarm you, ma'am," the freight driver said, apparently noting her reaction. "But you need to know what's been going on in your absence, and I'm sorry to say, it's only gotten worse."

"Worse?" *How much worse?* Shiloh wondered. "Well, best you tell me all you know. I can't be of much help unless I know what the problems are."

"Well, that's kind of my thought too, ma'am." He shot her a considering look. "Were you aware that Meeker's had his eye on plowing up a big plot of that rich pastureland in Powell Valley, to plant winter wheat in?"

"But that's the Utes' grazing area for all their ponies."

"Yep, and when Meeker sent Shadrach Price to start plowing, the Utes took it pretty bad. Meeker apparently ignored their protests, and the plowing resumed. Then some of the Utes hid in the surrounding sagebrush and fired some warning shots at Price. He hightailed it out of Powell Valley and refused to come back until the matter was settled between Meeker and the Utes."

"When did all that happen?"

"Just a couple of weeks ago, in early September."

Though she dreaded the answer, she had to ask. "And have things been settled?"

Joe sighed and shook his head. "Not for long. Chief John-son and Meeker had a big falling-out about a week after the Powell Valley incident. Johnson accused him of plowing up his land and writing lies to Washington. One thing led to another, and Johnson ended up grabbing Meeker, pushing him outside, and slamming him into a hitching rail."

Meeker had always considered Johnson a good friend and ally. What would happen now that Johnson had seemed to turn against him?

"Anything else happen since then?" she asked.

"Couldn't say. I headed back to Rawlins for another supply load the next day on the 9th, and this is the first chance I've had to return to the Agency."

Shiloh did some quick calculations. Johnson and Meeker's falling-out had happened on September 8th then, and today was September 24th. They should arrive at the White River Indian Agency tomorrow. Seventeen days would've passed by then, since the last incident Joe Collum knew about. She could only wonder what had transpired in the interim.

"Well, let's just hope, by the time we arrive tomorrow," she said, "that things have begun to calm down."

"I sure hope so, ma'am," the freighter said, though his somber tone didn't bode well. "Because if it hasn't, we're in for a heap of trouble. A very big heap of trouble."

14

Jesse had mixed feelings about heading out on the hunting party to Wyoming. But fresh meat was running low in their camp, and with Shiloh due to arrive any day, he needed more time to sort out his chaotic emotions about her. As a planned weeklong excursion, the hunting trip would be the perfect excuse to prolong his inevitable meeting with Shiloh. Hopefully, it'd also provide the time for thought that he craved.

However, in the past few weeks, things at the Agency had rapidly gone from bad to worse. After Jack and Douglas had discovered that, thanks to Meeker's incessant letter writing to his various superiors, the Colorado governor was trying to send soldiers to move the Utes to the hated Indian Territory, the two chiefs had their people stop all work on Agency projects. Jack had even paid Governor Pitkin in Denver a visit, complaining about Meeker. And, when Meeker found out about the visit, he told Jack he deserved hanging for his disloyalty. After that, things were never the same between the two men.

The attempted plowing of Powell Valley had only escalated the tension between the Agency and the Utes. With the hundreds of ponies owned by the White River Utes, the rich grasslands for grazing were imperative to protect. Yet it seemed nothing they could say to Meeker could convince him otherwise. Not even the agent's friendship with Chief Johnson seemed to make any difference. And when Johnson had failed to change Meeker's plans for Powell Valley, Johnson had finally washed his hands of the Indian agent.

Now, Meeker had no allies left with the Utes. Jack and Douglas had never thought much of him, and just paid lip service to the agent's plans as long as they could obtain the annuity goods. In the meanwhile, though, they went behind his back whenever it suited them. Johnson had truly tried to work with Meeker, but it seemed that he'd finally tired of always being the one to have to change, to compromise. And now, all the chiefs were becoming increasingly worried that soldiers were coming, that there might be war.

As much as he hated leaving the reservation right now, perhaps it was for the best. If it came to war, they'd need a good supply of meat and other provisions. And they certainly couldn't count on Meeker's generosity of late. Only yesterday, Jack had gotten into another argument with Meeker when the agent had refused to issue annuity blankets to their hunting party.

The People were sick and tired of feeling like beggars when it came to asking for the necessary supplies promised to them by the US government. To feel they had to ask permission to engage in activities that had always been their right, like ranging far from the reservation to hunt. And to have their traditional way of life not just belittled but actively destroyed at every turn.

The tension, the insults, and the degradations had been building for years now. No man who called himself a man could endure much more. Yet Meeker seemed not to see what was building, or even to care. He was like so many of his kind, puffed up with their own importance and sense of superiority over a race they felt was little more than ignorant, uncivilized savages. They took whatever they wanted and imagined themselves justified in doing so. In the end, Jesse well knew, no matter what the People did, the whites would win.

The saddest part was that the innocent would suffer in this clash of cultures and likely suffer the worst of all. The women, the children, the good-intentioned whites who championed the Indians' cause. Folks like Shiloh, whom Jesse knew truly wanted the best for the People. But she, in her own way, was as naïve as the Utes in imagining that the People and the whites could ever live together as equals.

Perhaps, if fortune smiled, Shiloh would arrive back at the Agency and realize how precarious things had become. Realize that all her fine teaching aspirations were a lost cause and that it wasn't safe for her to remain here. Perhaps, if fortune smiled, she might well be gone from the Agency, heading back to the safety of her home, before he even returned.

The solution to the problem of Shiloh was likely too easy, though. Fate, it seemed, was repeatedly forcing them together. Forcing them into a headlong course that Jesse feared might lead to him having to make a choice—a choice between Shiloh and his Ute family.

One of the last summer squashes, nearly hidden by the large green leaves, dangled from a thick, bristly stem. Shiloh squatted and gingerly felt for the vegetable through the leaves. When she found the squash, she twisted it gently from its stem, then placed it in her basket and rose.

A few yards away, Josie worked with a spade, carefully checking the potatoes. "Not quite ready," she called over to Shiloh. "Another week at most, though, and we should be able to dig them up."

"Let's just hope we don't have a killing frost in the meantime," Shiloh replied, adjusting the brim of her straw hat to better shade her eyes. "I'd hate to have to drag a mess of blankets out here to cover all these plants."

Josie gave a short laugh, then turned her attention to spreading dirt back over the potatoes she'd exposed. It was a nice warm day for it being four days shy of the end of September. Shiloh had been back at the Agency since yesterday and in the past day had struggled to come to terms with all the changes that had occurred in her absence.

Some things Josie had filled her in on, others Shiloh had just noted by quietly observing. Since early August, when Nathan Meeker had badly injured his arm when their wagon had overturned on the trip back from Rawlins, Josie had noted a decided change in her father. He now spoke disdainfully of the White River Utes, calling them cowardly and dishonest. He had been too good to them in the past and now was willing to use force—soldiers, guns, and even chains—to get the Utes to come around to his way of things.

And his foul mood wasn't just directed at the Utes. His whole personality had taken a turn for the worse. He was distant and moody with everyone around him. He even berated Josie for watching the Utes race their ponies.

"Everyone goes around with a long face these days," she'd informed Shiloh her first night back as they sought out the privacy of Shiloh's bedroom and gingerly sipped at steaming mugs of tea. "I'm really getting worried. After Father's falling-out with Johnson almost three weeks ago, I can't even get Susan to talk to me. And Douglas pulled his son out of school, so now I've no one to teach in your absence."

"It does sound bad." Shiloh paused to take a tentative taste of her Earl Grey tea. "Isn't there any way to mend things?"

"I don't know." Josie sighed and shook her head. "Not unless one side caves in to the other. And Father thinks he's bent over backward and says he refuses to bend any farther. The Utes, of course, feel pretty much the same way. I'm just afraid the soldiers from Fort Steele are on the verge of heading down here to settle this. If they do, the Utes might see it as an act of war. They're already pretty skittish these days, with a lot of meetings, braves riding back and forth between camps, and even some war dances near the Agency buildings on the night of the 10th. Most of us couldn't sleep at all that night."

The Utes suspect something, Shiloh thought. *Meeker's a fool to imagine that whatever he's doing to get soldiers down here hasn't been noticed.*

"Has your father sent for the soldiers?"

Though Josie hesitated in her reply, the look on her face gave the answer away. "Yes, but you must promise not to say a word to anyone, and especially not to any Ute."

"Well, that shouldn't be too hard a promise to keep," Shiloh said with a chuckle. "If Susan and Johnson won't speak to you, they likely won't speak to me, either. And Douglas and Jack have not been big supporters of mine in the best of times."

"There's always Jesse," her friend supplied, shooting her a sly look. "But he's on a hunting trip with some of the other braves from Jack's camp. He just left two days ago and won't be back for about a week."

So, Jesse found a convenient excuse not to be here when I arrived.

Shiloh leveled an intent gaze on Josie. "Did you tell him when I'd be getting to the Agency?"

"Yes, of course. You didn't say I couldn't, and I'd hoped he'd have taken the news well."

"But he didn't, did he?"

Suddenly, Josie seemed to find great interest in her cup of

tea. "Well, he thought it might not be the best or safest time for you to return, considering what's been going on of late."

"And that was all he said? That he was concerned for my safety?"

"Pretty much."

Shiloh grimaced. "I can just bet that's all he said. Well, it doesn't matter. I'm back and am here to stay!"

Josie set down her cup, stood, and rushed over to her. "Oh, I'm so glad to hear you say that! I was afraid that once you found out about the recent troubles . . . well, I'm just glad you're here."

"We've got a lot of work ahead of us," Shiloh said as she set aside her own tea and took her friend's hand. "Somehow, we've got to try and get everyone to make peace and start afresh."

"How exactly do you plan to do that?"

"I don't know," Shiloh replied, chewing her bottom lip in thought. "But just give me a day or two and I'll come up with something."

<hr/>

By the next day, it soon became apparent that the task before her and Josie had become even more difficult. Douglas came to Meeker, demanding to know if he knew anything about soldiers being in the area. Meeker denied any knowledge but assured the chief that if any soldiers did turn up, he'd have them halted at the reservation border at Milk Creek and then arrange a meeting with all the chiefs and the military commander.

The agent's assurances didn't seem to work, however, and soon the squaws in Douglas's camp were taking down their tepees and heading south. That evening, a messenger named Charlie Lowry arrived and Meeker took him into his office for a private conversation. The fact that he soon ordered the Agency employees to stand guard over the storehouse containing the annuity goods didn't bode well for the contents of the message.

Everyone went around with solemn expressions at best, and outright fearful ones at the worst. An air of foreboding hung over the supper meal, and there was little talk and even littler of the meal consumed. Shiloh helped clean up after supper and wash and put away dishes, then headed to her bedroom.

It didn't take long for the drums to begin a slow, rhythmic beat, the sonorous sounds rising from somewhere down beyond the Agency buildings. Singing soon followed.

Shiloh opened her bedroom window and peered out. Bonfires burned not far away, and she could make out many Ute braves dancing around the leaping flames, wielding spears, tomahawks, and other weapons. She slammed the window shut and locked it.

For the first time since her return, she allowed herself to admit they were all in grave danger. She didn't know whether to pray for the timely arrival of the soldiers or not. If and when they crossed the reservation border, the Utes might well attack them. And once the Utes did that, the die was cast for them.

At that point, there'd be nothing lost by also turning on the hapless Agency employees, slaughtering them one and all. The foolish act of placing guards to prevent the Utes from breaking into the storerooms and taking all the annuity goods was the least of Meeker's worries. Instead, he should be thinking of ways to protect everyone behind some defensible barrier. Or, better still, get everyone out of there under the cover of darkness.

But where could they go that the Utes couldn't quickly find them? Indeed, it was doubtful any large evacuation could be arranged and managed without the Utes knowing. Since the day she'd arrived back, Shiloh had been acutely aware that the Agency and its employees were being watched.

She paced her bedroom, her hands growing damp, her heart thudding loudly in her chest, as the first tendrils of fear ensnared her. *Why did I come back?* she thought. *There was never any hope of accomplishing anything here. Never. I was just a fool to think so, and now I may die because of that foolishness.*

If only Jesse were here. Surely I'd be safe with him. But he ran just as soon as he heard I was coming back. I can't depend on him for any help. If he even would *help.*

There was only one hope of help, and that lay with the Lord. Shiloh knelt by her bed, clasped her trembling hands before her, and began to pray. Pray for herself but also for all the innocent souls who worked at the Agency. Even for Nathan Meeker.

Ultimately, they were *all* innocent pawns in a battle for supremacy. A battle between the US government and the Indian people. A battle in which little, if any, mercy would be granted from either side.

After two nights of war dances that kept everyone awake, the 29th day of September dawned sunny and warm. Though feeling groggy from lack of sleep, Shiloh rose at sunrise, performed her morning ablutions, then dressed and headed downstairs to help prepare breakfast. By the time the morning meal was served to the boardinghouse occupants, a large group of Ute braves had gathered at the kitchen door, begging for food.

Arvilla Meeker exchanged a worried look with her daughter and Shiloh, then began to hurriedly butter some slices of bread. "I reckon they're getting pretty hungry," she said, "what with the squaws all packed up and moved away. No one's left to cook for them."

Shiloh moved to the cookstove to fry up some extra bacon. "Best we see to their needs then. No sense aggravating them right now."

The Ute men's hunger finally sated, the three women watched them walk away, then joined the others in the dining room. Everyone appeared tired, but the mood around the table was hopeful. The Utes appeared friendlier this morning, and several at the table thought things looked to be improving.

Shiloh kept her own opinions to herself. True, the braves had asked for and accepted food from them, but she didn't necessarily think that signified much of anything. Hungry people would take food where they could get it.

As she helped the other women that morning with the chores, she couldn't shake the feeling that this was just the lull before the storm. It didn't help her mood when Flora Ellen Price returned from her room and admitted her husband had loaded up their Winchester rifle and left it there. Even his attempts to ease her worry by telling her it was just ready as a safety measure didn't reassure Flora Ellen. And it certainly didn't reassure Shiloh, either.

Shiloh spent the time between breakfast and lunch preparation in her room. She read from her Bible for a time, then penned a letter home. In it, she told them of the current dire situation and assured them, if something were to happen to her, that she had made her peace with the Lord, and that she loved them all.

Then, after sealing the letter, Shiloh walked over to the storehouse, where Harry, one of the Agency employees, was getting supplies in preparation for his trip back to Rawlins. "Would you see that this letter gets to the post office in

Rawlins?" she asked, handing the letter to the man. Shiloh then offered him a coin to pay the postage.

Harry tipped his hat, pocketed the money, and shoved the letter into his shirt pocket. "Sure thing, ma'am. I'm also going to be taking a telegram from Mr. Meeker, to deliver to the Western Union station there. Guess he likes to keep up a steady correspondence with the Indian Bureau."

She wished she could read the contents of that telegram but knew it wasn't permissible. "I suppose it never hurts to keep one's superiors informed of things."

Harry finished stuffing his supplies into his saddlebag, then shouldered it. "Well, I'd best be on my way. It's a long ride back to Rawlins."

"Oh, and don't I know." With a smile, Shiloh stepped aside. "Godspeed."

"Thank you, ma'am." Once more, Harry tipped his hat and strode from the storehouse.

Watching him leave, she was tempted to ask if she could accompany him back to Rawlins. After the events of the past few days, more than anything she'd ever wanted, Shiloh desperately wanted to run, and run as far as she could, from the White River Agency. The admission of her cowardice shamed her.

Along with Nathan Meeker and his family, the rest of the Agency employees were holding steadfast. They seemed convinced that everything would turn out fine. And they had, after all, been privy to many events that she had not been there for. Surely their perspective had to be more accurate than hers.

So Shiloh choked back her plea to be allowed to leave with Harry and headed to the boardinghouse. As she did, she saw a Ute brave riding pell-mell toward Douglas's camp. Shiloh halted and watched as Douglas exited his tepee, and the two men began to confer.

Shaking her head, she entered the boardinghouse and made her way to the kitchen. Josie, her mother, and Flora Ellen Price were already there, busy preparing the lunch meal.

Shiloh took down an apron from its peg and quickly donned it. "What do you need me to do?"

Arvilla indicated a bowl of potatoes that Flora was already working on. "Help Flora Ellen," she said, replacing the lid on the beef roast she'd pulled from the oven. "The sooner we get those potatoes on to boil, the sooner we can get them cooked and mashed."

Taking a short, sharp knife from the drawer, Shiloh pulled out a chair at the worktable near Flora Ellen and picked up a potato. Ten minutes later, the two women finished peeling and cutting up the last potato. After adding them to the big pot of now-boiling water, Shiloh rinsed her hands, then wiped them on her apron.

"What's next?"

Arvilla paused to check the other pot of green beans. "Everything's going fine in here now. How about you start setting the dining room table? Oh, and set an extra place for Mr. Eskridge and Sowerwick. They'll also be dining with us."

Josie turned just then and caught Shiloh's gaze. At the mention of one of Jack's subchiefs, Shiloh arched a questioning brow. Her friend smiled and shrugged. Shiloh took that to mean Josie didn't know why Sowerwick was invited, but hoped it boded well.

A half hour later, the meal was served and eaten by all with great gusto. Eskridge departed immediately thereafter to join his two Ute guides on the trip to deliver another letter to Major Thornburgh, the commander of the military companies on their way to the Agency. Mr. Meeker retired to his office for some afternoon reading, and most of the other men left to work on the new building.

As Shiloh and Josie cleared the table of dishes, Mrs. Meeker and Flora Ellen, baby Johnnie perched on her hip, headed to the kitchen to get the wash water prepared. Shiloh was surprised, in one of her forays back to the kitchen with a tray full of dirty dishes, to find Douglas there, requesting some bread and butter. As she watched, he accepted the bread and butter with one hand as he patted Josie on the shoulder then shook Arvilla's hand.

As he turned to leave, he shot Shiloh a strange, assessing look. Something about his glance sent a prickle of unease through her. She shook it off and proceeded to carry the tray load of dishes to the sink.

"Well, I must go fetch May," Flora Ellen said as she untied her apron and removed it. "Shadrach's outside working with the other men. I can't leave her alone and I still need to wash some clothes."

Arvilla turned from the sink full of suds. "Yes, go get that precious little girl. We can all help keep an eye on Johnnie while you're gone."

Shiloh and Josie finished clearing the last of the dishes from the table. After Shiloh placed the loaded tray on the sideboard, she helped Josie remove the tablecloth and carry it outside to shake off the crumbs. Down the street, she could see the men working on the new building.

Arthur Thompson was on the roof, spreading dirt. Below him on the ground, Frank Dresser and Shadrach were throwing dirt up to him. Shiloh saw Flora Ellen walk back toward the boardinghouse, her daughter May's hand clasped in hers. For a long moment, as Josie helped her fold the tablecloth, Shiloh enjoyed the warm sunshine and deep blue of the cloud-strewn sky. For some reason, the blue of the sky always seemed to take on a more intense hue in autumn.

She walked back inside to the dining room, straightened

the chairs around the table, then pulled out a broom and pan from the nearby closet. As she began to sweep the dining room floor, she heard Flora Ellen singing as she began washing clothes, and May's childish chatter. A deep satisfaction filled her. There was something so grounding, so reassuring, about the routine of chores.

Josie reentered the dining room. "What's left to do?" she asked, glancing around the room.

"Nothing else, once I get the room—"

Rifle shots tore through the air. Men screamed. Utes uttered high-pitched war whoops.

From the kitchen, May began to wail. Josie and Shiloh locked gazes, and Shiloh was certain her own was as filled with terror as Josie's.

The broom fell from Shiloh's hand. "Come on," she cried. "We need to find cover and find it now!"

15

They sprinted into the kitchen to find Arvilla standing frozen, staring out the window in horror. Shiloh ran to the kitchen door to get Flora Ellen and her daughter to come inside, but they were nowhere to be found. She hurried back in, slammed the door shut, and locked it.

"I'll take Mother, you take baby Johnnie," Josie said. "Let's head upstairs to my bedroom."

Shiloh forced herself to calm, imitating her friend's surprising strength of mind. She grabbed up Johnnie and held him close.

"Okay. Let's go."

It was slow going for Arvilla, who at sixty-four was still feeble after a fall two years ago that broke her thigh. Finally, though, they made it to Josie's room. Gunfire was still reverberating around them, and a few stray bullets shattered the bedroom window.

Josie ran over and lifted the bed skirt. "Let's get under my bed. It'll be safer there."

Shiloh climbed under the bed first, with Johnnie. Josie helped her mother get down and crawl under next, with her following. About then Flora Ellen, May in her arms, ran up the stairs from the unlocked front door and into the room, followed by Frank Dresser with a Winchester in his hand. He helped Flora Ellen and May also climb beneath the bed, then locked the bedroom door and stood guard.

For a time, the sound of gunshots and window glass shattering was the only thing that filled the air. Then, ever so gradually, the scent of smoke began to trickle into the room. The longer they waited, the stronger it grew. Finally, Frank stooped down beside the bed and lifted the bed skirt.

"I'm afraid they've set fire to this house," he said, his expression grave. "We need to get out of here."

"But where can we go to be safe?" Mrs. Meeker asked as Flora Ellen and May crawled out. "They're still firing off their guns outside. They might shoot us if we make a run for it."

Josie climbed from under the bed, then assisted her mother. "The milk house is close. I've got the key to it and the walls are good, solid adobe. We'll be safe there from any bullets."

After handing baby Johnnie to her friend, Shiloh scooted from beneath the bed. "It's the best of all options," she said in agreement. "Besides the thick walls, there's only that one small window up high. No one can look in and see us very easily. And any bullets that might fly through it will be well above our heads."

Frank Dresser cautiously led the way down the hall and the stairs. When the coast was clear outside, he signaled them to join him.

"Josie, you go first and unlock the milk house door," he said. "Just as soon as you get the door opened, Shiloh, you head on over with Johnnie. Then next, Flora Ellen with May. I'll bring up the end with Mrs. Meeker."

All the women silently nodded. Frank gave one more quick glance around. Thankfully, it seemed the Utes had given up shooting and were now down at the storeroom, looting the annuity goods.

"Go, Josie!" he whispered.

She shot off like a deer and swiftly covered the distance across the street to the milk house. Once the door was unlocked, she waved. Shiloh took a quick scan around her, and when she saw no Utes, she raced across the street with baby Johnnie in her arms. Flora Ellen and little May soon followed, then Frank, one hand clutching his rifle, the other supporting Arvilla.

Once inside, Josie locked the door, then stacked milk cans against it as a barricade. Thanks to the adobe walls and small, single window up so high it didn't let in any discernable breeze, the milk house was damp and the air felt close and stifling. To further hide themselves from anyone who might try and get up to look in the window, they all hid under shelves placed against the walls.

It was miserable and warm, but there was nothing to be done for it. Periodically, Shiloh would hear another round of gunfire. Despite their mother's attempts to quiet them, both May and Johnnie wept for a long while until they finally cried themselves to sleep. Shiloh doubted anyone would easily hear them anyway, with the milk house's thick walls and all the gunfire, but she was still glad when the two children ceased their soft wailing. It was just one more stressor, in a day already filled with terrible stress.

Time plodded by, too much time in which to consider what was happening outside. Shiloh knew the Utes were likely killing the rest of the Agency employees. Eventually, she feared they'd find them as well and finish up by butchering all the women and maybe even the children. Frank Dresser's life, for certain, was forfeit when the braves got to him.

Please, Lord, she silently prayed, *save these dear people. I'll gladly be the one to die in their place, if it's Your will. Just please, spare them, I beg You.*

Over and over, Shiloh lifted her thoughts and petitions to

God, until she was so exhausted she finally began to doze. After a time, Josie shook her awake.

"W-what time is it?" she asked groggily.

"I'm not exactly sure," her friend replied, "but from the way the light's slanting in, I'd say we're about a half hour or so from sunset."

So, it's close to 6:00 p.m., Shiloh thought. *We've been hiding in the milk house almost four hours.*

A curious sound, like snapping twigs, caught her attention. She noticed the scent of smoke, but it was much stronger than it had been all day. Looking up, she could see flames licking through the roof. For the first time, she realized it was becoming hard to breathe.

"Josie!" Shiloh grabbed her friend's arm. "The milk house is on fire!"

"Yes. It's why I woke you. We can't stay here any longer. We've got to make a run for it."

Panic filled Shiloh, and with a great effort she tamped it down. "But where? Where can we go?"

"Frank thinks we can head west and hide in the sagebrush. We'll cross the street, then go through the Agency office for cover, then out the back door toward the sagebrush."

It wasn't the greatest of options, but Shiloh knew it was likely the best one they'd have. And the sagebrush *was* fairly high and should offer good cover. She crawled from the shelf she was crouched beneath and took Johnnie back in her arms.

"What's the plan, then?" she asked, looking from Josie to Frank.

"I'll go first to make sure the coast is clear and no Utes are inside the Agency office," Frank said. "Josie will follow with her mother, then you and the baby, along with Flora Ellen and May. Once inside the office, we'll decide when to make our break for the sagebrush."

Between the cover of smoke now billowing from the flaming milk house roof, and the fact the Utes still seemed to be occupied looting the annuity goods, they all made it safely into the office. Briefly, they considered hiding there but decided it was only a matter of time until this building was also set on fire. So, Frank leading the way, they ran, using the other buildings to shield them and headed toward the plowed field north of the Agency.

The women were slowed by the children and Arvilla, who was lame. They covered a good hundred yards when some of the Utes discovered their escape. Frank shouted, "Run, run! Now or never!" and fired his rifle at the approaching Utes.

Undaunted, the braves kept on coming, shooting at all of them in return. Shiloh's heart was pounding in her chest, but she ran as fast as she could with baby Johnnie in her arms. Bullets sprayed around them, sending up puffs of dirt. She tried to protect the baby as best she could but felt certain she'd be hit anytime.

Up ahead she saw Frank Dresser reach the sagebrush and disappear in its dense foliage. Behind and far off to her left, she heard the Utes still firing their guns and yelling "Stop, squaw! White squaw stop!" and "We no shoot. Come with us!"

But there was only one Indian Shiloh would've ever stopped for, and he was nowhere to be found. Though her breath was ragged and short now, she forced her tired legs onward. The sagebrush . . . she was almost there!

Then she heard Arvilla cry out. "I've been shot," the older woman screamed. "They've shot me!"

Shiloh stopped, wheeled about. Mrs. Meeker lay there on the ground, Josie hovering over her, trying to pull her up. At that instant, the Utes caught up with Flora Ellen and May, straggling far behind. Then they reached Josie and Arvilla.

Two braves stopped and aimed their rifles at Shiloh while the others grabbed hold of the three other women.

For a split second, Shiloh considered taking a chance and heading for the sagebrush, now so near. Some of the braves were quite evidently not very good shots, as evidenced by all the bullets fired that had missed their mark, until one finally caught Arvilla. If she hadn't had the baby in her arms, Shiloh would've tried to run for it. But she did, and she wouldn't take a chance on his life. Odds were, even if the women might eventually die, the Utes would likely take the two Price children and raise them as their own.

The sun was setting over the westernmost peaks as the Utes caught up with Shiloh. She suddenly noticed how fast it was turning chilly. Two of them took her by the arms and led her back to join the other women and little May. They all then headed to the Agency office, which had yet to be set on fire, to meet up with Chief Douglas.

Arvilla was shivering. "It's so cold. May I please have a blanket?" she asked Douglas.

He stared at her for a moment, then ordered one of his braves to fetch Mrs. Meeker a blanket. The man soon returned with a blanket, hood, and shawl. Arvilla wrapped the shawl around her, then the blanket.

Shiloh would rather freeze to death than ask for anything from Douglas, so she just walked along with the others. Josie took May, and Flora Ellen finally found a way to walk beside Shiloh.

"Thank you for carrying Johnnie all this time," she said. "But I'll take him now. He'll need his mother's milk, and if they eventually split us up . . ."

She hadn't thought of that. The consideration filled Shiloh with a renewed surge of fear. What would become of them, now that they were captives of the Utes? Though death wasn't a pleasant thing to look forward to, some of the other possibilities were even more horrifying. And if they were all separated and sent off with different groups of Utes, they'd lose the comfort of each other's company, and it would make it all the harder for all of them to be rescued.

As they rounded the corner of the Agency office, a man lying on the ground caught Shiloh's eye. He was stretched out, hands at his sides, and naked except for his shirt. As they drew nearer, she could see blood running from the corner of his mouth.

Arvilla must have recognized him at almost the same instant Shiloh did. With a soft cry, she broke free of the grip of the brave who held her and ran to her husband. She knelt beside him, leaned over to kiss him. Then as her gaze locked with her Ute captor, she hesitated and apparently decided it might not be wise to kiss her husband. Instead, she stood and, face stoic, walked back to join them.

Though Nathan Meeker's body didn't look mutilated, Shiloh nonetheless felt sick to her stomach. He may not have been the most effective Indian agent, but he had tried to do the job he'd been sent to do. He didn't deserve to die like that.

But then, neither did the other eight Agency employees whose bodies were strewn about. Many of them were young men with families still living in the Greeley colony where Meeker and his family had resided prior to coming to the White River Agency. They, truly, were the most innocent of all the victims of this tragic turn of events.

Before all this was over, she, Arvilla, Josie, Flora Ellen, and her two children might also be sacrificed on the altar of the US government's ultimate plan to steal all the Colorado lands from the Utes. Or, Shiloh amended that grimly, all the worthwhile lands anyway. And they would. Sooner or later, they would.

Perhaps the Utes knew this on some level, and it was part of the many reasons that had led up to this terrible expression of their deepest fears and frustrations. They had known the soldiers were on their way. The only uncertainty was the true reason for the army being called to the reservation. Had Nathan Meeker requested them solely to help keep the peace and settle the problems growing between the agent and the Utes? Or was the army's real purpose to round them all up and force them from their beloved mountains and out farther west to the Indian Territory?

Well, none of it mattered just now, Shiloh thought as they approached another group of Utes. Persune, upon seeing Josie, stepped forward and clasped her by the arm.

"Come, Josie," he said. "I take you with me."

She reared back, trying to break his grip. "No, please. Let me stay with my mother and friends."

He shook his head and jerked her toward him. "White squaws not stay together. You see."

As if on cue, Douglas grabbed Josie by the other arm and in Ute demanded Persune give Josie to him. Persune angrily refused, and for a moment, Shiloh thought the two men would tear Josie apart between them. Then, after another angry exchange of words, Douglas released her and stomped away. As he departed, however, he called to some of his own braves to bring Arvilla with them.

As Shiloh and Flora Ellen huddled there together, Arvilla and Josie shouted encouragement to each other as they were dragged in opposite directions. A Ute whom Shiloh knew wasn't of the White River band moved to stand before her and Flora Ellen.

"You squaws go with me."

"Where will you take us?" she asked him in his language.

"To Jack's camp."

As they all followed their captors down toward the White River, they passed burning buildings and Utes loading food, blankets, cooking utensils, and other contraband onto the Agency horses and mules. Eventually, the twenty or thirty Utes who'd participated in the massacre all joined down by the river. Knowing the soldiers would come sooner or later to punish them for what had transpired this day, they readied themselves for their retreat into the southern wilderness. And, late that evening, their captors put the two women on horses and headed them into the White River.

As they forded the gently flowing waters, Shiloh looked back at the Agency. All the buildings were burning now, and leaping tongues of fire lit the darkness. At the sight, a great sorrow filled her.

Meeker and all his men, save perhaps Frank Dresser, had perished. Tragic as their deaths were, at least their travail was over. But not so for her and the other women. The terror and uncertainty of their eventual fate would surely follow them for a time to come. It was a nightmare pure and simple, but a living one that would now dog them both awake *and* asleep.

They rode for five miles until they reached Jack's camp. Then the Utes took a short break in which they ate their meal. The women were all offered coffee, cold meat, and bread.

Though Shiloh had no appetite, she forced herself to choke down the food and coffee. The food would give her needed energy, in case there was ever a chance for escape. And escape was foremost in her thoughts, now that she'd had a time to calm down and think things through.

Indeed, she was the most likely one with a good chance of getting away. Arvilla was too old and feeble to run anywhere far or fast. Josie now had custody of little May, and Flora

Ellen had baby Johnnie, both of whom would only slow them down.

The break soon ended, and they followed their captors back out into the night, lit fortunately by a bright moon and blessed with mild weather. As they had done while eating their supper, the Utes kept talking and laughing about how many soldiers had been killed at Milk Creek, as well as the men they'd killed at the Agency. From their conversations, Shiloh pieced together that the soldiers had crossed the reservation border at Milk Creek late that morning and were soon set upon by the Utes who fired at them from the surrounding hills.

Apparently, Major Thornburgh, the leader of the soldiers, had been killed. The rest of his men were now trapped behind their supply wagons, outnumbered with no hope of escape. It was but a matter of time, according to her captors, before they'd all be dead.

She offered a silent prayer for the soldiers, begging God to spare them for their own sakes as well as for her and the other women. The soldiers were the closest help right now. If they were slaughtered, it would be a long while before any more help could get to this remote area, and the Utes could be long gone by then.

Around the middle of the night and after another fifteen-mile ride, they reached Douglas's camp deep in a canyon. It soon became evident this was where all his camp's women, children, and old men had moved to, that day they'd taken down their tepees near the White River and departed. Only a little over two days ago, Shiloh mused, and yet that event already seemed like weeks ago.

There were about eighty tepees there, and as Shiloh slid from her horse, exhausted and sore, much talk swirled around them. Some of the Utes seemed in favor of keeping their captives alive, in the hopes of using them as hostages in case the soldiers caught up with them. Others were adamantly opposed, wishing to put the women to death by torture. Douglas, Shiloh noted with some dismay, was one of the most vocal advocates of death by torture.

"He doesn't like us much," Flora Ellen, her eyes swollen and red from weeping, whispered as she settled down beside Shiloh and began to discreetly nurse a whimpering Johnnie.

Shiloh saw the direction of her gaze, and knew she spoke of Douglas, who was loudly arguing with some of the more seemingly peaceable of his tribesmen. She chose, however, not to reveal the true extent of the Ute chief's ire against them. Fortunately, Flora Ellen knew little of their language. Josie would've been able to understand enough, but she and Arvilla were sequestered somewhere else in camp.

"No," she softly replied, "it seems not, though we fed him often enough at our table, worked hard to try and school his son, besides Arvilla taking care of the boy when he was ill. But then, Douglas stinks of whiskey, as do many of the others. Let's just hope they don't decide to harm us while they're drunk."

"If it weren't for my children, I'd almost wish I were d-dead." The other woman's voice caught on a sob. "They k-killed my Shadrach. Killed him, stripped him n-naked, and left him lying there for the vultures!"

With a soft murmur of compassion, Shiloh turned and wrapped an arm around Flora Ellen's shoulder, pulling her close to lean against her. "I know. I know," she crooned. "I still can't believe it all happened. It was horrible. Just horrible."

For a long while, Flora Ellen, Johnnie still clutched to her breast, laid her head on Shiloh's shoulder and sobbed. Shiloh, in turn, just held and rocked her, her own emotions so chaotic and conflicted she thought she might be on the verge of losing her mind. But she fought her way back, knowing that a clear head and strong resolve would be their only hope.

"Hush, now," she said at last. "Time enough later to mourn family and friends. We've got to make plans. Plans to save our lives."

Flora Ellen reared back and stared up at her. "What can we possibly do, save try to escape?"

"Escape, at least for now, is likely out of the question." Shiloh inhaled a deep, considering breath. "I was thinking more like how to ingratiate ourselves with the Utes, so they'll view us more kindly. Not all of them are cold-blooded killers, or hate us, you know."

"Like that handsome half-breed you were friends with? I haven't seen him at all. Is he gone, fighting the soldiers then?"

"No—or rather, I hope and pray not." Shiloh shook her head. "From what Josie told me, Jesse's off in Wyoming with a hunting party. He should be back soon, though."

"Maybe when he returns, he'll rescue you and keep you safe." The younger woman smiled. "I always thought he cared very much for you."

Shiloh had tried as best she could not to pin her hopes on Jesse's return. Though part of her indeed wanted him to rescue her and keep her safe, another part feared what his reaction would be when he rejoined the others. He had made it more than clear that he considered himself a Ute and that his loyalties now lay with them. But she also knew he cared for her, and that might well place him in a difficult if not very dangerous position.

"We were friends once," Shiloh said by way of response. "After all that's happened of late, though, I don't know if we can be anymore."

Flora Ellen sighed, then paused to move her baby to her other breast. "Indeed, a lot has happened. It would be a sad thing, though, if he turned his back on you."

Hot tears stung Shiloh's eyes. It would indeed be a sad thing, but she didn't dare count on Jesse even returning in time. The Utes were drunk and half crazed with fear and bloodlust. She and Flora Ellen might not live to see the morrow.

"The loyalty of any man isn't what matters," she said. "Our lives are in the Lord's hands now. And I trust, whatever happens, that it's part of His plan for us."

"I wondered at your bravery, and now I know from whence it comes." The younger woman reached out and clasped Shiloh by the hand. "Your faith is so strong. I envy that."

"Not as strong as you might imagine." Shiloh squeezed Flora Ellen's hand. "But I keep trying, over and over, to surrender my will and place my trust in the Lord. That's all any of us can do. I think, though, He values even our smallest efforts, and that gives me comfort."

Baby Johnnie stirred. Flora Ellen pulled her hand free and gently patted him on the back, making little cooing sounds. Finally, Johnnie quieted and resumed his suckling.

"I cherish that thought—that the Lord loves and values us far beyond our true worth. Well, at least our true worth in our own eyes and the eyes of others," she said with an ironic chuckle. "I pray that I remember that, when things turn difficult or frightening."

"We'll both do that," Shiloh vowed, her heart swelling with a quiet but deep joy. "And we'll pray for the grace to be brave no matter what. No matter if all others desert or fail us. No matter what . . ."

16

Late the next morning, Shiloh awoke to much commotion in camp, as most of the men readied themselves to ride out to join the others in fighting the soldiers trapped at Milk Creek. She was greatly relieved to see that Douglas was in the group preparing to leave. Without his hostile presence, the odds improved that she and the other women would survive at least a few more days. And the longer they could stay alive, the greater their chances of rescue became.

At long last, their rifles in hand and loaded with a generous supply of ammunition, the Ute braves departed camp. In their possession, Shiloh could make out the latest models of Winchester rifles, as well as Sharps, Henrys, and Remingtons. She wondered where they had managed to purchase such weapons, as Meeker had always refused to sell arms to them. But then he'd also refused to sell them whiskey, and yet she'd seen liquor bottles in their possession from time to time.

People who didn't have the Utes' welfare at heart had sold them the illegal weapons and liquor. Sold them solely to make a tidy profit for themselves, never thinking of the long-term consequences of their actions. Actions that now put every miner, settler, and soldier within hundreds of miles in danger.

The soldiers at Milk Creek were likely fighting for their lives right about now, and no help for her and the other women would soon be forthcoming from them. Shiloh whispered a silent prayer for the beleaguered men's safety and that they might eventually overcome their Ute attackers. Then she turned her attention to the day ahead.

Squaws from Jack's camp soon took charge of her and Flora Ellen. With fists shaken in their faces and shouted insults, they were led down to a creek to draw water to fill the cook pots. After an hour or two of doing that, they were finally fed breakfast of biscuits and coffee. Then she and Flora Ellen gathered firewood and were told to bake bread. The weather was pleasant, the sun warm, but that was about all that could be viewed in any sort of positive way. The horrors of yesterday and the potential ones yet to come cast a gloomy pall over everything else.

Shiloh slept soundly that night, partly from the lingering stress and weariness of the long ride the night before, and partly because, as the time passed, she became ever more hopeful that the Utes wouldn't kill them. Though several squaws and even some of the children were cruel, taunting them and poking them with sticks, others—Jack's own wives, who had taken Shiloh into their tepee, while a squaw of one of Jack's subchiefs had offered hospitality to Flora Ellen and baby Johnnie—were quite sympathetic and kind. Some even wept over what had happened at the Agency, and for the loss of Flora Ellen's husband.

Wednesday, the next day, Chief Johnson came to Jack's camp and took Flora Ellen and baby Johnnie to live with him, claiming he'd made it all right with the other Utes. Though Shiloh was sad to see her companion leave, she was hopeful that, once safely away to live with Johnson and his wife Susan, Flora Ellen would be safe and receive even better care. From the start of their captivity, Shiloh had heard talk that Susan, behind the scenes, had been their champion, arguing against killing them.

Late that afternoon, after another full day of chores that seemed all the harder without Flora Ellen's sweet presence, Shiloh was finally able to sit down and eat a meager supper. As she did, several Utes rode into camp. One of them was Jack and another Broken Antler, one of her former suitors. From the bits of conversation she could pick up, they'd only come for the night and to resupply before returning to the battle.

The fact that the soldiers must evidently still be alive heartened her. She prayed they'd been able to send someone back to Fort Steele near Rawlins to get reinforcements. Otherwise, according to the Utes, the soldiers were greatly outnumbered and it was only a matter of time before they were all killed.

After putting up his pony, Broken Antler walked over and squatted beside her. She managed a friendly smile and greeted him, but when he reached out and stroked her face, Shiloh froze. When his hand next went to her hair, which had begun to fall loose from her braid, she couldn't help her instinctive response to pull away.

The Ute brave frowned. "Don't be afraid, pretty one," he said. "You're safe with me. I spoke with Jack, and he's agreed that you should be mine." He took her by the arm. "Come. You'll share my tepee this night."

Shock, then horror, swamped her. There was only one interpretation anyone could take from that statement. Broken Antler intended to bed her and make her his squaw.

Her mind raced, searching for some reason not to obey him. Her situation was still precarious. If Broken Antler was to take offense . . .

"I cannot," she said, resisting his pull. "I'm promised to another."

The brave released her and straightened. "Who are you promised to? I care not if you've made your vows to some white man. You are our captive now and we don't have to honor—"

"It's no white man," Shiloh cried, as a sudden, desperate inspiration struck her. "I'm promised to Jesse. Jesse Blackwater."

Broken Antler eyed her with disbelief. "How can that be? I never saw him court you."

"It happened when we journeyed to my home in the southern mountains. In the days we spent together, we fell in love."

The tale she spun, on the spur of the moment, wasn't entirely a lie, she told herself, though she did experience a twinge of guilt. She had fallen in love with Jesse. And, though he might not have fallen in love with her, on the journey he *had* admitted to his desire for her. Surely that was enough reason to claim she was Jesse's woman. Surely, he would take her into his tepee based on that desire, if not their old friendship. And surely it was enough to counter Broken Antler's claim to her.

"He never said anything about you when he returned without you those months ago."

"Jesse didn't need to," she said. "He knew I was coming back to the Agency, just as soon as my sister was better. It just took longer than either of us planned."

Hesitation, then indecision, flared in the Ute's eyes. "He'll return soon from his hunting trip. We'll talk it over then. I have many ponies and blankets now. If he's wise, he'll let me trade those for you."

She could well imagine where Broken Antler had gotten the extra ponies and blankets. She'd seen him that day at the Agency, along with many other Utes she'd recognized. Killing . . . burning . . . looting.

Jesse wouldn't want any of those ill-gotten gains. Shiloh knew him well enough to know that. But whether he would lie and claim her for his own was another matter entirely. Likely he would, if for no other reason than to protect her from Broken Antler. He was, after all, a good and honorable man.

At any rate, she was safe from Broken Antler until Jesse's

return. When all was said and done it might not matter, but at least it would buy her some time. And, in that time, there was always hope some other plan would come to mind. There was always hope that she might even be rescued.

The long hunt had been good for him, Jesse thought as he and the other braves drew near Jack's camp. He'd had time to think as well as distance himself from the issue of what to do about Shiloh's return, helping him clear his head sufficiently to sort out his true feelings about their relationship. Out in the striking mountains of northern Colorado and southern Wyoming, the sharp, tangy scent of pine trees, the crisp bite of the autumn weather, and the vast blue sky stretching overhead soothed and comforted him. And everything finally fell into its proper perspective.

The easy camaraderie of his fellow hunters, as they all engaged in the very important task of providing meat for the rest of their band, reminded Jesse how deeply he cherished their ready acceptance of him, and of the traditional ways that bound them all. These were things that mattered, that he deeply cherished. Things that he would gladly share with Shiloh, if she was willing.

Out there in his beloved mountains, Jesse had soon come to an admission that he loved Shiloh Wainwright. Truly and deeply loved her. The decision to actually acquiesce to the forging of a permanent relationship with her, however, had taken him a while longer. Though part of his hesitation had been his fear of what others would think of their mixed-blood marriage and eventual children, a part had also been his indecisiveness over whether he could give up the Ute ways and family for a life with Shiloh living as a white.

Now, though, he knew he could never leave the People.

And, though he had finally discarded his concern for the opinions of others regarding their marriage, Jesse also knew it'd hardly be an issue amongst the Utes at any rate. The solution to almost all their problems had always lain with staying with the People. He just had to convince Shiloh of the logic of that choice.

Jesse's musings faded as he became acutely aware of the unnatural silence. By now, they should've heard the everyday sounds of camp life. They should've long ago smelled the scent of cookfires.

He glanced at the brave riding beside him at the front of their party. "Something's wrong."

The other man nodded and urged his pony forward with Jesse's. The two men rode hard toward camp, and the closer they got, the greater the certainty arose that everyone was gone. Finally, they arrived at the big area where once had stood ninety tepees. The area was deserted. The pony pens were empty, the campfires long extinguished.

Gradually, he realized that all the talk and angry arguments over what to do about Meeker had finally progressed to some form of action. And there was only one reason to move camp at this time. Something terrible had happened.

Shiloh!

Unbidden, her name flashed through Jesse's mind. His heart twisted within his chest. And he knew. Knew without a shadow of a doubt that she was in mortal danger.

He reined in his horse and turned to his companion. "It looks like you and the others need to pick up the trail and find our camp. They'll be needing the meat and hides."

"Sounds like you're not going with us," the other brave said. "Why's that?"

"I'll catch up with you later. I want to see what's going on at the Agency."

His friend laughed. "By the look of things, I'm think-ing there's not much left of that place. Father Meeker likely pushed Jack one time too many."

For some reason, the other man's laughter didn't sit well with him. "Nonetheless," he gritted out, "I want to see it with my own eyes."

"Then be off with you." The brave pulled his pony about. "And catch up with us as soon as you can."

Jesse watched him rejoin the others and briefly explain things. Then the group turned around the ponies laden with deer and elk carcasses and slowly rode away.

He kneed his own mount forward and was soon riding hard and fast back toward the Agency. Less than an hour and a half later, before he even caught sight of the neatly aligned buildings north of the White River, he smelled the smoke lingering in the air. His pulse quickened.

The sight that greeted him, when he topped the last hill, sent ice coursing through his veins. All the Agency buildings lay in ruins, black heaps of burned wood and ash. Bodies were strewn around the buildings, and as he drew near, Jesse noted that nine of them were white. Some were unrecognizable, faces bloodied and bruised, and most were nearly naked. To his relief, however, he soon ascertained that they were all men.

No sight of any of the women or the two children. That could mean only one thing. They'd been taken captive.

By the looks of the buildings and bodies, the massacre had been recent, likely no more than two days ago. That heartened him. The odds were good that Shiloh might still be alive. How much longer, though, was the question.

He'd heard enough of the talk going around among the different chiefs and their braves to know emotions were high. High enough that some were eager to kill any and every white person who crossed their path, be they man, woman, or child.

And the Utes knew, when they'd attacked the White River Agency, that there was no turning back. If soldiers weren't already on their way, they soon would be. A few more lives lost, even if they were helpless women and children, wouldn't change anything.

Jesse didn't know if he could save Shiloh and the others, even if he did make it in time. Only one thing was certain. If it came to it, he'd die trying.

Late the next afternoon—and several hours ahead of the rest of the hunting party—Jesse rode into the big encampment hidden in the canyon. Though he looked for a sign of Jack's camp, he didn't find them among all the other groupings of tepees. Finally, he caught sight of Douglas's elderly uncle, rode over to him, and dismounted.

The other man gave him a disdainful look. "Where have you been? We could've used you in fighting the soldiers."

So, Jesse thought, the plan long bandied about among the chiefs had come to fruition. Things were getting uglier by the moment.

"Jack sent me and seven other men out hunting over a week ago," he replied. "We've been far up north."

"Well, likely it's a good thing you brought back fresh meat. We'll be on the run for a while and will need it."

Jesse frowned. "Is anyone chasing us?"

"Not yet, but you can be sure the whites will, sooner or later. They'll want their women."

Relief flooded Jesse. The women from the Agency were still alive.

"Where are these women now?" he asked, trying to feign just a curious interest in the information.

"The agent's daughter is with your friend Persune. My

nephew has the old mother. Johnson has the young one with the children." The old man paused, a knowing light in his eyes. "And Jack has the red-haired one you so admire. Not that it'll do you any good. Word has it that Jack's given her to Broken Antler."

Any lingering weariness fled Jesse in one sudden rush. "Where are they?" he snarled, grabbing the elderly brave's arm. "And when did Jack give Shiloh to him?"

The Ute's gaze narrowed, and he pointedly looked down at where Jesse still grasped his arm. For a fleeting second Jesse considered doing more than just grabbing him to get the information he desired, then decided against it. He released the man and took a step back.

"I ask you again," he said, burying his antagonism toward Douglas's uncle beneath a thin smile. "Where and when?"

The elderly Ute shrugged and rubbed the offended arm. "Jack's camp is about a mile south of here, down by the river. And, from what I heard, it happened last evening. So you're too late."

Jesse turned and lithely vaulted onto his pony. "Perhaps," he said, gathering the reins. "And perhaps not."

Without a farewell or backward glance, he urged his mount forward. As he guided his pony around tepees and people going about their work, Jesse seethed with barely contained anger. If Broken Antler had harmed Shiloh in any way . . .

But what cause did he really have to turn his ire on the other man? He'd made no public claim on Shiloh. Not once. Ever. If something had happened to her at Broken Antler's hands, Jesse reluctantly admitted he'd only have himself to blame.

Not that it should've come to this, that Shiloh would be a captive and fair game for any brave who cared to claim her. But it should've never come to a massacre at the White

River Indian Agency either. Or that the Utes were finally provoked to revolt.

But none of those were events he'd had any control over, Jesse thought as he finally cleared the camp and nudged his pony into a lope. Not now and, unfortunately, not all those times in the past when he'd tried to talk sense into Nathan Meeker before finally giving up and distancing himself from the moody, opinionated Indian agent. And there had never been much he could do to help the People find acceptance in what was happening to them—watching their lives slowly but surely constrained and diminished by the laws and lies of the whites.

There was one thing, however, he could control, and that was preventing Shiloh from becoming a squaw to any other Ute but him. To take her as his wife in the Indian way . . .

The thought appealed to Jesse more than he dared admit. There'd be no family of hers to interfere or stop him. No demands to turn from the People who'd always loved and accepted him. And, safe and protected within the Ute en-campment and customs, there'd be no one who'd judge or look down upon them.

He knew she cared for him, perhaps even loved him. Shiloh had never been one to hide her emotions well. And he loved her. In truth, had always loved her, though his feelings had changed from those of a boy to those of a man.

The admission on one level frightened him, yet on another filled him with such joy and yearning. Still, he'd be a fool to pass up an opportunity that might never come again. He had Shiloh exactly where he wanted her, and nothing—especially the minor obstacle of Broken Antler—would stand in his way.

From a distance, the smoke curling from the smoke holes of another encampment of tepees finally came into view. Jesse's heartbeat quickened. It was Jack's camp.

The task of finding the chief's dwelling was a simple enough matter. To his relief, Jack was standing nearby speaking with Shiloh, who sat at the campfire mixing what looked like the beginnings of bread. Jesse pulled his pony to a sliding halt and flung himself off it. In three quick strides, he reached Shiloh, who had seen his approach and scrambled to her feet.

It was hard to say who hugged who first but, in the end, it didn't really matter. Jesse pulled her close and rested his head on hers. For just an instant, he savored her warmth, the soft contours of her body pressed so close to his, her delicate, feminine fragrance.

"Oh, Shiloh," he breathed into her hair. "Shiloh . . ."

"J-Jesse." His name, uttered on a shuddering sob, was the sweetest thing he thought he'd ever heard. "Thank the L-Lord you've found me!"

"Yes, I have. You're safe now." He leaned back from her and searched her face. "Are you all right? Has anyone hurt you?"

She smiled up at him through her tears. "Now that you're here, I'm fine. Just fine."

"But has anyone hurt you? In any way?"

A look of puzzlement flitted through her eyes. "No. Not really. A few children poked me with sticks, but that's nothing."

"Broken Antler." Jesse forced himself to ask the question of which he dreaded to hear the answer. "Has he . . . has he taken you as his squaw?"

Sudden comprehension lit her eyes. "No." Shiloh firmly shook her head. "No. I told him I was already promised to you, and he decided to wait until your return." She chewed her lower lip, which Jesse knew she did when she was worried or unsure. "I hope that was all right. Me saying that about us. I didn't know what else to do, and if I hadn't . . ."

He laid a gentle finger on her lips. "It was fine. Just fine."

From behind him, a hand settled on his shoulder. Jesse

released Shiloh and, snaking an arm around her waist, turned them both to face Jack.

"I see you have eyes only for the red-haired woman," the older man said, "and no thought or greeting for your chief."

Jesse flushed. "I'm sorry. I'm glad to be back. Our hunting trip was a success, but the rest of the party is a few hours behind me."

"Good. We will feast well tonight."

The conversation died. The two men stared at each other. Finally Jack broke the silence.

"I gave the woman to Broken Antler." He indicated Shiloh. "He's wanted her for a long while, and until just now, you never said you had any interest in her."

Jesse pulled Shiloh closer. "She is promised to me."

Captain Jack arched a brow. "So she says. Now. But I'm not so certain either of you made any promises until it became convenient for you. And Broken Antler asked first."

He'd never known Jack to be so unyielding, leastwise not when it came to him. His chief's response troubled him.

"Broken Antler already has a wife," he said. "I have none."

The older man shrugged and gestured to Broken Antler, who'd evidently noted Jesse's arrival and was even then striding purposefully toward them. "You may work it out with him. I tire of this little game you play, Nuaru."

Jesse bit back a caustic response. Maybe he had been playing a game, but if so, it had been with himself. A game in which he'd done everything he could to convince himself he didn't want Shiloh, didn't deserve her. But now, faced with the possibility of losing her to another, he suddenly knew what he must do. What he had always been supposed to do.

"Shiloh is mine," Jesse said as Broken Antler halted before him, preemptively taking the offense. "We made our promises to each other months ago."

"But she is not yet your wife, is she?"

"No." Jesse met the other man's gaze with a steely one of his own. "But I will not give her up."

"Not even for twenty ponies, five rifles, and ten new annuity blankets?"

A goodly bridal offering to be sure. Extravagant even. But Broken Antler could offer all the ponies and other ill-gotten Agency goods, and Jesse would've still refused.

He shook his head. "She is mine, and not for the bartering."

The Ute brave standing before him scowled. "Then I will add three army mules, one soldier's jacket, a fine hat, and a pair of his boots."

Again, Jesse shook his head. "No."

Broken Antler narrowed his gaze, and his lips thinned. His hand moved to the knife hanging in its sheath at his side. "You'd do well to reconsider. While you still draw breath."

The barely veiled threat didn't sit well with Jesse. He released Shiloh and pushed her behind him. Then, one hand on his own sheathed knife, his other hand fisted at his side, he took a threatening step toward the other man.

"If you mean that as a challenge to fight for her," he growled, "then it's a fight you'll have. But, one way or another, you're not getting Shiloh!"

17

Shiloh watched in horror as Jesse and Broken Antler shed their buckskin shirts and drew their knives. Men and women, alerted to the pending fight, hurried over to form a large circle around the two men. She soon found herself standing in the back of the crowd, along with Jack.

"Do something!" she cried, turning on him. "Make them stop!"

He graced her with a disinterested look. "They both mean to have you, and Nuaru has refused Broken Antler's most generous offers. Now they will have to settle the matter another way."

"But does it have to be with knives? Someone could get killed!"

Jack shrugged. "It was their choice. A wrestling match is usual, but neither seemed to want it that way. Now, they must work out their disagreement as they decide."

She couldn't believe how uncaring Jack seemed over the possibility of losing one, if not both men, in a knife fight. She, however, wasn't about to helplessly stand there and allow that to happen.

"Well, if you're not going to stop this, I am." Shiloh turned, intending to force her way through the crowd and confront Jesse, when a hand settled tightly on her arm and pulled her back.

"Do you think to shame them both by interfering?" the Ute chief hissed in her ear. "It's too late for that. You should've thought more carefully what the consequences would be to play the two against each other."

"I didn't!" she cried, wheeling about to face him. "I never wanted Broken Antler. It's always been Jesse. Always. But I won't stand here and watch him get killed just to protect me."

"Then you'd give yourself to Broken Antler to save Nuaru?"

For an instant, Shiloh hesitated. The thought of becoming Broken Antler's woman filled her with revulsion. But to see Jesse die and still have to go with Broken Antler was worse still. Her possible fate with Broken Antler was in the Lord's hands. Jesse's survival right now, though, could well be in hers.

"Yes," she replied, forcing the word past a throat gone dry with both dread and resolve. "I love Jesse, and his life is worth that much to me."

A strange light flared in Jack's eyes. For a passing moment, Shiloh imagined she saw a look of satisfaction there.

"Though especially at a time like this I don't care to risk two of my best braves," he said, "I will not allow you to stop the fight. It is their right to choose how to settle this matter. But I also tell you not to fear for Nuaru. He's a strong and clever fighter. It's unlikely that Broken Antler will best him."

It wasn't what she'd hoped to hear, but she knew she had no choice but to accept the small comfort Jack offered. "I won't interfere. But please, let me be there for him."

"Then come." Jack indicated that she follow him. "They won't begin until I give the word."

As Shiloh finally cleared the crowd to stand in front along with Jack, Jesse met her gaze. He smiled grimly, but she knew it wasn't just an expression of determination but one of encouragement too. In spite of her best efforts not to embarrass him with an unseemly display of emotion, tears still filled her eyes. She smiled through them, though, and gave him an acknowledging nod.

"Begin!" Jack cried just then, and the two combatants pivoted about to face each other.

In the next instant, knives flashed and glinted in the day's waning sun. Broken Antler lunged at Jesse, and if Jesse hadn't nimbly leaped aside, Broken Antler's knife would've skewered him in the chest. For his efforts Jesse's stockier opponent received a glancing slash on his arm. With an angry snarl, Broken Antler whipped around and came at Jesse again.

It was soon evident that though Jesse intended only to wound and wear out his attacker, Broken Antler had far darker intentions. Jesse was taller by at least half a foot, leanly muscled, and fast. But Broken Antler was equally fast and used every means at his disposal, be they fair or foul. Several times, if not for Jesse's speed and accurate anticipation of what his opponent intended, he'd have likely received a serious if not fatal knife wound.

Despite the slowly falling temperature as the sun began to set, sweat began to glisten on Jesse's torso. Both men were superbly fit, and for a time, neither seemed to hold the advantage. Then, with one quick feint that drew Broken Antler off to that side, in a blur of motion, Jesse changed direction and thrust his knife deep into Broken Antler's right upper thigh, then withdrew it.

With a cry the Ute fell. Grasping his leg, he writhed on the ground. Jesse walked over to him.

"Do you agree the woman is mine?" he asked.

"Take her!" his opponent gasped, clutching his leg in an effort to staunch the bleeding.

Jesse squatted, wiped his blade clean of blood, then returned his knife to its sheath. "Then it is settled, once and for all?" He held out his hand to Broken Antler. "And there'll be peace between us, as before?"

"Be gone!" The other Ute pushed Jesse's hand aside and shoved to a sitting position. "You're no friend of mine. Not now or ever again!"

"As you wish."

Jesse stood and turned. Once again, his glance locked with Shiloh's and he smiled. Joy filled her and she began to walk toward him.

As she did, though, a surreptitious movement behind Jesse caught her eye. She saw a hand reach out and grasp a knife.

"Jesse!" she screamed. "Behind you!"

He spun about. Even then, Broken Antler was throwing the knife. Because of Jesse's quick reaction, the weapon missed him. It sailed past and directly at her.

A sharp pain lanced through Shiloh. She stopped, surprised and confused, and looked down. Broken Antler's knife hilt protruded from her right shoulder.

She lifted a befuddled gaze to Jesse. Horror widened his eyes.

"Shiloh!"

He moved toward her, but everything suddenly seemed to be in slow motion. Myriad tiny lights sparkled before her eyes, then the edges of her vision began to gray. Her strength fled. Her legs buckled.

"J-Jesse . . ." she whispered as he reached and caught hold of her. She sagged in his arms as everything—the sky above, the world around them, and even his dear face—disappeared.

Rage engulfed Jesse as he gently lowered a now-unconscious Shiloh to the ground. He pulled the knife from her shoulder and watched as the blood swiftly welled and stained her blouse. A red mist filled his vision, and he stood, turned, and advanced on Broken Antler.

His face gone pale with fear, the man raised a hand in supplication, but Jesse felt nothing but a hunger for vengeance. Then hands were on him, pulling him back, wrestling Broken Antler's bloodied blade from his hand as well as his own.

"See to your woman," Jack said. "We'll take care of this cowardly snake."

For a few seconds more, Jesse struggled against the hands restraining him. Then he stilled, dragged in a deep, shuddering breath, and nodded.

"Let me go. You're right. Shiloh must be my first concern."

Ever so gradually, they released him, though stood warily by as if suspecting some trick. But Jesse just wheeled about and hurried to where Shiloh lay, never once looking back. Some of Jack's wives were already kneeling beside her, one cradling Shiloh's head in her lap, while another patted her hand as if to try and wake her, while yet another pressed a wadded cloth over the knife wound.

He squatted at Shiloh's side. "Let's get her to my tepee," he said. "And someone fetch bandages, salves, and a burning stick, in case we need it to staunch the bleeding."

The women stood, stepped back, then hurried off to fetch what he had requested. Jesse slid one arm beneath Shiloh's shoulders, the other beneath her legs, and rose. With rapid strides, he headed to where his tepee had been set up, grateful to whichever women had seen to it once their own tepees were readied.

As he walked along, he glanced down at Shiloh. Her face was pale and skin clammy. She weighed little more than a feather to him, and he pulled her even closer.

The bloodstain continued to grow, drenching her blouse. Jesse feared she'd definitely need her wound cauterized and prayed she'd remain unconscious at least until that was accomplished. He also prayed, for the first time in many, many years, to the Christian god he'd long ago rejected.

If You're truly there, he fervently entreated, *spare Shiloh's life. And, whatever the purchase price You may demand for that, I'll gladly pay it instead. Just don't let her die. Please, don't let her die.*

By the time he reached his tepee and carried Shiloh inside to lay her on a soft buffalo robe, several women had crowded in behind him. After handing the burning stick to Jesse to hold, they set to work. He stepped back to allow them to care for Shiloh, knowing they were far more skilled in the treatment of wounds than he'd ever be.

They quickly stripped off Shiloh's ruined blouse until only a lace-trimmed chemise covered her. After a time attempting to stop the bleeding with pressure, Kwana, the oldest woman, took the flaming stick from Jesse. After wiping the oozing wound with a cloth, she immediately applied the stick to the cut edges.

A sizzling sound filled the air, then the scent of burning flesh. If it had been anyone else, the act wouldn't have affected Jesse. But he couldn't control his involuntary wince at seeing them burn Shiloh.

Kwana paused, wiped the wound clean, then watched as blood began to seep again, though this time far more slowly. She applied the still-smoking stick to the wound and held it there for a few seconds. This time, no blood flowed when she sponged the wound clean.

Shiloh was then most efficiently bathed to remove any blood that had spread over her upper body, a healing salve was applied, and her wound bandaged. Mercifully, she never woke. After covering her with another buffalo robe, the women gathered their supplies and began to leave.

"Build a fire to keep her warm tonight," old Kwana said. "And if she wakes, give her nothing but sips of water. I'll be back throughout the night to check on her."

"My thanks," Jesse said, grasping her arm. "I know you live alone, now that your man has died. I will hunt for meat for you as soon as I can safely leave her."

She nodded. "That will be appreciated. When you can safely leave her, of course."

Once he was alone with Shiloh, he scooted over close to her. For a time, he watched her closely, afraid her breathing would cease and she'd leave this life. Finally, however, as time passed and he became aware of the night's growing chill on his bare skin, he remembered the old woman's instructions to build a fire.

He climbed from his tepee to find his buckskin shirt folded and laying just outside. After donning it, Jesse went off to Jack's tepee to borrow some firewood. Tomorrow, he'd gather extra to replace it, knowing Jack wouldn't begrudge him what he took tonight.

It didn't take long to get a fire going, and its warmth soon filled the enclosure. Once more, he crawled over to sit close to Shiloh. She slept on, but a quick check of her bandage reassured him that the bleeding hadn't resumed.

She's so beautiful, he thought as he gazed down at her. *And she's now mine.*

The only obstacle that lay before him was convincing her to accept that.

Tomorrow was soon enough to worry about that, though. After two days without sleep, he was mightily tired. Jesse lay down beside Shiloh and closed his eyes. Tomorrow was indeed soon enough to deal with everything that lay before them. And with the massacre at the White River Agency and the women's capture, surely the least of his problems would be taking Shiloh to be his wife.

A terrible ache in her shoulder woke Shiloh the next morning. She opened her eyes and stared up the sides of a tepee until her gaze caught on a patch of blue sky through the smoke hole. A passing confusion swept over her. Where was she?

Then the memory of the fight between Jesse and Broken Antler filled her. The agonizing pain of the knife ripping through her shoulder. Jesse catching her as she fell. Blackness . . .

Her hand went to her right shoulder, which was covered by a thick bandage. Someone had treated her wound, and it didn't seem to be bleeding. If all went well, she thought with a touch of black humor, she just might survive.

Someone stirred on her other side. Shiloh levered to her good elbow and looked down. Jesse lay there, fully clothed, on top of the buffalo robe that covered her.

Her gaze softened. He looked so young and peaceful in his sleep, his mouth soft and vulnerable, his frequently tight jaw relaxed. A slight beard stubble shadowed his face, and his long, black hair lay tousled and free.

Jumbled emotions churned within her breast. Love, gratitude for what he'd risked in saving her from Broken Antler, happiness at being with him once again, and how comfortable it felt with him sleeping beside her. Indeed, everything about this precious moment in time seemed so right, so good.

As if wakened by the sense of someone staring at him, Jesse opened his eyes. There was an immediate alertness and realization of where he was, and with whom, in his gaze. Then relief brightened his face, and he sat up.

"You're finally awake."

Shiloh smiled up at him. "Evidently so." She glanced around. "Is there any water? I'm so thirsty."

Jesse reached over near where his head had laid and picked up a leather water bag. He uncorked it and helped Shiloh hold it to her lips. She drank deeply before finally lowering it.

"Thank you. That really helped."

"So, how do you feel?" He eyed her closely before stoppering the water bag and setting it aside.

"Except for this pain in my shoulder," she said, shrugging it gingerly, "pretty good. How about you?"

His mouth quirked. "Just fine. I wasn't hurt yesterday, if you recall."

"And I'm glad for that. If you hadn't turned when you did, though . . ."

He sighed and shook his head. "I'd have rather taken that knife than see it hurt you."

"And I would've gladly taken it than see it *kill* you."

Their gazes locked, and for a long moment, Jesse stared down at her with the most tender look she'd ever seen. Then someone slapped the tent flap from outside, and the moment was gone.

A head peeked through the partially lifted flap. "Everyone awake in there?" an elderly woman asked. "I've got breakfast."

Jesse immediately sprung to his feet and took the bowls of food from her. "Come in, Kwana. Shiloh's finally awake and she looks good."

The woman crawled into the tepee and over to Shiloh. "So, you're feeling better, are you?" she asked, her dark eyes brimming with friendly curiosity. "You gave us all a scare yesterday, before we finally got your wound to stop bleeding. Your man was almost mad with worry for you."

Your man . . . The words were startling yet nonetheless stirred a wild joy in Shiloh. She blushed and cut Jesse a slanting look. He sat there calmly, as if he accepted the title.

"I'm sorry to have caused you any trouble. I just wasn't quite as fast as Jesse was in dodging that knife."

Confusion clouded Kwana's eyes, and she looked to Jesse. He smiled. "That's Shiloh's name for me. My white name."

"Oh, of course." The old woman pointed to the two bowls of steaming mush. "Eat now, before your food gets cold."

The mush tasted wonderful, warm, and flavored with honey and goat's milk, but Shiloh found she couldn't finish even half of it. With an apologetic look at Kwana, she finally set it aside.

"Much as I enjoyed it," she said, indicating the bowl of mush, "I just can't eat it all right now. Guess I was so thirsty, I drank too much water."

"Eat the rest when you can," the old woman said, climbing to her feet. She looked to Jesse. "We break camp soon. We're heading to the valley near Rifle Creek."

Jesse shot Shiloh a worried look. "I don't know if she'll be able to tolerate such a long trip. That's a full day's ride."

"I know. But Jack said to tell you that, no matter what, your woman comes."

Shiloh saw Jesse's hands fist and his gaze narrow. "I can ride, if you hold me in front of you," she hurriedly said. "That way, if I get too tired, I can always lean back against you and sleep."

He looked at her, his brow furrowed in thought. "I suppose that might work," he said after a time. "Unless you think you'd do better on a travois."

She was quick to shake her head. Even with an injured shoulder, the idea of snuggling up against Jesse was far too attractive to pass up. "I'll be fine riding with you. You'll see."

"I hope so." Though he didn't look very convinced, he seemed to accept her plan.

A half hour later, now wearing Jesse's red shirt to replace her ruined blouse, Shiloh laid outside on his pile of buffalo robes and watched Jesse take down and pack his tepee, then place it on a travois he then hooked to his second pony. By the time the rest of the camp was ready to depart, Shiloh had finished the mush, drank a good amount of water, and felt almost normal again. She soon discovered, however, how weak she still was when she tried to walk the short distance to his other pony they'd both be riding.

"I don't think I can mount on my own," she said, giving him an apologetic smile. "Could you help—"

Before she could even finish her request, Jesse grasped her about her waist and lifted her up to sit on his pony. Then, with a quick leap, he joined her.

Shiloh glanced back at him as he reached around her to take up the reins. "Well, I suppose that answers my question."

"Just lean against me and rest," he said. "No matter what you might think, this is going to be a very long and hard day for you."

"Maybe so," she said, settling back against him and his strong, buckskin-clad body. "But it has to be done."

"Yes, unfortunately it does." He urged his horse forward until they reached where his other pony attached to the travois waited. Taking up the long rope tied to its halter, Jesse once more signaled his pony to set out.

Before them, a long line of Utes led the way, mostly women and children, along with the old men. A strange sense of contentment filled Shiloh. She was safe, now that Jesse was here. Though there was no assurance what tomorrow might bring, at this particular moment in time she no longer cared. All that mattered was that she was with Jesse.

❦

They arrived after dark that night, in a beautiful valley with lush grass and near a creek that ran with clear, cold water. Shiloh had slept off and on all day but was still exhausted when Jesse finally lowered her from his pony. Her legs nearly gave out beneath her. Only his quick dismount to grab her by her arms prevented her from crumpling to the ground.

It was too dark to set up tepees that night, so everyone hurried to build campfires to cook a hasty supper, then turned in beneath bear and buffalo robes with the star-studded sky as their roof. Jesse was more than happy to cuddle Shiloh against him and was glad when she didn't protest about the undue familiarity of their embrace. Of course, he thought, that was likely more because she was half asleep when he climbed beneath the buffalo robes than because she actually wished him there.

Still, the ease with which she'd snuggled against him most of the day, her ready smiles, and occasional bursts of happy chatter reassured him. He knew she felt comfortable being around him, and maybe even enjoyed it. But then the doubts crept back in to erode his earlier optimism.

Compared to her fate at Broken Antler's hands, or being beaten by some of the more irate squaws, or even being tortured to death as he'd heard Douglas had advised, Shiloh knew how blessed she was to now be under his protection. And she likely imagined the fact that he'd won the battle to possess her was in name only, just to keep her safe. After all, she'd never made mention of her being his woman now, or asked any questions on the subject.

But then, there were those times when she looked at him with those big eyes of hers, and that look bespoke more than just friendship. Yet were her feelings for him strong enough to cast aside the life she'd always known? Cast aside her family and friends to live the life he'd chosen?

A chill breeze wafted across the valley, setting the tall grasses to gently swaying. The usual sounds of camp life stilled as everyone took to their beds, the quiet broken only by an occasional snort of a pony, a dog barking, or the bleating of their small flock of goats and sheep. Good sounds, comforting sounds, familiar and beloved.

Shiloh stirred, mumbled something, then settled back against him. He leaned down, tenderly brushed her wild, glorious hair aside, and kissed her forehead. She was so beautiful, and he loved her so.

Surely that love would convince her, in time, to accept this life and him as husband. She was his now, leastwise in the Indian view of things. And, whether she liked it or not, that was the way it was going to be.

She was, after all, no longer a free woman but a captive. And he didn't intend ever to let her go.

18

"Please, Jesse," Shiloh said two days later. "I'm going crazy just laying around in your tepee and being waited on. Let me help with some of the work."

He didn't answer right off but busied himself stacking the firewood he'd been gathering into a neat pile nearby. Finally, though, he met her gaze. "You need to rest that shoulder until it's well healed. And that pretty much makes you one-handed for a while longer."

"A person can do a lot with one hand," she countered. "I could help gather wood. I could make bread and do a lot of the cooking. And I could even air out the buffalo robes and—"

"You also need to rest and regain your strength," he interjected. "You still tire easily, and you still look a little pale."

"And you're being overprotective! I'm not a child, you know."

"Fine," Jesse said with a roll of his eyes. "Come down to the creek with me while I fetch water. You can pick up any tinder you find along the way."

Grinning broadly, Shiloh shoved to her feet. "Good. It's about time I start pulling my own weight. You're doing squaw work, and all the men are starting to make fun of you."

261

At the sharp glance he sent her, Shiloh nodded. "Oh, don't think I don't hear things. It's my shoulder that was hurt, not my ears."

"Well, it doesn't matter anyway." Jesse picked up a large woven willow basket by its wooden handle, took her by her good arm, and began to head them down toward the creek. "How I choose to treat you is my business and no one else's. Besides, until you came, I had to fend for myself. It's not like I had women hurrying to help me whenever I called."

She smirked. "That's not what I heard. A few of the women told me you had several maidens all but falling over themselves to bring you meals, fetch your water, and gather your firewood."

He shot her a sardonic look. "And did they also tell you I put a stop to that as soon as I could? Encouraging that sort of behavior would've only gotten those young women's hopes up, and I was in no hurry to take another wife."

"Well, no, they didn't tell me that." Shiloh blew out an exasperated breath. "And here I thought I'd better watch my step around some of those pretty girls, in case they were jealous of me."

"And why's that?"

"Because I'm living with you now, and they're not."

"You're living with me because you're my woman now. They know that."

Shiloh halted and stared up at him. "I'm your what?"

"My woman." His look was quizzical. "What did you think that fight between Broken Antler and me was about? A way to get some knife practice?"

Her mouth dropped open before she managed to snap it shut. "Well, no, I never thought that. And I'm sure the others all think we're . . . er . . . married, but I didn't expect *you* to think . . . to feel obligated to me in that way. I know you fought for me because you're my friend, and that's the only reason you did it."

"On the contrary," Jesse said. "As far as the People *and* I are concerned, yes, you are my wife. Come on, Shiloh, you know Ute customs well enough to know what constitutes a Ute marriage. Sleeping together is considered enough. Though, if you want the full experience, I suppose we could have Jack throw a blanket over us."

"But . . . but *sleeping* together surely doesn't just mean sleeping."

His expression went solemn, and a light flared in his eyes. "Well, no, it doesn't. But I thought we might wait on that until you're well healed."

She couldn't believe what she was hearing. Jesse spoke so matter-of-factly about what he considered was their marriage. A marriage that wasn't sanctioned in a church by a minister, nor one that he'd asked permission of her brothers, nor one he'd even received her agreement upon.

Yet Shiloh also knew that every custom accepted by the Utes had been fulfilled, and in every way that mattered to him, Jesse considered himself a Ute. She was also a Ute captive and could be treated in any manner they wished to treat her. She had just never thought that Jesse, knowing her and the white man's customs, would imagine she'd accept such a marriage.

"I'm deeply grateful," Shiloh carefully began, "for you rescuing me from Broken Antler. Sooner or later, though, I expect to be rescued, along with Josie, Arvilla, and Flora Ellen and her children. Until then, we can pretend to be husband and wife to fulfill everyone's expectations. But, once I'm gone, you can marry whomever you really wish to wed."

"This is no pretend marriage for me, Shiloh."

For a long moment, Shiloh stared up at him, shocked speechless. Then, glancing around, she found a fallen log and walked over and sat down on it.

Jesse didn't move from where he was standing. "Say something," he finally demanded, his voice gone harsh and strained. "Don't just sit there and look sick and horrified."

"I-I'm not sick and horrified," she finally managed to croak out. "It's just all so sudden and unexpected. Are you saying you really wanted to marry me, or that now that you've committed yourself, you feel honor bound to see it through?"

"Would it matter to you either way?"

Shiloh gave a strangled laugh. "Oh, most definitely!"

He eyed her warily, then sighed and made his way over to sit beside her. "I really wanted to marry you." He didn't meet her gaze but continued to stare off in the distance.

"Why?" Though his words gladdened her, after all this time and turmoil between them, she couldn't help but find this surprising pronouncement hard to believe. "Why now, when you've made such a big deal of avoiding me and telling me not to come back?"

Jesse sighed again and rubbed his eyes with one hand. "Because, besides the fact I'd already made up my mind to court you, by the time I discovered the Agency had been overrun and that you were gone and in great danger, the thought of losing you scared me to death." He turned to steadily meet her gaze. The ardent look burning in his eyes all but sucked the breath from her body. "And because I've always loved you, Shiloh. Always."

"You certainly have had a most unsettling way of showing it," she said with a shaky laugh.

"Kind of comes from being pretty unsettled about you, I guess."

"How's that? When have I ever acted like I didn't want to be with you?"

"It was never you." Jesse looked away. "It was me. I thought . . . well, I thought it'd never work between us."

"Why, because you're a half-breed who hates white men and wants to live with the Utes?"

He eyed her with amusement. "Leave it to you to cut right to the chase."

"Might as well get it out in the open, once and for all." She scooted close to him. "Because you being a half-breed doesn't matter to me and never has. I love *you*. I don't care who your mother or father was. As I hope you won't hold it against me who mine were either."

Jesse stared at her blankly. Then the light dawned in his eyes. "Because they're white, you mean?"

"Yes." Shiloh grinned. "Knowing how much you hate the white man, of course."

"I don't hate all white men. Just the ones who lie, cheat, and kill my people."

Shiloh laughed and pushed him with her good hand. "Oh, well that really narrows it down to a very few people then. And here I thought you hated just about anyone who wasn't an Indian."

He managed a sheepish smile. "I suppose I might have exaggerated a bit. But, after some bad experiences, I just chose to take my chances with the People instead."

She took his hand and, lifting it to her lips, kissed his palm. "But now, because you love me, you're willing to open your heart to some white men again."

"Like whom would you be talking about?" he asked, his tone guarded.

"My family, of course." Shiloh smiled brightly up at him. "Surely you know you can trust them?"

"Of course, especially your brother Cord and your sister Jordan."

Her smile faded a bit. "Cord will come around sooner or later. And Jordan . . . well, she's changed a lot since her injury. She's softer, gentler, and I don't think she holds you to blame anymore." Shiloh paused. "I hope not anyway."

Jesse reached out and cradled her jaw in his hand. "Above all, what matters is that we work out things between us. And we've got plenty of time for that. Right now, though," he said as he leaned toward her, "I'm going to kiss you. Because, since that one and only time at the doctor's house in Carbonville, I've been dreaming of doing it again . . . and again . . . and again."

Shiloh lifted her face to him. "I would like that very much."

As his lips neared hers, she closed her eyes. His kiss, at first, was tentative, his lips brushing hers with the lightest, most gentle of touches. But when she arched toward him, hungry for more, Jesse groaned and took her mouth with a fierce, ardent possession. His arms encircled her, pulling her close. Shiloh came to him eagerly, and for a long, glorious moment, there was no one in the world but them.

A twig cracked loudly nearby. Jesse released Shiloh and his hand went for his knife. Captain Jack stood there, an enigmatic smile on his lips.

"So, I see your woman is doing well," he said. "She will soon be able to carry out her own chores again."

Jesse stood. "She is better but still needs to allow her wound to fully heal. I am honored you cared to seek her out to discover this."

"I came to speak with you."

There was something in Jack's tone that warned Shiloh the Ute didn't want her around when he did so. She stood, brushed off the bits of bark clinging to her skirt, and nodded to the Ute chief.

"I've a fire to tend and will leave you two men to talk."

With that, she made her way back up the path to the camp. As she did so, Jack turned to Jesse.

"It is good she can move about on her own. If she needs to ask for help from the other women, she can now do that," she heard Jack say. "Because you and I will be leaving here at first light tomorrow."

Jesse didn't like the sound of Jack's pronouncement. He watched until Shiloh was well out of earshot and sight, then met the other man's gaze.

"Where will you and I be heading?" he asked.

"The fight is still going on with the soldiers."

"Yes, I know that." A prickle of unease ran down his spine.

"Indeed? I was beginning to wonder if you did. You've not mentioned a desire to join the rest of the men in fighting them."

"Since my arrival from the hunting trip, and caring for Shiloh, there hasn't been time to consider it. And it's not like I haven't fought in other battles."

"Nonetheless, there's been grumbling about your absence." Jack shot him a considering look. "Some say your woman has convinced you not to fight her people."

"Shiloh hasn't said a word about that. She's been too sick until the last day or so."

"But, from where I found you two, and what you were doing," his chief said, "I'd venture that she's feeling a lot better now. Well enough to care for herself in your absence."

He supposed it would come to this, sooner or later. Still, Jesse had hoped for more time to solidify his relationship with

Shiloh before he was forced to join the other braves in fighting her people. That good fortune, however, was not to be.

"You know I'm not afraid of battle," Jesse said, trying one last time to find some way out of this particular predicament. "And, from what I've been hearing, we outnumber the soldiers three to one, besides have them trapped and unable to flee. Is it necessary that I fight this time?"

"Why? So you can spare your woman's feelings?"

Jesse sighed. "What we have building between us is still fragile. And Shiloh's so intimately connected to the events that brought these soldiers here. She sees them as having come to rescue her and avenge what happened to the others at the Agency."

Jack gave a disparaging snort. "Little good that'll do any of them." He paused, his gaze narrowing. "It is your choice, Nuaru. I only tell you this because you have fought hard to build your reputation among the People. They imagine you as totally devoted to them and our way of life. But if you step back from our ways by taking a white woman as wife *and* refusing to fight with the other braves . . . well, you may lose all you've worked so long to build with us."

They were painful to hear, Jack's words, but Jesse knew in his heart that his chief spoke true. He either joined the others and fought beside them, or his motives—and his commitment—would likely always be suspect. Yet another of his concerns over allowing himself to fall in love with Shiloh, he reminded himself, had raised its ugly head. His fear of someday having to make a choice for one side or the other.

"Your words hold great significance for me," he said at long last. "I ask for this night to decide what I must do."

"It is given. Will you speak with your woman about this?"

"I must. She deserves to know where I go, and why."

"Just remember, you are the head of your family. She must learn this if your union is to survive."

Jesse nodded. "I know." He managed a bleak smile. "Many white women, though, aren't raised with the same outlook."

"Perhaps you should've thought of that before you fought Broken Antler for her then. *He* would never have asked her for permission."

"No, he wouldn't have," Jesse admitted. "And I knew the problems that might confront us. Knew from the start."

"I wish you luck then." Without further ado, Jack turned back down the path leading to their camp.

When the Ute chief had finally disappeared from view, Jesse walked over and again sat down on the tree trunk. A long while later, he finally rose. With heavy heart, he headed back the way he'd come.

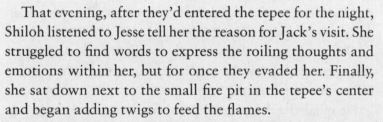

That evening, after they'd entered the tepee for the night, Shiloh listened to Jesse tell her the reason for Jack's visit. She struggled to find words to express the roiling thoughts and emotions within her, but for once they evaded her. Finally, she sat down next to the small fire pit in the tepee's center and began adding twigs to feed the flames.

"Say something, anything," Jesse urged, worry threading his voice. "I know you're not happy about this, but I'm duty bound to fight alongside the other braves. They are my people."

Shiloh nearly bit her tongue to stifle the first response that came to mind. That white men were also his people. That now that he had spoken words of love to her, that he wished to marry her, he had taken the first steps back into the world he had heretofore turned his back upon. Something told her, however, to go easy on that.

"And you know as well as I," she chose to say instead, attempting to make him see the logic of the situation if not yet the emotion of it, "that nothing good for the Utes will come of this. Even if they manage to kill these particular soldiers, more soldiers will come until the Utes are overwhelmed by their sheer numbers. And, this time, the soldiers will show them no mercy. Them and any who rode and fought with them, Jesse."

"It doesn't matter." He walked over and lowered himself to sit beside her. "I knew what would likely happen when I decided to join the People. That, unless some miracle occurred, the White River Utes would either accept reservation life, be sent to the Indian Territory, or be annihilated. But when they took me in and came to treat me as their own, I did the same. For better or for worse, as the saying goes."

Somehow, his use of a phrase spoken in taking marriage vows sent a shard of pain through her. She'd thought, when he'd finally admitted his love for her, that Jesse had worked through his conflicts over their differences. Now she wondered, and she was afraid. Very afraid.

"Where does that leave me then?" she softly asked, never taking her gaze from the fire. "With you about to ride off to kill some of *my* people?"

He inhaled a deep breath. "It leaves you safe here in this camp, along with all the other women and their children. Because I ride off with the other men to protect you and all the others. Because this is your life now as much as it is mine, and I'll fight to the death to preserve it."

Shiloh jerked around to stare at him in disbelief. "And who made that decision for me? That this is my life now? I didn't choose it. I was taken captive and forced into it!"

"When I fought for you and won, when you became my woman, this became your life. Surely you understood that."

The first tendrils of anger licked at her heart. "So, let me get this straight. Are you saying that, no matter who has me, I'm little more than a piece of chattel?"

"No, I'm not saying you're a piece of chattel." Jesse laughed. "Do any of the women in this camp act like they're subservient to their husbands? Or, at least the ones who have good husbands, anyway? But you could say that about white men's marriages too."

"That's not the point, Jesse Blackwater, and you know it!" Shiloh cried, frustrated at what seemed his obvious obtuseness. "For one thing, you can call me your woman all you want, but until we're married—church married—I don't have to obey you or follow you wherever you choose to go. And, for another, why does it have to be the Indian life for us? Maybe I don't want that kind of life for me or any children we might have. Did you ever think of that?"

"Actually, I did," he calmly replied. "But everything changed when you were taken captive. There'll be no church wedding. It's enough that we abide by the traditions of the People, which honor the Creator in the old ways, and honor marriage just as well. From here on out, those are what you'll live by, and no other."

Shiloh scooted back from him and awkwardly climbed to her feet. "And if I refuse? No matter what you say, you think I'm your property now. But how are you going to make me obey? By beating me? Ravishing me?"

Jesse looked up at her. "You know I'd never harm you in any way. In time, because I'm a patient man, you'll come to accept this life and all its traditions. Because I love you, and you say you love me." In one lithe, effortless motion, he stood. "Now, it's growing late, and I must depart tomorrow at first light. I suggest you go to bed."

"And where are you going?" she asked as he turned and headed toward the tepee flap covering the entrance.

271

"To tell Jack of my decision to join him and the other men. To fight the soldiers."

Jesse didn't return until very late. Shiloh had laid awake waiting for him, hoping for another chance to talk, but when the moment was finally upon her, her courage failed. What could she say to change his mind? He thought he had all the answers—and all the power.

In some ways it'd be easy to acquiesce to his demands. She had always loved him, and even in the face of Jesse's suddenly autocratic manner, Shiloh found it hard to let all hope die. It would be a decided adjustment to live with the Utes. Their ways were still very foreign to her. She had never been afraid of hard, physical labor or simple living, though. And, perhaps once they accepted her as Jesse's wife, they'd become more open to her teaching their children.

That had always been her goal, the dream nearest and dearest to her heart. Was the Lord's hand in this somehow? At least in Jesse's rescue and the claiming of her as his woman? The Bible spoke of God's ability to bring good even from evil.

Yet what good was there in her becoming Jesse's wife without the sanction of the Lord's church? It was bad enough that Jesse had turned his back on Jesus. Still, Shiloh had hope that someday he'd return to his Christian faith. Perhaps God was using her to that purpose as well.

Tears welled and spilled down her cheeks. Beneath the buffalo robe, she clasped her hands and lifted a silent prayer. A prayer for God to show her His will in all of this. A prayer to soften Jesse's heart enough to permit a church wedding. She could compromise on many things—including living with Jesse and the Ute people—but she could never go against her Christian beliefs.

Not even for Jesse.

Help him to understand that, Lord, she prayed. Help him to respect that, for my sake if not for his own. And please, please inspire him to have a change of heart, and not fight and kill those poor soldiers. Because if he does, then I'll know where his heart truly lies.

And it won't be with me.

19

Shiloh hoped against hope that Jesse would change his mind, but the next morning as the first rays of the sun streaked the sky, he rode out with Jack and several other braves. She watched him go, silent, hurt, and angry. Then she reentered his tepee, washed as best she could, then finger-combed her hair and gingerly plaited it into a single braid using her right arm as little as possible in the process. Finally, she tied off the braid with a strip of leather, happy to be able to do yet one more thing for herself.

Kwana came with breakfast, and they shared it together. After breakfast they helped each other gather firewood for the day and jointly carried up a big basket of water from the creek before beginning the day's baking. She enjoyed the old woman's company, for she seemed to know when to speak and when to remain silent. And, for most of the morning, her companion appeared to choose not to speak unless absolutely necessary.

Around noon, there was a commotion in Douglas's camp. Soon a rider arrived and ordered the old woman to take Shiloh into her tepee and not let her out until further notice. Shiloh considered refusing, then thought better of it. Without Jesse there, things might not go well for her if she created a stir.

Three hours later, a woman from a neighboring tepee poked her head inside. "It's all right for you both to come out now. The white man has gone."

As soon as she had exited and assisted Kwana from the tepee, Shiloh hurried over to grab her neighbor's arm. "A white man was here?"

"Yes," the other woman replied, pulling her arm from Shiloh's clasp. "Not that it's any concern of yours. He came from the great Chief Ouray, who sent a message for us to stop fighting the soldiers."

Excitement shot through Shiloh. "And will the Utes do so, do you think?"

The woman shrugged. "Who knows? Likely so, I'd imagine. Our chiefs respect Ouray. But we'll know more if and when all our men return."

If a rider had been sent out to the battle site, the odds were strong he might even catch up with Jesse and the other men before they had a chance to reach the soldiers. Which meant Jesse wouldn't kill any soldiers.

A passing joy filled her, before the cold, hard facts of reality returned. The problem between them was still there. The fact that Jesse had chosen to follow his Ute comrades, rather than respect her wishes in the matter. And, even deeper still, the issue of him choosing his Ute heritage over his love for her.

But wasn't that exactly what he was also asking of her? To choose her love for him over her own people? Problem was, they both loved the lives they were currently living, and it seemed one of them would have to totally give up that life, if there was to be any hope of any lasting relationship between them. And there were some aspects of her life Shiloh just couldn't give up.

The only bright spot in it all was that the soldiers would survive. And that Chief Ouray was involved now. There was hope that in all the negotiations that were sure to follow, she and the other Agency women would soon be freed. Still, when that occurred, it would complicate things with Jesse.

There were greater problems between them, however, than what he'd do when they were freed. Problems that included a clash of cultures and Jesse's seeming refusal to compromise on anything. Problems that threatened to destroy any hopes of a life together.

Shiloh almost dreaded their pending confrontation. And she seriously wondered now if those problems could truly be overcome.

Two days later, word came to move camp again. Jesse, along with Douglas, Jack, and all the other men, had returned from Milk Creek. Word now, though, was that even more soldiers were headed their way from Fort Steele in Rawlins. Most of the camp was unsettled, afraid of what would happen once the soldiers caught up with them.

A week later they moved camp again, this time traveling for nearly twenty miles in a very bad windstorm and ending up near the Grand River. The next day, they moved yet again to a place surrounded by high mountains where the Utes could watch the approaching soldiers with binoculars they'd taken during the Milk Creek battle.

They remained there for two days, and at noon of the third day, they traveled on yet again when scouts reported that the soldiers had passed the Agency and had come to within fifteen miles south of them. Everyone seemed to be in a panic, with squaws scurrying about taking down tepees and packing. Some of the ponies even got loose to gallop about the camp and add to the sense of urgency and fear. They made ten miles by the end of the day and set up camp on Roan Creek, where there was plenty of grass, trees, and water.

All the work of packing camp and moving so often, combined with multiple meetings with the chiefs to discuss what to do about the approaching soldiers, provided Jesse with ample excuse not to spend a lot of time during the day with Shiloh.

He imagined she was avoiding talking with him as much as he was with her. Since his decision to join the other braves in fighting the soldiers at Milk Creek, despite her pleas to the contrary, an almost palpable tension hung between them. He knew he had hurt her and that she thought he'd chosen the People over her, but it wasn't as clear-cut as all that.

Jesse wanted a life with Shiloh, living among the People. However, to accomplish that, he had to maintain the trust and respect he'd worked so long to build with the Utes. He had to carry his fair share of the responsibilities expected of all able-bodied braves, and that sometimes included fighting to protect the camp. That such expectations might at times put him in direct conflict with Shiloh's people was an issue they'd yet to come to terms with.

"We move out again first thing tomorrow," he announced that night when he finally crawled into his tepee to find Shiloh finishing up with the supper meal preparation. She looked hale and hearty now, and no longer wore the sling to protect her now-healed wound. Except for a bit of lingering stiffness in her arm and shoulder, she seemed as good as new.

Her expression of dismay, as she jerked her gaze to meet his, didn't surprise him. Everyone was weary of the frequent moves and long rides to the next camp. Tempers were fraying, squabbles amongst the braves—and even between some of the squaws—were happening more often. Talk was increasing of making a stand and having it out with the soldiers.

"Not another move," she said. "What's the point? The army can follow us all over the state if that's what's needed. And with a whole lot less effort than it takes us to break camp and move all this baggage so often."

"The point is—and you should be glad for this," Jesse said, "the People want to avoid any more fights with the soldiers. In the meanwhile, the chiefs are trying to use Ouray as a go-between to see what can be worked out."

"How about returning me and the other women for starters?" Shiloh began dishing their meal into bowls. "I can't think of a more obvious solution."

"And give away the one bargaining tool we have left?" Jesse shook his head. "You and the other women are more than captives now. You're hostages."

She paused in her filling of the bowls and stared up at him. "Hostages, are we? And what if the soldiers don't 'deal' with the Utes? Will we then be killed in retaliation?"

"No one's going to kill you or the other women." *How have I managed, with the first real conversation we've had since my return, to turn it into an argument?* Jesse wondered. "For one thing, you're mine now and no one would dare hurt you. And, for another, Ouray has forbidden any harm should come to any of you women."

"So, what bargaining power do the Utes really have then?"

"We won't return you, that's all. I mean, you're mine and Persune has taken Josie as his wife. So there's really only two women left to bargain for."

Her eyes grew wide. "Persune has taken Josie as his wife? Did she agree to it?"

Here we go again, Jesse thought. "It wasn't her place to agree or disagree. She's a captive, just like you."

"So, has he forced himself on her?"

He shrugged. "I can't say."

"Can't or won't?" Shiloh asked, her gaze narrowing in suspicion.

"Both." He threw up his hands in exasperation. "Look, I really don't know. It's their business, as what's between us is ours."

"You know," she said after what looked to be some thought, "you can't really and truly make me your wife unless I agree to it. No matter what Ute customs are."

A heavy weariness weighed down on him. Though he knew they needed to talk this issue through, or there'd be no hope for them, Jesse didn't think he could do so very effectively tonight.

"Yes, I suppose I do," he replied. "And I know we need to talk about this, but not tonight, Shiloh. I'm hungry and tired, and we've got another move tomorrow. Can't it wait just a little longer?"

"Time's running out for us, Jesse. The army's going to force some decision on us pretty soon."

She picked up one of the carved wooden bowls filled with some sort of savory meat stew. After placing a horn spoon and generous hunk of flat bread on top, she handed the bowl to him.

"But it doesn't have to be tonight, I suppose," she said, reaching for her own bowl of stew. "As you said, we're both so tired we'd likely not get much of anything accomplished anyway. I just wonder, if and when the time *is* right, if we will then either."

With that, Shiloh turned away from him and began to eat her supper.

✧～✦～◌

The next day's journey was long and arduous. It rained all day, hard and heavy, and everyone was soon wet, cold, and miserable. They traveled twenty-eight miles that day, and periodically scouts would ride in warning that the soldiers were drawing nearer and nearer.

Once camp was made, Chief Colorow, one of the other White River chiefs, rode in. A meeting was soon held with the other chiefs and some of their most trusted men. Jesse was asked to attend and eventually returned to inform Shiloh there was good news of a sort. They'd not be moving camp again. Chief Ouray didn't want them to come any closer to the two other Indian Agencies, Los Pinos and Uncompahgre.

The other good news, he informed her, was that the soldiers, who'd heretofore been advancing steadily after them, had halted any further forward movement. The time had come to negotiate, it seemed. Negotiate for the captives.

Shiloh, who had already snuggled down in her buffalo robe bed and fallen asleep, opened her eyes briefly as Jesse talked. Then, with a sigh, she pulled up the robe higher on her shoulders, closed her eyes, and went back to sleep.

Jesse watched her for a long while, too keyed up to take to his own bed. Instead, he wrapped a buffalo robe over his shoulders and sat there, trying to discern Shiloh's cryptic lack of response to the news. Was she happy that her captivity was nearing an end? Would she be glad to be rid of him?

She had said she loved him, that she wanted to marry him in a white man's church. That meant she'd been serious about a life with him. But those words had come before he'd ridden off to fight at Milk Creek. And, even though the battle was over before he even reached Milk Creek, Jesse knew his decision to fight was still a sore spot with Shiloh. A *very* sore spot.

When the time came, if she chose to leave with the other women, Jesse couldn't stop her. To do so would jeopardize the negotiations and all the People's welfare. He couldn't—and wouldn't—be that selfish.

His lips lifted in an ironic grimace. If he'd sided with Shiloh and not gone to fight the soldiers, he'd have lost the respect of the People. But, in ensuring his continued good relations with the People, he feared he might have hurt Shiloh past repairing. And now, when the time came, if he didn't let her go if she decided to do so, he threatened the safety of the Utes. And he also stood to lose Shiloh's love if he forced her into doing something she didn't wish to do.

It was beginning to appear as if having both Shiloh and the family and companionship he'd found with the Utes were mutually incompatible. Try as he might, he seemed caught in an impossible situation, a situation he'd feared from the start. Problem was, now that he'd admitted his love for Shiloh, and she her love for him, he wanted for them to be together no matter what.

The question had always been, how much of himself and the person he'd chosen to become was he willing to sacrifice in order to be with Shiloh? And how much was she willing to surrender to be with him?

It would be hypocritical of him to agree to a wedding in a Christian church. He had long ago turned his back on the white man's Jesus and all he represented. The Christian god had never been a friend of the Indian, no matter how some whites had tried to paint him so. Any marriage vows spoken in that god's church would be meaningless to Jesse. And Shiloh deserved a wholehearted commitment, one she'd never get from him in such a place or manner.

Still, Shiloh held great store in such a marriage ceremony. Jesse suspected she'd not feel sufficiently wed and blessed any other way. Frustration filled him. The difference in their spiritual beliefs was yet another stumbling block between them.

If only he didn't love her so much. In many ways, he loved her as a white man did his woman. That was yet another conflict raging within him. He knew too much of the white man's ways ever to imagine he could force himself on Shiloh in the hopes of making her his wife and think she'd ever forgive him for it.

Though he'd told Shiloh he truly didn't know what had happened between Josie and Persune, he did know Persune's outlook on such things was totally Ute. Persune now considered Josie his. And Jesse suspected that Persune had indeed bedded Shiloh's friend, whether she wished it so or not.

It was a hard admission, Jesse thought, to face that he was just as much white in so many ways as he was Ute. Until Shiloh had come back into his life, he'd managed to convince himself otherwise. There was no hope of doing so ever again. Leastwise, not if he wished to keep Shiloh.

His eyes burned with exhaustion, and he rubbed them with both hands in an attempt to ease the pain. It did little good.

There were some hard decisions ahead of him, Jesse well knew. Most of them, however, couldn't be made until he talked them over with Shiloh. And tomorrow had to be that time.

For he knew he didn't have much time left.

Later the next day, word came that a party of six white men headed by General Adams and thirteen Utes, including Sapovanero, Ouray's brother-in-law and spokesman, had departed Chief Ouray's home on the Uncompahgre River and were headed their way. With that news, the White River Ute encampments were again thrown into turmoil.

Shiloh heard the news from some of the other women even before Jesse, who had ridden out with a few other braves early this morning to hunt rabbits and other small game. Filled with mixed emotions, she busied herself with various chores of her own before going to help Kwana.

Over the past weeks, the old woman had become a friend and confidante. And, sooner or later, talk had turned, as it always seemed to, to her and Jesse.

"I'm trying the best I can to work it out with him," Shiloh said that day as they made bread. "But he insists I obey him in all things, and I can't. I just can't."

"Nuaru is afraid of giving up control over the things he deems important." Kwana paused to pour a bit more water into the dough that was forming beneath Shiloh's hands. "He has fought so long and hard to find a life that fulfills him that he's fearful of losing himself if he now surrenders any part of it."

"But he also wants me to be a part of that life," Shiloh cried, so frustrated that she could barely hold back tears. "He says he loves me, but I'm beginning to wonder if he even knows what loving someone entails."

"And that would be?" her friend asked with an arch of a brow.

"It entails putting the happiness of the other person ahead of your own. Of being willing to give and take. And, right now, Jesse refuses to give and is only taking."

"He has much to learn then. Things were so much simpler when he wed Onawa. She wasn't a firebrand like you."

"She was also a Ute," Shiloh muttered. "And I'll never be able to compete with that."

"Oh, little one!" Kwana reached over to pat her hand. "You wouldn't be who you are if you weren't just as you are. And, somehow, I doubt Nuaru would love you as he does if you changed. He just doesn't realize that yet."

"Well, he doesn't have much time left." Shiloh sighed. "Oh, if only he would compromise just a tiny bit!"

Kwana nodded sagely. "Compromise is indeed a vital component of a lasting relationship. Unfortunately, the compromises that are usually the most important are also the most painful."

"More painful than losing the one you love?"

"Sometimes, little one." The old woman smiled sadly. "Most unfortunately, sometimes."

An hour before sunset, Jesse and the other men returned. Their hunt had been successful, and Jesse's share of the game included three fat rabbits. Shiloh took them from him and proceeded to gut and skin them before sending Jesse off with one rabbit for Kwana's supper. By the time he returned, she had the cook fire down to hot coals, the rabbits spitted and roasting, and she was patting out flat bread dough to bake.

He took the news of General Adams and his party's impending visit far more calmly than she would've guessed. But then, Shiloh also knew Jesse had expected this visit sooner or later. Still, it rankled that he didn't seem too upset that she could be freed and leaving him in the next few days.

They ate their supper in silence, save for Jesse's compliments on how good she was getting at making flat bread and meals over an open fire. She acknowledged his praise as graciously as she could, considering the longer she sat there, the angrier she was becoming.

As they finished their meal, however, and Shiloh began to clean up, Jesse touched her arm. Startled by the first physical contact he'd made in days, she jerked her gaze to him.

"Leave those things for later," he said, his glance solemn and shuttered. "I'd like for us to take a walk down to the creek. It's time we talked."

Her heart skipped a beat, and Shiloh was suddenly terrified that the moment they'd both been yearning for and dreading was finally upon them. Still, their differences had to be faced or there was no hope for them.

She stood and straightened her skirt and the oversized shirt of his that she'd belted over it. "Yes, it's time we talked."

Though he held out his hand, Shiloh wouldn't take it. Instead, she just walked beside him as they made their way from camp and down the well-trodden path to the creek. If the truth were told, she was afraid to hold his hand or even get too close to him right now. Despite all their troubles of late, Shiloh still loved Jesse and feared the ever-present temptation he presented. The temptation to shed all her personal beliefs, to ignore her misgivings, and agree to whatever he proposed. Even, if necessary, to turn her back on her faith just so she could stay with him.

Yet just as that realization found expression in her mind, Shiloh squelched it with a fierce vehemence. No, she told herself, never would she turn from the Lord. How could she? He was her Savior, her Beloved, even before she had met Jesse and fallen in love with him. To betray her God was to betray herself and all she stood for.

Please, dear Lord, she prayed as they walked along, *don't let Jesse ask that of me. Most anything else I'd gladly give up for him, but not You. Never You . . .*

Then they were there, standing beside the creek's rushing waters, and Shiloh knew the time was finally upon them. She turned to look up at Jesse, her gaze hungry, her glance memorizing his handsome, bronzed face, his dark, piercing eyes, his beautiful mouth and jet-black hair.

I might not have much longer to look at him, she thought achingly. *To be with him. To talk with him. To be loved by him . . .*

"What will happen to us?" Shiloh asked, forcing the hardest words she'd ever spoken past her bone-dry throat. "When General Adams comes, I mean?"

His expression hardened. "It's simple, really. You can either choose to leave with him or stay with me."

A pained irritation filled her. *So, it is that simple, is it? Well, maybe for you, but not for me.*

"And that's how it's to be then?" Shiloh asked tautly. "Either I accept what you want, with no discussion or compromise, or I can leave?"

"You already know how I feel about staying with the People." Jesse impaled her with his dark gaze. "I can't—I won't—return to the white man's way of life."

"But where does that leave you and me, Jesse?" She choked back the rising frustration, determined to find a compromise in this that both could live with. "I love you and would live with you wherever that might be, but if you choose the Indian way, then it can pit you against my people, even my family, at some point."

"And living with the white man could eventually pit me against the Utes."

"That's not as likely, though. You could choose to stay out of that sort of conflict. Besides, the day is coming when the Utes will either remain on the reservation or be forced to move to the Indian Territory. You know that as well as I."

"So I should desert them because of possible hard times ahead?"

Shiloh expelled an exasperated breath. "No, and I'd never ask you to do that. All I was saying was that soon living as a white man won't require you to fight any of the People."

He smiled grimly. "Nor, if things go as you predict, will living with the Utes soon require me to fight the white man."

"Fine. I'll give you that. As far as our two peoples fighting each other, it's soon not going to matter much whether we live as Utes or whites. All I want is for you to be a man of peace and compassion. Is that too much to ask?"

"No, it's not. It's what I've always wanted. But some people won't let you live like that, Shiloh. And a man protects what is his."

"Yes, a man does," she agreed with a nod. "And so does a woman. But to have peace, you have to strive always to create it. And to have mercy, you have to be merciful even when it hurts to do so. Even when others around you aren't being very peaceful or merciful."

"And when has that attitude ever gotten me anything, except beatings, rejection, and ridicule?"

"And I say you're letting the past decide your future!" She moved toward him and gripped his arm. "We are all touched by what has happened to us, Jesse. The bad, as well as the good, influences us. But it's our choice what we do with those experiences. The cruelties of others can teach you compassion toward others, because you've lived that hurt firsthand."

"Do you know how naïve you sound, talking about turning the other cheek? About being thankful for the blessings of pain?" He gave a bitter laugh. "No one can do that, not unless he's some sort of fool."

A soft, poignant smile lifted her lips. "Jesus Christ did that, and He was no fool. Instead, He was wise beyond our meager comprehension. The only fool is the one who doesn't follow Him, doesn't try his best to live as He did."

"I gave up that crazy belief a long time ago," Jesse muttered. "And I'm not walking that path again."

"But why, Jesse?" she asked, her heart aching at the deep pain beneath his words. "What has the Lord ever done to you to turn you so against Him?"

He shook her hand away. "It's not what He has done," he softly replied, "but what *I* have done."

Confusion flooded her. "And what have you ever done, Jesse, to turn God against you? If it's your hatred of the white man, then confess it to Him and ask His forgiveness. He'll give it and welcome you back with open arms."

"It's not that simple. It's more than hatred. It's death. It's killing someone."

For a moment, Shiloh found she couldn't take in a breath. Then her constricted chest relaxed, and air rushed in to fill her lungs.

"Who, Jesse? Who did you kill?"

"A white man," he whispered.

She searched for some reason to justify what he'd done. "But if it was in self-defense, and you had no other choice—"

"It was my father." His face contorted in anguish. "I killed my father!"

20

This time, it took Shiloh a lot longer to come to terms with what he'd told her. Finally, she expelled an unsteady breath, took his arm again, and motioned to some large boulders at the creek side.

"Come, let's sit for a spell," she said. "I want to hear how and why it happened."

Gently, he extricated himself from her grip. "I'll tell you, but I can't sit while I do. There's just so much boiling inside me to keep still."

"Fine." Shiloh nodded. "You do what you need to tell me the story. I'll go and sit there, though."

Once she had settled herself on the edge of one boulder, Jesse dragged in a deep, unsteady breath and began pacing back and forth. "For most of my life, I hated him. Only when Brother Thomas taught me of Jesus and His love for even His enemies did I manage for a time to look upon my father with more compassion. No matter what I did, though, my father never changed. If anything, he got meaner. By the time I was fourteen, I was as tall as him, and I think he became afraid of what I'd do if he hit me. So he added what he considered my share of beatings onto my mother's."

His hands clenched and unclenched at his sides, and Shiloh knew, watching him, that Jesse was struggling with old, ugly memories. More than anything, she wanted to leap up, run to him, and enfold him in her arms. But she didn't. He needed to tell his tale and tell it like a man.

"Things came to a head the night my mother died," Jesse finally continued. Sweat began to bead his brow, and Shiloh sensed the agonizing toll that the telling was taking on him. "You know the events of that night. How my mother died trying to keep my father from beating me half to death because Brother Isaac kicked me out of school. But what I never told you about was the murderous resentment and rage I harbored for my father, in those days afterward, while we prepared to bury my mother. If he'd even once expressed regret or sorrow for what he'd done to her, it might have eased some of my fury at him. But he never did. He never did . . ."

His words ended on a strangled sob. Somehow, Shiloh knew Jesse's grief wasn't for himself, for never having the father he wanted, but for his mother. That she died as she had lived—unloved, unappreciated, and perhaps in some ways, even unwanted. Save for her son. A son who had also grown up feeling unloved and unwanted save for her.

To keep from saying something that might seem trite or unhelpful, Shiloh twisted her hands in her lap. "Go on. Finish it," she urged, for his sake as much as for hers.

"He got himself drunk that night of her funeral." Jesse's voice went hoarse with emotion. "And that suited me fine, for I'd made up my mind to leave and never come back. We had an old earthenware crock where we kept our money. Since I'd already started working for pay at a nearby ranch mucking stalls after school, I figured some of that money was mine to take. My father, however, wasn't so drunk he didn't notice me with the crock.

"First, he flung his now-empty whiskey bottle at me. I ducked just in time. Then he came at me with his hunting knife. We fought and I was finally able to turn his knife on him." For an instant, Jesse's voice gave out, then he forged on. "He died quickly. Too quickly for what he deserved."

Jesse turned to meet Shiloh's anguished gaze. "I buried him that night. The next morning I rode out. Since he no longer needed it, I took all the money with me."

For the longest time Shiloh didn't know what to say, and the silence stretched between them. Finally, she unclasped her hands.

"You were defending yourself. And it was an accident."

He shrugged. "Doesn't change the fact that I killed my own father." Jesse laughed tonelessly. "Makes me pretty much like him, it does. My father killed my mother, and I killed my father. All either one of us ever knew was killing."

Why, Shiloh wondered, did Jesse insist on taking all the blame for what had happened during that fight? It was as if he felt he had to bear the burden of not just his own sins but also the sins of his father.

Shiloh had opened her mouth to speak when Jesse picked up the thread of the conversation again. "He told me many times I'd never amount to much. That because of my mixed blood no one would ever want me. That I'd never fit in no matter where I went. But he was wrong. When I found the People, I found acceptance, respect, and love. I knew I'd come home. Where I'd amount to something. Where I belonged."

His words plucked at a memory. A memory of her brother Cord observing that Jesse was a very angry man who didn't appear to know where he fit in. Yet, that only seemed to happen—his anger and confusion—when he was in the white man's world, trying to find some way to be part of it. Part of it for her sake, and never solely for his own.

The realization that she could never ask him to leave the Utes filled her with a bittersweet pain. Sweet because Jesse was whole and happy living with the People. And bitter because either she adapted to that reality or there was no hope for them. She loved him too much to ask him to live any other way.

"I'm happy that you've finally found your heart's desire," Shiloh said softly. "And, because you're *my* heart's desire, I'll remain with you here. Be your wife. Birth, raise, and educate our children with a love and respect for what is best of both the Indian *and* white man. But I would ask two things of you in return."

"And what would those two things be?"

"That you would marry me in a Christian ceremony and allow me to teach our children of Jesus."

He stopped and looked down, and as the seconds ticked by, Shiloh realized he was fighting a battle within himself. Though she wished mightily to intercede, to utter all the reasons why he should acquiesce to her simple—her only—demands when she was giving him so much more in return, she forced herself to quietly let him work it through himself. Jesse knew, as well as she, that just as his need to remain with the Utes wasn't negotiable, so was her need for her and their children to live as Christians.

"I can't. I'm sorry, Shiloh. I just can't."

The words sounded torn from some deep place within him, and as he lifted his head and met her gaze, Shiloh saw the agony burning in his eyes. But she also saw the honest refusal there as well. It ripped open her heart.

Compromises that are usually the most important are also the most painful . . . Unbidden, Kwana's words crept into her memory. Somehow, Shiloh had feared this moment, this decision. Because if neither met the other halfway, there could be no hope for a lasting relationship.

"You can't have everything as you want it, Jesse," Shiloh said. "Your love for me has to be enough to transcend some of that pain you've suffered all these years. And if it can't, then I guess it's not strong enough."

She stood and met his burning gaze, something within her firming, hardening. "I'm sorry too. But it seems I'm not the woman you need."

His glance turned flinty. "And I'm not the man for you either."

Tears filled her eyes. She had finally hit a wall their love couldn't seem to overcome. But then, perhaps it had never been meant to. Perhaps, all along, it had only been her stubborn determination that had brought their relationship as far as it had come.

"So be it then." The words were torn from her heart, leaving it shredded and quivering. "When the rescue party comes for the other women, I'll be going with them."

"Shiloh—"

"No." She held up a hand to silence him. "It's over between us. Just . . . just let it go."

With that, she turned and walked away. As she did, Kwana's words, once again, echoed—prophetically now—in her mind.

Compromises that are usually the most important are also the most painful.

More painful than losing the one you love?

Sometimes, little one. Most unfortunately, sometimes . . .

Late the next day, General Adams and his party arrived. Much time was spent in stormy negotiations with the Ute chiefs before Adams finally won the agreement to release the White River Agency women and two children. That night, after Jesse informed Shiloh of her upcoming departure on the morrow, he escorted her to Johnson's tepee, where she rejoined the other captives at last. Their reunion was so joyous that Shiloh failed to notice when Jesse quietly slipped away.

The next morning after breakfast, Kwana rode over to Johnson's camp to say good-bye. The old woman already knew the reason why Shiloh had decided to leave, but still hugged her and cried all over again. Shiloh had hoped Jesse would come to say his farewells, so they could at least part on a cordial note, but he was nowhere to be seen. As the ponies were being saddled for their imminent departure, she hurried back over to Kwana.

"Would you give this to Jesse," she asked as she unfastened her chain and removed the tooled silver eagle, "and tell him I've worn it since the day he gave it to me? That I wanted him to have something to remember me by and because, along with my cross, it has lain so long over my heart. And that I cherished them both because they always reminded me of my two greatest loves."

Kwana put out her hand, and Shiloh dropped the eagle into it. "I will tell him. I will give this to him," the old woman said.

Then it was time to leave. With heavy heart, Shiloh mounted the pony lent to her and, as they rode from camp, she searched one last time for sign of Jesse. He wasn't there.

She had such mixed feelings, leaving the Utes. Though the reason for her captivity was indeed tragic and filled with hardship and fear for her life as well as those of the other Agency women, in the past three weeks she had also discovered that Jesse loved her. Yet, as much as she loved him in return, if he couldn't find it within himself to accept *her* people and beliefs as much as she tried to accept his, then there was no hope for them. It was as if he wanted her, but only certain parts. He just couldn't seem to understand that she could never be whole without the part of her that honored her family, her white heritage, and her faith.

Once again, Kwana's kind words plucked at her memory. She had said that Shiloh wouldn't be who she was if she wasn't just as she was. And that Jesse wouldn't love her as he did if she changed.

At the time, Shiloh had greatly appreciated the old woman's encouraging words, thinking that Jesse would quickly come to that same realization. But now, with the time to think on what Kwana had said in the long hours as they rode farther and farther from the camp, Shiloh delved deeper into herself. And she reluctantly admitted that true love wouldn't demand that the people involved give up their very personhood for the sake of the other.

Perhaps she was asking that very thing of Jesse in requesting they wed in church, and that she raise their children as Christians. But a church wedding, in which he repeated vows he surely meant even as he took her as wife in the Ute way, didn't seem such a threat to his personhood. Nor did allowing his children to learn of the Christian God.

But maybe that was the essential problem between them. Neither could see that what the other asked was fair and reasonable. One thing she *was* certain of, however. Her faith was an integral part of her. She couldn't turn her back on it for anyone, no matter how much she loved them.

As the sun dipped toward the west, a cool breeze began to blow. Shiloh hunkered down within the blanket she'd wrapped around her. Every mile they rode toward home and freedom was another mile away from a life she'd once thought would be hers. A life with Jesse.

The admission sent a shard of pain through her heart. She had always loved him, and always would. There was just no hope left for them. But love . . . there would always be love.

Jesse fingered the tooled silver eagle, silent and torn between pain and an unwanted sense of finality, of completion.

That Shiloh had worn this since the day he'd given it to her filled him with joy. But the fact she'd now returned it to him also ripped open wounds he'd thought he'd managed to close. Perhaps not yet healed but at least closed.

"That was all she said, that this had been with her since the day I gave it to her?" Jesse asked Kwana the evening of the women's departure.

Not certain he could watch Shiloh ride off, he had stayed away the entire day. It had been an excruciating sacrifice to let her go, but he'd done it for the sake of the People. The People, who meant more to him than anything he'd ever known.

Anything except Shiloh . . .

Furiously, Jesse clamped down on that traitorous thought, then crammed it back into the farthest recesses of his mind. The People were all that mattered. They *had* to be.

Kwana eyed him disdainfully. "And why would you wish to know more? Why make the parting even harder for yourself than it already is? You already know she loves you and would've sacrificed almost everything for you. And that still wasn't enough. So how could a few more words from her now make any difference?"

Anger flared, hot and bright, before Jesse was able to tamp it down. Kwana and Shiloh had become close in the past weeks. It was understandable that the old woman was on Shiloh's side.

Her words were also wise. What was the matter with him, that he seemed so intent on wringing the last bit of agony that he could out of this? To punish himself for his cruelty to Shiloh in refusing two simple requests? To flail his heart one more time for his selfishness, his fear, his inability to forgive himself? *Fool!*

"You're right," Jesse said with a nod. "Nothing's accomplished by dragging this out. And, as you say, it makes no difference."

He closed his fingers around the silver eagle. "I thank you for giving this to me." With a nod, Jesse turned to go when Kwana laid a hand on his arm.

"It's not too late to change your mind," she said, her dark eyes piercing clear through to his soul. "All it takes is for you to face your pain and see it through to its end. The soul pain. The spirit pain." She pointed north. "Go. Find your *poo-gat* and speak with him. Now, before it's too late."

With that, the old woman released him and hurried away.

Jesse watched her go, mystified at what she had said and meant. One thing he did understand was her instruction to find his poo-gat. The one who knows the way.

Frustration filled him. There was only one man whom he would ever consider his poo-gat, and Jesse had no idea how to find him. That man was Brother Thomas.

"What will you do with your life, Shiloh? Now that your dream of teaching the Indian children is over?"

Snugly ensconced in the library, with a fire blazing in the hearth to ward off the chill November day, Shiloh glanced up from the chemise she was mending. The lace border had finally come loose after many washings and was so fragile she was tempted to rip it all off and apply new lace. The frustration with the task did little to soothe her frayed nerves or the sudden surge of defensiveness her sister's question engendered.

Yet, when she met Jordan's curious gaze, she saw no smug sense of "I told you so" or barely veiled meanness. Her blue-green eyes were serene, if concerned. And that was all. No more, no less.

It had been nearly five weeks since her return from her captivity with the Utes, and Thanksgiving was in just another few days. After leaving the Ute camp, it had taken them a four-day ride to reach Ouray's house on the Uncompahgre River near the Uncompahgre Indian Agency. After resting overnight there, where they were most kindly treated by Chipeta, Ouray's wife, the other women and children continued their journey on mail coaches to Alamosa. There they boarded a train to Denver, eventually arriving in Greeley, where the Meekers had a home. Amidst tearful farewells, Josie had promised to write Shiloh just as soon as she got home, and the two young women made plans to visit each other.

Shiloh stayed behind while a telegraph message was sent to Ashton, which was delivered to Castle Mountain Ranch the next day. As she awaited her brother Cord's arrival, she enjoyed the hospitality and unexpected luxuries of Ouray and Chipeta's home. It had Brussels carpets, glass windows with window curtains, good beds, rocking chairs, mirrors, and an ornately carved bureau. Chief Ouray, Shiloh observed, had wholeheartedly tried to adapt to the ways of his white brothers. Unfortunately, it hadn't been enough to convince most of his people to do the same.

That time, if it ever arrived, would be long in coming, Shiloh thought as she pulled her attention back to the present. And, in the days that passed since her return home, she had long mulled over Jordan's exact question. What *would* she do with her life, now that her dream of teaching the Ute children was over? Or was it?

"I'm considering taking Ouray up on his offer to come to the Uncompahgre Indian Agency and teach the children there," Shiloh finally replied as she continued to industriously stitch the lace back on the chemise. "At least there, thanks to his influence, the parents are willing to have their children educated."

"So, you're bound and determined to become a spinster schoolmarm, are you?"

Shiloh chuckled along with her sister, even as a sharp, sudden longing for Jesse stabbed through her. The hurt would dull in time, she well knew, but it would take a while. A long while.

"Maybe so," she replied. "You just never know. In the meanwhile, I'll certainly have my fill of children. Day in and day out. I'll just be able to send them all home at the end of each day." She managed a weak grin. "Can't think of a more perfect way to have my cake and eat it too."

"That half-breed. Jesse," Jordan ventured, evidently catching some undercurrent of sadness in her sister's voice. "Whatever happened to him? Emma told me he'd brought you back from the Agency when you heard I was . . . hurt."

And what else did Emma tell you? Shiloh thought. *Well, no matter.* "He's still with the White River Utes. They took him in a long while ago, and he's happy there."

Jordan glanced briefly away, then riveted the full force of her gaze on her. "Emma said you were in love with him. What happened?"

Shiloh had hoped never to have to explain that to anyone. And, until Jordan's query just now, no one had asked. Somehow, they must have sensed that things hadn't turned out well between her and Jesse.

But Jordan, since her injury, had become far more direct and open, casting aside a lot of the social niceties. And Shiloh knew she asked now because she truly cared.

"It just didn't work out," she said, ducking her head and pretending to concentrate on a troublesome stitch gone awry. "There were some differences between us that we just couldn't seem to compromise on."

"Was one of those differences because of me? Because of what I did to Jesse all those years ago when I lied?"

Shiloh's head jerked up. Sadness darkened her sister's eyes.

"No." She shook her head. "Jesse understood you were

afraid of being punished, not to mention what being with him would've done to your reputation. If you'd willingly gone with him, I mean, and encouraged his kiss."

"So, it was other things then." There was an edge of relief in Jordan's voice.

"Yes," Shiloh softly replied. "Other things."

At one time, she had imagined that perhaps God had sent her to help both the Utes and Jesse. To help him back to the Lord. Help Jesse by her love, her compassion, and her self-sacrifice in the service of his people. But just as her dream of being Jesus to the Utes had failed, and failed miserably, so had her attempts to help Jesse.

Her sister sighed, and the sound jerked Shiloh's attention back to the present. "Well, I'm glad that he no longer hates me," Jordan said. "I just wish that I'd had a chance to apologize when he was here."

I wish you had too, Shiloh thought. *Maybe it wouldn't have changed anything between us, but at least Jesse could finally set that particular hurt aside. And know that one more white person was decent and kind, who saw him as a human being, a child of God, instead of someone beneath contempt because of his mixed blood.*

That long-held pain of Jesse's wounded her far more than their failed relationship. That he struggled still to find total peace and acceptance. And self-forgiveness for killing his father.

Shiloh wondered if he ever would, if he didn't turn back to his Christian faith and find what he needed most of all in the arms of the Lord. Find love, acceptance, and a tender mercy. Only there, cradled in God's embrace, would Jesse finally find his true self.

And there, drenched in the audacity of God's mercy, nothing else would ever make him feel unworthy again.

Thanksgiving Day, Shiloh got up early to help Emma and Sarah with all the preparations, while Jordan, with Danny's help, watched Ceci and baby Caleb. An hour before the big meal, with nearly all the food either done or cooking, the table in the dining room set in a grand fashion, and the house spic-and-span, Shiloh was finally free. She decided to go for a short ride.

The day was crisp and cold but sunny. A recent storm had covered the valley and the nearby mountain peaks in a pristine blanket of snow. The tangy scent of wood smoke filled the air, and she inhaled deeply, savoring the familiar smell.

It was a glorious day to be outside, with the anticipation of a fine Thanksgiving meal with family and friends only adding to Shiloh's pleasure. She loved this ranch and had from the first day she'd arrived here so very long ago. Loved the family who was always there for her when she needed them. Who had supported and comforted her in the past weeks as she'd slowly struggled to come to terms with the events of the White River Massacre and her parting from Jesse.

Above all, she loved the Lord Jesus, who had never left her even in her darkest moments. Especially those dark moments after the massacre that only now, when she was finally free of her Ute captives, she could finally and fully allow herself to relive and consider. And though the intensity of her emotions regarding those terrible days still sometimes staggered her, Shiloh also realized that, at the time, controlling and even denying them had been her only way to keep her sanity, to survive.

Leastwise, she added with a sad little smile, until Jesse had come to her rescue and staked his claim upon her. Only then had the unrelenting fear eased, for she had felt so safe and cherished with him by her side. So safe, cherished, and loved . . .

With a resolute, almost angry, shake of her head, Shiloh flung aside the pointless fantasy she was spinning. Nothing was served pining over what might have been. Though thoughts of Jesse still hurt, Shiloh knew she had made the right decision in choosing God over him.

She headed back to the barn after a time, anticipating that the supper bell would soon be rung, summoning her to the feast. After untacking her horse, she led her into a stall. Quickly putting the saddle and bridle away, Shiloh returned with a grooming box and began brushing her mare. Next, she turned to picking out the animal's hooves, her thoughts soon flitting off in aimless, scattered directions.

"We really need to stop meeting in the barn, you know?" a deep, familiar voice intruded just then on her reverie.

Shiloh froze, then lowered her mare's front foot to the ground and straightened. Her heart pounding in her chest, she turned.

Jesse stood there, casually leaning on the stall door. As always, he was dressed in full buckskins and his fur-lined buckskin coat, his black, shoulder-length hair gleaming in the light of the single lamp Shiloh had lit and hung on a hook just outside the stall. His gaze, as he avidly scanned her, was filled with love and yearning and no small amount of amusement.

"W-what are you doing here?" she asked, immediately struck by how inane and inhospitable her words sounded.

Jesse, however, didn't seem to take offense. He shrugged.

"I missed you and thought maybe there was still some way to talk you into becoming my wife. We'd have to get married in a church, though, as I'd like it to be done up right in God's eyes as much as in man's."

Gradually, Shiloh became aware that she was standing there staring at him with her mouth agape. She snapped her lips shut, swallowed to lubricate her dry throat, and then gave a shaky laugh.

"Well, I don't know," she began. "This is all so sudden, so unexpected. And I don't understand. What's changed that now you're talking about God and a church wedding?"

"Some of us are just slow learners, I guess." Jesse motioned to her. "Would you mind coming out of this stall so we can talk? I'm not keen on shouting out all my failings and stupidity for the whole barn to hear."

"Afraid the horses and other livestock will think less of you?" Shiloh gave a bemused snort. "Leave it to a Ute to worry more about the ponies than people."

Nonetheless, she did toss the hoof pick back into the grooming box, then picked it up and walked from the stall as Jesse unlatched and swung open the door. After depositing the grooming box on a nearby bench, she turned and waited. Jesse closed and latched the stall door then rejoined her.

"Kwana gave me the silver eagle you'd left with her," he said, coming to stand so close that Shiloh could smell his heady scent of buckskins and horse. "She didn't have very kind words for me or my decision-making ability, though. Told me I needed to hightail it north and get my poo-gat to talk some sense into me."

Her brow crinkled in puzzlement. "Poo-gat?"

He grinned. "The one who knows the way. One's spiritual mentor."

"I didn't know you had one of those. You never mentioned—"

Jesse placed a finger to her lips. "It was Brother Thomas. So I went to find him."

"And did you, after all these years? Find him, I mean?"

A Love Forbidden

"No, I didn't. He'd moved around these parts quite a bit over the years, and the best I could discover was that he died two years ago at a mission near Cheyenne. For a while after that, I was pretty devastated. But, one night while sitting at my campfire on my way back to Colorado, I was struck by the realization that I hadn't ever really needed to find him. I had all his words in my head and in the Bible he'd given me on my baptismal day."

"You've had a Bible with you all along?" Shiloh couldn't believe her ears. "But where? I never saw it in your tepee."

"That's because I'd wrapped it up and packed it away in my saddlebags a long time ago." He smiled. "At any rate, I sat there that night and began to think over all that he'd told me. Of why his words had so inflamed my heart with love of God that I'd finally begged to be baptized, to become a Christian."

Jesse laughed. "Not that I worked it all out that night, but it started me back on the right path. And I had plenty of time to think about a lot of things as I rode home. Long days and nights of nothing to keep me company but my thoughts. Yet, though the People had finally returned to the White River reservation by then, something kept drawing me southward. Until I finally realized I was on my way back to you."

He took her by the arms. At his touch, Shiloh shivered. Ah, but it was so good to see him again, to be close to him, to gaze up into his beautiful dark eyes! If he was a dream or some vision or figment of her imagination, she hoped it would never end.

"I love you, Shiloh," Jesse said softly, ardently. "I've never stopped loving you, even though I lost sight of what mattered most to me. I was just so confused, so afraid, and so unforgiving."

"Unforgiving?"

A wry smile lifted his lips. "Of myself, most of all. Because I couldn't find it in my heart to forgive myself, I became consumed with the inability to do that for others too. Others, meaning mainly the white man. I hated them first, before they could hate me, in an attempt to protect myself. If I received no mercy, I was determined never to give it either."

"And so it consumed you, until you wouldn't even believe you were worthy of love when you found it," she finished for him. "Not only from me but from God."

He nodded. "Guess that pretty much sums it up. Yet it was never you, never God. It was always me. Imperfect me who could never forgive his father, or the God-Father, or anyone who seemed a threat to me. And so, because I couldn't forgive or offer mercy, I never expected or felt I deserved any in return. Even from God, most of all."

"So you learned all this from Brother Thomas?"

Jesse smiled sadly. "I hated my father long before I killed him. And only Brother Thomas could help me make some sense of that, by telling me of the sacrifice, the love Christ offered when He died on that cross. The grace and mercy He won for us in the doing."

She reached up and stroked his cheek. "You're real, really here. You're not some dream."

"Yes, I'm really here." He grinned. "But I can well understand why you'd imagine this a dream. Some strange words have sure been coming out of my mouth in the past few minutes, haven't they?"

"Strange," Shiloh murmured as she stood on tiptoe to brush her lips across his, "but oh, so wonderful. So longed for."

As she settled back on her heels, Jesse grabbed her up and returned her kiss, though this time it wasn't just a gentle meeting of mouths. His kiss was hungry, searing, and covenant-sealing. And Shiloh kissed him back with an equal ardor and commitment.

"So, does that mean you'll be my wife?" Jesse asked huskily when they finally pulled away from each other.

"Yes." Her reply was breathless with emotion. "Yes, Jesse Blackwater, I'll be your wife."

From outside the barn, the dinner bell began to ring loudly. Shiloh gasped and stepped back.

"It's time for supper," she cried. "Thanksgiving supper."

She grabbed his arm and started dragging him to the barn door. "Come on. Everyone will be so excited to see you!"

Jesse dug in his heels. "Whoa! Hold on. I don't think this is the best time to spring me on your family. They're looking forward to a nice, happy, peaceful holiday meal. I'd hate to ruin it for them. I can come back tomorrow after you've told them about me."

"No, you won't." Shiloh tightened her grip on his arm and began pulling him forward again. "As my intended, you're now part of the family. The sooner they get used to it, the better. Besides, Emma's prepared the most scrumptious meal, and I want to enjoy it with my future husband."

"Is this just another one of those compromises you women seem to love talking so much about?"

She laughed, and the sound reverberated all the way down to her toes. "Oh, most definitely. Most definitely indeed!"

Everyone was already gathered around the big dining room table when Shiloh, followed by Jesse, walked in and closed the front door. As she took his buckskin coat from him and hung it on some hooks on the wall inside the front door, then removed her own coat, hat, and mittens, Jesse watched as eyes around the table grew wide and mouths dropped open.

Then, once again, Shiloh was dragging him forward.

"Emma, could you round up another chair and put it next to mine?" Shiloh asked brightly.

As the housekeeper, her eyes twinkling in delight, rose from the table and hurried off, Jesse, like a man going to his own execution, followed Shiloh around to the head of the table. Her brother Nicholas sat there in his wheelchair.

"Nick," she said, "Jesse's decided to pay us a visit. He couldn't have timed it better, could he?"

Her brother nodded. "Nope, he sure couldn't have." He held out a hand to Jesse. "Glad to see you again. Going to join us for supper, are you?"

Jesse accepted the other man's hand and shook it. "Shiloh's invited me, but if you don't have the room . . ."

"Nonsense." Before Nick could reply, Jordan piped up from her seat catty-corner to her oldest brother. "There's always room at the Wainwright table for family and friends. And you've always been a friend, though some of us didn't always know how to appreciate that." She grinned. "From the looks of Shiloh's beaming face, I wager that you'll also soon be part of the family."

Once again, all eyes turned to Jesse. He felt a surge of blood heat his face, but he forced himself to reply with a calm assurance he certainly didn't feel.

"We love each other, and I'd like her brothers' blessings on our marriage, if they'll give it," he said, meeting Cord's then Nick's gazes. "One way or another, though, we're going to be married."

Nick glanced down the length of the table to where Cord sat. "Well, what do you think, little brother? Shall we give them our blessing?"

Cord shot Jesse a disgruntled look. "Might as well," he grumbled even as a smile twitched at the corners of his mouth.

"If Jesse's even half as stubborn and hotheaded as our little sister, we won't have a chance to convince them otherwise. Even if we wanted to."

"Guess that means welcome to the family." As Emma re-entered the room just then with the extra chair, Nick swung around to grin up at Jesse. "Now, sit on down and let's say grace, so we can dig into some really fine food."

Jesse's eyes burned as he assisted Shiloh with her chair, then took his beside her. Maybe it was from the long ride and nights without much sleep—the burning, suddenly tear-filled eyes. Or maybe it was because he'd just found another home with some good people. People who accepted him and might even someday come to love him.

People who offered him mercy and forgiveness. As he must strive always from here on out to offer to others. It could be no other way.

Brother Thomas had taught him that many years ago, and now Shiloh had taken up that charge. It was the only thing of value he could offer back to God in atonement for all his sins and failings. But, as Brother Thomas had once told him, there was no truer test of love than to give back what one received.

Beneath the table, Jesse sought out Shiloh's hand and squeezed it. She squeezed back then, with a smile, bowed her head as Nick began to say grace.

Author's Note

I hope you've enjoyed *A Love Forbidden*. It was a very interesting if challenging story to tell. I did, however, want to clarify a few details for historical accuracy.

Shiloh, Jesse, the Wainwrights, Kwana, Onawa, and Broken Antler are all fictional characters. All the other characters mentioned in regard to the White River Indian Agency were real people, as were all the events leading up to the Meeker Massacre on September 29, 1879. Josie Meeker was actually the only schoolteacher at the Agency, and I of course took literary license with the interactions and dialogue between Shiloh, Jesse, and the other Agency personnel, as well as with them and the Utes. Only three women—Josie, Arvilla, and Flora Ellen in addition to her two children—were actually taken captive by the Utes.

After the Meeker Massacre, things didn't go well for the White River Utes. Though the Utes who'd fought the soldiers at Milk Creek were never prosecuted, as the fight was deemed a legitimate battle, attempts were made to apprehend, try, and punish the Utes who'd killed innocent people at the Agency.

However, though Arvilla, Josie, and Flora Ellen named twelve Utes whom they'd recognized during the massacre, none of the White River Utes would testify that they knew anything about the massacre or who had participated in it.

Even after Ouray got involved, only Chief Douglas was eventually brought in and punished by being imprisoned at Fort Leavenworth, Kansas. He was eventually set free and died insane, sometime later.

The residents of Colorado, however, were still up in arms and demanded that "The Utes must go!" Eventually, Ouray hammered out a treaty with the US government, and on September 1, 1881, the White River Utes began a 350-mile march to the Utah reservation—a "wild and ragged desolation valuable for nothing unless it shall be found to contain mineral deposits." Brokenhearted, the Utes left the lush, green Shining Mountains of their ancestral homelands in Colorado, forbidden to return.

Ouray never saw his people's banishment from Colorado. He died on August 24, 1880, of what was believed to be kidney disease.

KATHLEEN MORGAN is the author of the bestselling Brides of Culdee Creek series and *As High as the Heavens*, as well as the These Highland Hills series. She lives in Colorado.

"BE STILL MY HEART—KATHLEEN
MORGAN IS BACK,
AND SHE'S BETTER THAN EVER!"

—JULIE LESSMAN, author, the Daughters of Boston series
and *A Hope Undaunted*

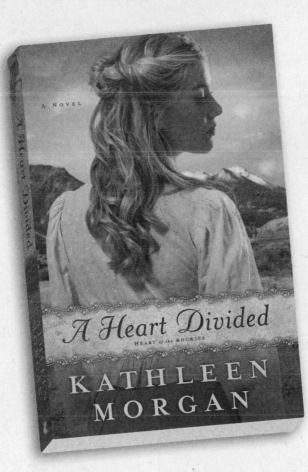

Against the beautiful and wild backdrop of the Rocky
Mountains comes this sweeping saga of romance, betrayal,
and forgiveness from beloved author Kathleen Morgan.

Catch the first book in
Maggie Brendan's new series
THE BLUE WILLOW BRIDES

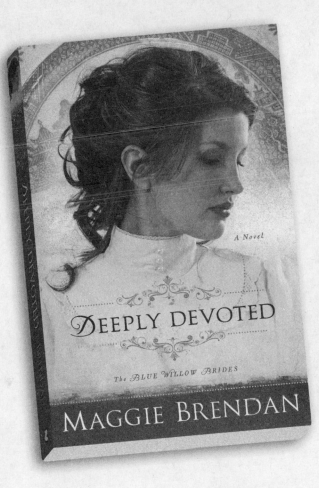

She is staking her future on a man she's never met.
Can she learn to love him?